Praise for *The Woodsmoke Women's Book of Spells*

'Captivated me from the very first page. It reminds me of why I love writing and why I love reading. It' [illegible] agical and grounding at the same time, otherwor[illegible] tural. I absolutely treasured it from beg[illegible]

Cecelia Ahern, *Sunday Time*[illegible]

'An atmospheric and cosy r[illegible]

Natasha J. Hastings, [illegible] *[illegible]t*

'Modern magic meets pe[illegible] one day. It is an absolute masterpiece a[illegible] te books of the year. It incorporates magic in[illegible] ay that feels natural. You will love meeting the Wood[illegible] women as much as I did.'

Frost Magazine

'An evocative and compelling story about lost love and the magic of coming home.'

Sunday Mail

'The characters are so raw and relatable and the mystery so intriguing that I hated slipping out of this magical world and back to reality.'

Kate Robb, author of *This Spells Love*

'Otherworldly, beautiful, and completely captures the imagination.'

Muddy Stilettos

'Spellbinding and starry, the Woodsmoke Women cast a spell on me.'

M.A. Kuzniar, author of *Midnight in Everwood*

'An enticing read.'

Belfast Telegraph

Rachel Greenlaw grew up in North Cornwall, surrounded by wild moorland. She studied English with Creative Writing at Falmouth University before moving to an island in the middle of the Atlantic, where she lives with her husband and two children. Her debut, *One Christmas Morning* was shortlisted for an RNA award. Rachel can be found on Instagram @rachelgreenlaw_

Also by Rachel Greenlaw

One Christmas Morning

YA

Compass and Blade

Shadow and Tide

THE WOODSMOKE WOMEN'S BOOK OF SPELLS

RACHEL GREENLAW

HQ

ONE PLACE. MANY STORIES

HQ
An imprint of HarperCollins*Publishers* Ltd
1 London Bridge Street
London SE1 9GF

www.harpercollins.co.uk

HarperCollins*Publishers*
Macken House, 39/40 Mayor Street Upper,
Dublin 1, D01 C9W8, Ireland

This edition 2025
1
First published in Great Britain by HQ,
an imprint of HarperCollins*Publishers* Ltd 2024

A catalogue record for this book is available from the British Library.

ISBN: 9780008708535

Printed and bound in the UK using 100% Renewable Electricity by CPI Group (UK) Ltd

FSC www.fsc.org MIX Paper FSC™ C007454

For more information visit: www.harpercollins.co.uk/green

For all the Morgan women in our world,
and for those still searching

Autumn

October

Chapter 1
Carrie

This is not a firsthand account. Or even a second, or a third. This tale has been passed down and passed down, discussed around hearths, embellished, and clipped until I sat down to record it in the book . . .

–Tabitha Morgan, July 19, 1929

I clutch the keys between my fingers. The cottage in front of me is quiet and watchful, small windows tucked into the folds of granite walls. I hesitate, taking a moment, feeling the edges of metal in my hand, the cold damp air as I draw it down my throat, the light as it snatches at the October clouds above. I needed this moment. It's grown inside me like a nettle, this need, curling around me all these years, stinging me as I turned the other way. But now that the moment is here, I find it is full of ghosts.

I turn the key in the lock and fumble with the handle, my fingers slipping over the worn iron, and push. The hinges protest, but the door gives with a low sigh. Inside it's dark and cold, so much colder than the outside world. I feel the cool air twine around me like an arm, guiding me in, pulling me past the doorway. Perhaps it is Ivy, my grandmother, welcoming me back. I let my eyes adjust, finding the wide flagstones, the crooked staircase.

And I step over the threshold.

My boots clatter on the floor, echoing down the hallway as I move past the staircase. I run a hand over the wood, feel the smooth varnish, then the rough patches where time has worn it away. It's familiar in the way a dream is upon waking. I haven't been in this house in ten years, and somehow it seems smaller. Frailer than it did ten years ago. Without the true owner of the place singing in her sweet, reedy voice as she potters around, the cottage holds an air of neglect. Of being left too long in the dark, all forgotten.

I shake off the cold, drawing my coat a little tighter across my chest, and take the door on the left into the front room. The fireplace is littered with the remains of a bird's nest, and a chair lies on its side, as though hastily tipped over. I reach out and right it, but a leg comes off in my hands.

"Oh, Ivy . . ." I sigh, dropping it back on the floorboards. I don't bother trying the light switch. The electrics won't work. Cora, my great-aunt, said as much in her letter.

In a rush, I move to the next room, to the kitchen spread across the back, circling the old farmhouse table and peering out of the back windows. And there they are, the giants that loom over me in every dream, every nightmare. The reason perhaps that I have been running for so long.

The mountains.

I lean over the sink, gazing up at them. The three peaks of the mountain range dwarf this cottage. Full of secrets. Full of stories and whispers and trails you should never wander from. Even now I can hear Cora's warnings, Ivy's old tales, the whisperings in the school playground, passed down and passed down. I dig my fingers into the ceramic edges of the sink and feel the first stirring of something. Something that perhaps I no longer want to run from.

Home.

I push away from the sink and cross back into the hallway. Then I climb the staircase, hoping with every tread that my boots don't crash straight through. The rooms upstairs are just as I remember. Peeling wallpaper, bare floorboards. The kind of rooms that hold so many memories, pressed like words into their walls. I trace the shape of a yellow flower on the wallpaper, and it bubbles up underneath my fingernail. Then I check the doorframe, feeling the notches marking our heights as we grew into ourselves. The ones marking mine and . . . hers. Jess's. I pull my fingertips back, stuff my hands into my pockets. The nettles curling inside me tighten.

The view is even more lovely from upstairs, and I move to perch on the window seat, bunching up my sleeve to wipe at the condensation gathered in the corners of the glass. Ivy's garden is choked with weeds. Even her roses have withered, their rambling limbs draped over an arch. It isn't just that it's October. Ivy used to sing to them, and I was sure they turned toward her as she moved around, taking a clipping here, a petal there. Now Ivy is gone, and her garden mourns.

My breath catches, and that ache, deep in my chest, sharpens to a point. I press my palm into it, close my eyes, and will my own memories away. The memories of what I have lost. What will never get a chance to grow. It all feels more vivid here, like a cut reopened, spilling scarlet.

In a moment, I'm up and back down the staircase. I bunch the keys in my fist and lock the door, then drop them into my coat pocket. I eye the caravan, still attached to my car on the other side of the field. I could go inside. Make a cup of tea. Figure out what to scrape together for dinner and start to make sense of it all. Ivy's will is in there, the terms laid out in precise black and white. The cottage and this muddy field are all mine, but I have to come back and renovate it. I have to stay a winter, a whole winter in this place. I have to return and make peace with Woodsmoke.

But . . .

No. Not yet. I turn to the north, to the mountains. If I don't greet them, if I turn away and pretend they're not there, I know what could happen. I know the old tales. It's a curse and a gift being a Morgan woman with this knowledge. But we all know, really. Everyone in Woodsmoke has grown up knowing that magic isn't some intangible, wonderful thing. It's real, it has consequences, and it echoes around this mountain range. This ancient place, where magic seems to grow thick and wild. Some people in the town like to think they don't believe, but I've seen them scratching at Cora's door. I've seen the outcome when her warnings are not heeded. We all have. I square my shoulders and start walking toward the mountains.

There's a trail that begins at the edge of this field, then winds up through the thicket of undergrowth and trees. My feet find it before I do, and I am careful not to step off it. The breeze ruffles the leaves, all russet and gold on the ends of spindly branches, surrounding me with a flurry of sound as I walk. I breathe in, out, drawing the sharp cold down into my lungs, focusing only on the path, my boots, the quickening thrum of my heart.

The world slowly dims, peeling back to twilight, but I don't stop. I walk faster, rushing up the trail that hugs the side of this mountain. My breath is ragged now, my lungs bloom with flame, burning all my other thoughts away.

I burst out of the trees and find myself on the edge of the world. A stretch of mud and grass slopes down and down, all the way to the little town of Woodsmoke. I lean against a tree, catching my breath as it fogs out in front of me. Dragon breath, we used to call it. On the walk to school along the familiar track, with barely enough space to walk side by side, every autumn, every winter. We would breathe out fire and laugh and laugh.

I miss Jess's laugh. Once I was sure I heard it, walking the streets of Paris at twilight four years ago, and those throaty notes lured me to a café with tables sprawling across the pavement. Of course, it wasn't her. But I stayed there all evening, nursing cups of hot chocolat and cream, listening to the ghost of her laugh on someone else's tongue.

Pushing my hair behind my ears, I walk slowly forward, testing each footfall, and take in the sweep of life below. Woodsmoke is a tapestry of tiny lights, chugging chimneys, and ancient, winding roads threading into its heart, the town square at the center. I watch as more lights turn on, picturing the families, the wood burners, and the cozy domesticity of it all. I thought that was where I was heading once, before I grew into myself.

The fire inside me smolders, charring my edges, but I focus on the town below. As I begin my next chapter in this place, the layers of memories drift through it like smoke. I stand over Woodsmoke, breathing in the scent of loam and wood, watching as the lights of the town blink below me like stars. And I tell myself I can do this. I can restore Ivy's cottage. I can do what was asked of me in her will and then finally, maybe, I can let this place go.

That will be my new beginning.

A noise, like footsteps, like a sigh, presses against my back and I turn sharply. For an instant, I believe I can see a shape. Someone rangy and tall. Someone almost familiar. But as I narrow my eyes, heart leaping against my ribs, all I see are shadows. I check my feet hurriedly, making sure I haven't strayed from the path. But it's still below me, trailing back down the mountain, the vein I will follow back to the real world.

I drag my gaze away, back to Woodsmoke and all the life spread out there like constellations in the dark. And the hope, so long extinguished, unfurls inside me once more. I carry that hope all the way down the mountain. Back across the muddy field, tangled with weeds and scrub. Back to the caravan I borrowed from my parents, with the chipped Formica table and stovetop kettle.

I create a makeshift dinner, the old saucepans and wooden spoons clattering in the eerie silence, then inhale an entire packet of rich tea biscuits with a cup of strong tea. I fold myself into fleece-lined pajamas, pile three blankets over my head, and get the letter out, smoothing down its edges. I should have gone to her first, I realize. She will know I've arrived and will wonder why I haven't seen her. Cora Morgan, Ivy's sister, is like that. After reading it through again, I tuck the letter under my pillow, turn out the light, and try to gather sleep to me. But sleep is just as elusive here as it has been everywhere else for the past ten years.

I worry all night that I strayed from the path without meaning to. That something followed me back, that the figure I glimpsed in the dark was real. I can hear scratching outside, and it follows me into my dreams. As though someone is tapping at the frost-laced window, bearing a warning to heed.

Or trying to get in.

I toss and turn, wishing I'd sprinkled salt and dried lavender around the caravan. It's all too easy for a vengeful spirit, for something other and twisted, to slither in if a proper warding isn't in place. And in the space between dreams and waking on this cold, dark night, it seems real.

Frost steals over everything in my dreams like a spell. Ivy's forlorn garden. Her roses and their withered, thorny limbs. The creaking, narrow staircase. The bubbling wallpaper. Even Ivy, her mouth full of warnings as she stands in the lounge in her cottage, her hands all twisted together, voice too quiet for me to hear. I try stepping toward her, try catching a single word. But I'm stuck, stuck to the floorboards, stuck in this spider's web of frost, just like her. It creeps down from the mountains, reaching for my skin, snaring my legs, my chest, tangling in my hair. Still, Ivy bellows.

And I cannot hear.

When I wake, winter has come. I fight my way out of the blankets, drawing in lungfuls of soothing air. It's stifling in the caravan, the walls too close, the ceiling too low. I drag a hand over my face, banishing the cobwebs of dreams, and shuffle around the small space, making coffee with the old whistling kettle, shrugging into my coat, pulling on my boots.

I clutch the rough ceramic sides of my favorite coffee mug in my hands, the one I found in a small pottery in Ireland many years ago. I let the steam curl around my face. Then I step out into the frost.

The field is a painting. All I see are droplets of glitter, the ground, the middle distance, the sky overhead, sparkling with dew. Frost is a scent you cannot bottle. It's sweet and sharp all at once, laced with memories from childhood, from early morning breakfasts, from the moments my heart thumped with the knowing that it was here at last.

I hold out my hand, my fingertips already nipped by cold. The chill draping the air is early for this time of year, not yet November. I smile for the first time since I arrived and breathe it in, that scent of frost and cold. And I'm sure in that moment that despite my long absence, despite the way I left this place and how it's haunted me ever since, this is my homecoming. This spell of early winter feels alive and wild with magic.

The mountains have welcomed me home after all.

Chapter 2

Cora

"She's back," Cora gasps at six that morning. She fumbles for the lamp, twisting the tiny switch until a glow bathes her bedroom. She smiles up at the ceiling, the one she has stared at for fifty-five years, ever since she moved into this house as a married woman. "She's back."

She cackles, forcing wakefulness into her limbs as she gets out of bed, smoothing her plait of hair over one shoulder. She knows she should cut it. That keeping it, this long rope of white and gray, is fanciful. But it's how she's worn her hair all her life, and she'll be damned if she'll change that now.

She pads out of her bedroom, leaving the indentations of two people on the crinkled sheets. She doesn't like to make the bed this early. It's not the first thing she wants to do each day, day in, day out, for time eternal. It's not the way she wants to begin her morning. The hallway is dark, but she detests using the electric just for herself. So she fumbles her fingertips along the wallpaper, feeling the familiar grooves, the slight ridge where Howard didn't hang it quite right. It used to annoy her, but like everything, time has smoothed that frustration away. She relents when she gets to the kitchen, flipping the switch to light the space where she has spent most of her hours, her days. She starts this day the way she likes to start them all—by making coffee.

She makes her coffee slowly, savoring each step. And as each moment passes, with every breath, she thinks of Carrie. How her arrival must have felt momentous, as it does to Cora. How Carrie will have stepped across the threshold of Ivy's cottage, her eyes snagging on every detail, snapping to the light switch she knows won't work. Standing in the kitchen at the back and staring up at the vast, all-consuming mountains. Cora hopes Carrie greeted them. She hopes they will welcome her grandniece home.

As she crosses her own kitchen, she wonders if Carrie will stay this time. If this cottage, Ivy's cottage, will be the glue that holds her here. If it's enough.

Cora reaches up, hooking her fingers around the handle of the four-cup French press in the cupboard, and pulls it toward her. She hums a tune that suddenly surfaces in her mind, a tune that conjures up scabbed knees and school dinners of lumpy mashed potato and conkers foraged in the woods, tied with string. She remembers how she and her sister would smash them together, enjoying epic battles that trailed across the autumns of her girlhood. Cora falters for a moment, picturing Ivy's narrowed eyes, her nimble fingers, her gray cardigan with the patches on the elbows and the hole on the left sleeve, right near her wrist. She blinks down at the spoon in her hand and forgets where she is.

Then the scent plumes up from the coffee bag and she resumes her humming as the kettle boils, thoughts of conkers and Ivy swept somewhere back to the recesses of her mind. She swirls the hot water into the press, the grounds coloring it like dirt. She gets two mugs out of the dishwasher. Her favorite. Howard's favorite. A smile tucks itself into the corners of her mouth as the back door opens, letting in a cloud of cold and dark.

"Carrie's at Ivy's," she says without turning around, knowing he'll be knocking off his boots, blowing on his fingers. She can taste the frost on the air that's just rushed inside, an early sign that winter is coming. "She must have got in late yesterday."

Howard shuffles to the sink, turns the tap on, and washes his hands with the soap Cora likes to make. It leaves the scent of lavender, which he hates, but he's never told her. "I'm surprised you haven't gone over there already."

"Before the poor girl has time to wake up? Nonsense." Cora tsks, grasping her own mug. Smiling again and staring out the window, she takes the first perfect sip. "These young people sleep in nowadays. And she's had a long drive." She nods to herself. "I'll go over there at nine-thirty."

"Of course you will."

"And what's that supposed to mean?"

Howard sighs, muttering about one of the chickens, Queenie, the layer he got last year. He doesn't stop muttering as he wanders off into the lounge to find his slippers, the sign that he's ready for Cora to make him his breakfast. Two boiled eggs. Soldiers. Another round of coffee to ward off the mountain chill.

But Cora is miles away. Years away. She's drifting on the current of a conversation she had the day Carrie left. The day the world came unstitched, when she and Ivy stopped talking and everything changed. She drinks the rest of her coffee leaning against the old Belfast sink, remembering the days and months that followed.

She wants Carrie to feel the roots of Woodsmoke. *Her* roots that bind her to this place, that bind every Morgan woman. She's not sure if Carrie has felt their tug while she's been gone, but she imagines this place hasn't quite let her go. The mountains don't like letting people go. Not before their time, anyway. She knows that even Lillian, Carrie's mother, feels that tug from miles away. She left Woodsmoke, and now she's too afraid to return and face whatever the mountains throw at her in reprimand for leaving. Wild places can be vindictive like that.

She wonders if Carrie is haunted still by the day she left. Or whether she's folded it away in her mind, let it slip all the way under until it's lost somewhere far away.

Cora clears her throat, reboils the water in the kettle. She sets about making breakfast, cracking the eggs to poach them, the way she likes them, and placing two more in a saucepan for Howard. She can't remember how Carrie likes her eggs, and for a moment that bothers her. Scrambled? Or perhaps fried, on slabs of white bread thick with butter? The corner of a slice of toast slips through her fingertips and she drops it, butter smearing the flagstone floor.

"Just my luck," Cora says, her eighty-year-old knees creaking as she bends to wipe it up. A blast of cold air finds its way through a crack in the window frame and she sniffs. The scent of frost burns her nose—too sweet, too bitter. She frowns, wondering if it means something after all, this early sign of winter. A decade on, and now everything, she realizes, is about to change again.

She butters more toast, cuts it on the diagonal, and places the slices in the toast rack. She knows you're meant to butter toast at the table, but it always goes too cold. She likes the butter melted in, turning to sunshine on her plate.

Cora brings it all to the table, and as Howard shuffles his way in, she thinks about how he used to look. How he seems to have crumpled like a tissue in the last few years. He used to bring her flowers, and she would kiss that shiny brown forehead, dipping her chin and patting his cheek. He was always shorter than her, even in school, a boy who never sat still, always moving, always talking and planning and sketching thoughts in the air with his hands. He wasn't intimidated by a tall woman, or by her last name. In fact, he embraced it. She kept her surname when they married, just as every Morgan woman does. And he kept his.

She pulls out a chair, the legs scraping against the floor, just as he does the same.

And she freezes.

Howard looks up at her, something like fear glinting in his

eyes, but only for a heartbeat. Cora looks to the door, as if she can see through it. Past it. All the way to ten years ago, when Carrie left and broke her heart.

The world seems to hold its breath.

Then a tap, quiet and hesitant, sounds at the door.

"She's here," Cora breathes.

Chapter 3
Carrie

Abigail had wildflowers left on her doorstep for a month and a day this summer.

—Clemence Morgan, December 18, 1875

Cora opens the door as though she is confronting a ghost, her own skin skull white, eyes glistening slightly. She's still wearing her dressing gown, the one she's always worn. It's pink and felted, with buttons instead of a cord. More of a housecoat. She opens then closes her mouth, and I can't help the smile bubbling up my throat. I've never known my great-aunt to be anything less than effusive, with a snap or a crackle to her words.

I say, "I can come back later or . . ." just as her arms come around me. I hesitate, her scent and the nip of her bones crushing me, before I bring my arms around her. She's all sage and coffee and snow, ribs too sharp, just like always. I still can't pass a coffee shop, even now, without picturing Cora and her kitchen.

"You got my letter?" she asks, finally letting me go. She stares up at me with those watery blue eyes of hers, the irises circled with a deep navy blue. "Did the mountains want you back?"

"I did," I say, my hand straying to my pocket. For some reason, ever since it arrived on that damp day three weeks ago, I haven't been able to put it down. I've scoured Cora's letter and the terms of Ivy's will as though searching for hidden meanings, secrets buried within secrets. "And they . . . I think so. I walked up to the lookout. But I thought I saw or heard . . . I don't know."

Her blue gaze narrows. She knows. "Did you leave the path?"

"Not once."

She exhales, her sharp edges softening, and the house at her back exhales along with her. "You best come in. Howard's eating his breakfast. You want eggs? Toast? There's a fresh pot of coffee, but if it's not enough I can make more."

Her words trail away with her as she turns from me, making her way deeper into the house. I linger for a heartbeat, remembering the last time I was here. How I pulled all the pins out of my perfectly tamed hair, leaving them in a snarled little heap on the sofa.

And then I left.

I step along the hallway. Past the old photographs lining the walls, the sepia-toned images of families long dead. The portraits of ancestors, of trappers and the men of the mountains. Cora collects them. She finds them in charity shops and junk sales around Woodsmoke. Dusting them off, she carries them back home like a magpie. She says they are the history that no one else will remember. That's up to us, up to every Morgan woman, she says, to remember the stories and preserve them. Because when a story is no longer shared, it becomes a secret. Then it all too easily either withers and dies or grows into something quite monstrous: a curse.

There is one photograph I remember, one that she acquired a year or so before I left. It chills me even now. A black-and-white photograph of a man, standing with his back to the mountains. It's actually not that old, taken just before Cora acquired it, which is why my eyes are drawn to it. His eyes, flint and hunger staring back, as though he will somehow reach out and snatch you in. A shiver curls down the back of my neck as I catch sight of it, and I walk a little quicker. It lingered at the corners of my dreams before I left, but now, glancing at that portrait with fresh, older eyes a decade later, I see he is around my age. Handsome in that rugged way that few men are nowadays. Perhaps his true story wasn't recorded by a Morgan woman, and that's why he's so hungry to tell it. Perhaps his true story withered and died along with him. That's all I know, all Cora told me. That the man in this portrait was lost to the mountains.

I walk into the dining room, and Howard raises himself from his chair. He looks at me the way he always does, with a slight smirk turning up his sunken brown cheeks. Like we have a private joke that only we know. He never shares that look with Cora.

"Good journey, my flower?" he asks in his cracked old voice.

I grin. I haven't been called that in so long. *Flower.* "Not bad. The car didn't give out on me, so . . ."

He shrugs, waving his hand at a seat. "Coffee's hot still. Good to see you, Carrie."

"Good to see you too." I take the mug from Cora, hovering next to me, and we all sit in uncomfortable, charged silence. I sip the coffee, trying not to look at either of them. Wondering why in these moments I don't have a single word in my head. Like I've forgotten the entire dictionary.

Cora opens her mouth, then closes it, as though conflicted. A sad frown appears in the grooves of her forehead before her gaze snags on mine. "You should have come sooner."

Howard releases an exasperated sigh, darting her a look. "Coraline—"

"Well, she should have. Can't all wait for a death to shake our lives up, can we?"

Cora folds her arms, knitting her lips together. Cora's always been like this every time I see her: taciturn, frustrated, and elated in equal measure, like she could shake me and embrace me all at the same time. Sighing again, Howard slides back into that slight smirk, just for me. He shrugs one shoulder, making sure she can't see it, as if to say, *You know how she is.* I know I should have come sooner. I know ten years was far too long to stay away. But I can't seem to admit it.

"The cottage—" I begin, attempting to change the subject, to shift the conversation from the past and my failings to the present.

"Howard will be along," Cora says, not meeting my eyes. "No need to fret."

I dart my eyes to his, and he raises his eyebrows. "Actually, I might try to find someone in Woodsmoke, or the next town over. Maybe you know of . . . I don't know. An electrician? Just to get that going at least."

Cora coughs. "There's only Tom now in Woodsmoke."

The coffee mug slips from my fingers. "Shit!" I say, leaping up as coffee drenches the lace tablecloth and splashes over Cora's pink housecoat. "I'm sorry . . . Cora, I—"

"Don't *fret*, girl." She leaves the room, muttering about how I've gone and got clumsier.

"I'm sorry," I whisper, to no one in particular.

Howard sighs, sipping his coffee in that contained, quiet way of his. "You'll have to ask in the next town. Or I can ask around for you. Tom, he—"

"I know," I say quickly, as Cora bustles back in with a wad of tea towels. "I can't ask him."

Cora looks at me, those lips knitting even tighter. I wait for it, sure it's coming. Then she looks at me, and I see it. All that frustration, all that love . . . She's as blunt as a butter knife and just *has* to speak her mind. She can't bottle it all up any longer. "Five addresses, Carrie. *Five.* I sent that letter, and it kept coming back, took six weeks to chase you around Europe, and you never updated us, you never said a *word*—"

"I had to move around a lot, for work. There was the gallery opening, and then I got a lead on some design work, but that fell through—"

"That's in one year! How many more addresses before that? Hmm? And are you even painting still? You haven't updated that website of yours in an age."

I sigh, the berating edge of her voice grating on me. She's right. I don't like admitting it, but it's true. I haven't painted in a year. The last images I uploaded onto my website were of the streets of Prague, the gray of them, the crowded squares littered with tiny tables, women sipping from espresso cups. I sold all of them. That kept me going on a backpacking trip around Croatia and Greece. Then I couldn't bring myself to even pick up my sketchbook. I've been drifting, scraping by on a little graphic design work, some waitressing. Nothing substantial. "It was hard to find a landlord I liked, and sometimes I just needed a change. It's just how I am, Cora."

"It is *not* how you are, my love. You can't run forever!"

"Coraline . . ." Howard chips in, warning lacing his voice in a way I've seldom heard. "Let the girl eat some breakfast."

"But the old ways, her heritage, the book—"

"Not the damn book. Not before the blessed sun's fully up, woman."

Cora clicks her tongue before disappearing with the tea towels. I shove some toast into my mouth, just for something to do, and eye the muddy coffee stain on the ivory white tablecloth. I wonder how many more things I'll ruin before I'm done with Ivy's cottage this winter.

"Does she still talk about the old ways . . . a lot?" I whisper to Howard, keeping an eye on the door. The book, as Cora calls it, is our history. The *Morgan Compendium*. It's the collected stories of every Morgan woman who's carried it, going back generations.

Tales of the mountains, of the seasons, warnings and curses and fables and recipes and spells, shared around the fire on winter nights. I can count on both hands the number of times I laid eyes on it before I left, a couple of times even turning the brittle pages. I fear it and yearn to read it again in equal measure, and that scares me. The magic of the mountains is a dark thing, demanding a price, demanding blood from a Morgan woman for every bargain made in its shadow, or so it's whispered around the town. And Cora has carried all of that with her for many, many years.

One day the book will pass to me. It always skips a generation, passed from grandmother to granddaughter. I know my mother wouldn't want it anyway. Any mention of spells and curses and she shrinks away or changes the subject entirely. She hasn't been back in Woodsmoke for years, and if she can, she'll avoid the place for the rest of her days. To her, our legacy is poison. But to me . . . I don't know. I'm still a little curious. I haven't figured out how I feel about the book and the old ways.

Howard chews his toast, then crosses his cutlery on his plate. Also eyeing the door before speaking. "Only every day, flower," he finally responds. "Only every goddamn day."

THERE ARE WILDFLOWERS on the doorstep when I return to the cottage. A bundle of them, tied with a length of twine. They're the kind you only find growing on the side of the mountain, under trees, in clumps, where the wild things wander. I nudge the bundle with the toe of my boot, then turn, eyeing the wide expanse around me. All I can hear is the thump of my own heart, the curl of fear lighting it like a spark.

Wildflowers in October, with frost coating the ground. They can't be from Tom . . . can they? I pull my arms around myself as I turn back to the door. No. They can't be from him. But my arrival, the fact that I am back, will have caught light by now. It will have burned through Woodsmoke like a wildfire, passed from tongue to tongue, exaggerated, lengthened into a story worth sharing. Could the flowers be from someone Mum and Dad knew? An old neighbor? A friend? I shake my head, picking up the bundle. There's herb robert, red campion, a handful of speedwell. And no note. They'll wilt in a few hours, hardly worth picking. Better to let them sleep in the loam and frost until springtime.

A twig snaps, and I whip around to find someone standing on the path leading up to the mountains. A man. My heart jolts, and we stare at each other, twenty feet apart on the frosted field. His dark hair and eyes stand out against the pallor of his skin. His lips are red, swollen from the cold, cheekbones sharp, jaw solid and chiseled. My breath catches in my throat as I regard him, and he me. He seems . . . wild. And not quite real.

"Did you . . . are these from you?" I call over, pointing to the flowers. But he just puts his hands in his pockets, eyes me quietly, then turns and walks away. Within a heartbeat, he's vanished as if he was never there at all. I exhale heavily, then wonder if he heard me, if I should go after him, demand to know if he was the one who left these wildflowers. A breeze stirs around me, and I pull my arms around myself.

There are tales in the book. Tales of beautiful people who are not quite real, stories from the mountains of the people of Woodsmoke being lured into the wild depths and never coming home. Perhaps the mountains are vengeful, perhaps just playful, perhaps in love with us. But it's been drummed into me to follow the paths and never stray from them. Most still follow the old ways here, even if they don't admit it aloud. But the hikers, the visitors, they don't know the rules. And some of them go missing. Some of them never leave the mountains.

What if that man isn't really a man at all?

I turn the door handle, shoulder my way into the cottage, and carry the wildflowers into the kitchen. Then I take down one of Ivy's old enamel milk jugs, fill it with water, and leave them in there. It's superstitious, but I can't shake it, even after all these years. You don't discard or scorn a gift from the mountains.

I want to believe these wildflowers were picked and left here by someone I used to know, but I can't be sure. Not with that press of unseen eyes I felt last night, or the faint finger tap on the window that echoed through my dreams. Not with the frost arriving today, early for this time of year. And certainly not with that man, that beautiful, quiet man who vanished up the mountain path, gone between blinks as though I might have imagined him.

My fingers tremble as I arrange the flowers, humming an old song Ivy used to sing, a song that's really a story, about a woman who had flowers left on her doorstep, who fell in love and disappeared into the vast mountains, never to be seen again. I bunch my hands into fists, the slow trickle of fear taking hold, the knowing that life is different in Woodsmoke. You can't be sure that a gift is always left with good intent. You don't stray from the path. And if you see someone stepping off the mountain trails, or hear a voice luring you away, never follow. Sometimes a gift is just a gift. But sometimes . . . I swallow.

Sometimes it's a warning.

Chapter 4
Jess

She can't tell him. She can't tell him that Carrie's back. That she swept in here with the frost last night, and she's heard this time Carrie might stay. He left for work at half past seven, as always, and Jess is watching the clock, knowing she's only got an hour before she has to walk Elodie to school. The school she and Tom went to . . . the school Carrie went to.

Elodie walks the same way Jess used to—along the track edged by high hedges, fields, and mountains beyond. For now, Jess walks with her every day, holding her hand and sometimes savoring those ten minutes with her daughter. But sometimes, like this morning, nothing goes quite the way it should. She boiled the kettle, made her cup of breakfast tea, allowing a dash of milk to whirl and bloom in the center. She made a cup for Tom as well, and then was irritated when he took only two small sips, made a face, and left it in the sink. How was he so fussy? It was tea, for goodness' sake. She'd been making it for him for years.

Then she forgot her own tea as Elodie began her day with one of *those* mornings. The cereal was too soggy. Jess hadn't found the right pair of socks for her to wear. The clouds in the sky, with their pattern of wisps like the marks of a skater on ice, were too crooked. Elodie lay on the floor in the hallway at twenty-five minutes to nine, her school shoes next to her, and that was when Jess took her first gulp of tea. Stone cold. Her irritation, at Tom, at the morning, at her six-year-old daughter who was going to make her late for her shift, only grew. It sprouted talons and claws, digging into her thoughts as she gritted her teeth and jammed the shoes onto Elodie's feet.

The walk to school was not to Elodie's liking. Jess walked too fast. She was hungry. Thirsty. She didn't like the frost dusting the ground. She had left behind her bear, Moonlight, who went everywhere with Elodie and smelled like spilled milk. Jess kept gritting her teeth until her jaw ached, nodding to the other mums and dads, trying to pretend this morning was going *exactly* as she had planned. But really, underneath it all, her world was a howling tempest.

It was on the tip of every tongue, the news of Carrie's return. She could feel the other mothers watching her with furtive little glances, marked looks, raised eyebrows. They all know what happened ten years ago—or at least, they *thought* they did. As Elodie muttered like a thundercloud at her side, Jess strode past all of them, sticking her chin in the air and making sure to avoid eye contact.

Her school mums WhatsApp group had been abuzz since dawn. The evening before, someone had seen Carrie's car pull up to Ivy's cottage, the caravan attached to the back. It didn't take long for the news to spread around Woodsmoke, especially with Facebook and WhatsApp groups, the embers of gossip shared with strings of shock-faced emojis. An explosion of whispers had fanned the news at the school gate, but Jess ignored it all. Ignored the thrum of her heart. Ignored the part of herself that had lived in fear of this day, when her best friend of so many years ago would return and see how the pieces had fallen since she left.

Jess was late for her shift at the library by six minutes. Dawn, the other librarian, barely glanced at her as she took the "hold" books from the shelves and stacked them with their printed white slips. The library, with the window seats, the faded blue-and-green carpet, and the dust motes gathering in the shafts of light, has been Jess's refuge ever since she learned how to read. When she was old enough, she would walk to the library by herself and spend hours on a beanbag in the children's corner, reading books about dragons and swoony heroes. Later, when she turned fourteen, she would stray to the romance and fantasy sections.

She's not sure what she would do without this place. It's one of the pillars that props her up. But today she feels exposed. Will Carrie turn up and demand that they talk? Jess jumps every time someone walks into the library, imagining her. Her face, her voice. The last time Jess laid eyes on her.

Jess gets through the morning on a wave of perpetual anxiety, then meets Tom at home for lunch in their hour off. She stuffs baguettes with ham and cheese, then with crunchy lettuce leaves and slices of cucumber, picked up from the supermarket three days ago. Jess and Tom don't talk much at all. She figures they haven't for a long time. It's all logistics after you have a child. Lists and dates for the diary, birthdays and anniversaries and cards you forget to post. He pulls out the slices of ham to leave them on his plate in a pink heap and chews his baguette. He never once asks her how Elodie was after he left for work.

She considers barraging him with details—the forgotten teddy bear, the clouds, the socks. Just so he can feel even an *ounce* of her irritation. But what would be the point? He's too lost in his own world today. Scrolling through Twitter on his phone, texting his dad about the football match he's arranged to go and watch later in the pub. It's clear that he hasn't heard yet that Carrie's back in Woodsmoke, that she's turned up to renovate Ivy's old cottage.

Jess eats the last of her baguette, dusting the crumbs from her fingers, and decides to let him find out for himself. Even though they got together after Carrie left, and there wasn't even a spark in all the years before, Carrie still casts a shadow over their relationship. They do not speak of it, how it smudges and darkens an otherwise perfectly respectable marriage.

"Can you pick up some more milk on your way home?" Jess asks, tapping a finger on the fridge door. Her voice sounds awkward, full of corners and edges that aren't normally there. "And some white bread for Elodie's lunches?"

"Sure," he says, not even bothering to look up. "I'll pick up your favorite chocolate too in exchange for one kiss."

She bites her lip, that old familiar flare igniting inside her. Even now, all these years later, Tom hasn't lost that cheekiness she fell for. "I'll text you a list."

"Sounds good. I'll collect my kiss later." He flashes her a grin, then turns back to his phone.

"Heard any . . . news today? Where is it you're working?"

"Mrs. Neal's," he says, pocketing his phone before swiping up his van keys from the table. "Big house on the edge of Goode Street? Electrics done by her husband thirty years ago. Bloody nightmare."

"Right."

"What kind of news?"

"Huh? Nothing. Nothing, really."

He'll hear it from someone, Jess is sure of it. He'll notice eventually the eyes sliding over him, alight with that tingle of gossip that only small towns know how to set off. And when he does, he'll know that Jess heard it first and didn't tell him. But she's not ready. She's not ready for that conversation, for Carrie to be alive again in Woodsmoke, breathing the same air as them. Stealing pieces of the life they have carved out so carefully together. Jess has pushed away the ache in her chest that Carrie left there, tamping it down to dwell alongside every other disappointment, every heartbreak, every loss she has experienced. But now Carrie is real. She's here, she's not a memory, and that ache is resurfacing like a ripped-open old wound.

She thinks about that night, what she did, and her heart quickens.

Carrie is back, maybe for good, and Jess's safe, ordered life is about to be set on fire.

Chapter 5
Carrie

Stir the salt and dried lavender under the light of the waxing moon and leave until at least the next full moon before use. Sprinkle liberally over every threshold, every window ledge, to ward against ill luck and spirits trying to get in.

—Abigail Morgan, March 23, 1871

Woodsmoke is just as I remember. As the drizzle begins, painting the pavements a darker gray, I tread the familiar path through the town. Past the greengrocers with punnets of imported grapes and strawberries outside, the inside overflowing with middle-aged women carrying baskets. One of them laughs as I walk past, a hearty clanging sound with the local twang laced through it. I wonder if she's someone I would remember.

I linger on the threshold of the bookshop, the crisp new editions fronting the jumble of secondhand paperbacks stacked up at the back. I'm sure old Mr. Winter will be around somewhere, searching for a book he hasn't laid eyes on in six months. They hide from him, I'm sure of it. Swap places in the night, pages ruffling with mirth.

There are layers to this town, with memories lingering on every corner—like the time Sally Nash swiped a tube of lipstick from the chemist in the main square on a dare. She wore the rose-pink shade on her lips the next day at school, planted a kiss on a napkin, and in second-period French passed it to Gregory Smith, whose ears turned the same shade of pink. Or when Jess and I would go Christmas shopping for our small circle of friends each year, the cold winter wind sharp on our cheeks, our breath frosting the air. After giving the shopkeeper in the trinkets and jewelry shop off the main square our exact budget, she would solemnly present us with a bundle of tiny treasures that we then carefully wrapped in tissue paper packets when we got home.

I glance up and see a couple of women my mother's age staring at me, one with a hand comically raised to cover her mouth. I smile uncertainly, and they quickly look away, rushing past me. It triggers another set of memories, another layer. Without Jess at my side, I always felt like an outsider. Like I was too different and didn't belong. The stories and whispers about magic and superstition were always intertwined with my last name, Morgan. I never knew exactly how to fit in, how to shake off my name. After I left, it all got too much for Mum and Dad, and they left too.

I carry on along the pavement and reach the shop that my grandmother, Ivy, ran. The candle shop is a tiny crooked thing with a narrow green door and a window with square glass panes. My breath hitches when I see the display, taking in how faded it looks. How tired and old the jumble of candles appears. This shop used to sparkle, luring in passersby with the scents of jasmine and fig, light spilling out in a golden pool over the pavement.

Now it belongs to me, another provision of the will. The lease, the stock. The extra pile of responsibilities. And I'm not sure what to do with it. I press my fingers to the glass, breath fogging up the panes, and feel as though I can almost see Ivy inside, see her smiling, plump little form peering around her old-fashioned cash register. Fingers of cold brush the back of my neck and I step away, thrusting my hands into my pockets.

I hurry away, even though I have the key in my pocket. I need to do an inventory, find the paperwork for the lease, and decide what to do with those two dusty rooms. Ivy leased the shop from Cora and Howard; it was Howard's mother's shop before it was Ivy's. Howard's mother, Mrs. Price, ran it as a haberdashery, a small treasure trove of ribbons, lace, and buttons . . . but that was before my time. I pause in the street, then turn back to the shop, my fingers closing over the large iron key in my pocket.

No. Not yet. I release my hold on the key, letting it drop back to the lint lining my pocket. Not today. One thing at a time. Today I need to find the old hardware store and work out what to buy for the renovation.

Cora, in her busy way, has arranged for an electrician to come over. All I had to do was leave the door unlocked and make myself scarce for a few hours. It wasn't hard. Especially when I heard who it was: a boy a few years above me at school, now a man who had moved two towns over. I wasn't quite ready for the small talk, the quiet judgment. One step at a time, I guess. There are plenty of months left to find out what Woodsmoke really feels about me and the choices I've made. To learn if anything has changed for the Morgan women, or if we're still largely outsiders, just as we have always been.

The hardware store is on a little side street off the main square, squat and wide, a labyrinth of items. I went in only once before, when I was a teenager looking for picture hooks to hang something of myself on my bedroom walls. Something *I* had chosen, not Mum. I came away with six hooks in a little white envelope, the price written in pencil on the front. I borrowed a hammer from my dad's workshop and put up six crooked pictures behind my bed. I can still picture Mum's pinched mouth, the way she folded her arms when she saw them. A thrill of triumph and rebellion coursed through my veins. Now I realize she was cross only because I pulled great chunks of plaster off the walls, using Dad's hammer.

The bell rings over the door as I walk in, echoing back and back. The shelves are stacked up to nearly twice my height, creating a maze of nails and screws, paint tins, and brushes in dusty packaging. I can hear the owner some way off, his voice muffled and far away. I breathe it in, the scent of purpose. Of wood polish and glue and the tang of metal. I pull the list up on my phone screen, mentally checking each item. It seems so inadequate, this little list, to face the work I have to do this winter.

The owner's voice cuts off suddenly, and I hear footsteps as he moves along the narrow walkways. When he spies me by the door, his eyebrows shoot up, creasing his forehead.

"Carrie Morgan. Ivy said you'd be by." He blinks at me, an HB pencil tucked behind one ear, as he dusts his hands off on the front of his royal-blue boiler suit. "You'll be wanting supplies."

I barely hide the shock of hearing my grandmother's name tossed around so casually, like she's still here with us. "She . . . told you?"

He nods as I hand over my phone so he can scroll down the list. "Before she passed. God rest her soul. Beautiful funeral, Carrie. Just beautiful. Cora made some lovely sandwiches afterward. Good cake too. That woman sure does know how to bake." He looks around as though checking to make sure there's no one else in the shop. No one listening in. "Between you and me, Cora gave my wife a remedy last year. A seasonal ailment. Bets had a terrible rash. All down her neck, her face . . . anyway. Doc didn't have a clue. Made us a consultant appointment, nothing came of it. Then she goes to Cora, quiet in the night like, and . . . well." His eyebrows raise. "I know plenty knock the Morgan name, but they soon all come calling if they need something, don't they? Helped my Bets no end. Ivy was a good woman. Cora is too in her own way."

"Right," I say awkwardly as he hands back my phone. And not for the first time, I wish my last name wasn't Morgan. That I didn't have this legacy dragging behind me. I can picture Cora making the spread for Ivy, ensuring everything was just so. They might not have gotten along toward the end, but Cora would never have seen her sister buried without a good send-off. And she would never turn away someone from the town if she could help them. "You think I need anything else? I just typed out the basics . . ."

He squints at me, humming discordantly. "How about I put together a few bits, and you can take what you can carry today? Howard can drop the rest over to you."

"I—sure," I nod, following as he skirts around teetering shelves laden with items as varied as rubber sink plungers, mouse traps, and boxed-up champagne coupes. It's an Aladdin's cave, and he seems to know exactly where each item is. I trail in his wake, breathing in the scent of wood polish as he collects screws and nails in little white envelopes, writing the numbers and prices on each one before sealing them. This small detail somehow reassures me. While the only constant in my life has been change over the past decade, this shop has managed to stand still.

"Have you been to see Cora yet?" the owner says, tucking the pencil back behind his ear. "I don't like speaking out of turn, but . . ."

"But?" I nudge.

"She's getting worse, Carrie. Almost reclusive. And when she does come into town, it's to tuck one of those recipes of hers inside a letter box, or to cast a warning. You know the ones. She helped my Bets, but some people . . . they don't take kindly to it. Not if they don't seek it out."

"I know," I sigh. Woodsmoke has always been divided over Cora. Those who think she's completely lost it roll their eyes and stuff her recipes in the bin. Sometimes that works out for them, but sometimes it doesn't go so well. When she tells someone to stir up honey and blackberries picked on the second Thursday in September for a tonic and to give it to their sickly child, they might bristle, but they usually follow her advice. Then some find their child becoming even sicker from some unknown illness even the doctor can't figure out. Because that's the thing about Cora—she's got a finger on the pulse of those mountains. When you live in the shadow of such an ancient place, full of stories of disappearances and cries in the night, it's best to heed any advice you can get.

"Howard told me the doctor's been by."

"He didn't say." I wonder what the doctor makes of Cora. Whether they believe in the old ways, or if they think she's lost every marble she ever possessed. "I'll keep an eye out."

When I leave the hardware store, laden with paint tins, brushes, packets of screws and nails, a hammer, and my very own drill, the drizzle has hardened to ice. Hailstones ping from the pavement, and tiny chips of them graze the back of my neck. I hiss, trying to shrug my jacket higher as the sharp little claws of ice burrow beneath my collar. The town square empties out almost immediately, with shoppers dashing for the car park or the sanctuary of the chemist and greengrocer.

That's when I feel it.

A change, a shift in the way the air flows around me. And when I look up, my eyes crash into his across the square. I falter, and the pounding of my heart lurching in my chest echoes through every inch of me. The ground tilts.

"Tom," I whisper, that one syllable carrying the old weight of a broken, restless heart.

He's got his hood up, half obscuring his features, but I'd know him anywhere. I'd know him as a child, as a middle-aged man, as an elderly man walking the winding road toward death. There are some people you just know that way. And as though he heard my whisper across the pavement and the wide, cobblestoned square, he takes a step toward me. But there's a child, a small, insistent little girl tugging on his hand, pulling him back. With another sickening, aching lurch, I realize that this child must be his. His and Jess's. I heard they got together after I left, but even if I had wanted to, I couldn't call Jess. I couldn't write to her. She didn't feel like mine anymore, she felt like another person entirely. And this man, this man I knew as a boy, is all hers now. A stranger.

I can't be here.

I run. I run as fast as I can, weighed down with the paint and the drill and everything else. I lumber all the way to my car, parked on a side street, dump all the supplies onto the backseat, and then sit in the driver's seat taking gulp after gulp of frigid air.

Twenty minutes pass before I feel able to drive. The tremors in my hands rattle and rattle, forcing me to turn inward. To relive the last few moments of our parting, when I ripped my world apart to save his. I haven't had a panic attack since the months leading up to the day I left. After leaving Woodsmoke behind, the attacks vanished too. Until now, I guess.

The engine turns over twice, three times, before the low rumble starts. The hail has stopped, leaving pockets of ice in the corners of the pavement shining like tiny marbles. The clouds still linger, though, pressing down on Woodsmoke, reminding us that winter is here. And the snow, the endless cold, will arrive with a finger snap soon enough.

It's not until I'm on the road and turning out of town that I remember the last thing on my list. Tea bags. And somehow, forgetting that one item, that simple, everyday thing, is what sends me plummeting over the edge.

When I return to the cottage, there's another bunch of wildflowers on the doorstep. For a beat, I just stare at them. I purse my lips, frustration building in my temples, and think about all the stories, the superstitions woven through Woodsmoke. About Cora and the book and her warnings. My heart thuds faster and faster, drumming up a tempest. I don't know if it's fear or anger or something in between, but I pick up those flowers and hurl them into the frost.

I slam the door to the cottage in my wake. It's not just about the wildflowers. Or the fear of who or *what* might be leaving them on the doorstep. It's everything. It's this crumbling cottage, it's being back here. It's the hole in my heart I've carried for a decade, wanting so desperately to fill it with a home that didn't seem to belong to me. I lean against the front door, gazing at the hallway. I should go back upstairs and carry on stripping wallpaper. That's what I should do.

But I have that feeling again. Like I'm being watched. Tested. Like every move I make is being weighed and measured.

I take a deep, shuddering breath, expelling my fear and frustration, and turn to open the front door. I bend down and carefully gather up the stems of the discarded wildflowers, making sure none of the buds are damaged. Then I go into the cottage, pull one of Ivy's old enamel jugs down from a shelf, and fill it with water. Looking at the flowers sitting in that jug on the farmhouse table, I can't help feeling like I'm losing. Like my homecoming is a test, and I'm failing so far. Like I'm cursed, cursed to never belong here. Like the mountains are filled with fury that I left.

I rummage in the drawers, then pull out an old tub with a

blend of rock salt and dried lavender buds inside. Peeling back the lid, I inhale the delicate fragrance, then carry the tub to the front door. Carefully, slowly, I pour the contents of the tub along the threshold. Along the windowsills outside. I close the lid, look up at the mountains, and squint, eyeing the path that winds up through the trees.

I can't ignore the stories here, not like some people in town try to. I can't ignore the signs or the warnings. I'm back in Woodsmoke, even just for the winter, and the old rules exist for a reason.

Chapter 6
Jess

He knows.

Jess realizes before Tom is even home. She knows before he leaps up the steps that lead to their front door, tugging Elodie in his wake. And when he throws the door open, letting it crack back on its hinges, her whole body runs cold.

He scrubs his hands down his face, his eyes wild and unfocused. She'd forgotten how he is around her. How he can unravel so easily. She'd forgotten this whole other side to the man she loves, the side that was there before she loved him, before Carrie left and they found their way to each other the year after. Jess's thoughts fracture and blur. Does he still care about Carrie? Is this just shock? Or . . . or . . .

Jess busies herself with Elodie, taking off her shoes, hanging up her coat. Her brown curls are plastered to her skin, her face a wide moon as her eyes dart to him. Her father. The man she has never seen in this state. As though he's rolled in a patch of nettle leaves and the spines have burrowed in deep, right to his very soul.

"Tom . . ." Jess sighs, frowning down at Elodie, who still hasn't said a word. Jess notices the green paint tingeing her hands. Tom picked her up from school and took her straight into town for a treat. She can smell the chocolate on Elodie's breath as she leads her into the bathroom, then turns on the tap, and pumps the soap into her pudgy little hands.

"There were hailstones, Mummy," Elodie whispers, drying

her hands on the towel on the back of the bathroom door. "I don't think Daddy liked them. I didn't like them either."

Jess swallows, staring down at her daughter. She's not ready to face what lies beyond the bathroom door. She thought she had exorcised those demons long ago. "Were they big?"

"Kind of like skittles?" Elodie says, considering. "Bigger than Coco Pops. I like the snow better."

"It's just winter beginning early, sweetheart. There'll be proper snow soon," Jess says, opening the bathroom door. Elodie starts her usual tinny tirade about another girl at school, about her shoes pinching her toes and how it's *so unfair* that she's allowed only one hour of TV time when her friend Gus gets two whole hours. But Jess isn't listening. Her focus is on Tom, standing next to the sofa, hovering over his mobile phone. It irritates her when he just hovers like that, and she wants to tell him to sit down on the damn sofa. But there's a charge in the air, in the silence that streams from him in waves. It plumes outward, like a cloud, engulfing her and their life together. She coughs, turning away, needing to form a plan, needing to do *something* . . .

"Are you, er . . . going out later still? The pub, was it?" she asks Tom carefully as she moves into the kitchen and reaches into the fridge for the ingredients for dinner. Her hands, automatically closing around the onion, the tomatoes, the mince, need to stay busy. She wants to make a Bolognese sauce from scratch. She needs this house to smell like a home. Like *their* home, the one they've built together. Then maybe Tom will snap back to himself. She needs him to make a joke, to wink at her and trick a grin from her lips. She needs him to be the Tom she fell in love with, the nineteen-year-old with the too-long hair who played bass in a band in the cramped back room of their favorite bar on the edge of town. The Tom she met up with on every university break, the one she couldn't stay away from. Who turned out to be less of a fling and more of a permanent fixture after she finished her degree.

Or maybe she's just fooling herself.

"I . . . after dinner? Are you okay to put Els to bed?" he asks, distraction dragging out every syllable as he pockets his phone. He blinks at her owlishly, as though just remembering who she is. And the choices he made.

"Sure," Jess says, her tone a touch too high and pitchy. She flicks on the kettle, needing the familiar comfort of her favorite mug warming her hands against this sudden winter chill. He's not being himself. "Be back before ten, though? That series is starting, you know the one—"

"What? Oh yeah. Yes. Of course." He lunges toward the staircase, still wearing his boots. Jess winces when he doesn't take them off, picturing the germs and dirt trailing their way up the stairs. She makes a mental note to steam-mop later. Her hands are already itching to snatch up a cloth and the disinfectant, to balance a reprimand on her tongue to shoot in Tom's direction. But it dies in her throat. Suddenly, she's treading on eggshells again. Wondering when he'll say her name, the name of his childhood sweetheart. The girl he offered his heart to before he offered it to Jess.

He doesn't get home at ten. Midnight comes and goes, and the hours creep ever closer to daybreak. She tosses in their bed, back and forth, back and forth. He's left her, she's sure of it. He's with Carrie. He went to her the minute he left the house. She pictures them, imagining their rekindling. How he will stare at her in reverence, closing the distance until she's in his arms. Then the past decade will melt away, and they'll both admit they made a mistake, that it was always Tom and Carrie, asking themselves:

How did we let it slip away? And Jess, with her meddling and her own wants and wishes, will be swept aside for this woman who has remained perfect in his memories.

Jess kneads her eyes with her fists, trying to banish her imaginings. He could be crashed out at his dad's, and not for the first time. Drank too much and stayed there with his sour breath and fogged-up head, instead of bringing that back home with him.

But she still can't help thinking Tom has gone to her. To Carrie. And that Carrie's return this winter is a repeat of what happened last time. Does he still think about her? Does he cling to her memory the way she does, never able to stop thinking about her? Jess has never asked. Never had the nerve to bring her up, to invite the ghost of Carrie into their home from the cold edges to sit wedged between them.

Jess finally gets a handful of hours' reprieve when her mind falls into a troubled slumber. She wakes at six, before Elodie is up, and shambles down to the kitchen in her old dressing gown and slippers. She finds Tom in the lounge, sitting on the edge of the sofa. His eyes when he turns to her are bloodshot and haunted. Fear clutches her insides, stilling the breath in her throat.

"Carrie's back."

Chapter 7
Carrie

When she awoke, the sky had changed. It was no longer blue. Everywhere she looked, blue was replaced with gray: her school dress, the wallpaper in her bedroom, the sky itself above her. Lillian Morgan had stolen the book and made a bargain with the mountains, and for that… she paid the price. Her bargain cost her the color blue, but it gave her the love of her life.

—Cora Morgan, February 15, 1984

"Bastarding thing," I screech, dropping the wallpaper stripper on the floor. I place my hands on my hips, take a deep breath, and close my eyes. My wrists, my entire hands, are cramped up and aching, however often I swap the tool from left to right. And this is the first wall. The first bedroom. I have two more to go after this one, and this wallpaper is sticking to the plaster, stubborn as shit.

I eye the curls of wallpaper littering the floorboards, the ones I've managed to scrape away from the decades-old glue. Tiny flowers peep up at me, forget-me-nots, roses, and sprays of baby breath woven over a cream background. As I grit my teeth, my gaze travels to the ominous patch overhead. Damp. The mildew is spreading like an ink blot, steadily taking over an entire corner near the window.

"That's a tomorrow problem," I mutter, checking the time. It's already eleven, and I've only had one coffee today. This feels like at least a two-coffee, one-tea morning. I push back my hair and knead my left palm as I clunk down the stairs. All the while, the to-do list revolving around in my head is growing longer. Wallpaper stripping. Sorting out the damp. New soffits and fascias. Replastering? I fill the little travel kettle with a groan, then watch it until it rattles to a boil and I can make a cup of bitter instant coffee.

I fidget in my pocket, pull out my phone, and perch against the old farmhouse table. Every inch of me wants to open Instagram, to gorge on photos of other people's lives, all the places they're traveling to, the food they're eating. To bask in the romanticized version of the day-to-day and let my own fall away. But I don't. Instead, I pull up the notes app and do what I've always done when I feel the world overwhelming me like a wave. Like when my exams were coming up and all I had was a pile of half-read textbooks, not enough class notes, and too many doodles in my sketchbook. Or like when I first left Woodsmoke, money in my bank account, passport in hand, and bought an interrail pass on a whim to travel through the major cities of Europe. I make a list.

1. Walk around the cottage and make a list of things that need work.
2. Read the surveyor report. Properly.
3. Go food shopping.
4. Avoid the wine aisle.
5. Buy chocolate instead.
6. Call parents.

I open a fresh note on the app and stand up. There's something about making a list that always grounds me. It reminds me of my purpose and gives me something concrete to focus on. I learned this trick—probably from the advice column in some magazine—

after my brain felt scrambled and overwhelmed getting ready for school exams. Now, whenever I'm planning a backpacking trip, or relocating to a new country, or getting ready for a gallery showing, I make a list.

I pour the coffee into a travel mug so it will stay warm, swirling in a heaped teaspoon of sugar to hide the burned and bitter taste. As I walk around the cottage, the anxiety built up inside me unspools, turning into certainty. A plan. The list on my phone gets longer, but I categorize each point by room, order them, then color-code them. Pink, blue, green, yellow. Each area of the house sorted, stored, and assessed in priority order. When I finish with the list, I take a few pictures, then upload them to Instagram with cheery captions. I drop my phone back into a pocket and take a sip of the coffee. There. I *have* made it.

This isn't all a huge mistake.

I'm staring out the window, up at the mountains, when I hear the faint jingle of a FaceTime call. I muddle through the pockets of my denim dungarees for my phone, only finding it after I've missed the call. It was Mum. Again. I haven't spoken to either of my parents since I left, haven't wanted to admit that this isn't going as well as I hoped it would. But I've been here a week. It's time to put on a brave face and cross number 6 off the list.

There's not enough signal in the cottage or the field for a proper video call, so I track farther from the cottage, toward Woodsmoke and the main telephone mast on the edge of town. When I've got it in sight, I down the last of the coffee (lukewarm and acrid—should have added an extra sugar) and press my lips together before clicking on her number. Mum answers almost immediately.

"Hello! Carrie? Blasted thing, it's just a blank screen—"

"Mum, I'm here!" I suppress a sigh. Every. Single. Time. "You just need to turn the camera on! That's it, yes, turn it on!"

They pop up on the screen, two furrowed brows with reading glasses perched on their noses, Mum's with a purple beaded cord draped around her neck. Their faces are pressed up to the camera, squinting at it like it's the world's most complex invention.

"Aha! We got it, Lillian!" Dad lifts his coffee mug, and we pretend to clink on-screen. I hide my smile behind my travel mug. Give Dad a car to fix or a map to read and he's brilliant. But hand him a laptop or a phone and he acts like he's defusing a bomb.

"How's the house going, love?" Mum asks, sipping her usual milky Earl Grey tea. "Not roughing up your hands too much, I hope. Hold them up to the screen, let me check . . ."

I roll my eyes, holding them up so she can inspect them. They're chapped and dry, a couple of plasters on my fingers. My nails are cut as short as I can bear, and honestly, it's the first time I've ever looked at them with pride. They aren't covered in nail varnish, perfectly smooth and well moisturized, or flecked with paint or chalk from hours with a new canvas. They're worker's hands.

Of course she winces, though she quickly looks away so I don't see. I catch the look she shoots off into the corner of her conservatory, wait for the ripple of admonishments poised on the tip of her tongue. Before she retired, Mum was a beauty therapist and an at-home Body Shop consultant. She would set up little parties in our lounge, invite all the mums around Woodsmoke in a bid to make friends with the gossipy mothers of the girls I went to school with. She would use me as a model to peddle the Body Shop makeup and skin care products, which I always wiped off at the first opportunity, feeling like an oily clown.

But it was the home beauty and health treatments she created that I loved. The ones she poured into little cork-stoppered glass bottles with labels tied around the necks with twine. Her own collection of recipes that Cora has carefully copied into the *Mor-*

gan Compendium. These were what the mothers all secretly wanted and would stash in their bags and coat pockets before leaving her parties.

"The house is . . . going," I say with a laugh, glad that they can't actually see Ivy's cottage, or the lack of progress I've made. "More work than I thought, but I should be done by the end of the winter, as planned."

"Are you sure you don't need help? I can drive up for the weekend, bring a few of the lads—"

"Dad!" I say, shaking my head. "You promised!"

He runs a hand over his forehead, his tell for all the nerves building under his skin. He's just worried about me.

"You should drive up in the spring," I tell him, "after the snow's cleared." I fix a smile on my face. So Dad won't worry. So he won't try to rescue me. "You know I want you to see the place when it's in good shape. You'll spoil the surprise."

He nods uncomfortably, glancing over at Mum. I'm not convinced she'll join him. I doubt she'll ever set foot in Woodsmoke again unless it's absolutely unavoidable.

"What is it?"

"Your great-aunt phoned."

"And?" I ask, shifting my weight to the other foot as a breeze ruffles my collar, sending a trickle of chill down the back of my neck.

"Cora's . . . worried. She said you haven't called round since you first arrived last week, and she mentioned the early frost—"

"I greeted the mountains, Mum. You don't need to worry. It was the first thing I did."

Mum blinks, and Dad shifts away from the screen. Mum has only admitted once that, after she left Woodsmoke, she finally felt like she could breathe. When you accept the magic of Woodsmoke and the mountains, either you embrace it, as Cora did, or like

Mum and Ivy, you fear it. There's no in-between place. Most of the folks of Woodsmoke are like Mum.

"Nothing else has happened? You know how I feel about Woodsmoke. I don't like to think of you there all alone. Don't meddle in anything, will you? Don't stray from the path—"

"Mum—"

"We both know what can happen," she says quietly. "We both know all the stories are true."

I think of the wildflowers left on the doorstep of Ivy's cottage and wonder if I should tell her. And should I confess that I felt like someone followed me down the mountain that first night and tapped at the caravan window? Should I mention the man I've seen? Or worse, admit that I'm not sure he's human? But I don't say anything. My mum left Woodsmoke for a reason. The magic of this place overwhelmed Lillian, frightened her with its enormity, its greed. After I left, there wasn't a weighty enough anchor to keep her here. She doesn't want to revisit the place or the stories woven through it. There is no wonder embedded in them for her, only fear.

"The man in the hardware store, he said Ivy had a good send-off. Cora made a spread and . . . I should have come back for it, shouldn't I? I should have just booked a ticket and come back for a couple of nights."

Mum frowns at the screen. "Ivy knew you loved her. Eating cake and avoiding talk of the book with Cora at her wake wouldn't have made a difference to her passing. She knew."

"Cora talked about the book?"

"She talked enough. We only stayed the one night, at Cora's," Mum says, looking away from the screen. "That was plenty. That my mother even kept the book for as long as she did . . . Better that it stays with Cora. Better it's buried with her when *she* passes."

"Still, I should have . . . I don't know." I blow out a breath.

"Everything all right, love? Really?"

"Everything's fine. I'll go and see Cora again. I've just been busy."

Mum nods uneasily. "Sure, love. Sure."

I capture her eyes with mine across the miles and miles that divide us, trying to pour reassurance over this thread of a connection. "You know why I'm here, why I had to do this." I glance away, at the field surrounding me, then farther still, my gaze traveling past the trees to the three mountain peaks dominating the skyline. "After all these years, I have to find out if I truly belong here. It's haunted me. I have to know if this is just the town where I grew up . . . or if it's home."

Chapter 8

Cora

The story goes like this. Sylba Morgan met a trapper as the frost glittered on the grass, on an ordinary Wednesday in October. The sky was the color of dirty laundry water, and Sylba was avoiding washday. No one else met him, this man who walked down the mountain path before vanishing after, back into the wild.

—Tabitha Morgan, July 19, 1929

There are no eggs laid by the hens in the yard for three days after Carrie returns. Every batch of Cora's muffins comes out either burned or undercooked. Their dog Kep barks at shadows, and that damn frost glitters over everything, like a taunt. Cora purses her lips as she finishes her morning coffee, swirling out the grounds from her cup in the sink. The mountains are unbalanced. Something has disturbed them, she can feel it. There's a sharpness on her tongue, coating the back of her throat, that reminds her more of a curse than of winter.

"This won't do at all," she mutters to herself as she makes their breakfast, stirring a pot of porridge on the stovetop. Even that comes out thick and gloopy, and she almost has to chew it. It's no good, she realizes. *No good at all.*

"It's just winter come early," Howard says as he winces through breakfast. "Don't fret."

"You and I both know the laying hens are like clockwork.

We've never gone this long without eggs," Cora says, enunciating her point by stabbing her fork in the air. "Like clockwork!"

"Even so."

She harrumphs. "The book will know. There'll be something in there, some warning, some tale—"

"I was wondering when you'd bring that up. Took you all of a five-minute conversation."

"Are you giving me cheek, Howard Price?"

Howard coughs, scraping the last of the porridge from his bowl, and rises to his feet. "Wouldn't dream of it."

Cora mutters darkly as Howard leads Kep out the front door, on their way to check the field boundaries and talk to the neighbors. Her husband has had the same routine for sixty years, and apart from the day of a wedding or funeral, nothing will shake him from it. He always takes Kep through the front door, never the back. Not among the chickens, and never through the yard.

Cora washes up quickly, stacking the dishes and spoons with the saucepan on the drainboard. She wipes down every surface, ensuring that the stovetop gleams. Then she folds her tea towel just so over the rail on the range cooker, cleans her hands with the soap she makes herself, and checks the time. Ten o'clock already.

"Time to get down the book, I should think."

She hobbles through to their bedroom, her hip giving her nothing but grief in this sudden cold snap, and pulls the book from its hidden spot. Then she takes it through to the lounge, props herself up in her armchair, perches her reading glasses on her nose, and opens it.

She finds an entry recorded by her grandmother, Tabitha:

This is not a firsthand account. Or even a second, or a third. This tale has been passed down and passed down, discussed around hearths, embellished and clipped, until I sat down to record it in the book...

Cora sags lower in her armchair, the ache in her hip receding as she's enfolded by the tale that could tell her what this sudden cold snap means. It's about the frost. It's a tale that begins as a love story and ends with a curse. When she finishes, Cora closes the book and stares into space. Then she clicks her tongue and gets to work.

"If someone in Woodsmoke has brought this upon us, there'll be nothing but heartbreak and sorrow come spring," she says to the walls as she moves through to the bedroom, putting the book back where she hides it. "They need rock salt. Plenty of it. Dried lavender buds, yes, but also perhaps some fennel seeds . . ."

She walks to the kitchen and pulls glass jars from the bottom shelf of her pantry. This is where she keeps the ingredients for any workings from the book. Unlike some of the Morgan women who came before her, she doesn't like to call them "spells." The word sounds fanciful, like the language used by a child playing dress-up. These ingredients, carefully combined and used correctly, are from recipes passed down through the generations from grandmother to granddaughter.

The workings in the book aren't all alike. For lesser workings, like this one, only a few ingredients are blended in the exacting conditions needed for them to work. Other workings require pieces of the Morgan woman performing them—usually blood. And promises. Ivy never took to those workings. She would shudder and quickly flip past those pages, fingertips barely brushing the ink. That was how Cora knew, deep in her bones, that the book should never have gone to Ivy. It was always meant for her, for someone who understood the true weight of a bargain.

Cora mixes twenty small batches of the salt, lavender, and fennel in the correct quantities, twists them up in little paper packets, and lines her wicker basket with them. She pulls on her purple wool coat and checks in the hallway mirror that her hair is set rigidly in a tight bun before tying a lilac headscarf under her chin. Then she picks up the wicker basket, sets it on the crook of her arm, and carries it to the passenger seat of the car. She pulls on her leather driving gloves and places her hands at exactly ten and two o' clock before guiding the car out of the driveway and onto the narrow lane into town.

She rarely bothers with the radio anymore. None of the songs seem like songs at all. They're all static and jumpy noises, or an awful lot of moaning about nothing. She much prefers classical music if she does turn on the car radio. Vivaldi is her favorite, but of course today the classical channel is playing a Mozart selection. She can't imagine that anyone with an ounce of taste *really* likes Mozart.

"It's these young people." She sighs, twisting the knob and filling the car with silence. Instead, she thinks about which homes she needs to pay a visit to. Which families need a sharper warning than the rest.

She pulls into Lemon Yard on the west side of town, closest to the snow-tipped peaks of the mountains, and pulls the wicker basket onto her arm. The family names of the women she knows can be wayward rattle through her mind: Evans, Peters, Simpkin, Gregson, Brookes . . . She makes her first stop twenty paces away. The sour-faced Cass Evans greets Cora with suspicion, her bottle-blond highlights looking brassy and limp.

"What am I meant to do with this? Eat it?" Cass waves the packet in Cora's face. "My Helen is a good girl. She's not chasing boys, she's not out at all hours."

"But she wants to fall in love, doesn't she?" Cora says, raising her eyebrows. "And we both know she wandered off into the mountains last spring. Or have you forgotten how you nearly broke my door down begging for a way to find her? Hmm?"

Cass's eyes widen with something akin to fear, something raw and faraway, before she sighs theatrically, rolling her eyes. "*Fine.* Sprinkle on the thresholds, I take it?"

"And Helen's windowsill, to be on the safe side," Cora says firmly. "And if you even suspect for a *moment* that she's met someone new, someone you've not heard of before, you tell me, Cassandra Evans. You come to *me*, you hear?"

"I hear you," Cass says grudgingly, accepting the packet between pinched thumb and forefinger. "We all bloody well hear you."

"And lucky you are too."

Cora leaves her, muttering about Evans women, how they always come in one variety: sour. But Helen . . . Helen's different. Cora remembers all too well finding her last year, a few feet from the path, her eyes distant, wistful, dazed . . .

Cora shakes off the memory, knowing she's doing right by the girl. She's doing right by *all* of them. She continues through the town, distributing twists of rock salt, lavender buds, and fennel seeds in the paper packets. Some of the women, especially the mothers, regard her with suspicion. Some are grateful, and some roll their eyes as she retreats from their front door. But all of them listen. None of them turn her away. And by lunchtime every paper packet has been left in the right place, with a warding sprinkled along the threshold of every household she has visited.

"A job well done," Cora says to herself smugly. Her hip is aching something fierce, making each step an effort as a fresh gust ruffles her headscarf. She collects eggs from the butcher's—muttering about the laying hens being off-color—and flour from the general store. At the newsagent's, she selects a new paperback. She walks past the library, but of course Jess and Dawn aren't on her list. Neither of them is from a wayward family. By the time Cora returns to her car, she almost has a spring in her step. The frost may have arrived early, but she'll be damned if she sees anyone else disappear up the mountains. Curse or no curse, this winter *will* go well.

Ivy would have tutted. She would have called Cora a fool for interfering and urged her to ignore the signs, to leave the mountains and their meddling well alone. She would have told Cora to close the book, to do no more workings. She would have reminded her sister of what she herself had had to give in return, of the bargains she had made. Of all that they had lost.

But Cora loves the people of Woodsmoke. The sour-faced Evans women, the Simpkins, the Brookes family . . . She loves the mountains and their magic just as much, but there's a balance to be maintained, she believes. The mountains have claimed too many lives. With this curse of early frost, this curse she hasn't quite put her finger on . . . well. It doesn't hurt to be careful. To dish out a few reminders of the old ways.

It's just Carrie she needs to fix now. Just Carrie she needs to check on, and all will be well.

Chapter 9
Carrie

My sister disappeared in the last blush of summer, and there have been no wildflowers left on the doorstep since.

—Clemence Morgan, December 18, 1875

The stranger from before is outside the cottage. He's carrying wildflowers—a small bunch of yarrow and evening primrose—in his fist. At first, I watch him through the windscreen, gripping the steering wheel, my knuckles turning white. I've just gone to pick up a steam wallpaper stripper; it's sitting in a box on the passenger seat at my side.

The man knocks on the cottage door, once, twice, then shakes his head. He places the wildflowers on the doorstep and thrusts his hands into his pockets. He's all angles, this stranger. Dark hair curving over his forehead, framing sharp cheekbones, his back curved like a sickle. He turns, walking toward the path that leads up the mountain. My gaze snaps to the yarrow and evening primrose, the haze of white and yellow that I know will wilt within an hour, and then to his retreating back. I get out of the car.

"Wait!" I call, slamming the car door shut. "Wait!"

His footsteps stutter as I hurry over to him, past the wildflowers, past the cottage. He turns, eyebrows raised in a question. And as I get closer to him, I see the true color of his eyes. Blue, a deep midnight blue, the deepest navy I've ever seen. Those eyes blink at me now, over his pursed mouth. "Who are you?"

Irritation nettles me. "I'm the woman you're leaving flowers for. Did you leave a bunch the other day as well? On this doorstep?"

"Yes."

"Well, don't. Do you think I need this? Here? I don't want these left here, I—"

His forehead bunches, tiny lines creasing his skin. "I left them for Ivy."

"Ivy . . ." I blow out a breath, relief pooling in my middle, replacing the irritation, the fear, the superstitious fear that I should be gathering up these flowers. The wildflowers were left by a *person*. An actual, living being. Not by the mountains. Not like some folktale that's been passed from tongue to tongue in Woodsmoke or written in the book. I rub a hand over my face, the tiredness of the last few days catching up with me suddenly. "Ivy passed away. I'm sorry."

"Oh," he says. He closes his eyes briefly, as though gathering himself. When he opens them, they're fixed on me. "Are you her granddaughter?"

"Yes, I am."

A faint smile ghosts around his lips. "She said you'd return."

Then he turns on his heel, setting off for the mountains.

"Wait!" I say again, reaching a hand out to him before I can stop myself. I don't know why I reach out to him. I'm wrung out, fed up with the wallpaper stripping, with this cottage that seems to be crumbling at its core. The more layers I peel back, the more I find. And these wildflowers, these gifts, have been bothering me for a week. Like a distant buzzing I can't quite tune out. But I can't ignore them, knowing the tales, the magic of this place. "How did you know her?"

He hesitates, turns partway, and fixes his eyes on the cottage at my back. A shadow passes across his face, but he quickly blinks it away. So quickly that I wonder if I imagined it. "I helped her last winter. A few repairs, just to keep the place going. I wanted to do more, but she said it wasn't time." He shakes his head in confusion.

"Ivy was like that," I say.

"Mysterious?"

"Cryptic. Stubborn. Even in her own sweet way."

He shakes his head again. "Sorry I disturbed you."

"It's all right," I say, shrugging. "It's good to know where the flowers are coming from. Even if they're not for me. You should have waited the other day, when I called after you. For a minute, I thought I'd imagined you."

He frowns, seeming to move words around in his mouth, reshuffling them, before he answers. "I should have waited and spoken to you. I guess I haven't seen anyone in a while. It's quiet up at the cabin, and I liked Ivy last winter. She didn't expect a lot, but she always loved having flowers in the house. Yarrow was her favorite. And anything yellow. Or pink. Like red campion, but I guess it's past its time. I couldn't find it the other day. Huh . . . I can't believe I'm already talking about her in the past tense." He smiles ruefully, his gaze slipping to his feet.

And I don't know why—maybe because I'm relieved these flowers are left by this person, or because I'm worn-out and lonely, or because of the halting, genuine way he speaks—but I share a piece of myself. "I know. She—she used to collect it for me. She kept a bedroom here, my bedroom, it was always in a jug on the bedside table," I add. "Anyway." I shove my hands in my pockets, feeling like I've said too much.

But his eyes soften. "I'm Matthieu, by the way . . . I doubt she ever mentioned me."

"We . . . we didn't speak much. A few letters, but she didn't like telephones."

He nods, clearing his throat. His skin still has that alabaster pallor, cheeks and nose tinged a faint blush color from the cold. I swallow, trying not to stare, suddenly very aware of my untamed hair, my jacket faded to a shade of brown that could almost be green. He looks unkempt in an almost deliberate way, wearing a lumberjack-style shirt, jeans ripped on one knee. There's a wildness to him. As though he's brought a piece of the mountains down with him. There's something about his eyes, the sculpted line of his jaw . . . I swallow, feeling heat rise up my throat as his eyes meet mine. "Well, if you need help with the cottage, I guess you're here to fix it up? Sell it on?"

"I—I don't know yet." I open my mouth to say more, dropping my gaze to the ground. The image of Tom with that little girl swims before my eyes. "I've only just got back."

He fishes in his jacket pocket, pulls out a battered black Biro, then an old receipt. He scribbles some numbers on the back and thrusts it into my hands. "Here's my number. Like I said, there's more that needs doing in this cottage than Ivy ever let me do."

I hesitate, then take the receipt from him, pocketing it. The irritation nettles again. Another person seems to think that I'm not cut out for this. That I need help, that I can't manage alone. Shouldn't I be the one to make that decision?

"I'm fine. But thanks, I'll keep it in mind."

He shrugs. "Your call. If you need help, I'm here all winter."

"All winter?" I ask.

His gaze locks with mine, the inky depths of them feeling almost familiar. As if I've seen the shape of this gaze before, though I can't quite pin down where. "I've rented the cabin just up the trail—the Vickers one?—for the low season, same as last year. It's booked up for spring and summer, but I'll be here as long as the frost holds."

I watch as he walks along the path, disappearing into the gloaming.

I DREAM OF Tom that night. I'm back in that long, trailing gown, the bells chiming in my ears. They're discordant. Distorted. Tom, his face ashy with fear, all pinched and wrong, is trying to say something. I look down at my hands, see the blood welling in them. Blood and petals, falling, forever falling. And when I look up, it's not Tom standing before me. It's Ivy, holding a bunch of yarrow. Asking me to fix her cottage. Pleading with me to stay.

Chapter 10
Carrie

The next morning I stand in the middle of the lounge of Ivy's cottage. I hug my arms around my chest and try very hard not to cry. It dawned on me upon waking in the caravan, the desolate fields stretching on around me, that there's so much work to do. I have no idea where to start. I've never renovated anything before, barely painted a wall or sanded down a surface. How did I think I could renovate a whole cottage? I can't ask Cora to fix this for me, and I absolutely refuse to phone Dad and ask him to bail me out. Whether I succeed or fail this winter, it's all on me. And the thought of failing, of not succeeding this winter, leaves me breathless with fear.

I pick up the drill, the useless, bloody drill. I need drill bits. A battery charger. And some clue as to what to do with it. My hand shakes as I set it back down on the floor, next to the pile of items I bought a few days ago. The paint, the paintbrushes. The pile of envelopes containing nails and screws.

"Not a bloody clue," I mutter, wanting to kick it all across the room. I swipe at my nose, which is already running. That's the thing, when I cry, my nose runs first. It's the warning sign I need to bolt. I release a jagged sigh, crouch down on the floor, and eye the fireplace. All dust and dirt and absence. I swipe at my nose again, frowning at that fireplace. Then I realize I've still got Matthieu's number on the receipt in my jacket pocket.

I stand abruptly, pacing the room. The receipt is slightly

smudged, but somehow, impossibly, it's still legible. I should have written the number down, saved it in my phone. But my mind was on fire, picturing Tom, that little girl. Wondering if Jess knows that I'm here, what she's doing, and where she works. I've spent so long trying to avoid even the thought of them that now I'm here my mind just burns and burns.

Should I call Matthieu?

I picture his inky blue eyes, the way he looked past me, toward the mountains, as though searching for something. I recognized that in him, that need to find something. Whatever it is, whatever has drawn him back for a second winter, I understand it. I reach for my mobile, tracing the bars of signal in the corner. I could call him. It's either that or give up. I can't leave, ignoring Ivy's last request, written in her will in that commanding way. And I can't ask Cora and let her take control, shaping this winter—*my* winter—as she likes. This is meant to be my homecoming. On my terms, at my choosing, to find if I truly belong here.

But . . .

I thrust the receipt back into my pocket. Asking for help feels like giving in, like conceding defeat. I sniff, drawing myself back together, and swipe to the notes app on my phone. Blinking down at the list there, I delete the item about not buying wine. I'm buying two bottles later. A red and a white, along with a big bar of chocolate.

I add "wallpaper steam and strip" to the list, then head out to the car to pick up the box still sitting on the passenger seat. I lug it inside, up the stairs, and within twenty minutes it's set up and ready to use. Carefully, I coax the wallpaper off the walls, letting it fall in limp swaths before I scrape it off.

"I can manage," I mutter to myself, pushing my hair out of my face. It's only wallpaper stripping.

But after a while, an ominous damp patch spreads across the

wall. In fact, when I press a finger into it, expecting to feel the plaster beneath, the wall feels . . . spongy. I step back, place the steamer attachment on the floor, and quickly google. As the internet slowly ticks over and connects, I see the search returns, saying you shouldn't steam a chipboard surface. I run my hand over the wall, feeling the rough quality of it. It could be chipboard.

That's when I snap. I release a feral, strangled sort of scream, the kind that rises and rises inside you, building, then catching in your throat. My stomach churns, and I blink furiously, eyes heavy with tears I refuse to shed. I place a hand against the wall, leaning into it and close my eyes. Suddenly I'm exhausted. Tired of running from this place, tired of forever returning to it in my dreams. Tired more than anything of fighting. I turn and walk carefully down the stairs to the kitchen at the back of the house. I make a big mug of coffee, stirring in twice the number of sugars I usually allow myself, and try very hard not to scream again.

I can't phone Cora and Howard. I can't call anyone I know from before and admit I'm in way over my head. But . . . I also can't walk away from this. A drawer I haven't gone through yet is slightly ajar, and I jerk it open, my mind a muddle of tired exasperation. And here I find a scatter of old photographs. The kind that are overexposed, taken on a disposable camera, then carried to the local chemist to get developed. The kind you used to pick up a few days later, and thumb through quickly, hoping that at least *some* of them weren't fuzzy or just blank. I sift through the pile, seeing some of Ivy's garden, one of her holding me on her knee when I was a toddler, face smeared with blackberry jam.

And then I find one of me, Tom, and Jess. My breath stutters as I pull it from the drawer. It's the three of us standing in the field just outside, the mountains behind us. We're all wearing backpacks and wide grins, arms slung around each other. Happy. I remember that day. I remember going on a hike with them, following an old trapper map of Tom's, eating our lunch in a clearing with mosquitos buzzing in our ears. I smooth my finger over us, each of our smiles, our sunburned noses. The summer before I left.

The summer before everything changed.

I can't give up now. I just can't.

I reach inside my pocket. Smoothing out the receipt on the old kitchen table, I set my teeth and dial the number scrawled across it in black biro.

It rings and rings, and my shoulders slump. An answerphone kicks in, a generic message from the network provider, and I cancel the call. I'm muttering again, moving around the kitchen, when my phone lights up in my hands.

"Hello?"

"Ivy's granddaughter," he says, his voice a crackle of static and syllables. "You know, you never told me your name."

I hesitate, wondering what he's heard about me and all the other Morgan women who have come before. What stories are whispered still to newcomers? What did Ivy herself tell him of the old ways? "Carrie Morgan."

"Well, Carrie Morgan, what can I help with?"

"The cottage. You said yesterday." I close my eyes, then open them to look out the window. At the mountains, at the way they loom up, eclipsing everything. "You said yesterday that you'd done some repairs on the cottage. That you wanted to do more, but Ivy never let you."

"Yes," he says. Then there's a *whoosh*, as though he's adjusting the phone against his ear. "It's an old place."

I turn my back on the mountains, pressing the phone a little too hard against my cheek. "Would it be possible for you to come over? Perhaps tomorrow? I think I need some help with a few things, and I'd like a quote."

For a moment, I think he's hung up. Then his voice returns, warmer than before. "Sure, Carrie. How's ten?"

"It's good. Thanks."

"No problem."

The line goes dead, and I pocket my phone. In the ringing silence, I allow myself a moment to cradle my fingers around the warm mug. Maybe this isn't beyond me. Maybe with a bit of help, with someone to check things with, like what the hell to do with that chipboard, I can make this work. A smile spreads over my face as I drink the coffee. The warmth of it threads through my chest.

No Cora meddling. No running from Ivy's request. I don't need to call on anyone from Woodsmoke, from the curling mists of my past. I can do this. I can knock this cottage into shape and find a fresh beginning.

Chapter 11

Cora

She walked to the town square with her sisters, perusing the ribbons in the haberdashery window. She saw his reflection behind her and turned, finding his eyes like ink as they trailed over her. Afterward, Sylba spoke of this man with eyes as navy as the night. But no one else could remember seeing him. It was almost as though she had imagined him entirely.

—Tabitha Morgan, July 19, 1929

What she never told anyone was what happened afterward. All they saw was a runaway girl that day.

But Cora knew different.

As she mutters, pulling on her warmest coat, tying her head-scarf, checking that she's stuffed some tissues into her pocket, she clicks her tongue at Kep, whose ears prick up, her gaze fixed on Cora. She needs fresh air to stir her stew of memories. She leaves the house, Kep at her heels, and drinks in the crisp morning air.

It wasn't winter when it all changed ten years ago, but spring, with the frost behind them, the fields no longer crackling with ice. Carrie seemed haunted, with dark crescent moons under her eyes. Skin white as porcelain, collarbone jutting from that dress. She looked fit to shatter, too fragile to be real. In the years Carrie grew silent, when too long passed between each letter, Cora wondered if she had somehow dreamed her. Imagined her. And she would speak to Howard, a great babble of incoherence, about

Carrie, her baby grandniece. Her girl. The one she wished, more than anything, was her own and not Ivy's.

And every time, Howard reassured her, though his patience was growing thin and frayed. Carrie is real. She'll be back one day. You have to have patience. You have to understand.

But eventually Cora could picture only the day Carrie left, seeing all those hairpins in a pool on her sofa. And the sight of Carrie, running as fast as she could, away from Woodsmoke, away from her legacy, her home.

Carrie kept saying, over and over, that she knew it would happen. That she knew it would come to this. She couldn't go through with it, she couldn't make everyone happy, she felt suffocated, trapped, she had to break *free.* As she pulled each pin out of her hair, her slight arms laced with blue veins, she trembled all the more. Shaking not just with sorrow but with relief.

Cora ponders it all now as she sets off on her walk, wending through the back ways, the cut-throughs between the fields. The silent ways. The narrow ways. The ones not marked on the maps detailing Woodsmoke. Whistling to Kep every once in a while, calling to the dog, her old voice grating against the silence.

"Come along, Kep!"

There's no one about, just her and Kep. While Kep nuzzles the mulch and leaves, Cora strides through the past, where she can usually be found these days. In a way, Ivy gave her sister a gift by leaving the cottage and candles to Carrie. Cora and Ivy hadn't spoken in six years, and the turn of each season had been marked with festering resentment between them. It had dug its claws into Cora and refused to let her go, even when she knew she should apologize for what she did. Even when she knew she was in the wrong. But every time she nearly walked this way with the intention of visiting Ivy to patch things up, to admit that the spell should have never been cast, she always stumbled and turned another way. It was envy really, all muddled up with pride. Carrie still made the effort to write to Ivy, but she seldom wrote to Cora. No. Cora was the one who was forever left out. Forgotten. The blood between her and Carrie wasn't thick enough, apparently.

But in leaving Carrie the cottage, Ivy had wedged a door open for her granddaughter to return. And Cora knew it wasn't just about Carrie. Ivy had left Cora something in her will too. Not that Carrie knew about that, or Howard, or anyone. Ivy had left her a quilt, the nine-patch she'd coveted for years. Stitched into the border on the left corner was a note: "Forever your sister."

Cora gasped when she found it, tracing the tiny stitches with her fingers. It was so Ivy. In life, she had been the one with the granddaughter to pass the book to. But in death, she had ensured that Carrie would have to return to Woodsmoke. Return to Cora, so she wouldn't be the last Morgan here. This was what caught her in the end, what pressed the grief into her. That careful, stitched note that took Cora right back to when they were girls. When Ivy was just her sister and there wasn't a whole lifetime of bad decisions and secrets between them. Ivy always seemed to have more—more love in her life, more luck. But with Carrie returned, perhaps Cora would get the chance to feel like a real grandmother. Perhaps now she wouldn't be the last Morgan woman left in Woodsmoke.

Forever your sister.

Cora sighs as she rounds the curve of the path, picturing those stitches, the hands that made them. Like chalk and cheese, her and Ivy. Ivy may have lured her back, but Cora doesn't know how to pin Carrie down and make her stay. It won't do to march over there and insist upon it, or to call in the favors that would bring the tradespeople running to the cottage. If anything, that would speed up Carrie's departure. She purses her lips and whistles to

Kep. It will take a more subtle approach. Far more subtle than Cora is suited to.

And she knows that Ivy is most likely watching from afar, having the last laugh.

The trees strangling each side of the path suddenly fall away, revealing the fields glinting with the first frost of winter. Cora halts, eyeing the light trickling over the blades of grass, how it coats everything with a layer of glitter. She loves this time of year. It's when the mountains are most alive. With the frost come the old tales, the ones about women who lose their hearts. It comes with sighs and longing, wending down the old, ancient paths. It comes with the tale that she rediscovered in the book only yesterday—of a man who appears as the frost shrouds the mountains, then disappears as the frost thaws in the spring.

It's a tale Cora can't shake. She's already reread it three times since yesterday, following the faded loops of Grandmother Tabitha's handwriting, fascinated not because it's a love story but because it's not. The story shows how treacherous these mountains can be. How they can beckon you with a sweet smile, a dark sweeping gaze. Then shred your heart come springtime, when their love melts away.

When she pauses to catch her breath, her eyes return to the mountains. Forever returning. She traces the height of them, the trees clinging to their sides. Then her eyes travel down, down, to the field just east of Woodsmoke. Where Ivy's old cottage is still stubbornly clinging to the earth. Cora knows she shouldn't, but what harm is in it, really? She nods, having convinced herself, and hands Kep a treat from her pocket. After handing out the warnings and the salt to all those other young women in town, why not Carrie? Surely she'll be more cautious than the other women in Woodsmoke, more aware of the mountains and their mischief. But Cora has to be sure.

"Just a small detour is all," she says to Kep. "Howard won't miss us."

Then she steps off the path to make her way across the fields, headed straight to the cottage she hasn't visited in six years.

Cora means to go in. She really does. But something keeps her feet stuck to the dirt, wedging her boots into the unforgiving ground. She stands rooted, just beyond the threshold, Kep sniffing around her as though it's just a regular day. But this isn't a regular day. Not for Cora. This is the day she's returning to her sister's cottage, knowing that she won't find her inside. She'll never find her again. She gasps suddenly, covering her mouth, and a single tear slips down her cheek.

Forever your sister. Those three little words echo inside her, thrumming in her heart, and she sniffs. Finding a tissue up her sleeve, she quickly wipes away the tear, annoyed with herself. She's not accustomed to this grief that's fresh and nimble and quick. It darts in when she least expects it, spilling out of her eyes and bleeding into her thoughts.

"I'm a silly old woman," she mutters to herself, shoving the tissue deep in her coat pocket. Kep sneezes, and Cora sighs, about to turn away. What's done is done, she thinks. Ivy's cold in the ground. We'll never get those years back now. But . . . she can see movement in the cottage, just through the window. Someone's there.

Cora dithers, wondering if she should knock on the door. Whether she should turn away, stop her meddling, her prying. She sees a single discarded yarrow flower, its stem sliced as though with a pocketknife. She knows yarrow was one of Ivy's favorites, but she can't imagine Carrie finding the secret patches on the mountains. Cora remembers the page in the book. The note Clemence Morgan left, about wildflowers and about the disappearance of her sister, Abigail. Cora hisses through her teeth, wondering as her eyes dart to the mountains, to the path at the edge of the field, whether she should intervene. Then she remembers the tale of Sylba. The young woman who met a man with eyes the color of an inky night . . .

Cora finds the remnants of salt and dried lavender sprinkled across the threshold and relaxes a little. At least Carrie hasn't forgotten. At least she knows how to protect herself, unlike those other young women in town. But wildflowers in October, and with an early frost . . .

Cora wonders if Carrie is indeed safe in Woodsmoke, or if she is the one unbalancing everything.

Cora wonders if it's already too late.

Chapter 12

Jess

Jess shakes her umbrella out as she crosses the threshold of the library. It's hailing again, and the snap of cold in the air has chilled her exposed skin. She shakes out a shiver as she closes the door behind her.

Dawn levels her with a look, and Jess shrugs. "Tom was late back. What was I meant to do?"

Dawn rolls her eyes as she picks up a bowl of popcorn (salted, not sweet) and indicates a bottle of nonalcoholic bubbly on the desk. "Bring that through, would you? We've got five minutes before Betty arrives. She's always early."

It's nearly seven o' clock on the fourth Thursday of the month, and on this Thursday, without fail, Woodsmoke library holds a book club. This month they've been reading *The Night Circus* by Erin Morgenstern, which has felt particularly apt for this time of year. Jess fell into the book the first week of October, inhaled it, and turned the final page five days later. She even ordered a hardback copy, deciding it was one of those books she wanted to keep around, like a favorite sweater or the family cat.

"I've written the questions down this time, made ten photocopies," Jess says to Dawn as she unscrews the lid on the bubbly and pours a few inches into ten plastic cups. "There. We're ready for them."

They always take over the crime section of the fiction area, dragging the comfiest armchairs and low tables over to form a haphazard oval. There's been a book club night at the library for as long as Jess can remember. Her mother used to attend when Jess was a little girl, and now she still comes with her quietly gossipy circle. These four of the original group—her mother, Sylvia, Hayley, Annie, and Greta—are all hanging on to middle age. Greta is the only one of the four to have given in to gray hair; the rest have embraced varying shades of auburn hair dye, liberally applied once a month at the hairdressers off the main square. The four friends have been thick as thieves since primary school.

The book club was one of the reasons why Jess so desperately wanted to work at the library one day. She had watched her mother's car leave the drive, the headlights dipping as she turned off toward that side of town. Jess would wait up, clinging to the railings of the banister on the landing, waiting for her mother to get home from the meeting. Waiting for her mother to tuck her into bed so she could hear her thoughts on the book the group was reading. One day Jess wanted to choose the books and host this club. She wanted to be a part of the life of the library, which as a child seemed like pure magic to her.

Newer members of the book group include Betty, with her thick green-and-red wool hat and truckload of opinions; Rashid and Diane, the couple who insist on bringing their aging black Labrador, Lucy; and Gregory, who Jess is fairly sure just turns up for the free snacks. Gillian, with her flyaway hair and absent-mindedness, is an occasional member who turns up so she can catch Jess at the end to gossip. Jess and Dawn make ten (occasionally eleven, with Gillian). The group hasn't welcomed a new member in years.

Betty shambles in first, slapping her dog-eared paperback copy of the book on a side table next to her favorite armchair. "I have *thoughts*," she announces, polishing her glasses with the edge of her cardigan. As Betty launches into a long-winded moan about circuses, Jess wonders if she should have shirked the library rules and brought along a bottle of wine.

Then Rashid walks in, Lucy rambling at his side before collapsing at his feet for a snooze. "Diane couldn't make it." He shrugs apologetically. "Got the sniffles, and she wants to be better before our ten nights in Fuerteventura."

Jess's mother, Sylvia, wanders in with Hayley, Annie, and Greta. They clutch matching Kindles with aubergine-polished nails and take small sips of the bubbly while reminding Jess of what a "very good job" she does keeping up the book club each month.

Gregory slinks in last, grabs the bowl of popcorn, and proceeds to eat half of it before passing it to Rashid.

"Cheers, mate. What did you think of the book?" Rashid asks.

"Can't say I'm a fan of World War I romances, but I tried my best," Gregory replies.

Jess stifles a snort as Dawn presses her lips into a thin, disapproving line. Then, unexpectedly, Gillian rambles in, rummaging in her tote bag for a battered paperback copy of the book. "Sorry, everyone, nightmare leaving the house. Good book, though, isn't it?" She takes a seat right beside Jess, and Jess is reminded of all the times at school when Gillian would sit too close to her, or bump into her as they walked side by side. Gillian never quite got the hang of personal space. Jess smiles at her, pushing down that old, familiar irritation, and lifts her chin to beam around at the gathering with her best librarian smile.

"Well, now we're all here, I'll just pass out the question sheets . . ." She shuffles around the circle, heading out the sheets of paper, as everyone pulls out reading glasses to have a look or, in

Gregory's case, to fold the paper into quarters to use as a coaster for his second glass of bubbly. "Who'd like to start?"

Jess manages to keep the conversation focused on the book for a decent fifteen minutes.

Then Betty mentions the frost. "Early this year. Everyone's saying it." She pops a piece of popcorn into her mouth. "I bet it's something to do with the Morgans."

"You blame everything on the Morgan women, Betty," Hayley says. "Not everything in this town links back to them. Didn't we all have a lovely summer?"

"Tricia Richmond lost her voice for a month!" Betty says, aghast. "I wouldn't imagine she called it a good summer."

"Tricia had a *cold*," Sylvia explains, side-eyeing Jess. "Now, shall we get back to the discussion?"

"Early frost decimated my squashes," Rashid says. "I'm with Betty. All seems a bit odd."

Jess sighs as Dawn tries fruitlessly to turn the conversation around. "What do we all think about the themes in the book—"

"Of course, it's because that young Morgan girl has returned," Betty says firmly. "I always said she'd be trouble."

"Always a little strange in school," Gillian agrees. "Haven't seen her, though, have we, Jess?"

"Carrie Morgan is just carrying out Ivy's wishes," Annie says, shooting Jess a reassuring look. "The Morgans may be a little . . . different, but you can't blame them for a change in the weather."

"What about Cora's warnings? The rock salt?" Betty clasps her hands in her lap. "Handing it out from a little wicker basket, she was. Knocked on almost every door in Lemon Yard. The Evanses, the Simpkins . . ."

"She has a point, I've heard that book is full of *spells*," Gregory begins. "*Actual* spells. And curses."

"Can we return to the *actual* book we're discussing tonight please?" Greta says, but then adds, "Cora Morgan gave me a tonic for my cat last year, perked her right up when the vet couldn't do anything. I'm sure that if we can't say anything nice, we shouldn't say anything at all, *hmm*? Besides," Greta says, her gray bob bobbing as she taps her Kindle with a nail, "I was about to make a *point*."

"You and your points." Rashid sighs.

Annie narrows her eyes as the four best friends draw together. "And what is that supposed to mean?"

As the book club descends into jabs and gossip, about the frost and Cora and Carrie, Jess sinks deeper and deeper into her armchair. She thought Carrie's return might not affect her. She thought that, just maybe, they might avoid each other all winter. But it's clear that Carrie is invading every part of her life already. Sylvia catches her daughter's eye, raising one eyebrow before winking at her reassuringly. Jess raises her shoulders an inch to shrug in return, as if to say, *What can I do?*

Gregory leans over to her. "Great popcorn tonight, Jess. Could we have some crisps as well next month, do you think? I'm very partial to prawn cocktail."

Chapter 13
Cora

Seventy Years Earlier

"You must understand, girls, this book is not a toy." Cora watches as her mother carefully turns the pages, showing her and Ivy the looping writing inside. She is consumed by it, by the sketched illustrations, the titles for each story, the added observations from different Morgan women, the annotated notes in the margins. The history is layered in the *Morgan Compendium*, a book containing multitudes, containing whole worlds. Containing, she believes, real magic. Cora leans in closer, sure that her mother is finally sharing the secrets she knows are just beyond her fingertips. Where the mountains touch the sky, where the trees lean together, whispering and hiding the old ways beneath them.

Grandmother Tabitha has died, aged one hundred and a day, on All Hallows' Eve no less, and the book will now pass from grandmother to granddaughter. It will pass to ten-year-old Cora or twelve-year-old Ivy, and Cora cannot contain the excitement in her chest.

But Ivy is fidgeting beside her.

"Stop that," Cora murmurs to her sister, digging her elbow into Ivy's side. She doesn't want Ivy to ruin this. Not this too, when she ruins everything else.

Ivy sighs, twirling a strand of fair hair like a ribbon around her finger. She lets it unwind, a faint corkscrew shape bending it into a loop, before shaking it back to pin her gaze on their mother. "It's just a book," she says. "It's the one Grandma Tabitha kept on her nightstand, with all the old stories and recipes in it."

"It is. Well observed." Her mother beams. Her eyes glitter, sharp little chips of blue that always seem to see the best in Ivy, even when Cora can see all her faults in plain sight. Her mother's approval nettles her, drawing out the sour blood between them. Drawing out the spite in Cora that seems to rise out of nowhere.

"I can look after it, Mother," she says, licking her lips. "Will you let us read it now? If we're careful?"

Cora's mother blinks, her expression shifting. She snaps the book shut, lips tightly pinched. "It passes from grandmother to *oldest* granddaughter. Ivy will have the book."

"What? That's not fair!" Cora says before she can contain the words. "Ivy doesn't care about anything, she makes a constant mess, she'll ruin it, or lose it, it isn't *fair*—"

"Sorry, Cora," Ivy cuts in quietly. She raises her hands slowly, and their mother beams at her as she passes the book into Ivy's outstretched hands. "Maybe we can read the stories together?"

Cora sits, fuming, as Ivy eyes her quietly like she's a lit match sparked by every argument, every fight she ever had with Ivy. Cora wonders what would happen if she pushed her, just gave her a good, hard *shove*—

"Cora, go to the step."

Cora takes a great trembling breath. The step. The place she has been banished to more times than she can count this week. The back-door step, beside the compost heap, where the chickens peck and cluck in inane, slow circles. Where she will be utterly, horribly alone. And Ivy will have the book all to herself. She hesitates.

"Go to the step."

Cora lets her eyes rest for one beautiful, full heartbeat on the book Ivy now clutches in her hands. The book that should be in *her* hands. The *Morgan Compendium*. The collected stories of the mountains, of generation after generation of Morgan women. She heaves a trembling sigh, stands with leaden bones, and drags herself out of the room, toward the back of the house, the lonely part. As she walks, she hears her mother slide off her chair to sit beside Ivy. She hears the excited lilt in the cadence of her voice as she shows Ivy the first story, telling her that it is all real, that every secret revealed in the book should be guarded now by her.

Cora makes a vow while sitting on the back step that day. She stares up at the mountains, looming like God above her, and promises that she will get that book.

It isn't Ivy's, it isn't mother's. It's *hers*.

Chapter 14

Cora

She can barely contain it, the thumping in her chest. It rattles her, setting her limbs to twitching, slicking her palms with sweat. She places them flat on the drainboard. Its metallic coolness bites into her skin, reminding her to breathe. To think.

"Easy does it," she says, thinking about her ticker. About the way her thoughts are leaping around, like the flicker of an old black-and-white film. "Easy now."

Cora wants to tell Howard. It's the first thing, the only thing, she thinks as she half runs, half walks, to the front door, beating Kep. But by the time she reaches the familiarity of her kitchen, she's not sure if she should. She's not sure if he'll understand. He has never liked her talking about the book, or the old stories woven through it. Howard's world is a practical one: You care for the chickens and get eggs out of them. You work a day and get paid a wage. The only thing Howard has ever lost his head over is her. Everyone warned him not to take up with a Morgan woman, especially not the prickly one. But he didn't listen. Didn't *want* to listen.

"Thought I heard you."

She jumps, a bolt running through her, and turns to find Howard framed by the doorway. His eyes crinkle, and she notes the slippers on his feet, the paper in his hand. He's been waiting for her.

"Did Kep behave herself?" he asks, bending down to pat the

dog's head, fussing her. All lean, like a small wolf, she's got one black ear, one white. They thought she was a collie when she was a pup, but now Cora's not so sure. Especially with the way Kep hunts on their walks, all rangy and focused, and the way she eyes the chickens like she's ravenous. "Did you do the usual route?"

"Not today," Cora says carefully, moving to the kettle, her old hands falling into the pattern of routine. "Circled around Ivy's field."

"Did you now."

"Don't say it like that," Cora says, filling the kettle from the tap. She bangs the top back on and presses down the switch to start the boil. "I can go that way if I like."

"Never said you couldn't."

She prowls around in uneasy silence, stewing in her own thoughts, her mind a tempest. And he waits, watching her cross back and forth, first for cups, then teaspoons. Then the sugar he hasn't had in his tea for a good fifteen years. He watches her make the tea, one for her, one for him, loading up both with two teaspoons of sugar. He resigns himself to how wrong it will taste. And still he waits.

"Only . . ."

"Only?"

Cora bites her lip, indecision giving way like a dam. "I couldn't help myself. I went up to the house and saw a discarded wildflower by the front door. Like Carrie had chucked it out. Like . . . like someone had left it there for her. It was yarrow. Only grows on the mountains in secret patches."

"And . . ."

"She's put wardings on the thresholds and the windowsills. She knows something's up, like that wildflower was a warning. Like—"

"You're worried."

"I . . . maybe. She's been a good girl, warded with salt and lavender. Even after ten years, she still remembers."

"Well, that's something."

Cora looks at him sharply. "Are you patronizing me, Howard? Because if you are—"

"Wouldn't dream of it."

"Hmm."

"Problem is, Carrie's return was always going to spark something," Howard says with a shrug. "This town's got a long memory. Mountains even longer."

Cora snorts. "A list of grudges and mischief more like." She hopes Carrie isn't already setting fire to Woodsmoke with her return. She knows it's as dry as tinder. All those secrets, stashed away in attics, in the cupboards, in the back of everyone's minds. Ready to light up, to burn and burn. And Carrie, with her long absence, with the ripples she's already caused, is the one holding the match. Everyone wanted her to wear that white dress, and no one wanted her to be accepted more than Cora. Finally accepted, not on the edge of things. Not treated like every Morgan woman who came before her.

"Grudges, a long memory . . . same difference," Howard says, making for the door. Cora knows he's thinking of Queenie, his layer. He wants to coax an egg from her, just one, and then he'll know she's all right. But Cora's not done yet. She needs to voice all this, to untangle the snarl inside of her. And he hasn't had his tea yet. Or the cake.

"I can't stop thinking of that story. I forgot my mother told me first, but I found it again in the book," she says. She loads the tea and two slices of cake, the fruitcake she baked just yesterday, on the tea tray, and he takes the hint, following her into the lounge. She places the tray on the coffee table, and they both sink slowly into their seats, bones shifting and aching as they find some comfort in the worn-out routine.

"Your mother told you a lot of stories," Howard says, side-eyeing his wife. She's flustered, has been since Carrie got back. Her hair has a frizz to it, no longer smooth and orderly. And she has barely looked at him. Instead, she looks right through him, or around him. She's not really here. And this makes Howard's bones ache even more than they do when he has to fold his joints into the old armchair he favors.

Cora waits until Howard picks up his tea, then lifts her own to her lips. Tea is like a homecoming. You know where you are with tea. There's a steadfastness to tea, the way it roots her in a way not many things can. The few times she's been away from Woodsmoke, when she and Howard have gone on holiday abroad or just on a day trip somewhere, she has always brought tea bags. Then hunted down milk and proper-sized mugs. Tea will always root her.

"It was the one about the frost I was thinking of."

"The frost."

"You know, Howard," she tsks. Then Cora's voice softens. "The one about a woman who meets her love at first frost, then he vanishes as the frost thaws in springtime. Never to be seen again, leaving her heart broken and forever cursed to search for him on the mountain. I—I tried to remember the exact way my mother told it. It's written differently in the book, all fact, no embellishments. Typical Grandma Tabitha. No heart to it." She sets down her cup in the saucer. Porcelain jostles against porcelain, rattling through the room. Howard watches her, knowing she's not done.

"When I saw those wildflowers, whole bunches of them, scattered outside the cottage, I knew, I just *knew*—"

"Coraline—"

"The mountains didn't welcome her home, Howard. They're tormenting her. Punishing her for—for leaving . . ." Cora takes a gulp of her tea, then instantly regrets it as it burns the roof of her mouth. The delicate skin creases like tissue paper, and she winces, rubbing her tongue over it. "I'm afraid the story is right. The one about the frost and the great love that will disappear. I'm afraid that—that it's happening to my Carrie. That someone—or something—is leaving her flowers. And the unbalance, can you feel it? It's because of her. She'll get her heart broken. Then she won't stay, will she? She'll leave again. Because she's cursed."

Her voice quakes, and Howard reaches for her, holds her skeletal fingers in his fist. He feels more and more that he is her tether to this world. Like she's a balloon, tugging on his hand, forever drifting. And if he makes one wrong move, utters the wrong words, she will release his hand and let go. Cora doesn't say the obvious—that maybe it's Tom, or an old school friend, or any one of a number of real, *breathing* people, who's leaving Carrie flowers. That's not the way her mind works.

"I'll go and see her, love."

"You will?"

He sips his tea, frowning at his cup. He's always hated this tea set. The edge of the fine porcelain bites into his lip, in such contrast to the warm blandness of the drink. "Today. I'll go there today. But Cora—pay no mind to it. The stories, the frost . . . I'm sure she's just had people round to help her out. Maybe they brought flowers. Maybe she's developed allergies and put them outside the house, and that single stem of yarrow didn't make its way to the compost heap. She can't do it all alone, can she?"

"She should have asked *me*," Cora says. "You could have been there, I could have made the lunch, come and checked on things, or—or I could have found her someone. Maybe someone she knew from school, someone she trusts, someone we *know*—"

"That's the point, love. That's the whole point. She doesn't want us there, underfoot. She wants to do this for herself. This is her homecoming, her way of finding her place here again. We've got to give her the time to work it all through in her head. She'll only bolt otherwise."

Cora seethes quietly, sipping her tea. Her heart is a storm, raging at Carrie, at Ivy, at the people of Woodsmoke, at the tea for burning the roof of her mouth.

"I'm not wrong, Howard. You'll see," she snaps, staring into the middle distance. She pictures the page in the book, the one with the frost tale written on it. She's not sure if it was her great-grandmother who recorded it or her mother. It would have been carefully transcribed, told around the hearths of a dozen households, before the young woman, whoever she was, gave in to her grief and climbed the mountain in search of him.

But the writing is faded now, only just legible. If it wasn't for the Morgan women, these tales would keep being brought to life—the women of Woodsmoke would continue to fall foul of the mountains and their strange ways. There would be no warnings at all. The story is pressed more firmly into Cora's mind than it is in the pages of the *Morgan Compendium*, and she worries that if Carrie doesn't see sense, there will be no one after her to pass it along to. To keep the stories alive. She sits back, features hardening, sure in her own mind of what she saw, what she knows. "I'm not wrong."

Chapter 15
Carrie

Over that winter, Sylba snuck out whenever she could, leaving only her footprints in the snow to mark her absence and where she had gone. She brushed them away each morning, eager to keep him a secret for a little longer. Not that anyone ever saw him, or heard a whisper of his name.

—Tabitha Morgan, July 19, 1929

I wake to a world turned white overnight. Rubbing my sleeve over the caravan window, I laugh softly as a snowflake catches on the other side of the glass. It shivers there in the corner, waiting. Waiting as more and more join it, icing the glass until there is nothing but frost. It's Halloween. The world should be full of crunchy russet leaves and pumpkins and toffee apples, yet it's white and cold. Full of frost.

The air is sharp as I trudge to the cottage, and I burrow deeper into my coat, pulling the hood low over my forehead. A set of boot prints is already leading to Ivy's cottage, all the way from the mountain path. I bristle, checking the time on my phone. It's just after nine, and I'm sure that, on our call, Matthieu said he'd be here at ten. I want a bit of time to myself, to prepare, but now I feel wrong-footed, flustered. My breath catches at the thought of him there in Ivy's cottage. He's gorgeous and rugged and has a soulful tilt to his mouth and eyes that my mind keeps straying to . . . I give myself a shake. This is absolutely not the time to be thinking about anything other than this renovation. I knock the snow off my boots and close the door against the crisp tug of all that white outside.

"Hello? Matthieu?"

"In here."

I follow his voice through to the kitchen, where he has already set up a makeshift tea station: two cups, a heap of teaspoons, a jar of instant coffee far nicer than the stuff I have been drinking, and a tin caddy stuffed with tea bags. It's quite an improvement on my scattered box of tea bags, used teaspoons, and small bottle of milk I decant each time I walk over from the caravan. The electricity is working now, thanks to Cora and the electrician, but there's no fridge yet. Only my small travel kettle, which is already on, rattling away on its tiny stand.

"I didn't expect you . . ." A blush flares across my cheeks as I picture the disarray he must have walked into.

Matthieu runs a hand over the back of his neck. "Sorry. I'm early, aren't I?" He glances at the tea station, then back at me as the kettle clicks off the boil. "And I'm meddling. You only wanted a quote, and I just let myself in—"

"It's all right," I say, moving toward the kettle. I swallow, avoiding looking at him directly. Now that I'm standing close to him in Ivy's old kitchen, I can smell woodsmoke. Citrus and loam and the sharp scent of snow. He smells like the mountains and I want to breathe it in. I give myself another mental shake. "Tea? Coffee?" I ask, my words coming out a little strangled.

"Coffee would be great, thanks." He darts me a look, and I'm sure I catch a suppressed smile, like he can see I'm flustered and finds it . . . amusing? I will my cheeks to cool as I fuss with the teaspoons and straighten the solitary tea towel on the oven rail.

"I should set it up properly, shouldn't I? Get a microwave, a few essentials . . . should we start in here first?" I turn to survey the kitchen and glance up at him. His head is slightly bowed, and I notice a slight blush tingeing his cheeks, the twin to my own. Is he . . . *nervous*? Surely I can't be making him nervous? I thaw slightly, checking myself. Perhaps I'm not the only one who feels anxious this morning, who wants this to go well. "I don't know when Ivy installed the kitchen, but I'm fairly sure it's considered retro now."

The cabinets are so old that they're yellowing on the inside. The worktops are chipped Formica, stained black around the sink. Ivy may have kept the kitchen ruthlessly clean to prolong its life span, but now, if I'm honest, it's aged past the point of retro. There's nothing to salvage here.

"We need to rip it all out, Carrie," he says quietly. I glance up at him. He's got a watchful look, as though testing what he should say. How far am I willing to go with this renovation? He's being careful around me, I realize. Considerate.

"You're worried I'm attached to all this, aren't you? That I won't throw it all out because it was Ivy's?"

He shrugs, burying his hands in his pockets. "She wouldn't throw away anything. Makes sense you'd feel the same way. And—and this place isn't mine. I don't have any memories attached to it."

I take a deep breath and frown down at the worktop. There's an old mug stain there, a perfect ring where the tea or coffee left an indelible mark. I rub my index finger over it absently. It's appeared since I left. I knew every quirk of this cottage a decade ago, just as you do with family homes. The doors that squeak on their hinges, the places where the wallpaper curls slightly, where you can dig a finger in and peel away another centimeter.

He's right, in a way. If it were possible, I would keep it all. Everything Ivy touched, everything she used. The ceramic pot with the collection of wooden spoons and spatulas still sits beside the range, coated in dust. I remember her using them, humming as she stirred pots of soup, flipped griddle cakes on the stovetop. I remember the scent of scones, the blackberry jam she made every autumn. I remember her sitting, glasses perched on the end of her nose, to scrawl on each label before sticking it carefully on another jar full of the sticky sweetness. I remember it all, and I swallow it all down. Because the memories are laced with bitter guilt that I left all this behind.

"I'll phone for a dumpster," I say, not meeting his eyes. "I agree, it all has to go."

He nods and makes for the lounge. I sniff, blinking back a fog of memories, and busy myself with the kettle and the mugs. I rattle the teaspoons around, my thoughts elsewhere—on Cora, on the dumpster I need to order, on the conversation I never had with Jess. On Tom's face, gaunt and aged compared to the one I hold in my head. On the little girl standing beside him, a perfect replica of them both, like the ghost of winters to come.

Then I gather it all inside and hook my fingers around the mugs.

Matthieu is tapping the wall that divides the kitchen and lounge, frowning as a clot of plaster crumbles away to the floor.

"Thanks." He accepts the mug, wraps his fingers around it. "This is just a partition wall. It's not holding anything up. How far do you want to go with this renovation?"

I sweep my eyes across the lounge, then step back to look through the doorway to the kitchen. "I guess we could take it down? Open this space up?"

"It could do with more light," Matthieu says, sipping his coffee. "And if we're ripping out carpet, wallpaper, stripping it all back . . . that is, if you want to—"

"Makes sense."

"All right," he says, reaching out to tap his knuckles against the wall again. "All right. Shall we start with an hourly rate? Or would you rather I quote for the whole job?"

"Do you want to see upstairs first?"

He smiles into his coffee. "I know what I'll find—more of the same."

"Okay. Well, I guess the whole job, then."

He gives me a figure, and I quickly calculate what that leaves in my savings, how much I'll have left to live on until the spring. It's just enough to buy some furniture to stage the cottage for selling, buy building materials we'll need, and pay for any specialist tradespeople. "Done."

We shake on it, awkwardly, avoiding each other's eyes, then hurry through the rest of the downstairs. Matthieu goes upstairs and taps his way through the chipboard walls of the bedrooms. To his credit, he says nothing as he eyes the discarded steam wallpaper stripper, and that simple kindness thaws me out even more.

By midday we're working our way through the bedrooms upstairs, carrying furniture down the crooked staircase. My lower back sends out a steady pulse of pain, and I rub it, kneading away the ache, before moving to the opposite side of a small chest of drawers as Matthieu reaches for the other side. We lift it, moving slowly toward the staircase, and I puff out a breath, a strand of hair falling across my eyes. Matthieu smiles at me and shifts his hands to take the bulk of the weight on the stairs.

"So you grew up here?" he asks, steadying the old set of drawers as we reach the hallway. I rub my hands together, stalling for time as I work out how to answer.

"Yes . . . I was born here."

"And you left?"

"A while back. But I wouldn't call this a return."

"No?"

I shake my head, moving back to the staircase. "No. How about you?"

"I grew up all over. Lots of moving around. Mum didn't like the people in this place, or my dad couldn't get enough work in the next town . . ." He sucks in a breath. "Anyway, I'm just here for the winter, like I said. Just until the season changes."

"And you were here all of last winter?"

"Yeah. Before—"

"Before?"

I turn to catch his frown, quickly erased as he smiles at me. "Before I had to leave for a while."

"And you like the mountains?" I ask as I reach the main bedroom. The one with the view out to the looming mountains, the ever-present giants.

"I do," he says quietly. "My brother and I . . . we used to come hiking here, years ago. The stories are interesting. You know, the old ones. Ivy started telling me some of them before I had to leave."

I nod, then move to the front bedroom, with the floral wallpaper. It was mine when I stayed here sometimes, the room where Ivy tucked me in with bedtime stories and silver tea. "Some of them you have to take with a pinch of salt."

"And the rest?"

I pretend I don't hear him. The last thing I want to do is talk about being a Morgan, about the book. About still heeding the warnings, though none of us will admit it. "We'll have to strip all this back next, I guess?"

"All of it," he says, leaning against the doorframe. "The bathroom suite as well, and I'll check the plumbing. It looks ancient."

"All right," I say, mentally calculating whether I have enough saved to cover the cost of a new bathroom suite as well. Ivy left me a bit in her will, along with her bequest, but it wasn't enough to hand the problem off by paying someone else to do the work. She knew full well that renovating the cottage would compel me to return, and also that I couldn't shirk her request. But I wanted to come home. Maybe she knew somehow, in that Ivy way of hers, that I just needed a good enough excuse.

Movement plays at the corner of my vision, and I glance up to the window. It holds the view over the fields, all the way to Woodsmoke. I can just see the tops of a few houses over the bump of the land as it slopes away. And there, shoulders hunched, cap pulled low over his ears, is someone crossing through the gate. He's shuffling more than he used to, dragging his feet through the thickening snow. He looks up, only once, and I raise my hand, in case he can see me standing here. But he just carries on, steadily trudging toward the cottage.

Matthieu comes up behind me, eyeing the man, who is nearly halfway across the field. "Best get going. I'll be back in a couple of days, you can manage until then?"

I nod, not taking my eyes off the man. "Sure, thanks. I'll be fine."

Matthieu mutters a farewell, swings down the stairs, and slips out the back door, leaving only that scent of citrus and frost and loam lingering in his wake. By the time the knock of knuckles cracks against the front door, he's gone. I tidy my hair up, smoothing it back as best I can, and stretch out the ache in my back before opening the front door.

"Flower, it's time," Howard says, mouth all twisted up like he's eaten something sour. "We need to talk."

Chapter 16
Jess

It's midnight again. And again, she can't sleep. But it's not Tom this time who plagues her thoughts. It's Carrie. Not the nightmare version she's grown into, the shadow of guilt and regret looming over her life, but the Carrie of before all this. When it was just the two of them and the whole world glinted with promise and magic. Before Elodie, even before Tom, they walked to school every day, arms linked at the elbows. They would stop in at Ivy's candle shop in town on the way home, sniffing all the candles, and Ivy would drop paper packets of lemon sherbets and chocolate limes into their pockets.

She smiles into the dark, the scent of Ivy's winter candle lingering, pluming around her in a cloud. She carried on buying them, every winter. Stealing into Ivy's shop like a thief, barely making eye contact as Ivy accepted the notes, handing over the candles for Jess to stow in her cloth tote. Her heart aches, knowing Ivy's shop is closed now. Knowing that there will be no candles this wintertime, no gentle flickering light on the mantelpiece. That the scent weaving through her house, the tenuous connection to her former life before all this domesticity, now wafts only through her memories.

Listening to everyone at the book club, she had the peculiar feeling of floating out of her own body, up above them all, and watching the gossipy twitch of everyone's heads below as they discussed Carrie Morgan's return. Betty had many opinions, of course, about how Carrie wouldn't last the winter, about how she was too wayward, too flaky. Jess's own mother tried in vain to lead the conversation back to *The Night Circus*.

Jess gave up in the end on steering the conversation back to the book. She cleared away the plastic cups, tuning out the discussion about Ivy's cottage and the sheer volume of work it needed, about how that girl would ever manage alone, about how every Morgan woman had an unpleasant streak of pride. They don't know Carrie, she thinks, not like she does. The Carrie of before, anyway. Carrie always felt like she inhabited the edges of Woodsmoke, she told Jess. She never felt like she completely fit in. But that Morgan pride will carry her through a winter of hard work, Jess is sure of it. That cottage will be renovated come springtime. Then Carrie will disappear once more.

Jess doesn't want Carrie to leave. She mourned the loss of Carrie for years, carrying it with her like a death. They were inseparable, as close as sisters, and since Carrie left no one else has come close to that, not even Gillian, even though she tries to inhabit the space Carrie left. It just isn't the same. You simply can't replicate that kind of friendship with someone else.

Jess rolls onto her side, bringing her knees up to her chest. She misses Carrie like she misses summer. It's as though the cold rolled in the day she left, and Jess hasn't been able to get warm since. She misses that person she just had to *glance* at to feel a bubble of giggles building in her throat. She realizes now that this kind of friendship is irreplaceable. And she wishes more than anything that she had reached out to Carrie in the last ten years, but now . . . now it's too late.

THE NEXT DAY is Saturday, and even though Jess is tired down to her very bones, she wants to create memories. It's Halloween. Elodie has started to understand what Halloween is, especially that it's another chance, like Easter, to fill herself with sugar. She wakes Jess up at seven, wearing her fairy wings and a black tutu dress.

"I'm Isadora Moon!" she says, twirling beside Jess and knocking a box of tissues off her bedside table.

Jess blinks down at the tissues, then back at Elodie. "So it seems."

"Aren't you going to ask me why?" Elodie asks, creeping closer, lowering her voice to a stage whisper. Jess can see eyeshadow smeared on her cheeks and forehead. She hopes it's not her new Charlotte Tilbury duo. "It's Halloween!"

Jess remembers to smile as Elodie flutters around the room, trilling in a silly singsong voice, but she wants to roll over and stuff her head under the pillows. She wants to pretend she has a migraine and blot out the day. But . . . she can't. She just can't. So she takes a deep breath, swings her legs over the side of the bed, and grins at her daughter, so small and unburdened by the tangle of worries that collect like cobwebs as the years pass. "We should have pancakes. And choose a pumpkin! Is Daddy downstairs?"

"He's on the sofa," Elodie says, already shimmying from the room.

Jess swallows, her heart thudding dully in the cage of her ribs, and glances over at the empty space beside her in bed. She summons up a wall, a shield to hide her thoughts, determined to create a perfect day for Elodie and for herself. Determined to ignore the fact that her husband is drifting away and that, internally, she wants to scream.

She thumps down the stairs, dragging her dressing gown around her body, and blearily reaches for the coffee machine as soon as she enters the kitchen. She has switched from tea to coffee over the past few days. She needs the kick in her bloodstream as soon as she wakes, to stir her, to make her seem present, real. It must be the time of year making her mind slower and more sluggish than usual.

"Coffee?" she calls to Tom, pulling the eggs and flour from the cupboards and fridge. She bites her lip, calculating whether there's enough milk left to make pancakes for all of them.

He ambles in, eyes bloodshot, hair a scruff across his forehead. For a moment, she's pulled back to when she first watched him play at the bar on the edge of town, after Carrie left and she was out with Gillian, one term into university and back for the holidays. He was on the scrap of a stage with the rest of the band, while the crowd pressed around her in the hot space. She wriggled to the front and his eyes drifted to hers, then lit up when he saw her. When he played, the bar, Woodsmoke, everything, slid away. And something, somehow clicked. She was lost.

The memory leaves a smile on her lips as she makes the coffee, hands him a cup, then sips her own as she heats up a pan on the stove. Elodie's cartoons blare from the lounge, cutting into the ghost of that charged, wild night, and she wishes for a minute's silence. But instead she gulps her coffee, so hot it sears the roof of her mouth, and melts tiny chocolate stars on the pancakes. She rolls the first one onto a plate for Elodie. On automatic now, she heats up the next pancake as Tom sets the table. She catches his wince as he drinks his coffee and has to bite her tongue. What is it this time? Too bitter? Too sweet? Or is it that it's not made by Carrie?

She coughs, that thought snapping her spine straight as she serves up the final pancake. She sits with Elodie and Tom, cutting up Elodie's pancake into perfect, bite-size chunks and listening to her talk about the pumpkin she wants to find today.

"Thought we could go to that farm? What's it called, the one with the shop and indoor jungle gym . . ."

"Edgewood."

Jess nods. "That's the one."

"Sure," Tom says, rubbing his eyes. He smiles at Elodie. His whole being lights up when he looks at her, just as he used to do when he looked at Jess. He's a good dad. Doting, in his own way. But Elodie tires him out so much. Fatherhood seems to have smoothed out all his corners, making him as bland and amenable as the rest of the men in Woodsmoke. Jess can't remember the last time he picked up his bass guitar, but she wipes off the fuzz of dust beneath the strings every month, just in case. "We'll make a day of it, get lunch . . ."

They're on the road an hour later, and as they leave the confines of Woodsmoke, the snow recedes, revealing the autumnal day Jess was hoping for. Elodie babbles in the back, holding a pink plastic wand, with vampire fangs drawn on her face with black eyeliner. Tom focuses on the road, Jess sits in the passenger seat, and they avoid making eye contact with each other. Jess papers over the fractures in her fatigued heart by talking excitedly with Elodie, pointing out the sheep in the fields along the way, playing "I Spy," singing along to the *Moana* soundtrack when Tom cranks the volume.

When they arrive, Tom follows Elodie to the pumpkin patch while Jess, thinking of the family photos she wants, stays behind to check her makeup in the pull-down mirror on the back of the sun visor. Then she strides across the pumpkin patch and sees Tom pushing the wheelbarrow toward Elodie. Jess stops to watch them both. Her daughter has her hands on the biggest orange pumpkin she can find. Tom, his skin the color of ash beneath his eyes, puts his daughter in the wheelbarrow and then wheels her around, pretending to tip her out, back and forth, making her shriek and giggle as she cries for him to do it again. Tom is relaxed and laughing as he wheels Elodie back and forth between the pumpkins, and Jess sees the glimmers of the man she fell in love with, the cheek of his humor shining through.

She stuffs her hands in her pockets, breathing in the crisp air, letting it cool the bile collecting inside her. This is perfect, she tells herself. This is always how it was supposed to be. Her little family, brought up in her hometown, minutes from her parents, from the school she attended growing up.

They flag down a passing family and ask them to take photos. Jess hands her phone over to them, then joins Tom and Elodie to pose for the photos. When they return her phone, she flicks through the photos, smiling in satisfaction. Her golden hair is carefully tousled, the blond streaks catching the low autumn light, Elodie looks fit to burst with elation with her pink wand and vampire fangs, and Tom—Tom is actually smiling. Jess sniffs, pocketing her phone. She'll send the photos off to get printed. She wants the day to be perfect, and if she has these photos, then maybe in a few years she'll forget how she was feeling. Maybe she'll convince herself that it really *was* perfect.

"Shall we get our pumpkin to the car and get some lunch? Maybe a chocolate milkshake?" she says, raising her eyebrows at Elodie.

Elodie whoops and they high-five, then help Tom get the pumpkin in the wheelbarrow. They make their way off the pumpkin patch, nodding at the other families doing the same. Jess purses her lips, keeping her eyes focused on the horizon, thinking only about the next step, then the next. No one would think they weren't perfect. This is everything she always wanted: Tom, a family, these Instagrammable days caught and pinned in a photo album as real memories.

This is exactly how it was always meant to be.

Chapter 17

Carrie

I'm putting off the inevitable, and so is Howard. I can feel the nervous energy seeping from him. His churn of thoughts, probably a host of reprimands planted by Cora, waiting in his throat to bubble up, admonishments for every little thing I've done wrong. He *hmms* and nods as I rattle off the changes I'm planning to make to the cottage as I give him a tour of the rooms he knows every inch of. He probably installed the kitchen in the first place, thirty years ago. And now it'll all be ripped out, exposing a patchwork of brick and plaster.

"Always did like the view from this room," he says, stopping my ceaseless babble. He's standing in my old bedroom, the one at the front of the house, looking across the fields. "You can't see the mountains from this side. It's like they don't even exist."

I hesitate, hovering on the threshold. I see his shoulders slump as he tucks his hands into his pockets. Howard has thickened in the years I've been gone, not just his waist but his dark brown skin, which seems to have grown extra layers. But he is somehow still the same. Like a tree that has just grown more roots, tangled out of sight under the earth.

We used to play cards together, Howard and I, for endless hours at their dining room table, a pile of pennies at our sides, a heap of hearts and spades in our hands. He taught me to play poker. He taught me how to hold all my excitement on the inside, to keep my features passive, even when I held a straight flush. Poker face.

That schooling, how to hold myself in, how to hide my emotions, has been the most important lesson of my life. Howard taught me how to never show my cracks and fissures when it is time to walk away. How to keep my dignity, even when inside I am lost.

"Flower," he says now, turning from the window, "Cora's worried."

"Cora's always worried."

"I am too."

I open, then close my mouth. Howard has always stayed out of Cora's way. He gently guides her, keeping her on track, but he never intervenes. Not even on the day I left, ten years ago.

"You know I couldn't ignore the will," I finally tell him. "Ivy was clear: I got the cottage, the lease on the shop, and she expected me to return and handle it for her. But, Howard, this is it. I promise. A final goodbye, one last winter to fulfill her wishes, to do the right thing, then—"

"That's what I'm afraid of. That's what Cora is afraid of." He sighs again and rubs a hand down his tired features. "Carrie, you can't run away like you did, then dip back in when you want to. It doesn't work like that, and you know it."

I try again, sticking stubbornly to the same words. "I'm just trying to do the right thing."

"Stay this time, my flower," Howard says suddenly. "Stay. Ivy didn't leave you everything so you could get it ready to sell. She was giving you a way to return, an open door, a way to come back to us. You can see that, can't you? Surely you've missed Woodsmoke. Surely you've wanted to come home."

"Howard . . ." I say wearily.

He smiles at me, and all his warmth, all that sunshine, spills out of him. "It's all right to stop running, Carrie."

"I did the right thing ten years ago," I say, raising my chin, even as my poker face slips slightly. "I'm doing the right thing now."

"According to you." He changes tack. "Look, I know it's not easy. I know it won't be easy, being back here . . ."

I blow out a breath. "You could say that again."

"And those ten years you've been gone might as well be a day to folk here. You know how it is." Howard levels me with his gaze. He sees all of me, every tell, every stumble, just as he always has. "Everyone in Woodsmoke has a long memory, Carrie, same as all small towns, I imagine. Gossip holds for generations. I still hear whisperings about my dear mother and her shop. How she sold faulty ribbons one season." He cracks a grin, then blinks. "They count their blessings, but they also count their slights. I know Morgan women are treated differently here; I know there's gossip. But . . . you should stay. As long as you're prepared to start anew. Carve out a place for yourself. Leave the rest of it in the past."

I sniff. "This is my home too, isn't it? I have just as much of a claim to being here as any of the gossips."

"It was, my flower. It was. And it can be again, if you let it." Howard's face softens some more. "You have someone helping you here. Someone from the mountain. When did he show up, Carrie?"

"I—how do you know that?" I search my memories, but I've never mentioned Matthieu to anyone. I want to keep him a secret, to get it all done without the help of anyone from Woodsmoke.

"Let's say I've been married to Cora long enough for some of those old stories to rub off. My dear mother believed it all, and perhaps I've come to know there is some truth in it. Did he arrive with the frost?"

"This is about Cora and the book, isn't it? The Morgan book of spells and curses. That's why you're really here!" I shake my head. "Tell her to stop worrying. I did as I was told; I did everything I was supposed to. I went straight to the mountains when I arrived,

I didn't stray from the path, *not once*, just like I told her, and they welcomed me back. I haven't stirred up any shit with Tom, and I don't intend to. I'm not falling for a man who isn't real, like in that old tale, and clearly I haven't gone missing, like in some of the other old tales. I've hired someone to fix up the cottage. That's all. That's *it*. You tell her that. You tell her I'm fine and I'll be gone by spring."

"That's what she's afraid of," Howard says softly. "That you're coming here, cleaning off the dust, and then disappearing again when the whole place catches fire."

"You're acting like I'm back here to settle a score."

"Are you?"

"No," I snap. "Of course not."

Howard shrugs and walks past me. He takes his time going back down the stairs, his old bones creaking as he reaches the hallway at the bottom. "I did what I came to do. I've asked you to stay. I've said my piece, Carrie. You can't carry around all this guilt your whole life. Nor can you be rootless. This is where you belong." He shrugs again, and a crooked half smile quirks his mouth. "Your move, flower."

Then he's gone, leaving me with nowhere to throw my emotions.

My phone beeps, and I pull it out, stabbing at the lock screen. It's a message from an unknown number, but I know it's intended for me. I haven't changed my number all this time, transferring it from contract to contract. The short message holds a world of meaning and shatters the tension in my head, in the room Howard just left. I deflate, sinking to the floor, all my fight gone. If Howard can cut to the heart of my thoughts, this message cuts to the center of my soul, bringing it all back, every moment. And suddenly my heart is aching.

Meet me tomorrow at nine, our usual place.

I tip my head back against the wall as I drop my phone to the ground.

Remembering all the times we met there.

Remembering how it was to be the two of us.

I SIT IN the car the next evening, waiting for Jess. I could be seventeen again, my fresh driver's license burning a hole in my pocket, waiting for Jess to get here so we can sit in the car, drink hot chocolate from a thermos, and revel in the thrill of being on our own in a carved-out space in the world. I had a secondhand Ford back then, cherry red, and it lasted a year before giving up the ghost. When I left, I didn't bother replacing it. The car I have now is the first one I've owned in ten years.

Headlights glow as another car pulls into the car park on the edge of town, highlighting an arc of snow and absence. There's a field beyond that's used for football and rugby practice and a small play park where parents take their children between bursts of rain in the autumn and spring. I remember swinging there next to Jess when we were six, daring each other to go higher and higher, my heart soaring at having a best friend. Someone who didn't care who my family was or believe the gossip about us.

Now, as the car stops a few feet away, the engine cutting out and the headlights killed with it, butterflies flutter in my belly. What if this isn't Jess's attempt to reforge our friendship? What if there's too much between us now? What if—

I gasp softly as a figure gets out of the car. It's not Jess at all.

It's Tom.

Chapter 18
Cora

Fifty-Six Years Ago

"Does she need feeding?" Cora asks pointedly. The baby's little face is turning puce. Ivy walks back into the room, arms outstretched for the cross little bundle. Cora gladly hands her over and picks up her mug of tea as Ivy sinks into the sofa, getting ready to feed.

Lillian. A name Cora had on *her* baby list, the one she keeps at the back of her diary. But she bit her tongue when Ivy told her what she named her baby, even when she said she first heard it from Cora. Really, she's been biting her tongue her whole life, keeping her temper in check, knowing that any sharp words, however little, won't endear her to her family. She's nothing like Ivy. Sweet, mild Ivy with the perfect baby, the cottage in the shadow of the mountains, and the husband she doesn't mind working away all the time.

The clock ticks away the seconds on the mantelpiece, and Cora feels the gloom settling like a blanket over her shoulders, the autumn turning as slow as treacle to winter. She has begun to hate winter, to hate how the world dies off around her. What she wants right now is life—life around her, life to grow within. Not that she and Howard have been married *that* long. There's plenty of time. It isn't a competition, as her mother likes to say.

But with Ivy, she can't help it. She's always comparing herself and measuring her achievements against those of her older sister. The perfect sister.

"You haven't asked about the book," Ivy says, piercing the silence. She hushes Lillian, swapping her over to the other side with a slight grimace before cooing at her, the baby's fist gripping her blouse. "You *always* ask about the book."

"Maybe I've given up asking."

"You know, I've been reading some of the stories inside it." Ivy leans forward, eyes suddenly wide. "Did you know that the mountains will let you make a bargain? A kind of . . . trade? Like for like? They ask for certain ingredients from you. At least that's what Grandma Tabitha's own grandma recorded in *her* account. But she says she was able to reverse a terrible harvest one year. For a price."

She lets that hang in the air between them. Cora swallows her tea, meeting her sister's gaze. With Ivy, there is always a reason to bring something up. She thinks over things for days, weeks sometimes. But this subject, so casually mentioned . . . she may have been turning it over for months. Cora's skin prickles, and she clutches her mug tighter. "What of it, Ivy?"

Ivy swallows, as though preparing herself. A flicker of sadness sparks in her eyes, but is quickly blinked away and hidden. "If you really want the book, Cora, if it still means so much to you, we could make a trade."

It seems to Cora that the entire world stills at that moment—that the very mountains open an ancient eye and hold a collective breath. "What?"

"A trade," Ivy says, smiling tentatively. Then, "Ooo, she's done!"

Cora holds out her arms instinctively as the tiny, well-fed Lillian is passed to her. She maneuvers the warm, milk-drunk bundle up to her shoulder, then gently pats her back to bring up the trapped air. Smelling the baby scent on Lillian's hair, the tiny wisps of it curling over her skull, she thinks that Ivy's baby is almost perfect. Almost. But Cora longs for, obsesses over, only one thing, and it isn't made of soft curls and warm milk. It's made of paper and magic.

She stands, shifting her weight to rock Lillian, and fixes her attention on Ivy, now reclining on the sofa. "Explain."

"You're always so *sharp*, Cora," Ivy says with a troubled sigh. "Good thing Howard loves all those jagged edges."

"This is about Howard, isn't it?"

"In a way." Ivy fidgets with her blouse buttons, not meeting her sister's frank stare. "I want you to be happy, Cora. You have Howard now. You have a home . . . you should be happy. Content. But you're not, are you?"

Cora continues moving around the room, swaying with the warm, fidgeting bundle in her arms. "What do you mean?"

"I think you'll only be truly happy when you have the book. When all those stories, all the old ways, are yours. And I want that for you. I want for you to be happy with your life."

Cora narrows her eyes. "But Mother gave it to you, not me."

"There's a way," Ivy says softly. "I can give it to you, break my bond with the book so it's yours, so you're the keeper of it all. You know I do not use it. You know it's not for me. But you will have to pay the price . . . by giving up someone you love."

"And you're worried that'll be Howard."

"I am."

Cora moves toward the Moses basket and pours the sleeping, flushed-cheek bundle into it. She rocks the basket gently, watching the rosebud of Lillian's mouth opening and closing. Howard wanted children; she knew that much. How many did he say when they first started courting? Four? She pinches her lips, trying not to think of Howard. Trying not to think of his needs, his wants. If she takes the book from Ivy, what love will she lose? A future child? The prospect of *ever* having children? The mountains extract payment somehow, she knows that much. Sometimes in ways you don't see coming.

As she watches Lillian sleep, still gently rocking the Moses basket, she thinks of how much Howard would love this. Their own child in a Moses basket in the front room, Cora pottering around the kitchen getting the supper ready. He's that kind of man. But what she wants, what she has always wanted . . . is the book. The old ways. The tales of the mountains, the closest thing on this earth to real magic. "I guess we'd find out," she murmurs to herself.

Ivy sighs, a frown pinching her forehead. "I was afraid that would be your answer."

"Why now? Why would you hand it over to me now?" Cora glances at Ivy, noting how tired she looks around her eyes, how limp and a little thin her hair is. How she slumps on the sofa like she'd be happy to nap for half the day.

"Because . . ." Ivy stops, biting her lip. "Because when I look at Lillian, I see everything I ever wanted. I have this deep peace within me, this certainty. And I want you to be happy, Cora, more than anything. I want you to have that same peace, and I don't think you'll get it from having children. I think the only way is if I give you the book. But—but it won't be my price to pay, and that's what I'm afraid of. That you'll lose something, or someone, either now or in the future, and the price will be your happiness, when that's what I'm trying to fix."

Cora turns to Ivy, fixing her with a look. "Someone I love for the book. That's the price."

"Yes. That's what the book says. That's what the mountains will ask of you."

"Done."

Ivy blinks, sadness flooding her eyes, then finally she nods. "All right then, if that's your decision. I'll follow the steps and break the bond. On the next full moon, the book will be yours."

Winter

November–December

Chapter 19

Jess

"I thought she married some fashion designer in Paris. Had five kids and got really into hemp."

"No, that was Suzie Riley. And it was Milan, not Paris."

"Well, I heard she moved to New York and runs a bookshop. There was lots of competition from a bigger bookstore, and she nearly got closed down."

Jess snorts discreetly into her scarf. "You're thinking of that film. *You've Got Mail.*"

The other mums all raise their eyebrows. Gillian snaps her fingers, and her carroty hair flies around her face with a sudden gust from the north. "I can't ever keep these things straight in my head. I swear I lost half my brain after the third."

Jess sighs, wishing not for the first time that she had someone to turn to, someone whose eye she could catch for a fraction of a second, who would know in that trace of a heartbeat how ridiculous she finds Gillian. How ridiculous they *both* find her. But she's never found someone to fill that gap, not since Carrie. And now these women, these friends, are all having a pop at Carrie and she feels a weird twinge of protectiveness. Of melancholic annoyance.

"I'm sure she's only back to sort out the cottage. Then she'll be off again," Jess says briskly, checking her watch. She's still got a few minutes before she has to leave for the library, and after book club the other night, she's really over all the fresh gossip and intrigue stirred up about Carrie. "I doubt we'll even see her."

"Has Tom seen her?" Amy asks slyly, eyes narrowing like a cat's.

Jess clears her throat, bunching her fists in her pockets. "Why would he?"

"It was all so long ago, Ames. Seriously," Gillian says, trying unsuccessfully to tame her wild ginger mane with a claw clip. "Let it go."

"You're not worried then, Jess?" Amy asks.

Jess takes a minute to reply, hoping whatever answer she gives will snuff out a rumor before it's had time to catch fire. "Tom hasn't talked to her, or about her, in years. Not since she left. And they were eighteen, remember? Kids, basically. What does it even matter if she's back for a couple of months?"

"Huh," Amy says, shrugging. "I guess so."

"Cora Morgan's been at it again, though. Told my second cousin Jenifer she was cursed the other day," Gillian says.

"A curse she placed on her?" Amy laughs.

"Your second cousin Jenifer isn't cursed," Jess snips irritably. She doesn't like all this poking and prodding at the collective knowledge about the Morgan women. It sets her teeth on edge wondering what will be dug up next. "The girl's a damn flake."

Gillian stops laughing, eyes darting from Jess to Amy. "Well! I better get going," Amy says. She rolls her eyes, not bothering to say goodbye before turning on her booted heel and walking back to her car. The tight gossipy group disbands. Gillian shrugs and walks away, and Jess turns toward the lane that leads to the library, feeling slightly sick and hollow.

She replays over and over what she said, what Amy and Gillian said, trying to find the gaps, what they didn't say out loud. She's mostly annoyed at Gillian, who does try, in her own way, but is so easily influenced by the crowd. So ready to turn on someone she used to be friends with and believe every silly little white lie about her.

Without thinking, Jess lifts her hand up to glimpse the silvery scar on the edge of her palm, from the day she and Carrie became blood sisters, when they were fourteen. After watching *Practical Magic*, they pinched Carrie's dad's pocketknife and went up to the lookout, high above the rooftops of Woodsmoke. She remembers how odd and exhilarating it felt, the shock of blood, the press of Carrie's skin to her own, how they grinned at each other in the dark and promised to be sisters forever.

Jess is so in her own head all morning at the library, constantly and absently rubbing a thumb against the silvery scar, that she doesn't fine someone who's had a book out for over six months. She drops a full cup of coffee in the tiny kitchen behind the desk and lets someone take out a book without remembering to stamp it. She forgets to change the sign from OPEN to CLOSED when she and Dawn go on their lunch break, and she finds a disgruntled note tucked under the door from a resident when they return.

"Get it together, girl," Dawn huffs on her way to the back stacks with a trolley of books to reshelve. "Or take some annual leave. Get yourself a haircut. Do *something*. But stop being so damn *absent*. Yes?"

Jess knows Dawn means well, but it's not good that she's noticing her absent-mindedness. Jess doesn't want to appear any different, to give away that Carrie's return has had any effect at all.

But it has.

She asks her mum to collect Elodie from school for her, vaguely citing a need to pop over to the shops in the next town. But really, she's avoiding the other mums. She doesn't want to find their eyes sliding away, gossip hot on their tongues about her and Tom. So she drives over to the next town and loses herself for an hour in the pre-Christmas throng of shoppers. Walking along the parade of high street shops, she sinks into anonymity. She buys a takeaway coffee with too much extra cream and feels the lump of overprocessed dairy and sugar heave like a rock in her stomach the whole drive back. She isn't comfortable. Not in Woodsmoke, not in her own skin, not in her own *life*.

"Damn you, Carrie," Jess says inside the silent car as she pulls onto her road. "Damn you."

The big problem, what's cutting her up and dividing her in two, is that she misses her friend. Acutely. She doesn't want anything in her life to change by stirring up the past, but she wants just as much for Carrie to be here. She can't marry the two sides of herself, and it's leaving her immobile. Disconnected. Desperate.

Still preoccupied, Jess barely registers Tom saying he has to go out that night. She's wrangling Elodie into bed, going through the nighttime routine of a cup of water, finding Moonlight the bear, kissing her the same number of times on each cheek . . . then she hears the front door close and realizes he's gone. Just . . . gone.

And so Jess spends another evening alone. Another evening stewing over Carrie, unable to close the division cracking her apart. She wonders if she's made the right choices, if this life is what she's always wanted. Or whether, without Carrie, it's like winning a coveted prize and finding out it's all a lie.

Chapter 20

Carrie

Memory lives in our skin. We experience it with our whole being, a touch awakening a moment from years before. I remember how his kisses felt. How they shivered along my skin, my mouth. How every moment waiting for him to call would stretch as long as an hour. The tinny landline would trill downstairs, and I would go still, every fiber of my being straining toward that phone as my mother picked up the receiver. I remember how my heart would race as she called up the stairs for me. How every step on that staircase felt like a victory march as I walked to the corded phone receiver, lying ready for me on the side table in the hallway. How I would cradle it to my ear, a slow smile spreading throughout my body. How we would arrange to meet, and I knew he would kiss me again.

I sigh, then snap back to the present when Tom taps on the window. I nod slowly, the first fingers of unease crawling over me. He's not smiling. This is not a fond reunion. He slides quietly into the passenger seat and closes the door. I don't turn to look at him. I keep the headlights on, watching the light pool over the snow outside, pushing against the darkness beyond. The air is thick with all the words we never said to one another. The conversation I never had—*couldn't* have—with him before I left.

"You could have warned me," he says finally, brushing his dark, tousled mass of hair back from his face with his fingers. He's grown it longer than he used to wear it.

"What good would that have done?"

"I would have had time. To prepare, or—I don't know. To think."

I swallow, shifting in my seat. "You don't seem so thrilled that I'm back."

Tom stares moodily out at the night. "I guess I didn't expect you to come back, Carrie. Not after what happened. Not after you left so suddenly. Jess is . . ."

"Jess is what?" I ask quickly.

"She's not herself." He sighs, flicking a glance at me, before turning back to the night. "She's jumpy, and quiet. You haven't seen her, have you?"

"No," I say quietly. "No, I have not."

"Are you going to?"

"Wouldn't it be the right thing to do? Call on my old best friend, arrange to meet up—"

"I don't think so."

"Look, Tom, I get it, my presence is an issue for you. I didn't leave in the best way, and I didn't get in touch . . ."

"You left me at the altar, Carrie."

I blink steadily, feeling the weight of his words. Feeling the ghost of a long-extinguished relationship sitting between us. We never got any closure, we never closed that chapter, and yet . . . there is nothing. We nearly got married, and I feel nothing for this man. He's a near-stranger sitting beside me.

"Do you need me to apologize for leaving? Is that it?" I look at him sadly. Not for the first time, I wonder what it would have been like if I hadn't run that day, if I hadn't left, if I'd become Thomas Gray's wife instead of Jess's. The old scars on my heart are still there, still present, and yet, looking at him now, the way his face has slumped ever so slightly over the past decade, the unkempt hair, the pattern of crow's feet around his eyes, I know for sure we wouldn't have worked. I didn't belong with him then, and I don't belong with him now. I thought that if I married him, the whole town would accept me for who I am. But at the last minute I realized that wasn't good enough. I couldn't marry someone, tie myself to someone forever, just to appease the small town I grew up in. You can't fit yourself into a box that wasn't built for you.

He rubs his hand over his jaw, the prickly stubble making a scratching sound. I remember when he grew his first beard. I remember his first shave. I remember so many things, so many details, and it seems strange that they belong to me. It seems strange that *he* ever belonged to me.

"How long."

"How long?" I frown at him.

"Until you leave again. Until you're gone. Surely you won't stay."

A flash of anger so lightning-quick my fingers tremble forces me to pull in a breath. "Are you asking me how long I'm staying in *my* hometown? Like it's your right to be here but not mine?"

He works his jaw, as though he's chewing on his words. "For Christ's sake, Carrie, just tell me."

"As long as I like," I say, crossing my arms. "Why does it matter?"

"Carrie." He sighs, deflating further. "You agreed to marry me, then you ran. On our wedding day. In front of everyone, the whole town. All our families, our friends. You never looked back. Never—never sent me a message. Never wrote. I had to beg your mum to tell me you were all right. And yes, I see now that we wouldn't have worked. I do. We were too young, we both got caught up in it, and it was a thing that should have run its course. But weren't we friends? Did it . . . did it not deserve at least a postcard? Or a text message?"

"This wasn't the place for me back then," I murmur, pushing down my guilt. Pushing down everything but the residual bitterness that lingers like the tea leaves in Cora's teapot. Bitterness about feeling that I didn't belong in Woodsmoke. That Tom had no intention, as it turned out, of leaving Woodsmoke with me, as we had planned. I wanted to be accepted by Woodsmoke, but that didn't mean I wanted to stay. Not back then anyway. "I always intended to leave and travel."

I pull in another breath, feeling once again that constricting dress across my ribs, how it felt that day to put it on, remembering how I stared at myself in the full-length mirror in my bedroom. I looked too skinny, and my mum placed her hands on my shoulders, as if to stop me from floating away. I remember what she whispered: *You don't have to do this. You know that, right? Your whole life is ahead of you, Carrie. I know you think you're doing the right thing by going through with this, but you're only eighteen.*

Our eyes met in the mirror, and I think she knew as well. The secret that I hid, under all that white and tulle. The secret that my heart wasn't here, wasn't with him, that it wanted to wander very far away. And Tom had decided, quietly, without telling me, that he wouldn't leave Woodsmoke. Once we were married, once we were tied to each other . . . I'd have to stay too.

I repeated my mum's words in my head all the way to the church. I felt the kisses on my cheeks, the bouquet thrust into my fingers. The eyes on me, so many eyes that I flinched. Did they all know too that if I married Tom I wouldn't be leaving Woodsmoke? My shoulders began to shake under the veil, and all I could hear was a constant, tinny whine. As soon as my feet carried me all the way to the altar, they'd see me. *Really* see me. Tom would pull back my veil and find all that pretty makeup smeared down my face. The eye shadow, the mascara, the layers of foundation plastered on my skin.

I wondered if he'd say, *Sorry, I'm not leaving.* Or if he'd deny what I'd heard, tell me it wasn't true, that we could still go traveling together and see the world. Deny that he had secured a full-time apprentice job as an electrician, that his mum and dad had put down a deposit on a house for us. Or if he'd finally tell me the truth at the front of that pretty old church, giving everyone a good look at how afraid I was, how trapped. How not right for each other we were. How much I wanted to bolt. How Thomas Gray, my childhood sweetheart, the boy I had so publicly given my entire being to . . . didn't love the real me. He wanted a version of me that didn't exist. A version that would marry at eighteen, stay in our hometown forever, and be perfectly content with those firmly built boundaries around my existence.

Something snapped inside me that day. I picked up my dress, wrapped those layers of tulle in my fists, turned to my dad, and looked into his sad, hooded eyes.

"I'm sorry," I gasped. "I can't."

He blinked at me, surprise flaring briefly on his face before he covered it up. Then he nodded in that slow way of his. He knew that I'd always felt like I didn't quite belong in Woodsmoke. And he was the one who had told me, hesitantly, calmly, that Tom had a job and a house all lined up. "Go to Cora's. I'll hold them all off."

I cried then, real wailing tears and sobs that caught in my throat as my dad pulled back my veil, kissed my forehead, and told me quietly, "You're free. Run."

I ran to Cora's without looking back. She didn't believe in church weddings and never attended them, not even family ones. So I knew she'd be there, getting ready for the reception, for the big party we had planned for afterward in the orchard of Mum and Dad's back garden. With the wind tugging at the pins in my hair, I discarded the bouquet in some hedge along the way. I took the back ways, the narrow lanes between the fields, the old ways Cora had taught me. When I got to her house, she pulled all the pins from my hair and listened to my heart. She cried softly when my dad showed up to drive me away from Woodsmoke.

That was ten years ago. That's what everyone remembers. They remember only what *I* did, how I fled. How I stood Thomas Gray up at the altar and broke the poor boy's heart. How the big party never happened, the bunting and the tablecloths were packed away, and the wedding feast was boxed up in Tupperware, then eventually thrown out.

"I'm not here to rake up the past," he says, more softly than before. Like he's rewinding his memory too, working his way back to the days before the wedding. Maybe even the years before that. The years when it was him and me, Tom and Carrie. The years when Jess was my best friend, as close as a sister.

"Then why are you here?"

"I—" he swallows. "I need you to stay away, from me, from Elodie, and from Jess. Do whatever you need to do, then go. I can't . . . I can't have you upsetting them. Not that I think you'd do it intentionally, but—"

"Elodie, she's the girl I saw with you in town? Your daughter?"

"Yes."

I sniff, staring out at the endless cold. The frost inside the car, the frost that's built up between us is icing up my veins. It used to be the three of us. But now the two of them have shut the door, and I'm very much on the outside. "Understood."

"You were never meant to come back, you know that? We didn't think we'd ever hear from you again. You broke Jess's heart, leaving like you did. She's spent ten years getting over it."

My breath hitches, and I shrink inside at the thought of Jess upset, the thought of her sad at my leaving. But when I ran, it was never to get away from her. I just needed to be free. "You talk as if I'm your ghost."

He sighs, reaching for the car door. "It sure feels like you are, Carrie. It sure feels that way."

"For what it's worth, I'm sorry I didn't want this life with you."

He hesitates, looking back at me. And slowly nods.

Then he's gone, walking across the drifts to his own car, leaving me in a pool of silence and snow.

Chapter 21
Carrie

He asked her if she liked the ribbons. She said she did, but she had no coins to pay. He smiled at her, the kind of smile that caught at her imagination, and she kept seeing it, hours later, as she was scolded for shirking her work on washday.

—Tabitha Morgan, July 19, 1929

The frustration grows inside me. Over the next few days, I pace up and down Ivy's cottage, the conversation with Tom swirling around the walls like a storm. It needles me, the way he expects me to leave again. Like this isn't my town too. Like Jess wasn't *my* person before his. They were both mine before they were each other's, but he's erased that entirely. It's all been conveniently swept away, along with the ghost of my very existence.

I'm the one who left, but now I'm the one left behind.

On the third day, Matthieu shows up, all smiles and mugs of tea and talk about the progress I've made. I swallow down the bitterness, the unease Tom has stirred up inside me. We make small talk, and he tells me about a migrating bird he found that blew in with the snowstorm. But with every hammer blow, every chunk of plaster I remove, I imagine all the things I should have said to Tom. And to Howard. One wants me to leave, and one wants me to stay. It's as though the town is divided, and that same divide sits in my heart. I wonder if they're all talking about me, gossiping in shop aisles and over café tables. I picture them stoking the embers of the past, just as Howard predicted.

As I imagine my presence lighting a match and casting it into these perfectly honed lives, for the first time I want them to burn. I want them to feel the cold as they flee their smoldering homes, driven away with ash in their lungs. Sniffing, I reach for the next length of skirting board and grip it so tightly that my knuckles flare white. It's my choice, isn't it? Whether I stay or go. I want to belong. I do. I want to feel that deep, rooted comfort of home that others seem to feel so easily, so naturally. But what if Woodsmoke and the mountains just don't love me back?

"Carrie . . . your hand," Matthieu says quietly.

I look down to see a lone trail of blood, beginning in the soft folds of my palm, extending toward my wrist.

"Oh," I say, a dull ringing beginning in my ears. "Oh, right."

Matthieu takes the board, gently prying it from my hands. He's peering down at me in that calm, steady way some people have, his whole being focused on me. I sag slightly as the ringing grows louder and my skin flushes hot under the layers of my clothes. I was so deep in the past that I wasn't focused on the present.

"You need to sit," he says, his voice seeming far away. I think of how different he sounds from Tom. There is no razor at the edge of his syllables. No tiny cuts at the end of each word. Only a low, soft roundness that wraps around me. I drop down, bringing my knees up to my chest, and he hunkers down next to me, keeping a polite distance. As he hands me a clean rag to press into the folds of my hand, I can't help it. Maybe because he's not from Woodsmoke, or maybe because he's just here, in this moment, and there's something about him that feels almost familiar. Comforting.

It all spills out.

"It's getting to me, being back here. I can't move without memories exploding around me. That man who was here the other day?"

"Yes."

"He's my great-uncle. Howard. He's basically my grandfather. I've always thought of him that way anyway. But—but he's worried about Cora, my great-aunt. He told me I should stay and not flit in and out, and I don't know, maybe he's right. But now, if I leave, it'll upset Cora, and then I think maybe I shouldn't have come back at all. Maybe—"

"Carrie," Matthieu says, holding his hand out for the rag before passing me a bandage. I take a shuddering breath and look at him, feeling foolish for unburdening myself. "That's up to them, how they react to you. You can't control them. You can only take hold of how *you* feel. How *you* react. Yes?"

I nod, tearing my gaze from his. The tears are threatening, closing up my throat, and I swallow them back down as I carefully place the bandage on my palm. I must have caught it on a loose nail or a splintered piece of wood. I'm not really present. Haven't been since I arrived back here. I have one foot here in the present and one all the way back a decade ago. And I wonder if it's the same for Tom. Was that what Howard meant? Have I pulled everyone I've ever cared about in Woodsmoke back to ten years ago, making them relive the moments that have led to my return? That's what I was afraid of with my homecoming. That it would cause such a ripple that it would be more like a tidal wave.

"I spoke to Tom as well," I say quietly. "It didn't go well."

"Who's Tom?"

"My—my ex. Well, more than an ex in some ways, I guess. An old friend as well. At least, I thought of him that way." I take a deep breath. "I was meant to marry him, but I let him down. He wanted the family here, the house, the life . . . and I wanted to explore the world. Now he has all that with Jess . . . who used to be my best friend. And I guess . . . I guess I thought it wouldn't matter. I thought maybe I'd run into them, but it's not that simple. You can't snap your fingers and vanish ten years of absence. It feels like I'm still suspended in the decision I made that day to leave. Still eighteen and having to defend my own choices. Even if they're not what other people wanted for me."

Matthieu is quiet for a moment. "I understand that, going against expectations. When Henri—" He swallows, glancing at me. "I told you I had a brother, and we loved hiking the mountains here? Well, when I was sixteen, he went missing here. Never found a body, never found any answers. He just . . . vanished. We were staying at a guesthouse, and when I woke up I was alone."

"Oh, Matthieu, I'm so sorry," I say, blinking quickly. "Are you here to . . ."

"For closure, I think," he says with a shrug. "And maybe answers? My family didn't want me to come here. They thought I should leave it all in the past. But they weren't here when he vanished. It was just me and him. And I can't shake that feeling I had when I woke up in the guesthouse and he was gone. That . . . fear." He smiles ruefully. "So I understand . . . well, searching. For answers. And not doing what everyone expects of you."

I look at him, the angles of his face, the way he's hunkered over, still keeping a respectful distance from me. "I'm assuming the police . . ."

"Yes, all that happened. It was a long time ago, but lately, just in the last couple of years, I can't shake this feeling about the mountains. Maybe I won't find anything this winter, or maybe I'll finally put the ghosts to rest." He bites his lip. "I think we should stop for today, take a break. I need you to see something."

I nod as he gets up. He offers me his hand, pulling me up so we are standing next to each other. I take a few steps away, readjust the bandage, pull my jacket sleeves back over my wrists.

"Shall we?" he asks. He raises his eyebrows, and I look up into his eyes. All inky darkness below dark, thick brows, his hair a tousle of black. There's a tiny piece of plaster dust above his left ear, but I refrain from mentioning it. It strikes me suddenly how very tall he is, and how when he's not smiling his features appear haunted. It's the swollen mouth, the deep-set eyes. He seems at once present, standing right beside me, and yet a thousand miles away. I wonder if this is what losing someone to the mountains does to a person. I don't know how to tell him about the book, about all the stories pressed into it, all the warnings. Should I tell him? But then his mouth widens into a tentative smile, small crow's feet appearing at the corners of his eyes, and my stomach does a little flip.

Despite the sting of my tears, as well as the sting of Tom's words, I smile back. Matthieu is the only person in Woodsmoke I don't have some kind of history with. Spending some time with him is like taking a break from the muddle of my thoughts. It's the distraction I desperately need, and being near him feels like a balm. Like he's the coolness I needed to calm my flames. Perhaps today is not the day to talk about the old ways and the stories. "Lead the way," I say.

We take the path up the mountain. The one that winds up to the first lookout over Woodsmoke, the one I followed the night I arrived. Except, instead of gazing over the quiet, watchful town, as I did, Matthieu turns his back on it and heads west. We take a trail that's seldom used in winter. Even the creatures that live on the mountain range are rarely seen on it.

"Mind the branches. If you knock one, you could upset a snowdrift," Matthieu says over his shoulder. "I did it the other day. Feels horrible when the snow gets under your collar."

I shiver, imagining the snow melting against my hot skin, water trickling down my spine. "Thanks for the warning."

We continue in silence but for the sounds of the world around us. Slowly, inch by inch, I give in and stop looking inward. As we walk deeper into the secret heart of this mountain, I wake up. The scent of snow is different up here, colder and threaded with loam. Without the constant chug of cars and fumes, it tastes like a tall drink of water. I breathe it in, letting it pool on my tongue, trickle down my throat. And I feel more alive than I have in weeks. There are heavy snowdrifts packed in under the trees, marked only by the occasional scatter of bird tracks. The bright blue of the sky is piercing the thick pine trees around and above us and is so clear it feels like it goes on forever.

"We're nearly there," Matthieu says quietly. I notice he's being more careful, treading only where his footfalls will make the least sound. I do the same, weaving under branches, hunching my hands up inside my jacket to protect my fingers from frost. It's almost silent, in a heavy way that seems weighted and timeless. These mountains hold so many tales, so many secrets. It's rare for them to give them up, rarer still for them to be recorded and passed down. I think of Cora and the book.

Matthieu stills suddenly, and I hold my breath. He looks back at me, a grin lighting his features, and points through the thicket to our left. "Just where I left it," he says in a soft hush that almost carries his words away and past me, like the breeze itself. I look to where he is pointing, narrowing my eyes to search for anything that stands out in the world of white and pale wood.

"Amazing," I breathe. I track the fluttering movement of the tiny bird, the bright plume of fiery feathers across its chest. When it flits to a higher branch, its wings stretch wide, the charcoal depths of them like ink against the snow. "How?"

Matthieu shrugs. "I got lucky, I guess. Looks like this chap is lost. Maybe he'll be gone by morning? It's a varied thrush. Rare here, usually seen on the Pacific Coast of the US. My—my brother was a birder. Loved researching different species."

We hunker down to watch the bird as it moves between the branches. Then, in a flurry, it finds a higher branch, puffs up its tiny chest . . . and sings. It's a haunting cry, as though the bird is searching, forever searching. My breath catches in my chest, leaving a dull ache. I reach out to steady myself and find Matthieu's hand held out to steady me. My fingers, cold and small, flex within his warm grasp, his hand tightening around them as I regain my balance. I listen to the sad song of the little bird and let everything else fall away.

I dare not look at Matthieu. Dare not move in case he releases my hand. In this dead, white world, where this tiny bird is so lost and alone, I feel the heat from Matthieu's skin. It reaches through me, around me, firmly burying the memories I've been restlessly circling. I am grounded. And somehow I belong in this moment. I am no longer alone.

Chapter 22
Cora

Twenty Years Ago

This is how it always starts. With tea and the night and nerves too close to the surface of a person. With someone placing their hand on the door, hoping Cora will open up and make one more bargain with the mountains for them. Just one more, whatever the cost.

Whatever the price.

Tonight it's Brenda Haggerty, a woman who lost her baby last spring. She miscarried, as many do, but now she hears the baby's cries at night. When the wind whispers from the east, when it flows past the mountain, all she can hear are the thin wails of a newborn.

She scratches at the door and Ivy lets her in. Cora notices her hands first. How they're red and swollen, with small cuts in the skin between thumb and forefinger. Brenda catches Cora looking at her hands and balls them into fists.

"I wouldn't ask if I wasn't desperate," she says to the two sisters.

"I'll get the kettle on," says Ivy, leaving Cora and Brenda to talk.

Cora leads her into the lounge, glad at least that Howard is out in the fields. Milly, their jersey, is calving, and Howard will check her every hour until dawn breaks. Her eyes slide to the kitchen as she ushers Brenda into the lounge, still wringing her hands. Cora's and Ivy's eyes meet, and Ivy turns away first. But not before Cora sees it, the disapproval. But what did she expect when she gave the book to Cora? That she would hide it in the attic?

"What can you give me for it?" Brenda asks as Ivy brings in the tea. She sets it down, adding a tot of brandy to Brenda's, who sighs when she sips on it and briefly closes her eyes. "A potion? Maybe a spell?"

"Earwax," Cora says firmly. She doesn't touch the tea, since she can't stand caffeine past eight in the evening. She likes to sleep as soon as she's finished her twenty minutes of reading in bed. "Stopper your ears, don't open your bedroom window tonight. Leave the rest to me."

"Ear . . . what?" Brenda says, forehead wrinkling in confusion.

"It'll be tonight, it's a full moon," Cora says firmly. "Drink your tea, there's a love. Tonight, Brenda, you close your bedroom window and you stopper up your ears. Don't follow the sounds, there's no baby out there on those mountains waiting for you."

"But what if there is, what if—"

"Earwax," Cora says with a nod. "Stuff it in, you won't hear that husband of yours snoring either. More brandy?"

After Brenda leaves, politely shutting the door behind her, Cora turns to Ivy. "Don't start."

"Is there any point?"

"You think I shouldn't interfere."

"I think Brenda Haggerty needs to get ahold of herself."

"You don't believe her, then."

"Cora . . ." Ivy sighs. "I do believe she's hearing things, of course I do. You can't live here and not believe it all, not when there's proof every which way you turn. I know, if she follows the sounds, she could lose herself to the mountains tonight. But that's not what . . . What I'm most afraid of, really, is you going up there tonight and doing a working to save her."

Cora shifts past her sister to place the stone-cold mugs of tea on the tea tray. Ivy hasn't drunk hers either. "If I don't interfere, who will?"

"All I'm saying is . . . be careful."

Cora fixes her sister with a look. "And all I'm saying is, at least one of us Morgans has to do what's right."

Ivy bites her lip. "We don't know yet what you have to give up. What love you'll lose—"

"Not now," Cora says sharply. "Now, are you coming with me, or will you go home?"

Despite how Ivy feels, she still walks the old ways with her sister. They go up the mountain with the moon brimming and full, and in the silver haze Cora cuts her finger. She lets the blood well and drip, speaks a few words over it, kindly words, asking the mountains to forget about Brenda. Ivy is resigned to this casual, secretive horror. But she worries for Cora. She worries for her mind, for her soul. She stays in the shadows as her sister does the working, giving up a small piece of herself in exchange. As they walk back down the path, Cora sways and Ivy clamps an arm around her waist.

"What did it take to protect Brenda?" Ivy murmurs.

"Not sure yet . . ." Cora says and swallows carefully, as though it pains her. But she knows she's done the right thing, the best thing. For a brief moment, the barest thump of a heartbeat, she could feel the magic, and touch it, like touching thread or wool, golden and silken, reaching for her. These flares of magic, these tiny glimpses into something other, something that seems almost absent from the world, are worth every piece of herself she gives.

The following morning Cora wakes and eyes her braid in the

mirror. Her twirling hair, once an ashy blond, has silvered overnight. She brushes her fingers down it, loosening the braid into waves over her shoulders. When she learns later that Brenda slept soundly, that she didn't hear a single wail, she knows in her soul it was worth it.

Chapter 23
Carrie

"We need bags of plaster, a few buckets, and a hawk and trowel," Matthieu says, tapping the end of a pencil against his mouth as he studies his small notebook. He's in the passenger seat while I drive, and hot air from the engine is warming our faces and feet. As the road straightens out, I tune the radio to a station that doesn't play dance music on repeat.

"Lengths of skirting?" I ask, glancing over at him. His face is all serious, pinched in concentration, and my blood heats just looking at him. I pull air down into my lungs and drag my gaze back to the road as I tell myself to *stop* checking him out. He's working with me on the cottage, that's all. He liked Ivy, and he's got some time this winter. He might have held my hand as we watched that bird—his touch sending flutters of lightning through my veins every time I think about it—but there was nothing in it. Nothing. Just two people sharing a moment on a mountain. And in his search for answers about his brother, he's still stuck in the past. This is not the time for either of us.

"Carrie?"

I dart a look at him and see that he's turned his whole body toward mine, a small smile tugging at his mouth. "Wh-what?"

"I asked you twice if we could put it on the roof rack. You seem . . . distracted?"

I mumble something about concentrating on the road and out of the corner of my eye catch him turning back to his notebook, his smile growing slightly. He is a distraction, plain and simple. But the thing is . . . I kind of like being distracted by him.

"Take the next left, the builders' merchant is next to a coffee shop and a tractor dealership," Matthieu says, pocketing the pencil and notebook.

"Do you want to place the order," I ask, "and I'll pick up a couple of coffees? I fancy one that doesn't require stirring in granules and a kettle."

He chuckles. "Sure. I'll have mine black, if that's okay."

I pull into the car park in front of the builders' merchant, a squat building with stacks of blocks outside on pallets. The tractor dealership is surrounded by large, expensive farm equipment and the coffee shop is huddled in next to it.

"The Pit Stop. Cute," I murmur, hopping out of the car. Snow has been shoveled away and piled up in the corners, and with the sun at full strength in a deep bowl of blue above us, I see it's already melting slightly. There's still snow and frost everywhere, coating the fields and hedges for miles around us, and the mountains, the looming backdrop, are capped in white.

I turn my back to them, call over my shoulder to Matthieu, "See you in a few," and make a beeline for the terra-cotta brick building with the fogged-up display window. A bell jangles over the blue door to mark my entrance. Once inside, I find a whole display wall of ticking cuckoo clocks and, on the other side, a long counter accommodating a shuffle of men in lumberjack shirts. They're taking coffee from a woman with thick plaited red hair, while a skinny man who moves like a spider brews cup after cup of coffee with a big, silver coffee machine.

There are a few tables, but most of them are empty. The customers seem to favor standing up while they talk, taking great gulps out of large takeaway cups or mugs. I go to the back of the line, eyeing the display of cakes and doughnuts on top of the counter. I haven't had a treat in . . . weeks? Not since Halloween, when I bought a couple of black-iced spider cakes from the bakery in Woodsmoke and inhaled them in my car. The doughnuts are pistachio cream, and when I get to the front of the line I order two with coffees to go.

"You want them in one bag?" the woman asks.

"Two bags, please." I hope Matthieu likes doughnuts.

I collect my order, leave the sweet-scented café, and cross the car park to my car, balancing it all in my hands. Matthieu isn't by the car, so I place the doughnuts on the dashboard and carry our coffees to the builders' merchants. When I push inside the door, I don't see him. The list of things we need is on the counter, in that little notebook he carries, yet there's no sign of him. I breathe in the scent of new wood as I look around the space. The floor is concrete, and the space behind the counter is filled with racks and racks of items like packs of screws, lengths of piping, safety hats, and a stack of brochures.

"Hello?" I call out, wondering if Matthieu is off in the recesses of the building, looking at lengths of skirting board. I place the coffees on the counter and walk toward the back of the building, along walkways filled floor to ceiling with timber, sheets of plywood, insulation board, skirting . . . "Hello? Anyone here?"

A distant voice calls back, and I retreat along the walkways back to the counter, hoping I'm easier to spot there. A sudden shadow dims the space, and I look out of the window to see clouds swirling over the sun. The first flurries hit just a moment later.

"Sorry, stacking up an order," says a woman my age with brown frizzy hair and black dungarees as she marches over. She blinks at me and grins. "You've got a list there? I can check what's in stock?"

"Oh, brill—yes, thanks . . ." I say as she pulls the notebook toward her, tapping on a tablet and frowning. "Was there a man in here? He must have left the notebook on the counter? Dark hair? Tall?"

The woman looks up, tapping her chin with a finger. "No one that looks like that today, I don't think," she says. "Unless he's looking around the warehouse?"

"Maybe." I shrug, reaching for my coffee.

The woman finds everything I need and rings it up, and I hand over my bank card for her to scan. Then we wrestle the lengths of skirting out together, and she helps me strap them to the roof rack. I pile everything else in the boot, eyeing the flurries settling on the road. It'll turn icy soon, and there's no grit down. I need to get back soon.

"Thanks for your help," I say to her, and she waves, already running to get back inside the warm warehouse.

"Hey, sorry, I had to grab something." I hear Matthieu's voice behind me, turn, and find him leaning against the car. He has a wild look to him, hair disheveled, eyes sharp and watchful. I blink, wondering what it is about him. Why he looks like Matthieu but somehow . . . different. Like he did the first time I saw him, leaving the field by Ivy's cottage for the mountain trail.

I pass his coffee to him. "It'll be cold, but still caffeinated."

"Thanks." He smiles and shivers. "Shall we get going?"

"Sure." I hand him his notebook and place the doughnuts on the backseat without thinking.

It's not until later, after Matthieu leaves for the mountain trail, that I find them. And realize he never told me what he had to grab, or where he disappeared to before the frost re-formed.

Chapter 24
Carrie

Sometimes he would be gone for days, and she would wait for him. Wait for him to court her and bring her back pieces of the mountain. Stone, leaf, flower, a sketch of some forgotten, wild place up there.

—Nora Morgan, May 20, 1918

The snow falls steadily for the next two weeks as we glide further into November, my heart falling with it. His hand occasionally brushes mine as we pass each other, like when we converge on the kitchen at the same time to make a hot drink. Sometimes I catch him looking at me, a small smile on his face, and the heat instantly floods my veins. We call out the wrong answers to the quizzes on the tinny radio and have endless debates about what's better, doughnuts or cookies. When I have to climb a ladder to reach a second-story window, the feel of his hands bracing my waist leaves me dizzy.

We talk about everything. Slowly at first, then more openly. About our childhoods, our families. He asks me hesitantly about the *Morgan Compendium*, and I tell him about reading it when I was younger, about Cora keeping it hidden now. He grows thoughtful, a frown pinching his features, when we talk about the stories of people going missing in the mountains, like Henri. Hikers, the brokenhearted—tales of the lost are scattered throughout the history of Woodsmoke. But he brightens when he shares details about his brother—his auburn hair and wicked sense of humor, how he liked cricket and reading. We discuss the winter in the mountains, how fresh and renewing it is. He tells me about the other birds he's found on his walks, and he shows me the pictures he managed to take before the flame-colored thrush we watched finally left.

What I don't tell him is that he is becoming the siren call to the cottage each day, luring me deeper into this winter. When I woke up two days ago, my fingers had found my set of pencils and sketch pad and were tracing the shape of a dream on the paper before I had even fully greeted the morning. I don't tell him that I hadn't picked up my pencils since I returned here—longer than that even. I don't tell him that he is coaxing out my true nature in the midst of all this frost.

I don't dwell on the conversation with Tom, and no messages from Jess show up on my silent phone. I realize that our friendship is never going to restart and I have to accept that. On the few trips I make into Woodsmoke, I keep my eyes pinned to my boots and sweep in and out of shops like I'm stealing. No one tries to strike up a conversation or even shows that they know who I am. I wonder if Jess has changed, if she's spread some poison about me among everyone in town. Or perhaps the other girls I knew back then, Gillian and Amy, did that. Then I shrug off my suspicions and find myself again as I drive away from the center of town.

One day in the second week after we saw the thrush, Matthieu leans over me as I chatter about something inconsequential—maybe paint colors? And I feel his fingers brush the shell of my ear. My heart stutters and I falter, electricity zipping through my veins.

"Some plaster dust. It fell in your hair," he says, his voice low and close.

I swallow, tilting my head toward him. His face is so close to mine, I can see the depth of color in his eyes, the kaleidoscope of darkest blues and charcoal and gray . . .

"Thank you," I say softly, my eyes flickering to his mouth, then back up to his eyes. If I leaned in a little closer, if I closed this small distance between us, what would he taste like? What would his mouth feel like on mine?

My phone trills suddenly, breaking the moment, and I fumble for it in my dungarees pocket, heat flooding my face. Matthieu moves away, and I answer a call from my dad, who's checking in on the renovation, asking how it's going. After I hang up the call, I realize I don't remember a single word of what was said.

In the third week after we saw the thrush, the sun brightens a little, the wind stills her temper, and the frost thaws on the ground. As I begin the work for the day, clearing out the kitchen so the carpenter can fit the worktops, I don't worry that Matthieu doesn't turn up. Not even as the sun climbs higher on the bright late November day and the snow melts into sullen sludge.

It's not until I leave the carpenter to it and check my phone for the time that I see it's three o'clock. Matthieu hasn't messaged. It still nettles me when I change clothes later back in the caravan, and later when I start tracing the lines of the pencil drawing I worked on at dawn.

"It's just not like you . . ." I say as the sky darkens outside. I peer out, narrowing my gaze, seeking out the blurred edges of the field. My fingers slip over my phone, light it up, then pocket it again. I'm not going to call him, but I feel a little let down. I thought we'd reached an understanding since the day we walked up the mountain and saw that bird together. I thought that maybe we might be more than friends.

When I search for tea bags and realize I'm out, I take that as a sign. In minutes, my boots are on, my coat shrugged over my shoulders, and I'm setting off, into the gloaming.

My knock is less hesitant than the first time several weeks ago. When Cora opens the door, her surprise is genuine.

"Witchy intuition failing you?" I ask with a smile. She crumples slightly, as though she'd been bracing herself for this.

"Carrie," she says, relief softening her. She's aged in a few weeks. Her features are dimpled with deep wrinkles, and her skin is gray as porridge. I blink, hiding my shock, and she reaches for my hand, my arm, grasping me as though she's drowning. As though this moment is her first gasp of air in a month. "I didn't know if—I didn't think—"

"Kettle on?" I ask, moving past her, pulling off my boots to walk through her clinically clean home. "I'm out of tea bags. Figured it was time I stopped by."

She fusses around me in the kitchen, pulling out mugs and tea and milk. When we settle in the lounge, the loudest sound in the house—just as it's always been—is the ticking clock on the mantlepiece, marking the steady buildup of seconds. I can't understand how it doesn't drive Cora completely mad.

"How is the cottage coming along?" she asks now as she spoons sugar into her mug, even though she doesn't take sugar anymore. Not usually. She clatters the teaspoon in swift little circles, placing it precisely back on the tray when she's done.

"Quickly. It's . . . there's not much left to do." I take a gulp of tea. "I can get it on the market in January or February most likely. Should be ready for photos by then."

She sighs, taking an efficient sip of tea. "I suppose you've had help."

"Matthieu? Yes, he's been a great help." I steady my voice, bracing my hands around the mug. I remember Howard's words, how he asked me when Matthieu appeared, how I told him Matthieu seemed to arrive with the frost. I take a sip, then set the mug down on the coffee table. "Couldn't have done it all without him."

"Not there today, though, I imagine," Cora says in clipped tones, turning beady eyes on me. "I expect you haven't seen him since yesterday."

"How . . ."

She places her cup on the coffee table and points at the window. It's dark outside, but she hasn't drawn the curtains. Still, I know what the window would show. The perfect picture of a thawed driveway, rivulets of water pooling at the edges.

"What happens when the frost thaws, Carrie?"

I shake my head, a tiny puffing laugh escaping me. "Come on, Cora—"

"I'm right, though, aren't I? You haven't seen him. I bet he hasn't messaged, hasn't called." She leans toward me. "It's why you're really here. You believe because you're a Morgan. You can't deny your own blood. It's who you are. Those stories, the mountains, are what both of us are made from. The stuff of our blood and bones."

"Cora, please—"

"Could you even tell me his last name?"

I shake my head, pursing my lips.

Cora sips her tea, watching me. "I don't say it to hurt you, dear one. Quite the opposite."

"They're not all real," I say suddenly, picking up my mug with a jerking swipe that makes the tea slosh out. I stare for a moment at the tea splatters pooling in clouds on the coffee table. "Sometimes—sometimes someone really does go missing, and there are reasonable explanations. A slip from the path, a twisted ankle—"

Cora cackles. "Don't be so daft, girl. Of course they're real. Every tale in the book is true, every working, every potion written down, passed from hand to hand . . ." Her eyes soften, growing misty. "It'll be yours one day. You can pass it down to your granddaughter—"

I stand abruptly and go to the kitchen, where I grab a cloth, hold it under the running tap, then squeeze it out. My breath is coming a little too quick, and my shoulders are hunched around my ears. I've had a lifetime of Cora's warnings, Ivy's too. She even included one in her will, reminding me to greet the mountains on my return. Her letter now echoes in Cora's words.

It was Cora who told me on my twelfth birthday that I was about to meet my first love in the orchard. My mum's eyes darted to her aunt in warning as she quickly lit the candles on my cake, then drew everyone around to sing "Happy Birthday." I met Tom in the orchard three days later. He was stealing apples from the tree in our garden, five of the best ones my mum had been saving for an autumn pie, letting them ripen up before picking. I knew him from school, but not that well. He was one of the kids who populated the backdrop of my life—or rather, I appeared only in the backdrop of theirs.

I pelted him with conkers that day, and he just winked at me as he took a big, juicy bite. The tartness made him gag, and I doubled over laughing. He spat out the apple bite, and rubbing the back of his hand over his mouth, he started laughing too.

"Cooking apples!" I said, walking over to him. "What was it, Tom Gray? A dare?"

He nodded, dropping the rest of the apples into my hands. "Billy bet me a fiver I wouldn't even climb the wall. Said you Morgans are all witches who eat your husbands' hearts."

"And you didn't believe him?" I asked, tossing my hair. I had outlined my eyes perfectly that day with a sweep of dark kohl and thickly applied mascara I'd stolen from Mum's dressing table. I looked the part. "You should see the book."

"It's true, then," he said, his grin lighting him up. My heart skipped as he placed the last apple in my arms, then leaned forward to kiss my cheek. My blush was instant, and scarlet heat flushed my skin. "That was the second bet. That I wouldn't kiss you."

Then he was gone, racing for the fence, slipping over it to sprint up the lane. I remember that first kiss every time I smell apple pie. Cora didn't mean to curse me, but in a way that's exactly what she did.

I march back into the lounge to clean up the spilled tea and drag my mind back into the present, back to Matthieu. I eye her, this woman with her stories and her curses, and I draw in a breath. Cora is old. And in light of what Howard told me about her, and what the man in the hardware store said . . . I pause, stilling any retorts before they burst out of me. It would do no good to upset her by letting them out. It would just be noise.

"Cora, I respect all of it, truly. But this is different. I'll go and find him—tomorrow, at first light. He lives in the first cabin up the mountain trail from Ivy's field, the Vickers cabin. I found it with Jess and Tom when we were younger. It's not far," I say to her quietly, decisively. "Thank you for the tea."

"Be careful, Carrie," she says. "Please, my girl, if you must go there, don't stray from the path. Don't follow any shouts or calls. Don't . . . don't believe everything you see and hear."

I don't wait for her to say anything more. I don't wait for her to tell me I'm wasting my time, or that I shouldn't go looking for someone who is not even real. I don't want to hear her tell me that he's some vengeful spirit, the mountains made flesh. I don't want to hear any more curses fall from her lips, or any more stories of broken hearts and lost loves. I pull on my boots and set out into the gathering night, making my way back through the mud-slicked fields to the caravan.

Chapter 25

Jess

Jess's life is a series of moments. The precious, solitary moments before she drags Elodie to school in the morning, her time spent in the hushed library stacks, then the moments afterward when she collects Elodie from school and Tom gets home from work. She can divide up her days into sections, compartmentalize them like her to-do list. And right now she knows which moments in her day she prefers.

It all began with the chicken. After her shift, she stands in the line at the butcher's in town, one street down from the library. The thawing snow has left streams of water running through the square, and now it pools in the heel of her boot, soaking her sock. She can feel a cold coming on, a thickening in her nose and throat, an itching in her ears. And her limbs, her very joints, ache and fizz, every fiber of her longing for a bath and a mug of hot chocolate to hold in her hands. It's the same every December, in the run-up to the festive season, when everything seems to get so busy, when she can hardly find a moment to *breathe.*

She has already canceled on Gillian, sending a quick text to let her know she can't meet for coffee after the school run tomorrow. The very thought of carefully deflecting Gillian's attempts to gossip about Carrie for half an hour leave her wrung out and irritated.

When she reaches the front of the line, Adam Monks, with his white hat and striped apron, has only chicken thighs and lamb cutlets left. She sighs through her nose, eyeing them both before pointing to the chicken. She hands over her bank card, listening for the high-pitched tap that signals her account being drained just that little bit more.

Then she smiles a vacant half smile at Adam, the boy who is now a man. She remembers him picking his nose in year three, when he sat on the classroom carpet next to her. That's the thing about staying in your hometown into adulthood: each day and every conversation is layered with memory upon memory. Some days she feels like she's wading through a stream of them.

After Adam bags up the chicken, she leaves the shop and hurries to her car, dodging the rivers of meltwater and being prodded by umbrella spokes as she brushes past people. She dashes across the main square, feeling the damp squelch in her left boot, and unlocks her parked car with a whispered "At bloody last."

She doesn't usually drive, since she's always thinking about getting her steps in for the day. But just like the past few days, she woke up this morning with a bone-deep weariness. She has fought against it—swimming against a current of fatigue—but this morning it tugged her under. She hustled Elodie into the car, warmed her hands on the hot air choking out of the vents by the steering wheel, and decided to sign up at the gym instead of battling the dwindling minutes to squeeze in her usual walk to school and then to the library.

Now Jess rummages in a shopping bag and pulls out a paper packet, shiny with grease. She dips her hand inside, breaks off a piece of cinnamon bun, and exhales as she chews. She has a full twenty minutes before she has to pick Elodie up from school. She dusts crumbs off her hand and reaches into another bag on the passenger seat, then pulls out the hardback that's just come into the library. The latest in a series she loves, it's a book she's been waiting for. She takes another bite of the bun, settles into the car seat, and loses herself contentedly in the first chapter, the heat still blasting out of the vents, the chicken still sitting on the passenger seat.

After picking up Elodie, after listening to the other mums complain about the number of sweets their children were given on Halloween—about how it's become such a *toxic* part of our culture—she drives home, listening with only half an ear to Elodie talk about the boy called Phillip in her class who stole her seat at lunch. What Jess is really thinking about is how long it'll be before she can settle into a bath and read the next chapter of her new library book. Reading a new book is the quiet place of joy she's slipped into ever since she was little. The rustle of the pages and the tug of the characters' lives feel so vivid, so real. When she finds a good book, a gripping story, it's like winning the lottery. She hopes Elodie will find that same joy when she starts choosing books of her own.

Sometimes Jess wishes that Tom would pick up Elodie from school. That it wasn't always her job to race from the library, pick up dinner, and then rush over to the school to collect their daughter. She wishes he could be the one who remembers to send a birthday card to his aunt, or the one who packs the rucksack when they go out for a day trip as a family.

After she hustles Elodie inside, Tom arrives home earlier than usual. He has that wild-eyed look he gets nowadays, as though his thoughts are forever wandering across the fields to a certain cottage, to a certain person. Jess wants to say something. She wants to open her mouth and let it all pour out—all her feelings about Carrie, about him, about how he never picks up his damn socks off the bathroom floor when he showers, about knowing he's looked up Carrie on Facebook. He's probably stalking her Instagram account as well, seeing all the pictures of the renovation, her morning walks, her perfect existence. Not that Jess scrolls her feed at all. Obviously.

But she doesn't say any of these things. Jess just sniffs at the chicken, forehead dimpling slightly. "Does this smell okay to you?" she asks, turning to him. She places the thighs on a baking tray, intending to roast them and make a rice dish on the stove with some veggies. But something smells off. And even now, twenty minutes after getting out of the car, she still has a feeling of motion sickness. As though she is still traveling forward, propelled in a way that her body is revolting against.

It has to be the chicken.

Tom bends over it, his forehead pinched like hers, and breathes deeply. "Smells normal to me. Do you want me to do dinner? Maybe go up and take a bath, or—"

Jess is gone before he finishes the sentence. Soon she's wallowing in a cloud of marshmallow bubbles, ducking her head under the surface so she can no longer hear the rumbling of her husband's voice or the tinny notes of the TV program Elodie is watching. She drifts, imagining a weekend of being totally alone, answerable to no one but herself. Then she dries her hands, carefully turns to the next chapter of the library book, and loses herself once more in the pages.

She lingers too long in the bathwater. Finally admitting defeat, Jess pulls herself out of the tepid water. She brushes her hair back, pulls on joggers and a hoodie, and breathes a sigh of relief when she catches the scents of garlic and chicken. At least Tom is actually cooking dinner. At least there's that.

Jess goes downstairs, idly searches through the fridge for the half-empty bottle of sauvignon blanc, and, spotting it, pours herself a few inches in her favorite wineglass. Tom is thumbing through the TV channels, and Elodie has already tucked into a plate of chicken and pasta with a few circles of cucumber on the side. Elodie won't eat rice, so they always have to cook pasta separately for her. Just one of the many Elodie-isms Jess half hates, half loves.

"I'm going out in a bit," Tom says to her, not even bothering to turn around. Not even bothering to offer up an explanation.

Jess tenses and takes a measured sip of wine. It's sharp on her tongue, all ice and crisp citrus. "Right."

"Don't be like that." Tom sighs, abandoning the remote control next to Elodie, who still sits glued to the TV, her dinner on a lap tray, her little legs poking out like sticks.

"I'm just tired, Tom. Just tired," Jess says quietly.

Tom says nothing for a moment as he gets up, stretches, then looks at her. "I went to see her. When she first got back."

Jess's heart stops. "What?"

"I thought it would help. I didn't think she would stay this long, to be honest—"

"And you didn't . . . tell me?" Jess says, clutching the stem of her wineglass so hard it could snap. Fear and anger war inside her, tying her stomach in nauseous knots. "Is that where you're going tonight?"

"No! No, of course not. Just meeting Billy for a drink." He brushes a hand down his face. "I guess I wanted to know why. Why she left like she did, why after all these years she's back now. I'm sorry, I should have told you."

Jess takes another sip of wine, then another. She's trying very hard to hold it all together, to hold the shriek of rage and hurt inside. "You shouldn't have gone at all."

"I realize that now. Dumb move. I'm sorry."

Jess closes her eyes, a dull thumping beginning in her temples. This is what she'd been afraid of with Carrie's return. And really, with what she did all those years ago, did she have any right to be cross?

She snaps her eyes open and finds Tom looking at her uncertainly. As though she could explode at him, blowing up their carefully constructed life. Her fear deepens, beating back her anger. Does she want this argument? Does she really want to damage what they have? She takes a quick breath, breaking her gaze from his. "It's understandable you'd want answers, I suppose. As long as that's all it was. Just please . . . *please* don't go behind my back again."

"I'm sorry," he mutters again.

She eyes him as he moves around the kitchen, pulling out plates and piling up the roasted chicken and veggie risotto he's pulled together. She winces at the oily tideline around the edge of the pan, but says nothing. She'll have to soak it overnight.

He places the two dinner plates with careful, clipped precision on the dining table. "Glass of water?"

"Please," she says, sitting down. A wave of nausea overtakes her as she looks down at the food, but she begins to eat it anyway, almost mechanically.

Tom sits beside her, and she notices the creases appearing in his eyelids as he tenses his jaw, chewing and staring into space. When did they become so distant? So unattuned? She tries to tell herself that his going to see Carrie is nothing, that they were together so long ago, it means nothing now. But Jess's heart skips, a dull thud echoing through her like a stone dashed across the surface of a lake. She can't help picturing their limbs tangled together, Tom whispering promises into Carrie's ear. Jess's stomach twists, bile rises up her throat, and she pushes back her chair roughly.

Tom looks up. "Jess?"

"Just something stuck in my teeth," she murmurs.

"Jess, I'm sorry, I don't need to go out—"

She closes the bathroom door, cutting him off, locks it, and braces her hands on the edge of the sink. She counts to ten, slowly, mouthing the words as the storm clawing through her begins to subside. Then she blows out a breath, takes a drink of cool water straight from the tap, and dashes the back of her hand across her mouth.

When she looks up into the mirror, she can't find herself. All Jess can see is a tired woman with skin too pale, eyes a little bloodshot. She grips the edge of the sink again, staring at herself. This is what she chose: domesticity, simple and orderly everyday calm punctuated by quiet joys—like reading a new book. But she's off-kilter, unbalanced, and it isn't really about Tom or Elodie. It's about her.

"You know what you've got to do," she says to her reflection. "You *know*."

TOM LEAVES AFTER Elodie is in bed. He insisted on doing the whole bedtime routine and fussed around Jess with medicine and an extra blanket until she told him to please go out. Now he's definitely gone, and she calls her mum to come over and sit in the lounge. "Just an hour, Mum. I need to pick up a few bits at the supermarket. I was rushed off my feet this week."

She's already driving before she changes her mind. She picks up that item down the aisle she usually avoids, the one in a slim box, and hustles into the supermarket loo. The queasiness claws at her, making her feel just the way she did the last time, and she wants to be certain. It might be the chicken, but she doesn't think so. Afterward, she's not doing a big shop. There's somewhere else she needs to go, a place she has to keep secret. She's going to the one place she's avoided, down the old country lanes she knows better in the dark, or on foot, than in the daylight.

She steels herself for a night that could change everything.

Chapter 26
Cora

Eighteen Years Ago

Lillian's garden is riddled with giggles. Cora keeps glancing out of the kitchen window, and every so often she spies a dash of pink gingham or a flutter of blond hair. She chuckles to herself as she pulls out the old Mason Cash bowl she gave Lillian as a wedding present and stirs the muddled mint and rose petals into the infusion. Carrie and Jess, toting matching wicker baskets on their arms, are picking petals and leaves that they think smell the nicest and look the most beautiful, as instructed by Cora. She sighs happily as she gently stirs the potion with a wooden spoon, all to keep the girls entertained for the afternoon.

And if Carrie takes a shine to the magic, well . . .

Would that be such a very bad thing?

Ivy seems to think so. Ivy, the true grandma, the hesitant one who gave up the book and all that came with it. She doesn't want Carrie inheriting the magic. If it were up to her, it would be buried in the back garden, deep in the loam, to make worm feed.

"We think we've got enough!" Carrie says breathlessly, rushing in trailing the scent of pollen and grass. She pushes her hair behind one ear, still giggling as she turns back to Jess, whose eyes are glittering, a wide grin on her face. Cora can't help but chuckle again as she moves to inspect their baskets.

"Verbena, good, good, and plenty of petals, some honeysuckle . . .

Carrie, is that a nettle leaf?" Cora asks, searching for something to pluck it out of the basket with so she won't be stung. That would not do at all, not for what she is brewing. Not for a love potion.

"I like them," Carrie says stubbornly, sucking her index finger. "And I had to move it so Jess could reach the yellow rose."

Cora's eyes shift to Jess's basket, all pale pinks and yellows and creams. She frowns, looking back at Carrie's. Her basket holds a mishmash, with no clear color or texture, no clear pattern, to any of her choices. Now, that would *not* do.

"Run back to the garden, girls," Cora says softly, dragging the baskets toward her across the kitchen table. "I need an apple from each of you. Either plucked from the tallest branch or foraged from the ground. Still whole and perfect."

Jess nods solemnly, then races after Carrie, who lets out a long holler as she sprints for the walled orchard at the far end of the garden. Watching them run, Cora tuts. Carrie is barefoot and covered in grass stains, with wild hair and a tear in the back of her dress. Jess is a whole different story. Neat hair, neat dress, little Mary Jane pumps still clean as a whistle on her dainty feet. "Chalk and cheese," Cora murmurs with a sigh.

She pulls two saucepans out of the cupboard, sparks up the stovetop, and places one pan at each end of the range cooker. The sprawling, farmhouse-style kitchen has cream-colored cupboards, worktops made of thick slabs of wood, and knickknacks covering the windowsill. Most of them are Carrie's creations. Tiny paintings in heart-shaped frames, a Mother's Day card from three years ago, and quirky egg cups and porcelain thimbles. It's a lived-in kitchen. Scarred and scratched and well used. Looking around this kitchen, listening to the shrieks of the girls as they balance ladders against the trunks of the old apple trees, Cora can't understand why Lillian is considering leaving when Carrie is older.

Why would she *ever* want to leave Woodsmoke and this magical, homey life?

Cora splits the potion between the two saucepans, sets both burners to a gentle simmer, and then turns each pan a quarter anticlockwise before tipping the contents of each basket into each saucepan. This potion is a recipe from the book, a harmless way to coax out Carrie's curiosity. Jess's potion glows pink momentarily before dulling to a rosy tint. Carrie's potion, however, gleams as green as a forest. Cora stirs them both, watching as the petals dissolve and the leaves curl and vanish. Then she turns off the heat and steps away from the stovetop.

The girls run in again, out of breath, carrying an apple each. Carrie's is green, of course, one of her favorites with a tangy crunch. Jess's is a rosy red, too small to be ripe, but it fits perfectly into her palm.

"All right then, Jess, you place your apple in the saucepan on the left, and Carrie, yours goes on the right," Cora says, washing her hands in the sink and watching out of the corner of her eye as the girls drop the apples in. Carrie's, she's sure, flashes, while Jess's doesn't even wink. Cora dries her hands and inspects the saucepans. "Very good. Now you must leave these saucepans in a patch of moonlight. Tomorrow you'll pluck the apple out with your own hand, not with a spoon, or a fork, or any other implement."

"And then?" Carrie asks eagerly, already picking up the saucepan off the stove.

"Then you eat the apple and make a wish to fall in love."

Carrie's nose wrinkles. "What if I don't want to fall in love?"

"Everyone wants to fall in love," Jess says quietly, eyeing her rosy red apple. "You just don't know it yet."

Carrie shrugs, turning to Jess. "Let's leave them on the garden table. Mum says it's a full moon tonight."

Jess nods eagerly and carries her saucepan carefully down the back steps. Carrie has already rushed to the trestle table, her potion spilling out over the sides of the pan. Cora smiles and then begins clearing up the kitchen.

Lillian feels the same way as Ivy about the book, about the magic, about all of it. But Cora needs Carrie to feel differently. She needs her to see the whimsy in it first, the charming nature of potions and moonlight. Not just the warnings, the rules, the curses, and the cost of the sometimes necessary bargains.

There are two sides to the mountains, and Cora wants Carrie to know the joy, the freedom, the *beauty* of such a wild, ancient place. She reaches down to pick up a fallen rose petal, then rubs the silky sunshine blush between her thumb and forefinger. She looks out of the window and sees the girls practicing their cartwheels. She hopes, desperately, that Carrie's life will always be like this. That she'll spend her life in Woodsmoke, a little life surrounded by love and hope and magic.

Deep Winter

December–January

Chapter 27
Carrie

But when he didn't reappear for three weeks, everyone thought he had broken off the courtship. Everyone except Edith. She was sure he was lost somewhere, that he just needed to find his way back.

—Nora Morgan, May 20, 1918

I leave for the mountain trail as dawn whispers through the fields. Tendrils of breeze stir the exposed grass, stinging my skin where my hat doesn't quite meet the collar of my coat. It's cold enough to snow again. I can smell it on the air. But on this cool December day, the sky is lightening to a deep blue without a cloud to mar it. My breath hangs in foggy clouds as I hit the trail that will take me away, up the mountain.

If he is there, what will I say to him? That I believed Cora when she suggested that he might not be quite real? Perhaps I can say that I was concerned. When he didn't turn up and never called back, it made sense to check on him. Yes, that's what I'll say. I reason it out, turning over different scenarios as I round the mountain path and the lookout over Woodsmoke. I pause for a moment, catching my breath, and brace my hands on the straps of my rucksack. Woodsmoke is peaceful today, a tapestry of brown and gray, the square in the center full of fidgeting little forms.

My eyes track right, away from the center of town to follow the winding road to Cora's. She will be drinking her morning coffee and pestering Howard about some minor detail of their lives, and he'll be indulging her. Am I doing this to prove to her that she's wrong? There's always been a bit of tug-of-war to our relationship, as though she is forever pulling at my loose threads, wanting to unravel me. Yesterday I prickled with it. She's so sure that all those stories, all those tales passed down in the *Morgan Compendium*, are facts. I want to believe they are no more than fairy tales. Fables spun from thin air to explain away something unexplainable. But now, being back here and in the thick of it, it's hard to hold on to that idea. The stories in the book feel all too real.

Guilt needles me suddenly. I should be spending more time with Cora. That's all she's ever wanted from me—just *more*. More of my time, more of my love. And I've always been so hesitant to give it. That's why she's so focused on collating the past, collecting these tales and hoarding them like jewels. She uses them to lure me in, I'm sure of it, and it might have worked when I was a child. But now I am older, and the mysteries of this place no longer thrill me or fill me with wonder. I'm no longer interested in exploring every inch of the mountains, taking field notes, and marveling at the heady freedom of such an ancient place. The hidden mysteries of the mountains used to fill me with wonder, but now I am older, I fear their sinister edge.

I turn to the rest of the world, with my back to the view, and consider the three trails that branch out from this lookout. I know which cabin Matthieu is staying in; there are only a few scattered throughout this mountain range. The ones that are known of, anyway. And the one he is renting from the Vickers is the closest; he can reach it quickly with his long strides each day. I pull my bottle out of the side pocket of the rucksack, sip on the water, and let it wash my uncertainty away. He will be there. He will be there in the cabin, and maybe he hasn't been well. Maybe he will appreciate someone reaching out when he's so alone up here in the vast, cold nothing. Cora has just unsettled me in her usual tug-of-war with me, and I'm off balance. I allowed her into my head, and for the briefest moment she made me question if the frost tale is real.

That's all.

The walk takes longer than I thought it would. The path sometimes peters out into nothing but stones. The only way I know I'm on the right trail is from the broken branches on either side, where the encroaching wild has been pushed back. I picture Matthieu shoving back branches as he walks, keeping this path through the mountains his own. But there are patches where the wild has begun to steal pieces of the path, where no one seems to have passed in a while.

I remember when I used to tread this path with Tom and Jess. We would walk and walk, exploring the trails trickling like veins down the mountainside, marking them on our map and imagining we were the first explorers. Like sunlight on ice, the flashes of those moments dazzle me now, again and again. With every curve in the path, every place where the trees dip and sway, showing the view of the landscape far below, I remember.

The last time was a month before I was meant to marry Tom, a few days before I was turning eighteen. The three of us walked up to where the trees part, where we could see for miles and miles, far beyond the edges of Woodsmoke. We stood shoulder to shoulder and gazed out over the world.

"We don't have to stay here, you know," I remember saying to them both.

Tom kept quiet, but Jess frowned, a furrow appearing between her brows. "Why wouldn't we want to?" she asked.

"Look how big it is, Jess. Look how much we still have to explore."

I told Jess then that Tom and I planned to travel. That she could come with us, that this new future, this one without Woodsmoke at the center of it, was a possibility opening up to her too. Something new and wondrous and wholly attainable. She grew quiet, then mentioned university, the holidays, her summer job at the library. I dropped the subject after that, wondering why Jess didn't get it, and why Tom was so quiet.

I think I told Cora that same night, cheeks still flushed like roses from the glow that Tom and Jess gave me just from being nearby, just from being alive. My fiancé and my best friend, the people I was going to conquer the world with. Cora grew still for a moment, then snapped on a smile. She offered Ivy the first plate of pasta she was serving up at the table, and Ivy muttered her thanks in return.

That certainty of belonging with the two of them, with Jess and Tom, is a ghost that haunts me now as I walk to find Matthieu's cabin. After I left Woodsmoke, I chased that ghost, that deep sense of belonging I craved elsewhere. I searched for it down the many steps of Positano and in the cramped streets of the Gothic Quarter in Barcelona. I sought it out in tiny flats, in a two-bedroom house on the outskirts of Manchester, even in a rented cottage by the harbor in St. Ives.

But I didn't belong in any of these places, or with anyone else.

No one else I met while I was gone gave me that glow, that certainty, that feeling like I was exactly where I was supposed to be—the feeling I'd had with Tom and Jess. I mourned the loss of us for too long. Always wondering if I should have stayed in Woodsmoke, if that sense of belonging was still there. Maybe it hadn't died between us, maybe I only imagined it had. Maybe if I had stayed, Jess and I would still be best friends now. But then Ivy told me—in a call I took on a tinny landline in a bar in Crete—that Jess and Tom had gotten together. Seeing him the other night, with his shoulder pressed against the car window as if he couldn't stand to be in the same car with me, just confirmed that the connection was long gone. I wasn't wrong. It did die between us, and it was never meant to continue. I didn't belong to him just as he didn't belong to me, and I did the right thing to keep searching all those years.

I stop on the trail and take a minute to breathe. It hasn't leveled out for a while, and the air in my lungs is burning. I place my hands on my hips as I feel the burn in my chest cooling, inch by inch. My legs are beginning to shake with each step, and I can feel my body slowing, needing rest. I drink more water and mentally measure the distance I've come and the distance up the winding path to the cabin. It's not a lot farther. But I hope there are no more memories laying snares for me on the way.

Thirty minutes later, my chest is burning hard, a furnace I can no longer cool. Just as I am sure I will need to sit and take a break, the path stops. A clearing opens, flat and wide, with trees looming over it in an oval. In the middle, as though sprouted from a Grimms' fairy tale, is the cabin.

It's a single-story building built of wood and granite, wearing a chimney on top like a too-small hat. The windows are dark and seem to watch me as I hesitate on the edge of the clearing. There are raised beds, but whatever thrived in the spring and summer has been cleared away. Now the beds are barren and cold. I walk between them, weaving my way to the front door of the cabin, and let my knuckles rest on the wooden door. Cora and her superstitions nudge at me, beckoning me away from the cabin. I inhale sharply, pushing those thoughts away, and rap my knuckles against the door.

Silence greets me.

Silence yawning so loud it's deafening. I knock again, louder this time, my mind a scatter of questions and answers:

He might not have heard—

Maybe he's out—

Maybe he's really sick—

Maybe, maybe, maybe.

I close my eyes, leaning my forehead on the door, wishing for once my head was a quiet place. Then I hear it, a gentle click. And the door opens.

"Matthieu, I'm so sorry, I didn't meant to disturb you, but—" My words seize up in my throat as I look up. There's no Matthieu. No towering man with kind eyes, capable hands, and an instant smile. There is only a doorway, open now, and darkness beyond. "Matthieu?"

When he doesn't answer, when no one answers, I plant my boots on the threshold. Then, pushing aside every warning, every discordant alarm bell, I step inside the cabin.

Chapter 28

Carrie

The darkness rearranges itself. As my eyes adjust to the strangled light, I see a shamble of kitchen cupboards, a fireplace, an old chair. The wood floor has no rugs to cover it. No comfort to offer bare feet. I decide to keep my boots on and the door open wide to the outside. When I step farther in, I hear no movement from anyone inside. Matthieu doesn't appear in a doorway. I suddenly long for his voice, to break the curse that seems to linger inside these walls.

"Hello?" I call, louder this time, as though that would banish this feeling of being watched. But no one answers. Instead of retreating back outside, I throw off my fear, stride forward, and thrust the bedroom door open. It holds a bed, some covers in a heap, and half-drawn curtains that have peeled away from the pole. "Matthieu?"

He's clearly not here. And from the smell of damp and loam, he might not have been here for some time. I step toward the window at the back, brushing my hand over the curtain. Dust motes dance through the thin shafts of sunlight, the only movement in this place. I turn with a sigh, wrapping my arms around my body. I know one thing for certain. I am not welcome here.

As I move back to the front door, to the outside world that I can make sense of, something nags at me. Calls to me. I look over to the far wall of the living room and see something huge and rectangular covering the wall. I frown, trying to make out the shape of it, tracing the drawn lines with my eyes. Finally, I see that it's a map.

Plastered the whole width of the wall, marked with gold pushpins connected with twine tied to each one. As I study the map, the cabin seems to grow colder, as though wanting to push me out. But I can't move. I stare, transfixed by the map, by the seemingly haphazard trails and tracks marked across it with lengths of twine.

It's the mountains. The entire range, all three peaks, every clearing, every marked trail. And all the trails that are unmarked. Trails that most visitors will never find, never stumble across. Visitors come back year after year to hike new sections of the range, and hikers participate in challenges to conquer all three peaks.

To try to cover it all, *see* it all, in just one winter . . . I don't know how that would be possible. It would take days to reach the other side of the range, and it's all too easy to step the wrong way. The trees are dense, navigation is tough, and the old trails are not clearly marked, like those for amateur hikers. Those old ways, the older trails . . . I shiver. What is he looking for?

"Matthieu, where are you?" I murmur. I break away a few moments later and walk back out into daylight. I turn in a circle outside the cabin, searching the clearing, searching the looming trees crouched around like sentries. "You could be anywhere."

I brush my hair back from my face, trying to think. If he's stuck somewhere, will he be able to call someone? I bite my lip, my thoughts growing frantic, leaping from outcome to outcome. That map was old. Faded. What if it was an old map, something that was already there when he arrived for the winter? There is very little sign of anyone living there, though. The cabin holds an air of neglect, of hibernation. What if this isn't the cabin Matthieu is staying in? I hug my arms around myself again, the chill of the place still permeating my bones.

I force my feet to follow the trail back down the mountain. I barely take it in, the views, the trees, the mud-slicked paths. I place one foot in front of the other until I reach my field and Ivy's cottage. Then I feel it—a change. As though the world has shifted a quarter inch. A flurry of snow shivers down around me, falling in lazy, soft arcs. I put out my hand, collecting a couple of flakes as they fall, and then look up into the vast abyss of white. The snow falls faster, drifting as I stand there and smothering the field in a crisp sheet. My phone beeps in my pocket and I lunge for it.

It's Matthieu.

My heart thumps, once, twice, thundering as I read the message. He's been tied up for a few days. Back tomorrow. A breathless, fleeting laugh escapes from me, and I pocket my phone. Sniffing, I crunch across the crème brûlée of snow, making my way to the cottage to begin the work for the day.

I should feel only relief, should be able to shrug off my earlier fears. But that cabin, the map, the lingering quiet of that clearing—it all keeps breaking through, haunting me. And I wonder about that story, the one that Cora warned me about. At the very back of my mind, in the darkest, least-visited corner, I turn over a question as the snow flurries thicken. One that should have no place in this world. What if Matthieu is something out of one of the tales in the book? What if . . . what if he did appear with the frost? What if Cora is right?

What if Matthieu isn't real?

"I RECKON YOU'LL be in by Christmas," Matthieu says, running a hand over the countertop in the kitchen. I'm doing the same, marveling at the thick slab of wood. It's a honey color, carved and fitted beautifully, blending with the character of the old cottage and the Shaker-style cupboards I chose. The kitchen is finished; even the flooring is down. It's two weeks until Christmas, and we just have some work to do upstairs and the furniture to collect and build. I decided to stage the cottage for selling, reasoning that it would sell for more than an empty house. Who can imagine creating a life in a few well-painted boxes? But all the furniture is a reflection of my taste, my dream life, reminding me of what I still can't fully admit to myself. That I could picture myself living in this cottage.

"I'll set up an appointment with the estate agent," I say, looking up at Matthieu. "It's time."

He nods. "If you're sure."

"I—yes," I say, gazing across the kitchen, taking in the brushed-chrome door handles, the gray-green cupboards, the range cooker built into the old fireplace. The kitchen is perfect, reflecting that heritage quality of true craftmanship, traditional and solid with the sleek and built-in modern appliances hidden behind cupboard doors. "I'm sure."

Matthieu straightens and moves a few feet away from me to run his hand over one of the cupboards. "It'll fetch a bit. You can open an art studio and get back into painting. Travel the world—go even farther than Europe. Do whatever you want. You'll never have to return to Woodsmoke again."

"Yes," I say, my throat thickening. I smile up at him, not saying what I'm really thinking. That I can do all those things now, that Ivy has given me that gift. But the one thing, the *only* thing I keep turning over in my mind . . . is whether to stay.

"Carrie, we should celebrate. We should, I don't know . . . go out for dinner. Would you like to go out for dinner . . . with me?" Matthieu's voice pulls me out of my brooding, and I turn to him.

"Are you asking me out?" I smile, stepping closer. My stomach twists with a delicious fizz as I eye his smile, the angles of his face.

He ducks his head, not quite meeting my gaze. "Yes, Carrie. I think I am."

"Huh."

"You haven't said yes."

I reach for his hand, then think better of it, suddenly awkward. "I would love to."

"I'll book somewhere. There's this place in the next town over, or we can get takeout and drive to the lake, make a picnic—"

"Wherever. Whatever you want to do," I say, still smiling. "Or we can go to a café, or . . ."

"I've found a trail near the cabin that leads to this clearing. It's not marked on any of the newer hiker maps, but it's beautiful." His eyes finally find mine, all smoldering edges that make my pulse quicken. "If you like."

An unmarked trail. A clearing. Suddenly the image of that map and all that twine surfaces in my mind and I hesitate. Perhaps he's just exploring the mountains, the trails he can remember from when he was younger. But I'm remembering the other reason for his explorations, the person he's talked about who's a part of his memories. His brother Henri. Who is no longer with him.

"Matthieu, can I ask you something?"

"Yes?"

I swallow, glancing up at him. I figure it's time to ask, to put my niggling worries aside, especially if we're stepping away from just working together. I have to know. "The cabin, where you're staying . . . it's the one just up the trail, right? The one straight up from Ivy's field, the nearest one, past the lookout point?" I know those cabins have a separate access for vehicles, but Matthieu always arrives on foot. He always takes the trail down to Ivy's field . . . I have to be sure it's the same one.

"Yeah, I rented it for the winter. Off a friend, I told you. The Vickers cabin." He's walking around the kitchen now, checking the hinges on the cupboards, checking they're hung just right.

It is the right cabin I went to. I swallow, picturing the damp, the cold of that place. The map on the wall, the pushpins, and the twine between them. "And it's . . . okay for staying in?"

He frowns slightly, drawing his hand away. "It's just right for me. For now, anyway."

I nod, but somehow I can't bring myself to mention Henri. Or to mention the map, or that I've been there, looking for him. Doing that now feels . . . intrusive. I swallow guiltily, thinking maybe I shouldn't have gone looking for him. "Well, shall I finish off in here?"

"Sure," Matthieu says. His features have clouded over a little, as though he has drawn himself back in. And I did that. I did that with my prying about the cabin. I curse myself. I should never have listened to Cora.

"Matthieu . . ." I pause, searching for the words to set us back in the moment when he asked me to dinner. When I felt like I could twine my hand through his, almost taste his kisses on my mouth . . . "I can't wait to have dinner with you. Truly."

He gives me a fleeting smile, then turns to go upstairs.

For the afternoon and into the evening, I choose to work downstairs while Matthieu finishes some painting in the main bedroom upstairs. I want to be honest with him, to tell him I went there. That I went to the cabin and it looked as though it hadn't been lived in for months, perhaps even years. But maybe I got it wrong, maybe I imagined that air of neglect, the scent of damp and loam. I've let Woodsmoke get under my skin, let the old ways and the stories twine around reality until I've actually believed Matthieu might not be real. This isn't down to him. It's all me.

In these past few weeks, something has been planted between us, something new and green in this sea of winter, and I'm beginning to realize I want to nurture it. I don't want it to fade before it's even begun. I want to go for dinner with him and watch his mouth break into that happy smile. I want to see what it feels like to share more with him than old memories from our childhoods and mugs of tea.

"Carrie," he says, and I turn to find him in the lounge, a smile on his face as he runs a hand over the back of his neck. "If dinner feels too serious or something, just say . . ."

"No, no," I say quickly, shaking my head. He's picked up on it, this cloud that's formed between us. He thinks it's because of him. I nearly tell him I went up to the cabin. Nearly ask outright, but then he steps toward me. Takes my hand in his and tiny sparks explode in my chest.

"I . . . I like you. But if it's too much . . . I know coming back to Woodsmoke is a lot and you're figuring things out—"

I squeeze his hand back and look up into his eyes. The sparks flitting through my chest spin out, filling me with warmth. With want. "It's not too much. It really isn't."

"All right," he says. "See you tomorrow, then."

When he releases my hand and turns to head for the front door, I know this is the moment to ask. I need to know about the map, whether it's about Henri, why he keeps disappearing, why he always disappears when the frost thaws . . . but the words die in my throat. I just . . . can't. Not when asking could break this fragile thing between us. Not when it feels like the start of something more.

The front door closes, and I release a breath, scrubbing a hand down my face. I walk back and forth across the lounge, telling myself I should follow him, I should just *ask*—

So when the door creaks open, when boots thump on the hallway floor, my breath hitches, catching on the hope that he's returned, that he's ready to share more with me, that he's not full of secrets at all and he won't cloud over when I ask him. That I won't shatter what's building between us.

"Look, I'm sorry, really—" My words stutter out as I reach the hallway. It's not Matthieu standing there but a woman, chin lifted, a proud glint to her features. Dread pools in my stomach, and I hang back, eyeing her quietly.

"Expecting someone else?"

Chapter 29
Cora

Seventeen Years Ago

A Morgan girl was born under a full moon, as is the way of every Morgan, on the hottest night of the year, with the crickets singing their song.

—Cora Morgan, February 1, 1995

Cora set the final cake on the farmhouse table and stood back. A heap of meringues, cream and plump strawberries, a vanilla sponge with scattered white chocolate shavings, a peach pie, lemon meringue tarts, dark chocolate gateaux . . .

"You've outdone yourself," Ivy says, plucking a strawberry from the heap of meringues and popping it in her mouth. "Lillian will be thrilled."

"Is this a curse of early onset diabetes?" muses Ivy's husband, Ralph, home for a rare long weekend in August.

Cora swats at them both, her cheeks flushed from the praise. "It's a curse of gluttony," she says with a sniff. "Now get in the garden and string up the bunting. Carrie will be here soon, and we want it to be *perfect*."

They all troop outside, Howard squeezing Cora's shoulder as he walks past. Ivy leans in, whispers, "Thank you," and Cora sniffs again, blinking furiously, her throat thickening suddenly.

Lillian's kitchen is all set for the best party of Carrie's childhood, her eleventh birthday party, and half the town is invited.

Cora fusses around, setting out cake plates, turning the main three-tier chocolate cake so that Carrie can see the *Happy Birthday Carrie* written in pale lilac icing when she walks in. Guests start arriving, and children rush out to the garden, mums and dads and grandparents pour glasses of Pimm's and sparkling elderflower, fanning themselves and agreeing that it has to be the hottest August on record.

Cora smiles, greeting the women who in the past have secretly asked her for potions and spells, occasionally even curses. They all squeeze her hand, or wink, or pat her arm as they pass. Cora believes she has finally convinced this whole gossipy town that the magic threaded through it is truly wonderful, and she's sure that the Morgans are finally accepted.

"She's here!" Jess says, leaping into the kitchen with her mother close behind. "She's getting out of the car, still doesn't have a clue!"

"Quick, everyone!" Cora says, waving to Ivy in the garden. There's a general rustling and commotion as everyone spills out the back door to find somewhere to stand under the wide bowl of the summer sky.

Lillian's voice echoes from the front door, joined by Carrie's, and Cora can hardly contain herself. Her heart gives a giant leap as Carrie walks in, gasps, and covers her mouth with her hands as all those gathered yell, "Surprise!" and then break out into the birthday song. Lillian grins, laughing, her eyes glistening with tears, and Cora finds herself sniffling, her cheeks growing wet.

Then Howard is at her side, pressing a handkerchief into her palm, murmuring, "Well done, love, well done," as Carrie blows out all the candles and laughs and laughs.

It's not until the party is in full swing and everyone's bellies are stuffed with sugar that Cora notices. Carrie, hovering on the edges, never quite joins in. Cora dries her hands on a tea towel as she watches Jess dash from tree to tree in the orchard, two boys chasing her, three other girls laughing and trying to snatch the tag from her belt loop. They played this game in the playground when she was a girl, and she can remember so vividly being like Carrie. Awkward. Unsure. Unable to step in and be like the rest of the children.

Jess pulls Carrie into the game, gasping for breath from all that darting around, and the Gray boy . . . is it Thomas? . . . holds out the tag to Carrie. She blushes and shrugs, tucks it into her belt loop, and raises her chin in a look of pure Morgan grit. Cora smiles as Carrie runs off, leading the others merrily around the old apple trees. She wonders if there is something there. Perhaps Carrie just needs a nudge over the next couple of years.

She chews her lip, picturing that day in this very kitchen when she mixed up those love potions with Jess and Carrie.

What if . . .

What if she turned that Gray boy's head toward her Carrie? Not just yet, she's too young, but maybe in a year or so, maybe when she begins to think of boys as more than just an irritation.

It wouldn't do any harm, Cora is sure of that. And if Carrie has both a school sweetheart and a best friend in this town, maybe she'll feel like she fits in. Cora hums to herself as she cuts a slice of cake, leans back against the sideboard, and takes a big, contented bite.

Chapter 30
Carrie

"Jess," I croak, finding my voice.

I step toward her, and she sniffs, scrunching up her nose. "You were expecting Tom, weren't you? Don't lie to me. Don't you bloody lie."

Her anger, hot and quick, catches me like a punch. I jerk back, blinking rapidly. "Jess, what—"

"He's been here, hasn't he? I know you saw each other. I know you've met up. Was he here again tonight? What is this, Carrie? After all these years, you want him back?"

I swallow, staring at her, the way her features are all twisted up. Her cheeks are flushed, her eyes smarting, and I wonder if she's about to cry. "Jess, that's not—"

"Well, he's *mine*," Jess says, her voice cracking. "You can't have him. You made your choice that day you left him. Remember that? Remember your wedding day? I was there afterward. Me. I've been here ever since. You can't just, you can't just *breeze in*, you can't just change *everything*—"

"I'm not, Jess. Please, I promise I'm not," I say quietly. She blinks, caught off guard. Surprise flares in her features, as though she wasn't expecting me to say that, but it's gone in an instant, quickly stamped out.

"What?"

I lick my lips, feeling the ghost of that knife of pain as I left, knowing I wasn't coming back anytime soon. Knowing I was leaving everything—Tom, Jess, my whole life in Woodsmoke—firmly behind. And I didn't know if I'd ever be coming back. "I'm only here to renovate Ivy's cottage. I guess I hoped I'd find my place here, find I belong . . . I don't know. But I promise it has nothing to do with Tom."

"You met up with him, though. You came back here, not once thinking to come and find me, but him? You met up with *my* husband." Jess narrows her eyes, like we're picking up a conversation that's been going all this time. Like we haven't been apart for a decade and we've been batting these words back and forth. "You made your choice, you left. I didn't. We're married, we have a child, we—"

"—have all the trappings. I get it. I know. You did the right thing, and the whole town loves you for it," I say, pinching the bridge of my nose. "You stayed. That's old news, Jess. I'm not here for him, and I think if you were *actually* honest with yourself, you'd know that. I haven't carried him around with me for the past ten years. Leaving was right for both of us, and I don't regret our breakup. It should never have gotten as far as it did; we shouldn't have gotten engaged. I am *not* here to break up your family."

Jess tucks her hair behind her left ear, agitation marking her staccato movements. "Is that what you talked about? With him?"

I frown. "Yes. But also—"

She sucks in a breath, blinking hard. "Why? Was it closure? Couldn't you have just come over, not all this sneaking around, discussing me and my marriage without me present?"

"Jess, come on—"

"Nothing's changed, has it?" she says quietly. "You don't see it. You left everything behind, your entire world. Like it was nothing. And now you expect to move back and for everything to be fine. You know I can't move in this town without hearing people talk about you, at the book club, on the school run . . . you're everywhere. And yet I haven't seen you. It's been ten whole years, Carrie, and you went and met with Tom and not . . . and not . . ."

I close my eyes for a minute. "This isn't about Tom at all, is it."

"No. No, I guess it's not," she says, blinking quickly.

"I left you."

Jess draws in a haggard breath, pressing her fingertips to the dark smudges under her eyes, and says nothing.

I gather my thoughts as I stare at a point over her shoulder. "That's what this is, isn't it? I left, and you can't see past it. But you have to understand, I was always on the edges here. Because of my family, because of what we are, even being engaged to Tom and with you at my side, I never felt like I quite belonged. I wanted to see the world, Jess. I wanted more than Woodsmoke."

"And now?"

"Now . . . I'm trying to find my place. I want to see if I can belong, if this is the home I've been searching for the whole time. I'm not going to take anything from you. I'm not trying to change anything."

Jess fidgets for a moment. "You left without a backward glance. You—you say you don't want to change anything, but you've already changed things, Carrie. Your presence changes *everything*." She finally fixes her gaze on me. "All I wanted was a normal life. And I've got that."

My breath catches again in my throat, and my eyes begin to sting. When it comes to Jess, I can't hide a damn thing. Not even from myself. I forgot that about her, about us. "You don't want me back here. That's it, isn't it? I'm—I'm disrupting your dream. This dream life you built without me."

"I—"

"We were practically sisters." I pause, pulling in a cooling breath, hot hurt sliding up from my chest, the tears already clouding my vision. "Remember that night we cut our palms? Remember how we swore we'd always be us? Never mind him, never mind Tom. We were meant to be forever, me and you. Yes, Tom and I weren't meant to last forever. He never wanted to leave. That's what I found out before I left. That's how I knew for sure it was all wrong between us. He had already agreed to his apprenticeship, and I guess he would have told me after we married. And I'd have been stuck and stifled. But me and you . . ."

I look up at the ceiling, trying to hold myself together. I press my fingertips into my cheekbones, as though I can erase the tears. As though I can close up the fissures reopening inside me. "You were my sister," I whisper. "You were my sister, and I've come back, and you're choosing to throw me away."

"Carrie, you never called, never wrote, not in *ten years*—"

"I couldn't, Jess! What would I say? You got together with my ex and started this whole life without me. I didn't have a place in your orbit anymore." I swallow, wrapping my arms around myself. "It's all I wanted. To come home, to have you back. There, I've said it. I know I should have come over sooner, but I . . . I was scared. For good reason apparently. Look at us!" I sniff again. "I got over Tom years ago. But *us*? How could I ever get over that?"

"Well, maybe you *should* have made the effort when you got back nearly two whole months ago instead of—"

"It's like we can't even hear each other," I say, shaking my head. How did we grow so far apart? "Just go," I say, furious at her, at myself, at the tears tracking down my cheeks. Every moment with her flashes between us: the sleepovers and film marathons, the walks to school on the old dirt track, the times we snuck peeks at the book and read the stories aloud to each other. All those moments, so rose-tinted, as though lit up by fairy lights, now lay cracked and broken at our feet. "Go back home. You've got everything you ever wanted. Go and enjoy and forget about me and you. But you have to know, I'm not leaving. I'm finishing up what I started here, this renovation, this winter . . . This is my home too." I realize, for the first time, that this is true. "I'm sorry it's creating gossip. I'm sorry the town has so little going on that I'm causing such a stir. Now you know how it is to have the last name Morgan."

"Carrie . . ." Jess says, taking a step toward me, her hand reaching out, as though she finally sees it. Sees that I couldn't have reached out to her. That just being here in this town is like crossing a vast ocean and I just needed her to take the last few steps to meet me. But she retracts her hand and stumbles back to the doorway. Standing there with both hands splayed across her belly, she gives me one final look.

"Go," I gasp, covering my face with my hands. I'm not sure I can stand any more arguing. This feels like a breakup, like a knife slipped between the ribs. Why is losing a friend always so much harder than losing a love? Especially when I've hoped, for so many years, to return here and find our way back to each other. I realize now how foolish that hope was. When I pull my hands away from my face, she's gone.

I DON'T LET myself fall apart, not like I used to. I pace up and down the living room, pulling in breath after aching breath. As I walk, I flex my fingers, forming them into fists, clenching and unclenching my jaw. Even after all these years, even after the miles and miles I've put between us, one conversation with Jess rips it all open. Like it's fresh and pulsing and I'm bleeding all over again. Like I'll never stop bleeding, never stop grieving the loss of her.

The loss of us.

There's a tap on the window, and I startle. Matthieu's face appears, his eyes widening when he sees mine. Then he's through the door, standing next to me, pulling me into his arms.

I cry like I did on my wedding day. As though the whole world is raining with my tears.

"I came back to tell you something," Matthieu says quietly, "to explain, but . . . Carrie, what's wrong? What's happened?"

I sniff, pressing my face into his chest, warm and safe. And even with Jess and Tom and everything, it feels so right. So right for his arms to be around me, so right that I don't register surprise that they're there. That he's here. "Nothing. Everything . . . I can't explain. It all happened so long ago, and she just came over, and I should have had a handle on it, but I didn't, and . . ." I gulp and take a steadying breath. "Me and Woodsmoke had a bad breakup a while back, and there was never any closure. Let's put it that way."

"Who came over?" he asks, smoothing his hands over my back.

"Jess," I breathe. "My former best friend. I guess—I guess the real person I had the breakup with."

Matthieu says nothing. He gently pries me away, putting the smallest distance between us so he can stare down at me. He brushes a hand down my face, running a thumb through my tears. I close my eyes, shudders rippling through me like waves. "Oh, Carrie. Loving someone—caring for them and losing them . . . it is a distinct kind of grief. One that's hard to shake."

Fresh tears course down my face, and he sweeps them all away. His touch, achingly gentle as he wipes at my cheeks, leaves a faint trail of heat along my skin. I sniff again, leaning into his warmth, and he brings his face down to mine. His mouth moves carefully, hesitantly, as his kisses cover my tears. I keep my eyes closed, focusing on that, on Matthieu, on his scent, all pine and frost and midnight. And the tight knot inside me begins to loosen.

"Matthieu," I whisper, bringing my hands up to his face.

"Carrie," he says back. And then he brings his mouth to mine.

My heart explodes.

Everything around us, everything else boiling up inside me, fades away, leaving only him, only his mouth, his touch, the warmth of him wrapping around me. It's as though I've been lost in a blizzard with no end and no beginning. And now suddenly I'm no longer cold.

His hands move to my waist, pulling me closer, tracing slow circles with his thumbs along my ribs. The circles move lower, curving down my sides, to the small of my back, and I press my body into his, wanting more.

He comes up for air, his lips slightly parted as he stares at me, transfixed. "I've wanted to do that since the moment I first saw you."

I smile, the ache in my chest easing as I look up at him. Sniffing, I rub away the last of my tears and look at him. With the work nearly done, I don't want this to end. It feels too much like it could be a beginning.

"Kiss me again," I whisper, and he presses his mouth against mine. His arms encircle me, and we give in to this *something* between us.

Chapter 31
Jess

She knocks on the door, two days after Christmas, heart tapping against her ribs. She knocks once, twice, feeling the desperation fizz and heat. The night air is cold, with a bite to it. She presses her palm flat against the tiny pane of window set in the door, silently pleading that someone will hear her. Her other hand gravitates to the familiar spot where she's been resting her hand for a week, ever since she drove to the supermarket and then to Carrie's. Right over her belly button. Where something smaller than a plum pulses and thrashes.

A light flickers in the hallway beyond, and Jess holds her breath, stepping back to smooth down her nerves, to tame the desperation in her features. There is a jangle of keys, a creak, and the door is pulled open, Cora outlined on the threshold. Expectation lifts all of Cora's corners, as though she hoped for someone else. Then she sees Jess, and her arms cross over her chest like a barrier. Like a silent *no* that has not yet left her lips.

"Please," Jess says. This is just like the last time, ten years ago. Even the night air tastes the same as she breathes it in. "*Please*, Cora."

Cora sighs, her arms unwinding, her frame deflating. "I'll get the kettle on."

Because this is how it always starts. Cora has been doing this for so long now that she knows how it will end before it even begins. She knows that, if she agrees to help, she will pay the price for the person who comes knocking, whatever the cost, however steep.

Jess walks in, closing the door behind her. She shrugs out of her coat, pulls off her boots, and tiptoes to the lounge, where she sits on the sofa. Howard must be out. Or maybe he made himself scarce as soon as she pulled up to the house. She fidgets with the cushion next to her, running her frantic hands down the soft beige fabric over and over until she thrusts it away from herself.

Cora walks in, the tray balanced in her hands, just as always. She places it on the coffee table, her quick, practiced movements producing a mug of tea exactly as she knows Jess drinks it—with a dash of milk and half a teaspoon of sugar. She prides herself on remembering how every person who crosses her threshold drinks their tea.

"It's decaf," Cora says gruffly, not looking Jess directly in the eye as she passes the mug to her. "You shouldn't be drinking caffeine."

Jess splutters, placing the hot mug on the coffee table. Her heart is thumping now, panic poisoning her body, drawing the anxiety up and out of her. "How—I haven't told anyone—"

Cora cuts her off with a barking laugh as she stirs the amber liquid in her own mug. "Woodsmoke never changes. None of you ever learn. A secret never stays a secret long. How many weeks along are you? Twelve?"

"Ten, I think. Just over maybe," Jess mutters, picking her mug back up. She lets the steam roll over her face, lets it calm her, soothe her. "It's Tom's, if that's why you're thinking I'm here."

"So you're not hoping to have the baby later. To cover up a slip."

"No," Jess says indignantly. Her hand strays to her belly, to the tiny life growing inside. "It's very much wanted and very much ours. I just haven't told him yet."

"But you are here about Tom, aren't you?" Cora fixes her eyes on Jess, not bothering to coax it out of her.

Jess sips her tea, remembering the last visit ten years ago, when Cora held the book and was running a finger down the pages. How her brow creased, mouthing the words, and she told Jess to leave it with her. To dry her eyes, to stop her fretting. That all would be well, all would be right. That Carrie and Tom wouldn't be leaving Woodsmoke together. And Jess wonders, not for the first time, whether she was wrong to have come here a decade ago. If she should never have trusted in the old ways, in knowing that the mountains hold far more than just earth and trees and shadow. Perhaps . . . perhaps she shouldn't have interfered at all. Because Tom did stay and Carrie left. Creating a chasm between them that they can't cross even ten years on.

"I need Tom to stay. With me. With Elodie and—and the baby." Jess stops herself from splaying her fingers across her belly, from hiding what doesn't yet need hiding. She takes another sip of tea, the bland comfort of it hardening her. Reminding her of who she is, of what she wants. Of all she has fought to claim.

"But I can't live like this, not anymore. Especially not with Carrie back. I need your help—like before. Because at some point it's all going to come out. It's all bubbling to the surface and I can't . . . can't lose him. I need you to reverse it. What we did, ten years ago. I need to know that he loves me for *me*, not because of some spell or whatever deal it was that you made with the book. I need to know that the life we've built is solid. I need it reversed. All I wanted was for them both to be happy. For everyone to be where they were supposed to be."

Cora grows silent, watching her as she fidgets. "Is that all?"

Jess hesitates, then nods. "That's all I ask."

"It can't be reversed."

"What?"

"You made your choice ten years ago. We both paid the price. Tom saw the love he had for you eventually and didn't leave. But *Carrie* still left. Carrie never came back, and I'll never get that relationship back with her, not after all these years." Cora sighs. "Nor, I imagine, will you."

Jess blinks back tears as she places the mug on the coffee table, then balls her hands into tight little fists in her lap. "He chose me. Of his own free will. But I need to know I didn't—that I didn't drive her away with that spell you did—"

"Like I said, we paid the price."

"So you won't help me?"

"Are you even listening, girl? I *can't* help you. What's done is done."

Jess shudders, closing her eyes. "I don't want this looming over me for the rest of my life, wondering if I should have left well enough alone. He was going to stay, did you know that? He was never going to leave. He—he had an apprenticeship lined up, his parents had already put a deposit on our house. It was only Carrie who wanted to go off and explore the world, but maybe if they'd stayed together, maybe he would have persuaded her . . . But then he wouldn't have been mine, would he? He would have still been with Carrie, and they would have been miserable."

Cora smiles, the warmth not quite meeting her eyes. The love potion she used to nudge Thomas Gray toward Carrie fresh in her mind. The one she reversed that night Jess came to her, scared of losing them both. Of course, Jess doesn't know it was a reversal. If Cora has her way, no one will ever know that secret, not until she's cold in her grave with the book safely in Carrie's keeping. "Perhaps that's the price you'll have to pay. Forever looking over your shoulder. Forever wondering what might have been."

"But the cost was losing Carrie, wasn't it? Isn't that enough?" Jess says, her desperation surfacing now. Carrie was right the other night. Jess did choose Tom over her. And now with Elodie and the baby, she would have to do it again. Was losing Carrie—her closest friend—the price? She betrayed Carrie horribly by going to Cora behind her back. By asking the mountains to make sure that she and Tom were with the person they truly loved, and that they were where they both belonged. And it turned out that Tom was meant to be with her, in Woodsmoke.

But was Carrie meant to wander? To feel constantly adrift and unsure of her place in the world? Carrie was meant to cut ties with everyone and everything in Woodsmoke, and yet she's back. Jess needs that spell reversed; she needs to know that it would have all worked out the same, even without the mountains and the magic.

"Get the book, Cora. Get the book and tell me what to do. I'll go to the mountains. I'll deal with this. Then I'll know that Tom loves me for me, and that Carrie was always meant to wander and I didn't ruin both their lives. Just tell me—"

"It wasn't you that paid the price last time," Cora barks. She stands up suddenly, tutting down at Jess. "It wasn't only *you* who lost Carrie."

Jess's eyes burn, her whole being burns, and she flushes with the guilt, with the knowing. "I'm sorry. Cora, I'm truly so sorry."

"Time for you to go. Time for you to go back to little Elodie, back to the nice life you've built here. Time for you to weather the storm. And perhaps . . . perhaps you need to tell Tom. Perhaps it's time to fix things yourself and tell the truth—that you meddled. No book. No bargains. No magic. Just you, Tom, and Carrie, figuring this out. You have to trust that your love is enough that he won't leave you."

Cora gestures to the door, then watches Jess as she crumples. She's reminded of Howard, of how he drags his feet through each day, how he holds it all in, all his disappointment. Jess rises to her feet, not bothering to hide her burden, or the fatigue so obvious on her sagging face, a fatigue that seems to have penetrated her very bones and taken root.

"You'll have to weather it too," Jess says, walking past Cora. She pulls on her boots and her coat, then turns back. "If it can't be reversed, if it all comes out, what you did that night, what I asked of you . . . you'll have to weather that too."

Jess makes it halfway back to Woodsmoke before she has to pull over. She kills the engine, leaving the lights on, the soft glow revealing a frosted hedge and ground glittering with ice. She wipes at her eyes, staring without seeing, replaying her conversation with Cora. Finding all the holes in it, where she could have pressed more. Maybe she needs to steal the book. Break in when she knows Cora and Howard are both out, take it, and find the passage or story inside its pages that will help her. That will tell her how to reverse what she did a decade ago.

She brings her fingertips up to her mouth, gulping in air as her nose begins to run. She feels sure that Tom loves her, that he would have loved her without her meddling, but there's doubt and guilt tangled up in all that history. Knotted like poison, choking her now that Carrie is back.

She has carried this guilt with her for ten whole years, carried it alongside her elation that Tom is all hers. She has traced Carrie's journey. Like running a finger over a map, she has tracked every place Carrie has stayed, visited, or painted, checking her Facebook profile, then Instagram, even searching her website for any details she can glean. But she never felt brave enough to message her, to open the door onto their past. The past is so mixed up with love, guilt, and longing that she can't see a way back to it anymore.

And now that Carrie is back, all of Jess's guilt is resurfacing.

She supposes that's partly why she went over to see Carrie. She's so wrapped up in her guilt, in her fear of losing the life she's built, but she's also missing her friend. Desperately. Now that Carrie is only a mile or so away, it all seems so immediate, so unresolved.

Gradually Jess's tears subside, leaving streaky paths of salt stinging her skin. Checking her reflection in the mirror, she dabs concealer under her eyes and on the tip of her red nose. She checks her phone, finds a message from Tom asking when she's getting back, if she's okay. Then she takes a deep breath, turns the key in the ignition, and begins the slow drive home.

Chapter 32
Cora

Ten Years Ago

She doesn't tell Jess about the potion. She doesn't mention the little nudge, how she meddled in Carrie's and Tom's lives, thinking it would fix everything. For a time, of course, it did. Carrie had a first love, a best friend, and a wider circle of other people who accepted her, cared about her, and gave her the kind of teen years she craved. But now it's all unraveling, and all she can do is try to reverse it.

Cora pauses for a moment, takes a deep, unhurried breath. The air is swampy and thick, promising a thunderstorm in a few days, and with every step up the mountain crickets sing to mark her way. It's the kind of night she lives for—the velvet dark so close it feels like a caress, the song of wild things, the mountains bathed in silver from a full, beautiful moon. But she doesn't appreciate it tonight. All she can think about, all she sees, is Carrie.

When Jess tapped at the door, eyes red, skin pale and taut, she fed her homemade lemonade and cookies and promised her she would take care of it. Promised her that her two best friends wouldn't leave Woodsmoke for good. She held Jess's hand, then sent her on her way before leafing through the book, poring over workings and stories. It all came back to this, back to her. Back to the potion, the little nudge, and the fact that she had to undo it all . . . then cross her fingers that Carrie and Tom's love was real and Carrie would stay in Woodsmoke for him.

She rounds the corner in the trail, reaching the lookout, and leans against a tree, staring down at the town below. Five days. Just five days until Carrie will marry Tom. If she doesn't truly love him, it could be the biggest mistake of her life. Cora knows she shouldn't have let it get this far. She should have reversed the potion long ago, allowed Carrie to view Tom with clear eyes and see for herself whether she truly loves him. But it was so easy to let it be between them. So easy to see the path before Carrie winding forward into the future, a future of love and acceptance and the book.

But . . . love doesn't work that way. It can't be forced; it can't be tricked.

She opens the book, which she's been clutching against her chest, and turns to the page containing a reversal. It was recorded by Tabitha, her grandmother, to reverse a working for a dry season. There had been a drought in Woodsmoke that year, she wrote, and she lost ten years of her life to the working to bring the clouds. When she made the bargain to reverse it, the rain pattered on Tabitha's head, gathering in the deepening wrinkles lining her face. When she got home, she looked in the mirror and realized that the mountains had taken ten more years from her.

Cora pulls out a pocketknife, pierces her thumb, and lets the blood drip, drip, drip into the loam. She makes her request of the mountains, just as it says to do in the book, and braces herself for what they will take from her.

Chapter 33
Carrie

Our first date is meant to be dinner. Getting all dressed up, putting lipstick on, and hoping it will be kissed away later. But we can't wait, don't want to wait. So we take the day off and carve our first date out of a January Tuesday.

Matthieu offers to drive my car, and we travel away from Woodsmoke, away from the clutter of collective stares and speculation. His hands drum on the steering wheel as he drives, and I sing along to old songs that the local radio station still plays, staring out of the window to watch as the landscape peels open, the mountains drifting away to linger on the horizon.

"Nearly there. Twenty minutes," he says, and I glance over at him, catching his grin as he keeps his gaze fixed on the road.

"Any more hints?" I've been trying to guess all morning where he's taking me. We began our first day off from working on the cottage in months by making pancakes in the cottage kitchen and toasting the day with fresh coffee in the French press I bought. The only details I've wrangled are that it's best to wear thick socks, a hat, and gloves and to pack a thermos of tea. We've got biscuits, a thermos of tea, and enamel mugs in a basket on the backseat, and I've been asking questions ever since. "Is it . . . outside?"

"Yes."

"Is it in the mountains?"

"No."

"Are we going skinny-dipping in a lake?"

That grin flashes again as he shakes the black wings of his hair from his eyes and my stomach swoops, remembering that mouth on mine the other night. There's something about making Matthieu smile. I love the way his smile lights up his whole being, how his angles smooth and the shadows under his eyes vanish.

"Do you want to go skinny-dipping?"

I laugh and he shakes his head, taking a turn off the main road onto a track that tails off, toward the mountains. I scrutinize the track, my heart thrumming in my chest. I can't remember the last time someone surprised me like this, staking out a whole day of their time to hand over as a gift. Matthieu is the kind of person who makes you feel like he has all the time in the world, just for you. The kind of person who leans in intently, listening to every syllable you utter. I snuggle back into my warm coat as sparks fill my veins for the hundredth time in the last few days.

"So not skinny-dipping, and not in the mountains . . . are we cross-country skiing? Husky riding?"

He barks out a laugh. "Keep guessing, I love it. How many huskies have you seen around Woodsmoke?"

I chuckle and shrug, trying to guess again where we're heading. We've barely been apart as we take our time with the last handful of fixes to the cottage. It feels like we're squeezing out more time, so that we can linger in the bubble that has suddenly formed around us. He leaves only to sleep at his cabin each night.

I don't want to ask Matthieu about his future plans. About what he intends to do after he has to give up the cabin. But I hold on to a hope that this bubble of time is like a promise, a binding promise. That Matthieu will linger on after the renovations, and the frost, and that somehow we will find a new routine in a summer in Woodsmoke together. I haven't voiced any of this. I don't want to upset the delicate newness of the "us" that might be. But it's on my mind, it's filling my thoughts in a smoky haze, and for the first time in a decade I feel like I'm home.

"Penny for them," he says, glancing at me. "You're lost again. You do that."

"I—well, I'm just . . . thinking about Woodsmoke. About the cottage and . . . us."

"Us?"

I smile and suddenly I want to gauge his reaction, to see what he might be thinking. "I don't know, I'm thinking about my roots here. About . . . staying."

"Staying."

I nod, looking over at him. "Staying."

"Well . . ." he begins, then his face clears as he pulls over onto a narrower track. "We're nearly there."

I sit up, taking in our surroundings, trying to place it in my memories. It's not long before we pull up into a tiny car park and Matthieu cuts the engine.

I get out of the car and scan the horizon, then start grinning as I realize where we are, what this place is. "Ice-skating?"

Matthieu nods, assessing my reaction. I gaze over the lake, now frozen over for another month at least, and breathe out a sigh of vast contentment. "We don't have to, if you'd rather not," he says. "We can walk, and watch the skaters—"

"It's perfect," I say and tentatively hold my hand out to him. When he grasps it, another knot inside me loosens and heat washes through me, right to my core. "Let's go."

At the lake's edge, another couple sits on a bench outside a gift shop, lacing up their shoes. A few people are already out on the ice—a man skating in smooth swoops, a tartan scarf tied around his throat, and a woman holding the hand of a child, coaxing her slowly across the ice. We go over to the gift shop to rent skates, and I tell the shop assistant my size. She hands me a pair of skates a size too big.

"Thick socks," Matthieu whispers, winking at me. "They never have exact sizes. It's potluck what you get."

I leave my boots behind the counter and sit on the bench outside beside him, lacing up my skates, my breath forming puffs of cloud. "How have I never heard of this place?"

"It's a secret?"

I raise an eyebrow. "I'm a Morgan. Secrets are what we do."

"It's fairly new, I think. So maybe they weren't doing this when you were last home."

I love how Matthieu has surprised me, shown me a different side to the mountains. A playful side, a side not closely guarded and full of tricks, like those in Cora's book. I feel like the mountains are mine again, that seeing this side of them is reclaiming a piece of the home I wasn't sure would be mine to come back to.

When I step out on the ice, Matthieu's hand is there to guide me. We glide slowly at first, my heart beating in my ears at the thrill of trying to stay upright, trying to find my center. Then, after a while, after our slow spinning, I gradually find it. I let go of his hand, trusting myself to find my own way across the ice, the smooth mirror beneath me reflecting back the sky.

I laugh, breathlessly, moving a little faster, getting as close as I ever will get on the ground to flying. Matthieu circles me, laughing as well, and we move farther out, where it's just the two of us. I slow, almost to a stop, breathing in the cold air, tasting the scent of the mountains on my tongue. I turn slowly, taking in the mountains, the vastness of them. The hulking shapes ruling this corner of the earth. And I know in that moment that somehow they have given Matthieu to me. That somehow they knew. That the mountains, my home, just *knew.*

I turn to him.

He is still spinning in circles, absorbed with the feeling of flying, of freedom. There is no one like him, I am sure of it. No one who glows quite as he does with such a steady, warm light. I take another breath and push off to skate beside him. There's no one else on the ice, I notice distantly. There's only us.

"Hey," I say, smiling at him.

"Hey," he says.

He slows, reaching for my hand, and we slowly spin to a stop.

"You know, I've always wanted to be kissed on the middle of a frozen lake."

"What, like this one?"

"Just like this one."

"Oh," he says, his eyes growing dark. "Who are you going to kiss?"

I shrug, looking round. "I don't know yet . . ."

Matthieu chuckles, turning my chin toward him with his fingertips. "Hey."

"Hey," I murmur.

Matthieu raises his eyebrows in question before leaning in to kiss me. I laugh against his mouth, drawing my arms around his neck and giving in to this moment he's created, just for us.

"Carrie . . ." he says softly, running his mouth gently along the line of my jaw. "I think we should do this first date thing again. It's pretty good."

I tip back my head, sighing in delight as his kisses trail down my throat. "I agree."

And right there, under the watchful eye of the mountains, with just the two of us on this vast frozen lake, Matthieu's mouth on my skin, and his arms wrapped around me, I fall a little.

I fall into that place of perfect first dates, of dappled light and frost and slow dances. I fall into it with Matthieu.

We build the last of the furniture the next morning. He's in the upstairs front bedroom, and I'm in the lounge putting a set of shelves up in the alcove next to the fireplace. He drops something and I hear him swear. There's a thump, like an angry fist or a boot, then silence. I pause, place the screwdriver on the floor, and walk to the hallway.

"You all right?"

"Yeah, just . . ." He mutters something I can't quite catch.

I take the stairs two at a time, turning on the landing to rush into the room he's in. I push the door open and find him sitting on the floor, one hand cradled in the other as he stares absently at the wall. There are shadows beneath his eyes, like charcoal with the edges smudged. "Your hand?"

"Caught it between the slats." He shrugs, attempting a smile, then closes his eyes. "Didn't sleep well. I don't know. Careless." There is a heaviness to him. A tiredness I haven't really seen before. Perhaps caused by hurting his hand, or not getting enough sleep. Then he blurts out, "It's the anniversary today."

"Anniversary?" I sit down beside him, taking his injured hand to check it over. It's just as rough as my own are now, and there's an angry red mark along the joints of his thumb and index finger.

"You know I told you I used to come hiking with my brother? Henri?"

I still, wondering if this is the moment. The moment when I'll find out more about the map, the twine, the cabin. "Yes."

"Well, this is the day we lost him." Matthieu sighs. "I heard it gets easier, and I guess it has over the years. But this day . . ."

I bring both my hands around his, looking up at him. Noticing the way his hair is a little wild at the edges, his eyes dull beneath his heavy brows. I try not to register any surprise and instead allow him a moment to collect himself. That's the thing with Matthieu. He's quiet, thoughtful. In his manner and in the way he treats me. I don't want him to feel rushed in this moment. I want him to share a piece of himself with me.

He keeps his gaze trained on the wall, as though seeing a thousand memories there. "Henri was older than me by a few years. But now I'm older than he ever . . ." He swallows. "He would have teased you. Relentlessly."

I lean my head on his shoulder. "I'd love to hear more about him. If you want to tell me."

Matthieu takes a minute, and I wonder if he's not quite ready. But then he blows out a breath, his fingers curling back around mine, and begins to talk. To tell me about Henri.

"He played guitar, and he spent hours working out each song, finding the right notes to something we heard on the radio. And . . . he was the one who made my whole family laugh. Real belly laughs, the kind that tip you backward in your chair at the dinner table." He huffs a laugh, looking at me. And I leave the space for him to keep talking.

As we sit there, with the sun wending its way through the sky, I figure Cora can't be right. He's just the quiet type, someone who chooses not to go into Woodsmoke too often. Or maybe he shops the next town over, perhaps avoiding memories of Henri. I do know how that feels, but I can imagine him being caught in cobwebs of memories if he traipsed through town.

He has to be real. How could someone who carries this much love and grief and promise not be?

Chapter 34

Cora

The next day Cora is sure that the mountains will take more from her. That there is always a higher price. Maybe she never understood the bargains she made to begin with. Howard is shuffling more slowly, and his breath is raspy and thick, as though the mountains have taken root in his lungs, using up all the space, all the air. She tries to make him sit still so she can keep him anchored here with her and fully assess the extent of the damage to his body caused by the passage of time.

"Give over," he says gruffly, yanking the pail of chicken feed out of her hands. "When have you ever done the feeding? Not in all the years we've had the layers."

"Maybe I should learn. Maybe it's about time you showed me. You know full well I'm twice as capable as those young'uns in town, Howard Price." She fidgets, pulling on her coat, following him out into the yard. The cold pinches everything, making her shrink back down inside herself. She chews on her lip as Howard slowly paces the yard, throwing out feed to the clucking mess of feathers at his feet. Cora steps over chicken shit, eyeing him as he stops for a moment to take a long, wheezing breath. "The winter isn't good for you. You should be in the warm, by the fire—"

"Coraline, for the love of . . ." He pulls off his cap, shaking his head. He's far more stooped over than last winter, closer to the ground, as he places the pail on the dirt. "It's just age. We're getting older, and there's no use in just sitting inside and waiting for death to come knocking, is there?"

"You need a checkup. When was the last time you went to the doctor? That nice receptionist, the one with the mole, you know? She always finds you a good appointment time. I can phone her; you could be seen tomorrow . . ." Cora trails off as Howard shakes his head again.

He places his cap on his head and picks up the pail again. "When will you learn? Meddling. Always meddling. I know that Jess Gray was here last night. I'm not dumb as well as old."

"I refused her this time, if you must know."

"That book is the real killer," he says, shaking his head. "Your superstitions have grown a life of their own. Look at your mother. Your grandma Tabitha. All bitter and gray and cheated in the end. Like they'd been stuck with a jack when they really wanted the queen. The only one who escaped was Ivy, by giving the damn thing to you. The best thing you can do is throw it on the fire, where it belongs. Should have been turned to ash years ago." He pauses, surveying the yard thoughtfully. "Would make great compost."

Cora splutters, readying her sharp tongue. But Howard suddenly clutches at his shoulder. "Howard?"

He makes a noise that sounds like a deflating beach ball and bends over almost double, clutching his arm to his chest.

"Howard!" Cora hobbles over to him, prodding and poking at him to make him walk inside. She can't help thinking of all the chickens, how they'll peck at him if he falls, how she won't be able to lift him again, not with her knees, not with this gnawing cold—

"Woman!" he says gruffly, pulling his arm away from her. His glare could light a match, and she stumbles back, startled. "It's just my shoulder, just my *useless*, bloody body giving up, bit by bit. And before you say it, *no doctors*. No nice receptionist with the mole. And no bloody bargains with that book!"

She watches him for a moment, the blood still heating her cheeks and throat. "Fine."

Then she turns on her heel, marches back into the house, and slams the door so hard the picture on the opposite wall rattles and falls clean off. She jumps when she sees it staring up at her from the floor. It's a picture of Carrie and Lillian, back when Carrie was so young that she would still curl up in Cora's lap like a kitten. Cora bends down and scoops up the framed picture, her hips clicking and protesting at the effort. She feels every movement now, every twist, as though a knife is probing her joints.

She pulls the back door open and eyes Howard critically for a heartbeat. His suntanned skin isn't as full of life as it used to be, but drawn and gray. She worries. Is this the cost of one of her workings? Has the price been drawn from the one she loves?

Carrie. She could speak to Carrie. Howard might not talk to doctors, but maybe he'll listen to Carrie. Howard has always had a soft spot for his grandniece. Besides, Cora needs a reason, an excuse, to reach out . . .

"Just popping out!"

She's off, hobbling through the house on purposeful feet, checking that she has tissues in the pocket of her coat, grabbing her hat, her gloves, putting the mobile phone she never switches on into the other pocket. She leaves before he can question her, before he untangles her thoughts and realizes where she is heading. She can't wait until the moment he collapses, until he has no will of his own and it's too damn late. Carrie is the last of the Morgans in Woodsmoke with her. The only person besides herself she can really trust. And who else will persuade him to take it easy? Meddling, he calls it. Well, she calls it *fixing*.

Ivy's old cottage is silent when she arrives. Too silent, too watchful, swollen with memories of years past. Cora has avoided this cottage, just like she avoided Ivy in the end. Just like Ivy avoided her. After Carrie left, after she admitted to Ivy what she'd done the night that Jess came to her, they argued one final time and never spoke again.

But now, she doesn't wait for an invitation. As she steps over the threshold, the scents of new wood and fresh paint envelop her, jarring her out of the past. The cottage has been reborn, stripped bare of the past and made ready for the future. But the familiar still lingers and haunts the corners of the rooms. As Cora walks through the lounge, marveling at the way Carrie has transformed the place, she can still see flickering images from before. The day Ivy, as she fed Lillian, offering her the book, telling her there was a story inside, a way to break its bond with Ivy and form it anew with Cora. For a price. Cora can see the day she was last here, the day of their final row, how Ivy ran her hand over the mantelpiece as everything came crashing down. Ivy never forgave her for all her meddling, and she blamed her for Carrie's departure. Then, when Lillian left, Ivy drew even further away, and Cora knew they would never reconcile.

She shakes off that day with a shudder, reminding herself that Ivy forgave her in the end, with that will and that message stitched into the quilt. Death is the greatest leveler of them all.

As Cora walks through to the kitchen, discovering a space that looks like a showroom, she sees Carrie's handwritten list on the counter. Her neat little loops and swirls, the handwriting Cora always hoped to find peering up at her on an envelope, slipped through the letter box one day. It's a to-do list, of sorts, with more items crossed off than not—*plaster back bedroom*, for instance, and *paint skirting on the ground floor.* Then she sees another person's scrawl along the bottom of the list. A stranger's handwriting, all spiky and uneven and wrong. It says simply, *Take a day off with me.*

"He's back, then," she murmurs to herself. Then she looks out of the kitchen window, eyeing the mountains and their white crowns. "Back with the frost . . ."

She taps a fingernail on the handwriting, wondering where he's taken her Carrie. She searches her mind, trying to remember the stories, the echoes inside other stories, of people disappearing in the snow and cold. Of people disappearing with the frost who shouldn't have. She draws in a breath, suddenly restless, wishing she could still walk the old trails, follow the veins and arteries into the beating heart of the mountains. But her hips, her knees . . . Age robs people of many things, she thought, stealing little pieces of a person until all that's left is so shrunken and small that it can hardly be called a life. And now Howard, with his strained, drawn features, his crumpling over, his refusal, his pig-stubborn *refusal* to concede even the smallest inch of ground—

Her heart thumps once, twice, pulling her back to her own needs, her own body. Her mind turns soft at the edges, and she throws out a hand, gripping the wall. Palpitations. Endless reminders of her own edges now, the boundaries of her shrinking world.

Cora hobbles out of the cottage slowly, closing the door with a quiet click, like a visiting ghost. She came to speak to Carrie about Howard, but instead of being able to ease her mind by having that conversation, her worries have doubled. She mutters to herself, frustrated with her own mind, how it wanders back and forth far more than it ever used to. First Howard, now memories of that last fight with Ivy, now Carrie, her Carrie, and the curse that seems to have settled over her.

"Where are you, my girl?" she asks the air, the frost. "Where have you gone with him?"

Chapter 35
Carrie

"Are you sure you want it all . . ." Matthieu holds up the tin of paint . . . "*timeless*?"

"Sure," I say, tipping a glob of off-white paint into the tray. I move the roller up and down in the tray to coat it with the paint, then move to the nearest wall in the kitchen. I glance at the place where I left the to-do list on the counter and smile at the note Matthieu scrawled along the bottom. "I'd rather it was a blank canvas."

"For you, or for a purchaser?"

I pause, resting the roller on the wall, and turn to him. "I guess . . . well."

He smiles, eyes glinting. "You're considering keeping it."

"I . . ." I swallow, staring around at the lounge.

"You don't have to make a decision straightaway." Matthieu shrugs, grabbing the edging brush. He's doing the cutting in for the first two walls, and I'll do the final two.

"All right, well, you know I told you last week when we were ice-skating how I feel . . . rooted here?" I hesitate, but decide to tell him. "It's partly the cottage. I've fallen in love with it. But it's also you."

"Me?" he says, eyes darting to mine.

"You."

He looks away, but I catch his grin. "That's not a terrible thing, I guess."

"What about you?" I ask way too casually. "Are you going to stay for a while? When spring comes, I mean."

His grin dissolves into a frown as his gaze drops to the paintbrush in his hand. "I don't know yet, Carrie."

"Is it work elsewhere, or—"

"I'm torn. Let's put it like that," he says. Then he leans toward me, those inky eyes glittering and brilliant. "I think you've got a little something there . . ."

"Oh," I say, wiping my hand down my cheek. It comes away with a streak of white paint and I laugh. "How does this stuff get everywhere?"

I only just catch his grin before he flicks his paintbrush, splattering my arm and hip. "Looks like you've got some there too."

I chuckle, checking out the flecks on my old denim dungarees and long-sleeve top, then raise my eyebrows at him. Reaching out with the roller, I paint down his chest. "Oops."

His grin cracks wide as he drops the paintbrush and closes the distance between us. My heart stutters, heat flooding me as his hands rest on my hips, pulling me closer. "I think you did that on purpose."

The roller hangs limp in my left hand as his mouth comes down to mine. His kisses are soft at first, lips fluttering against mine, but I want more. More of him, more of this winter, and I drop the roller to the floor, move my fingers to his jawline, his hair, and deepen the kiss between us. His hands move around my waist, circling the small of my back, the length of his body pressing into mine. I groan, and his mouth moves to my throat as I arch my back, electricity crackling between us.

Then he pulls away. His hands leave my body, and he steps back, putting too much space between us. He's breathing heavily, eyes dark with desire as they lock with mine. "This can't be the first time, Carrie. Not like this. Not"—he casts around—"covered in paint in this cold room."

I nod, pushing back my hair, my whole body still pulsing. I place my head in my hands and groan loudly. "You're right. You're right—"

"When it happens . . ." he says, taking a step back toward me to thread his fingers through mine, that intense gaze never leaving my face, "I want to take my time."

I swallow, look up at him, and feel the ground shift beneath me. "You know I have at least a three-date rule."

He chuckles, eyes glittering as he brushes one final kiss over my mouth. "I think we both know this has gone far beyond dating, and I promise you, I'm thinking about staying. I really am."

I spend the rest of the afternoon highly aware of him. Of myself. Of the air between us, crackling and heavy as we move around each other, painting the kitchen and then the lounge. And I realize that you can belong with a person as much as you belong to a place. Matthieu is the one I want to belong with.

Chapter 36
Jess

They press harder on your belly than you'd like them to. Jess remembers this from the first time. She wants to ask them to be more careful. It's a new life, she wants to explain. I've guarded it so carefully, and now you're pressing into it like it's a peach that will never bruise. But she doesn't say that. She lies back, half propped up on the hospital-style bed, as the nurse rubs the thick, oozy jelly across her belly. It never feels right to keep her boots, leggings, jumper, and jewelry on for these moments. She feels overclothed, overdressed, for the occasion.

"Will you find out?" the sonographer asks as the picture warps into view. "The sex. At the twenty-week scan."

"No," Jess says quickly, blinking at the tiny screen. This is the twelve-week scan, the first. She remembers the anticipation of Elodie's first scan so clearly, how the room was so stuffy, how Tom couldn't sit still on the blue hospital-issue chair in the corner. "I'd rather have the surprise."

The image on the screen floats up, as though from some black and gray underwater abyss, and she blinks again, startled at the image. The head, the arms waving, trying to catch something. She imagines eyes, a nose, toenails, and a flickering little chest—

"It's your second?" the sonographer asks, smiling down at her. "All present and correct. I can't see anything concerning, but we'll send the letter through anyway with the statistics. Just so you're informed. Congratulations."

Jess bunches her hands into fists, staring at the screen as the sonographer takes a couple of images, talking her through what she can see. But Jess can't hear her. She can't hear anything over the static inside her head. She grits her teeth, trying not to cry, forcing her breathing to stay even, unhurried. If only this moment was joy, unbridled, perfect joy. It should be. After all, this is what she wanted. The family, Woodsmoke, the home with a tangle of shoes by the front door.

But Tom isn't here.

She didn't tell him. She couldn't. Not when she peed on the stick alone in the bathroom at that supermarket, nor when the tiredness overtook her over the past two weeks like she'd slammed into a wall. She didn't explain, and he didn't complain, when she got rid of everything that smelled funny or musty in the house, including his favorite, worn-out slippers.

She should tell him; she knows this. She'll have to eventually. But she's too full of guilt, and she's also still cross with him for seeing Carrie behind her back. Even if Cora wouldn't help, and even if Carrie decides to stay, Jess is afraid he will find out what Cora helped with all those years ago, that Carrie's presence has sparked a series of emotions she can't stop or control. Mostly she has regrets, deep regrets that she's built a wall out of, a wall she can't break through. A baby should be a celebration, but she doesn't feel ready to share the news yet. She doesn't much feel like celebrating.

Now her body inhales sharply, as it often does of its own accord, without her volition. Her eyes burn with tears, and she hurriedly searches for a tissue in her pockets.

"It's always overwhelming," the sonographer says kindly, handing her a box.

"Yes. It really is." Jess sniffs, pulling a tissue from the box and pressing it into her eyes until she feels the numb pain in her eye sockets of pushing a little too hard. The sonographer fusses around, handing her more tissues and a length of blue roll to wipe away the jelly, then tells her she'll give her a moment to get redressed. Jess is left alone, but as she cleans the jelly off her skin, pulls down her jumper, and wipes the stinging tears from her face, she knows there is only one person she wants to share this moment with.

Carrie.

She catches the flash of silver scar on her hand, the ever-present reminder of Carrie and what they meant to each other. It's a horrible conflict inside her, this wanting and not wanting her friend to return. She gulps, fresh sorrow flooding her, a wound ripped open that startles her with its fangs and claws. More than anything, Jess wishes that Tom had been hers all along, that he hadn't been Carrie's for even a moment.

She reaches for her phone and nearly dials the number. But then she pictures Carrie's face, hears her again saying, *Just go*. She should have handled that all differently. It doesn't matter what everyone whispers about Carrie returning, at her book group, at the school gate, in the shops where she still sees the same faces. It matters what *she* thinks, and somehow she needs to put it right.

THE ULTRASOUND PHOTOS are sealed in a small white envelope. She tucks them into her bag after she gets back in her car and then stares without seeing at the car park in front of her. It takes her ten minutes to start up the engine and pull away, blinking furiously to keep herself focused on driving. Instead of on the past.

When she walks through the front door, Tom and Elodie are there, eating cut-up carrot sticks and crisps on the sofa. She stops herself from tutting and passes them a tray, eyeing the crumbs already littering the cushions and the floor. Tom glances at her and winks, an arm slung around his Elodie, who's glued to the TV as she mindlessly reaches with a hand into her crisp packet. Jess stands there for a beat, watching them, her world. At Tom, with his tired, older eyes, and at Elodie, with her sudden bursts of giggles at the TV. Elodie snuggles in closer to Tom, and he presses a kiss to her forehead. Watching them, warmth flickers in Jess's chest.

"Hey, can we talk later?" she says to Tom, sotto voce, and he glances back at her, head tilting as though trying to read her.

"Of course," he says. "I was going to take El over to see Dad—"

"Not tonight," Jess interjects, already in the kitchen pulling food from the fridge to cook dinner. "Can we go over and see them at the weekend instead?"

"Okay." Tom frowns. "Did you . . . have a good day? Is everything all right?"

"Super, thanks," Jess replies, pausing for a moment as a wave of nausea engulfs her. She closes her eyes, her hands straying to her belly, and pulls in a breath, waiting for it to subside. It's the onions. Like before, with Elodie, the scent of them sets her off. "Can you make tea? I might . . . take a bath."

"Sure." Tom looks back at the TV, gets his phone out, and begins scrolling.

"Now?"

He eyes her again, sweeping his gaze over her. "Sure you're all right?" he says as he gets to his feet. Elodie shuffles into the warm patch he's left on the sofa as Tom crosses the room to run his hands along Jess's arms. "I can get us takeout if you prefer?"

"Actually, that would be great." Jess sighs, moving away from Tom to run the tap. She fills a glass with water and gulps most of it down. "Chinese?"

"I'll get the menu." He turns to the lounge. "Hey, Els, fancy some special rice and chicken?"

JESS TAKES HER time, combing out her hair, washing away the feel of the hospital still clinging to her pores. When she hears the doorbell and the scuffle of feet and voices signaling the arrival of their food, she pulls on her pajamas and dressing gown and pads down the stairs in her slippers. Tom makes a show of scooping up everything with chopsticks, and Elodie giggles as she tries to copy him. Jess tries to let go of the tension in her shoulders, to lean in to this moment with them, but she feels like she's watching them through a screen. Like this is another version of her life and she's not quite a part of it. All the while, the ultrasound pictures are in that neat little white envelope, burning a hole in her dressing gown pocket.

When Tom takes Elodie to bed, she sits in silence on the sofa in the lounge, feet tucked up under herself, the white envelope sitting on the coffee table in front of her. She doesn't turn on the TV. She doesn't read a book. She sits and waits for Tom.

"What's up?" Tom breezes in, sinking onto the sofa next to her. He grabs the remote and flicks through a couple of channels before realizing that his wife is silent next to him. "Jess?"

She sighs through her nose, fidgeting for a moment. "Look in the envelope."

He half frowns as he reaches forward and lifts the photos from inside. All at once his jaw slackens and his features take on a puce cast, then a blanched white, like skim milk. He rubs a hand over his face, blinking at the images, as though he can't comprehend them. He turns to Jess, shock etched into his features. He regards her, this woman he's known almost his entire life, and knows she's holding a whole world inside her. One she keeps entirely separate and secret from him. "I—I don't understand. These aren't Elodie's. The date on these is today."

"They were taken today. At my ultrasound."

"But . . . this is a baby. A *baby*."

"Yes, it is. Our baby."

Tom regards her, seeing a stranger sitting beside him. A stranger with Jess's eyes, her body, but it's as though someone else has slipped inside her skin, or like the real Jess, the true Jess, has suddenly slipped out. Her features are pinched and, she imagines, fairly dull. "I—I don't understand. You're going to have to help me out here, Jess. What do you want me to say? Surely this is great news?"

"I—" she begins, but stops with a sigh. "I should have told you sooner. I went there today, and all I could think was that Carrie's back, she's in town, and in another life she might have been there with me." Her throat tightens and she closes her eyes, gathering herself back together.

"Oh, Jess . . ." He looks back at the ultrasound photos, the bulbous head, the tiny body, shifting through the image in shades of black and white. It was different when they found out about Elodie. So different. She can still remember that swell of pride and wonder they shared, as well as the utter, utter terror at the enormity of it all. He shuffles the photos back into the envelope and places it on the coffee table. "I'm sorry. I don't—I don't know how to fix that. I told her she should leave, and that isn't going to help, is it?"

"Not really," Jess says, sniffling. "Especially because we argued. I saw her for the first time in a decade, and we argued. I—I've been so cross with you, so angry that you went and saw her without me—"

His face crumples. "I'm sorry if I made it worse."

She gets up and moves to the kitchen, needing space in her mind, in her soul. She knows she's still not being entirely honest. This isn't the whole truth, but only a piece of it. The thing she's not ready to say—can't say—is that she thinks she's the reason why Carrie left ten years ago. Why she ran out on their wedding, and why everything is so fucked up now. She wants to tell him. But she feels like she's in too deep—a decade too deep. What if Tom would have chosen Carrie? What if she had stayed? "I'm not finding out the sex. I don't want to know."

"Okay. That's absolutely fine. But you have to tell me about the next appointment; we should go together, surely—"

"We've just been so distant, Tom." She pushes a hand through her hair. "I don't know. I'm going to bed. I'll—I'll make sure you're at the next appointment. Sorry." She leaves the room, and as she trudges up the stairs she already wants to take it all back. All her sharp edges, all her gloom. All her guilt and fear and longing. Her gloom seems to be about Tom, but really, it's not at all. She's scared that she'll lose him if she tells him about that night, about what Cora did. What she herself *begged* Cora to do. But she's also scared that if she doesn't tell him, she'll lose too much of herself.

She doesn't go back downstairs. She brushes her teeth, picks up her Kindle, and loses herself in a story about someone else's life.

Chapter 37
Carrie

She snuck out under a sickle moon, her shawl wrapped around her thin shoulders, and spent a night with him talking about the stars and their stories.

—Tabitha Morgan, July 19, 1929

The sky is a wilderness, brimming with starlight. We carry a midnight picnic, taking the trail I haven't walked along in years. It veers off in the opposite direction to Woodsmoke and Matthieu's cabin, toward the other side of the mountain range facing the sea in the far distance. We both wear head torches and layers of coats and hats and boots. I'm bundled up so tightly that I can only shuffle along in the near-dark, following Matthieu's back as we make our way to our picnic spot.

"All right back there?" he says over his shoulder, his voice muffled by the coat pulled up over his mouth. "In a minute, you'll see why this is the best spot."

I giggle and place a hand on his coat. He stops to turn round, and I catch a flash of teeth as he pulls his coat down and lowers his mouth to mine. The brush of heat as he touches my lips with his sends a jolt of starlight through me. I pull him closer, deepening the kiss, reaching up to run a hand over his jaw. He laughs, grabbing for my hand and pulling me farther up the trail. "I promise you won't want to miss this. I promise."

In only a few more steps we arrive. I stop in my tracks to stare at the clearing, the trees melting away, at what Matthieu has created. "When?" I breathe, letting go of his hand to walk closer. I turn in a circle, taking in what he's done, and find him staring at me, grinning. All around us are battery-operated fairy lights on copper wire, woven in the trees. Peeping out from the boughs, the tiny glowing lights in the dark mingle with the starlight overhead. And in the middle of the clearing is a huge rug, piled up with blankets and cushions. It's the setting for either a fairy tale or a photo shoot.

I walk over to the nearest tree and run a finger over a snow-draped limb. "You did all this. All for us. For . . . for me." My chest tightens, and I smile back at him, the soft glow of the fairy lights highlighting his features. This is technically our second date. After that perfect afternoon of ice-skating, I didn't think it could get any better. But this . . . I swallow.

He sets down the backpack full of picnic food and points to the sky. "Look up, Carrie."

"Oh." No words are adequate. The stars are piercing on a clear night when viewed from the field and from outside the cottage, but up here they're dazzling—brimming, bowls of molten light dripping from the heavens, so bright and clear they cast an eerie silver glow over the world. And beyond them are a million starry pinpricks, the whispers of light so far away that they can only murmur their presence.

I clasp my hands together and gaze up, and as I do a shooting star flares in a white line. I gasp, laughing, and Matthieu comes to put his arms around me. He nuzzles into my neck, and I relax back into his warmth, torn between wanting to close my eyes and bask in the heat from his touch and not wanting to miss a single moment of the brilliant midnight sky. It's all so new with him that every contact, every touch, sings electric.

"The clouds will cover it all in an hour," he says, "so don't take your eyes off the stars."

I smile and pull him down onto the blankets and cushions, pressing my mouth to his before looking upward again. "Can you name any of the constellations?"

"The major ones," he says, frowning. He points across at Orion. "We all know that one. I always search for Orion's Belt, then the bow and arrow. And the plow, of course. But my favorite is the Pleiades."

"The Seven Sisters?"

"Yes! You know it too?"

I grin, still staring skyward. "It's the first constellation I always search for, wherever I am, wherever I've traveled to. I always hope I'll see it, because it'll make me feel like I'm home."

"Have you heard the myth?" Matthieu asks.

"Tell me."

He bites his lip, then pulls me closer. "Well, they supposedly represent the seven daughters of the Titan Atlas. As he held up the world, he could no longer protect them from Orion . . ." He points to Orion, and my eyes track to the constellation. " . . . so Zeus turned them into stars. It's the brightest cluster in the night sky."

"Who told you about them?"

"My mother," Matthieu says softly. "She loved stories of all kinds, myths, legends, the ones that traveled the world appearing in many forms and languages. They were the ones she sought out, and then she would tell them to me. And . . . Henri."

"She sounds wonderful."

Matthieu hesitates. "She was."

I take in the enormity of the past tense, keeping my gaze fixed on the stars. He's told me a little about his brother, but I didn't know his mother had also passed.

"She—she liked it here. She said the mountains are so old that they are somehow alive. Neither malignant nor good, but with moods and stories of their own to tell." He sighs. "She would have liked you."

I let those words hang in the air between us, not wanting them to blow away.

"If you could wish for anything, what would it be?" I ask, glancing at him.

"Anything?"

I lie back against the pile of cushions, and he settles in beside me. "Anything. The next shooting star we see, we both have to make a wish, then remember it until tomorrow. And if we do that, it'll come true."

"All right," he says, reaching for my hand. "And we don't tell each other?"

"We keep it a secret. Or it won't come true."

Our breath fogs up in front of us, the sounds of the mountain becoming louder in the silence. I listen to the scurry of hidden creatures, to the creaks as the mountains shift and stretch. And then, under that blanket of starlight, the longest trail of a shooting star I've ever seen crosses the night sky. I breathe in softly, hurriedly whispering my wish in my mind. Then I close my eyes and smile, letting that dream sink in, hoping with every fiber of my being that it will come true.

Matthieu's arms come around me, and I feel the softest kisses gently grazing my mouth. "I made my wish," he says before giving me one final, longer kiss. Then he moves away to pull his backpack toward us and starts to unpack the thermos of hot chocolate and the cookies. He pours me a mug, and I sip it slowly, savoring the bitter richness of the chocolate.

"I never talked much about what it was like growing up in Woodsmoke," I say, realizing it's time. That I can't shy away from it, that someday he'll find out, and I want him to hear it from me. He shared about his brother Henri, and I feel like he's been making this space for me to share when I'm ready. That this is the way this relationship works, with a transaction of shared details about our past lives. "My family has a complicated history in this town, and it's part of the reason why I left."

He pours his own mug of hot chocolate, giving me the space to speak. "Tell me."

So I do. I tell him about the *Morgan Compendium* and Ivy's neglected candle shop. He asks if Cora still has the book, and I say yes. I tell him that one day it'll pass to me. Then I tell him about Jess and how we grew up glued together. How I thought it would always be that way between us. I show him the sliver of scar on my hand, the twin to hers, carved the night we promised to always be sisters.

And then I tell Matthieu what happened in the end with Tom. My voice cracks as I recount the moment of realizing that we were too different, that we weren't meant to be. But then it hardens like granite when I tell him about hitching up my wedding dress and running. About how I've been running ever since then—seeking, never stopping, trying to fill the gaps in my heart. I tell him that I was afraid of coming home, even though I desperately wanted to, and that finally doing it has been both a breaking and a healing. I admit that I haven't been able to reconcile those divided feelings.

Then I stumble and go quiet as I think about trying to tell him that meeting him has changed me, enabled me, like some wayward weed, to plant myself and take root in the harsh winter ground. This homecoming has not been easy. But each day I wake in Woodsmoke, I feel the thrum of the place in my bones and my restless heart settling. I feel that I belong here now in a way I never felt growing up. Maybe, as I learn to love this place and embrace every facet of it—and myself—I will accept the magic and the mountains as a part of me in a way I never did before.

I will tell him. I will. But tonight is for starlight, and tomorrow belongs to the future.

He listens to it all, and by the time we finish our hot chocolates, the mugs are cooling to stone in our hands. When the clouds plume over the stars, casting us in a thicker darkness, I am renewed—whole in a way I didn't think I'd ever be again.

"Carrie, the more I learn about you, the more I see how you're meant to be here. How much you love the place." He takes the mug from my hand and turns to me, trailing soft, fluttering kisses over my mouth. I relax into him, into his touch, his warmth, as he lays me down on the blanket. And under that velvet sky, he takes his time, as he said he would. My heart fuses to his as I wrap my arms around him, knowing that I belong.

Later, as we take the trail back down the mountain, making our way home to the cottage and the caravan, I ask Matthieu if he wants to stay with me tonight instead of returning to his cabin.

Inside the caravan, as we close the door, I feel the mountain sigh around me. As though it has also unburdened its heart beneath the bowl of stars and night.

As though it's releasing a decade-long breath.

Spring

March

Chapter 38
Carrie

Edith burned the candle by the window, and the trapper came back to her. But not as a person, as a voice. Calling her. She followed that voice, stepping off the mountain paths.

No one has heard from Edith Tucker or the trapper since.

—Nora Morgan, May 20, 1918

Three weeks later, as we tip into March, I realize I'm ready to claim my home. The cottage is finished, and only a few small pieces of furniture are left to acquire. I move in, taking several trips from caravan to cottage, lugging my stuff across the glittering field.

There's only a light frost today. The snow has melted away, leaving the glitter of ice painted on blades of grass. It crackles as I walk, and the scent of newness envelops me. Suddenly, I'm hopeful for spring, aware of what that means. The decision I've reached. The cottage isn't going on the market, and I've made no plans to move on. I'm staying in Woodsmoke, perhaps not forever, but definitely for right now. I find it hard to deal in absolutes. But with every day, every moment I'm back here, I finally feel like my feet are on solid ground. As though I'm where I'm supposed to be.

And Matthieu, with his quiet ways, his solid presence since I returned, is a big part of this feeling. Not the only reason, but important enough that I can no longer ignore what it means. As we lay in the caravan the other night, limbs entwined, I realized it was time to carve out more space for myself. And doing that will mean also making space for him. By laying my cards on the table and asking him to stay in Woodsmoke with me.

The caravan was too small that night. He had to stoop to shuffle around the space, and as we clutched mugs of coffee the next morning, I pictured him preparing the morning coffee in the cottage. Heating the kettle on the stovetop, spooning the earthy granules into the French press, and carrying the hot mugs up the staircase to the bedroom at the front of the house.

In the afternoon, I close the door on the cottage, pocket the key like a secret, and drive into the center of Woodsmoke. There are only a few huddled figures around, and so less gossip than usual plumes in the air. A few half-familiar faces acknowledge me with a nod, and the butcher, who I went to school with years ago, even asks how I'm doing as I pass. I guess the gossip has quieted down now, and folks are accepting the fact that I've come back. It all feels so . . . ordinary.

So wonderfully ordinary.

I slip a second iron key from my pocket as I approach the shop. It slips inside the keyhole, and a soft click tells me I can enter. For the first time since I arrived, I step over the threshold of Ivy's old candle shop.

I breathe in the scent of dust and lavender. My footfalls are cloying thuds in the hollow quiet as I cross to the counter and drop the key next to the till. It's one of those old-fashioned ones, with the number 9 rubbed out from overuse. I place my index finger on the ivory circle, feeling the ghost of Ivy's finger in the smooth indent from years of use. I picture her here, standing where I am now, giving me that knowing look before shooing a customer out to the bank around the corner. She only accepted cash, bills and coins, and sometimes she would write out a receipt by hand if someone particularly riled her, taking her time as they swayed impatiently from foot to foot. My grandma was a force of nature despite her sweet, reedy singing voice. You never, ever said no to her. Woe betide you if you did. I guess in that way she was just like her sister Cora, and like every Morgan woman who came before her.

Staring around the shop at the shelves lined with old stock, the patterned crimson rug in the center worn down to blush in some places from many feet, I feel more than nostalgia. It's as though the shop has been waiting for me, and now it's leaning in, inch by inch, with anticipation. Listening to the patter of my heart as it syncs with Woodsmoke again. I never could help longing for this slumbering town in my dreams, my nightmares. It's followed me through airports and train stations, crisscrossing continents with me, trying to pull me back.

I've resisted for so long. I've walked the earth with the broken pieces rattling inside my chest, hoping someone, anyone, would be able to heal the pain. That another place would become my new home. Yet I'm here again, back in Woodsmoke, wearing my heart on the outside of my chest. And now there's Matthieu. Even though I told myself, *promised* myself, that renovating the cottage would be the final chapter. The ending I'd been waiting ten years to write.

I haven't been in this shop this winter because even entering it feels like beginning a new chapter. If I reopen the shop, if I change it into something full of things that I want to sell, then I'm making a statement. I'm staking out my place in this town full of secrets and old magic and memories. I'm proclaiming that these things are mine too. Until now, I haven't been ready to even contemplate doing that. I heave a breath, lean my forearms on the counter, and gaze out into the middle distance.

Then I realize that a woman outside the window is watching me.

I blink, pulling myself up to stand straight and tall as she pushes open the door, the sharp breeze cutting the lavender-scented shop with the smell of car fumes and snow.

"Cora," I say, swallowing back my nostalgia, my faint stirrings of hope. "Thank you for coming."

"I'm not accustomed to being summoned."

"This won't take long."

Cora sighs, wilting slightly, and shuffles to the armchair by the window. It has been used for many years by long-suffering partners, and children have scrambled over it while their parents sniffed at the waxy pillars on the shelves. It's been neglected for many months, sitting in this relic of a shop that no one wanted to claim. Until now.

Until me.

"I want to reopen the shop."

Cora says nothing for a moment, merely staring at me, her left eye twitching, with moisture gathering at the outer corner. Then she clears her throat. "You . . . want to stay?"

I feel that secret smile tugging up the corners of my mouth. "I think so."

"Well," she says carefully, her gaze sliding away as she blinks furiously. It's the slightest slip of composure, so slight that it could easily be overlooked. But I notice. "This is a turn-up for the books."

"Ivy used to say that," I blurt out before thinking. Before I can push the words back into my mouth.

Her left eye twitches again, but she says nothing.

"Anyway . . . I need you to sign off on the lease. She rented it from you."

"She did."

The familiar sense of treading on eggshells around Cora surfaces. Like there's a layer of history between her and Ivy that I will never quite understand. "I can . . . pay you in advance? How do you want it to work?"

"We're selling it," Cora says, her eyes swiveling to the shelves opposite. "You can purchase it, if you like. But not candles. Make something else. That was Ivy's thing, and I think it's time this town had something of yours in it. Don't you?"

I think about the sketchbook I left on the kitchen table. Half filled this winter with pencil drawings of the mountains, of Matthieu, of the details I notice more keenly being back here. "I'm thinking of selling my artwork. I started . . . started sketching again."

Cora's eyes flare briefly. "At last."

"It's a start. I haven't painted in a while, but the back bedroom at the cottage is a good space. I've been thinking, with the afternoon light, it might be a good place to set up an easel."

"Ivy would have liked that," Cora says quietly, turning her gaze toward the window. She sighs, watching as a mother walks past, pushing a buggy and putting a snack in a red mittened hand reaching out. "She would have liked that very much."

I nod, watching her. "I should have come back when she was alive."

Cora stands, pushing herself up slowly, and the chair groans from her absence. "What's done is done. She left you the cottage and the lease for a reason. She always knew more than she let on." Her features soften. "I want you to stay. Desperately. I wish you'd never left to begin with and created this—this hole. But what's done is done. We all made our choices." She hesitates, placing her fingertips on a candle in the window display. "Just . . . do it differently this time. Carve your own path and don't cling to the past. That was always my mistake."

She walks toward the door, and I feel a weight settle between us. Like this is a door she will close behind her and I will never be able to walk through it and find her again. "Wait," I say. "I want to tell you about him. About Matthieu."

She stops in her tracks before turning sharply. "You can start by forgetting him. Don't make him the reason why you're staying."

"Cora, we've been over this—"

"He's not *real*, Carrie." She closes her eyes, like she's trying to explain something to a stubborn child. "He's not real. He will leave with the frost and never return. It's the curse the mountains carry. He will break your heart, shatter it, and this time you won't be able to mend it again. This time it will haunt you, it will hound you, as you try to find peace, searching for him across the mountain—"

"Stop," I say. I rub my hands down my face. "Just stop. If we're both letting go of the past, then the stories—that book—"

"—is the only true thing I have." Cora smiles sadly. "You can hate me for it. Sometimes Ivy hated it. You can curse the book and all the stories it holds. But one day it will be yours, and then you will understand."

"I love him."

Cora draws a jagged breath, and her hand flutters to her chest. "Then it's already too late. You're cursed. You've returned, and the mountains have cursed you for leaving. You'll have to work out how to break it, before—"

"Cora, *stop*. Just stop. You could meet him. You'll see then, you'll see what he's like. I'm not cursed. He's been searching for clues about his brother who went missing, he's been here to get some closure, some peace—"

"Has anyone met him, Carrie?" Cora cuts in. "Anyone at all?" I open and close my mouth, wanting to retort that of course someone other than me has met him. But the day Howard called in, Matthieu left before he reached the door. And at the ice-skating lake we went to, I can't remember whether he spoke to a single soul. Or when we went to the builders' merchant, when he disappeared for a time . . .

I frown, but say nothing, not wanting to let that seed of doubt take root. Then I remember. "Ivy," I blurt out. "Ivy knew him. He helped her with the cottage last winter."

"Convenient that we can't ask the dead." She sighs and kneads her temples with the tips of her fingers. "Look, my dear, Howard's unwell. He's slowing down, he doesn't want me to notice, doesn't want me to do anything it seems . . . but still. He's not well, and I thought you ought to know."

"What kind of unwell?"

"The kind where you should be dropping by each day." Cora sighs. She inhales, then blows out a breath, and suddenly I have a fleeting glimpse of the world inside her. What I see is a tempest, a whirl of torment and sadness, so different from the hard and aloof exterior she presents to the world. "We've missed you. It wasn't just your mother or Ivy you left behind. It was me as well, dearest. And now you've been back for a few months, and it's like you're still gone. Still absent."

"You're right," I say, moving toward her. I hold out my hand, take hers in mine, and feel the papery cold of her skin. "I haven't been over enough. I've been too wrapped up in the cottage and my own feelings about being back here . . . I'm sorry. I'll come by. Tomorrow. I'll come by every day for tea. I'll bring Matthieu . . . if you like."

She searches my features, as though trying to find something she's misplaced. Then she nods, gently removing her hand from mine. She doesn't mention Matthieu. "Eleven. Don't be late."

Cora leaves the same way she arrived, with a gust carrying the smell of frost and fumes from the cars snaking past outside. I watch her through the window as she walks stiffly down the street and feel the sharp little needles of guilt I always feel. The unnerving sense I always have with Cora that something has been left unfinished.

But as I turn back to the shop, back to the small slip of a space, to the walls and shelves and dust, I can't stop the smile spreading through me. I can buy this space from Cora and Howard and make a living in Woodsmoke. I can paint and create and live in that cottage under the watchful eye of the mountain, finding my way through every season of the year. I feel like I'm starting more than a new chapter. It feels like a new book, a fresh story all of my own making.

Chapter 39
Carrie

He wasn't at her wedding day. She pulled the flowers from her hair, desperate tears in her eyes, and under that same sickle moon, she went searching for him. She searched for him everywhere, all across the mountains, calling his name to the spring.

—Tabitha Morgan, July 19, 1929

I'm staying, and I want you to stay too.

The words thump to the rhythm of my heart as I walk, run, *fly* to the cottage, hoping he will be there. Now that I've spoken it out loud to Cora, saying it like a spell in that dusty, crooked little shop, I know it's true. I want to stay. As soon as I said it, as soon as I visualized my artwork filling that space, I knew I wanted Matthieu to stay in Woodsmoke with me.

And just like a spell has been either broken or cast, the frost begins to thaw.

As I cross the field, the grass no longer crackles like splintered glass. It's softening, rolling over and curling in a languorous wave as the sun spears great holes in the clouds, setting the world on fire. Spring has come and is shivering over everything, the landscape waking up with the kiss of heat and light. I laugh, breathless and dizzy, as memories tumble around in my head. Moments flash through my mind—the midnight picnic, his mouth on mine, paint flecking his features as we finished the last room. Each moment, each memory, turns into a molten haze and lights up the winter as I crash through the cottage door, calling his name.

"Matthieu! Matthieu, I have to tell you something! Where are you?" I pull off one boot, hop on one foot as I pull off the other, then scurry through the lounge, into the kitchen—

He's not here. He was here, just an hour or so ago. We woke up together, made coffee and toast. He didn't mention going anywhere. I turn, rush back through the lounge, cross the hallway to thump up the staircase, one tread, three, five, and burst into the main bedroom.

"Matthieu?"

Silence. Deafening, ringing silence. I drop down in a sigh on the four-poster bed, allowing my heart rate to slow as the light trickles across me. I turn my head to the window, the panes filled with a soft glow, and wonder what it will be like to wake here each day with the sunlight streaming in. Every day I have woken up since returning, I've struggled in either gray light or complete, velvet darkness until I'm already up and ready. I draw in a breath, allowing it to fill every inch of my lungs, the words still beating like a promise through my veins. I want to say it aloud. I want to say it to *him*.

I want you to stay.

My phone rings downstairs, the distant tinny tune breaking into the warm fugue of my thoughts. I get up and move quickly down the stairs to find my coat and dig into the pocket for my phone. As I draw it out, it rings off before I can answer, and I'm sure, so sure, it was him, telling me he popped out, asking if I want him to pick up something for dinner—

But it's a missed call from Cora and Howard's house phone. Probably Cora phoning to remind me I'm expected at eleven tomorrow and to bring shortbread or cake. Or maybe it was Howard phoning to apologize, in his shuffling, roundabout way, for Cora's sharp manner.

I walk into the lounge and sit next to the Wi-fi router I've had installed so that the call will be as clear as I can get it. I return the call, slumping in the armchair by the front window, knowing one of them will pick up on the third ring and not a moment before.

"Carrie," Howard answers on an exhaled breath. "Cora isn't herself. I don't know what to do. The doctor said this might happen, but I can't get through to her . . ."

My whole being deflates. "What do you mean?"

He hesitates, as though he's watching Carrie, wondering how much he can impart. "She just got back from town, and she's—she's saying the frost has broken. She just keeps repeating that. And she's talking about her baby, she's been going through each room, trying to find her baby . . . you know we never . . . Carrie?"

"I'm still here," I say.

"Can you . . . come over? Talk to her? I can't, I don't know if she can even see me, hear me . . ."

I begin to move, casting one last regretful look around the empty cottage, as though I can summon an absent Matthieu from the walls. "I'll be there in ten minutes."

"Hurry." He hangs up abruptly, leaving me in stewing silence.

I TRY MATTHIEU's number five times, and five times it rings out and out and out. On the drive over to Cora's, I stare at the landscape, seeing only green and brown. The white has melted away, retreating for another year and leaving the mountains bald and bare. As though they are ready to be reborn.

I chew on my lip, drawing pinpricks of blood, and the copper taste swills in my mouth. I'm trying to pin down the details of our ice-skating trip in my memory. Did he speak to anyone? Did

I collect the skates, or did he? All of Cora's warnings worm their way into my thoughts. In each of my memories now, Matthieu seems transparent. Ghostly.

When I pull up at Cora and Howard's in a spray of gravel and haste, Howard is already hobbling out, his creased face bent low, his chin tucked into his chest. For a handful of heartbeats, I don't get out of the car but sit there, wondering. If the magic is real, has Cora done something? In her twisted way of trying to protect me, has she banished the frost from the mountain? What baby is she searching for?

I glance at my phone screen once more, as though I can conjure a message from the silence. But the fact is I haven't seen Matthieu since yesterday. Haven't heard from him at all today. And the shiver running through the fields finally reaches inside me, all the way into my bones. In this new spring light, I finally feel the cold of winter.

"Where is she?" I ask, my voice strained and reedy as I step out of the car. "Where's Cora?"

"Now, before you go after her—"

"Howard—"

"No, you have to listen." His mouth puckers. "You have to *know*. When I got back, she was talking about a baby crying, like she couldn't even see me. Like I wasn't there, or she was somewhere else entirely. She's been searching everywhere for . . . for her baby. Our baby. But, Carrie, she's never been with child. Not once. She never lost a baby, and she's adamant it's not Lillian or you. She won't admit she's just muddling things in her head . . ." He takes a breath. "She's not herself. She's in one of those moods, talking faster and faster, and I'm worried for her, Carrie. All she wants, all she's ever wanted, is to love you. I can't, I *cannot* have her broken. Not again. Even if she shouldn't have—"

"What did she do?"

"She—"

"Howard!" Cora's shriek rips through us. "Howard!"

His face drops, and he hobbles fast around the side of the house, throwing back the gate in his wake. I rush after him, heart in my mouth, wondering what I'll find, wondering what Howard was finally about to admit—

Cora is holding Kep's lead as the dog strains toward the chickens clucking and fighting to get into the henhouses, a mess of feathers and fright. Howard takes the lead from her, pulling it into his chest, and growls something I don't catch as he pulls Kep into the house. He slams the kitchen door closed and turns, breathing heavily, and I notice for the first time the tremor in his hands.

"Cora. Never, *ever* . . ." He swallows, catching his breath. " . . . *ever* bring Kep out back. She'll kill the chickens. You know that. You *know* that, woman!"

Cora blinks down at her hands, then at Howard, not even registering my presence. Her hair is a snarl, fanning out around her head, and her eyes are both wild and vacant. She's wearing nothing but stockings on her feet, and I notice a food stain on the cardigan she's wearing. I recall the conversation with the man in the hardware store when I first arrived, when I walked into the shop with the labyrinth of walkways between overstocked shelves with a list on my phone, picking up packets of screws and a hammer. He warned me about how she's been, but I didn't truly listen. He was talking about Cora, after all. She's always been slightly out of step with the rest of the world.

I walk toward her now, taking her arm gently in mine, and guide her toward the house.

"I—I don't remember . . . there was a baby crying, Kep was upset, we were going to find the baby, it was mine, I know it was . . ."

"It's okay, Cora," I say, my heart breaking a little at how forlorn she seems, this woman who has always been like steel. How lost. "Let's make some tea, have a biscuit, a sit-down—"

"Don't tell Carrie. Whatever you do, you *mustn't* tell her." Cora suddenly grips my arm, bony fingers stabbing into my sleeve. "She has to come back. It's all wrong here without her. I made a mistake. A *dreadful* mistake that night. That working, in the moonlight . . . Ivy won't forgive me. But—but—you *can't* tell her."

I turn cold.

"She's not been herself for weeks," Howard says quietly. "Maybe even months, but I guess it's been so gradual I didn't . . . hadn't . . . It's never really around anyone else, but it's like her mind wanders. I just thought she was daydreaming, just wandering . . . but today is different, Carrie. It's like something inside her has snapped." Howard takes Cora's other arm and guides her to the sofa. "But in the past week it's gotten worse. She's been babbling, not making sense. I didn't know what to do, so I phoned the doctor. He's coming here today after his appointments. He said to keep an eye on her, keep her safe. Not leave her alone at all."

I swallow, stepping away from them both, a dark sense of foreboding sweeping over me. "I'll make the tea."

The clatter of the teaspoon jars me out of myself, and ten minutes of silence brings Cora back. Her gaze sharpens, her words turn more lucid, and I realize she's been stuck between two worlds, with one foot in the present and one in the warm, coaxing pool of the past. Maybe in a dream of wanting a baby. Wanting one so much that it became real in her mind.

But it's Howard who worries me. Howard, with his brown skin turning gray. He rubs at his left upper arm occasionally, a frown dimpling his features. He's a little older than Cora, I know that much. She was a young bride when they married. In marrying Howard, she chose stability, a comfortable home, the town where she grew up. I heard stories about how he had his own farm, his own land, and the quiet confidence of a young man who knew how to handle life. Now they rent out the land next to the farm, keeping only the yard for the chickens and a field surrounding the house, left fallow. All I remember of Howard growing up was his calm, steady voice, his patience. How he never uttered a cross or unkind word.

I fuss with my mug as it grows cold in my hands, the glazed sides slipping against my fingers.

"Oh, Carrie," Cora suddenly says, eyes snapping to me. "Have you had any shortbread? Howard, get her some cake. You're here for elevenses, aren't you?" As her eyes widen, darting between me and Howard, the ground tilts and there's a sharp ringing in my ears. Howard is right. She thinks it's the next day.

"Shortbread, yes . . ." I nod, my eyes meeting Howard's, both of us thinking the same thing.

"And would you get my housecoat? It's a little cold today." She shivers and draws a blanket over her knees, but the heating is on full blast, and the house is warm against the slight chill coming off the mountains. I rise to my feet and slip into the hallway to find her housecoat, hanging on a hook by the door. When I turn, my gaze lingers on the scatter of sepia-toned photographs, seeking out the one that has always haunted me, that I am always drawn to.

The face of the trapper.

I stifle a gasp. I've been working with Matthieu for several months, but never noticed before now that the trapper looks so similar to him. The planes and angles of his face, the haunting quality of his eyes, the dark smudges underneath, the thick brows above. I take the photo off the wall, angling it to peer at the date in the top right corner. It doesn't give the year, only the date. October 19.

The day after I returned . . . the day the frost formed over Woodsmoke.

I replace the frame on the wall, unease chilling me in this warm, quiet house. Returning to the lounge, I face Cora, after helping her into her housecoat, and take her papery hands in mine.

"Cora, I need to ask you . . . or I need to tell you. I can't get ahold of Matthieu." I take a breath, avoiding the full force of her pinching stare. "The frost has thawed, and I'm worried that you were right. That the frost tale . . . is true."

Her features soften, turning almost wistful. "Forget him, my love. He was real to you, but he was never meant to stay."

I shake my head, not wanting to believe it. But for the first time, her warnings sting me, like hidden nettles, worrying away at me with their poison. But there all the same, on the edge of my mind, and now I can't shake them off. "You think . . . you truly believe the mountains . . ." I draw in a breath. Continuing quietly, I start again. "If the old stories are true, then Matthieu . . ."

"Has disappeared as the frost has thawed, yes," she says. "Don't go chasing after him up those mountains. He's not coming back."

"But what does the frost tale say?" I ask, desperately searching for some reason, any reason, to make sense of this foreboding, this terrible knowing that he might not . . . that he isn't . . .

Cora leans forward suddenly, grasping my hands in hers. She presses with surprising strength, and her sharp bones grind into my knuckles. My gaze darts to her face, and I find her eyes are clear and unyielding. "He's a spirit. A spirit of the mountains and the lingering magic in this wild and ancient place. Perhaps guided by those known as the fair folk, the ones leading people to stray from the paths. Maybe he was here once, maybe he did lose his brother. But, Carrie, you do not meddle with those who are lost. Promise me you won't go looking for him."

"Cora—"

"You must *promise*," she says, an anxious edge to her tone. "Spirits, fair folk, curses, and bargains . . . they are not to be trifled with."

I swallow, tearing my eyes from hers. "I promise."

Chapter 40
Jess

Jess's head begins to throb. A prickle of pain at first, like the patter of tiny feet behind her eyes, or the first sporadic drops of rain from swollen, bruise-colored clouds. It grows in intensity as the storm finds its center, thumping louder and louder, cracking like thunder across her skull. It reaches down the back of her neck, hugging the top of her spine, and she breathes through her nose, breathes through the pain of it. She sits across from Tom in their lounge, an ocean between them, and begins.

"Ten years ago, Carrie told me she was going to leave after the wedding and take you with her. I would be left alone, and I couldn't stand it. I guess I was hurt . . . shocked . . . and it almost felt like a betrayal. She just said it so casually, like it was something we'd talking over before, but we hadn't." Jess takes a breath, massaging her temples with her fingertips. "It felt like my world was caving in, knowing both of you were going to leave completely. Neither of you seemed happy. It didn't seem . . . right. I didn't want to lose her. Honestly, I was *terrified* of losing her. It was always meant to be us, me and Carrie in Woodsmoke, and when she told me she was rejecting all of it . . ." She swallows, eyes flicking to Tom's. "I went to Cora."

"Wh-what?"

"I went to Cora and asked her to make it right." Jess draws a cushion toward her and hugs it to her chest. "Cora went up the mountain that night and did a working. I didn't think it had worked at first. You both carried on up to the wedding day, kept preparing. But Carrie seemed paler. Drawn. Like the life was trickling out of her, even as the town seemed so happy. I knew she was just doing it to make folks happy, to make them accept her. I wanted you both to see what was right in front of you, and had been all along, without the wedding. Woodsmoke, your home, the place you're meant to be.

"I don't know how, but I woke up before the wedding day, and it was like the world had shifted a quarter inch. You both seemed different that morning, free. Then it was your wedding day and I felt so sure it would all be fine, that she wasn't going anywhere. But then Carrie ran out of the church, the wedding was called off, and I couldn't find her afterward. Her mum told me she needed space, and I accepted it. Tricked myself into believing that she would just be gone for a few days, that it wasn't about the spell that I begged Cora to do, that it wasn't because of *me*. And you . . ." she says quietly, "you stayed. It wasn't meant to happen like that. You were both meant to stay. *Carrie* was meant to stay. When she didn't come back, it crept over me. The dread, the guilt over what I had done. I didn't mean for any of it to happen. But somehow, I made it so much worse."

The stunned silence rolls in like the fog between them, and for a moment Jess believes that all will be fine. Then Tom takes a breath.

And hurls lightning at her.

"How could you?" he rumbles, pinching the bridge of his nose. "Of all things, Jess, meddling in that stuff. You know it's dangerous. We both know hikers have gone missing. You don't mess with it, Jess! And Cora, of all the *people*—"

"It was desperation, stupid desperation. I couldn't bear for you both to leave—"

"But to go to Cora? That *witch*?" Tom laughs, without humor.

Getting to his feet, he paces across the narrow width of the lounge as Jess seems to shrink. "I thought we fell in love because we chose it, not because you drove off my ex with a spell. Did you go to Cora for us? Jess, tell me you didn't—"

"Of course not! Look, it's nothing, it's just whispered words and gossip. Magic isn't real. It can't be real, can it?" Jess spreads her hands out, attempting to defuse the situation, to salvage it. If she downplays Cora's involvement, if she pretends it hasn't haunted her, maybe they'll survive this.

"You never should have gone to her in the first place!" Tom shouts. Jess flinches. With her fingers tightening over the cushion, she stands and takes a step toward him. She swallows and glances up at the ceiling, thinking of Elodie, her precious baby, up there, waking, hearing this storm in their home . . . she shudders, pain dancing behind her eyes. She regrets what she did. The intensity of that regret sends her anxiety spiraling as she thinks over and over again about going to Cora and asking her to make sure Tom and Carrie didn't leave Woodsmoke together. She never meant for it all to happen the way it did—for Carrie to run from her own wedding, never to return. Jess never realized at the time the guilt she would feel, the unending, ceaseless *guilt*—

Her stomach tumbles, over and over, and she thinks she might . . . she might just—

"For God's sake, sit down. You're pregnant."

"You're . . . *yelling* . . . at me!"

"For good reason!" Tom shouts, but then he stops, scrubbing his hands over his face. He steadies his voice, like he's speaking to a child or a pet. "Sit down. Go through it again. I—I'm cross, Jess. I am. But not just at you. It's Cora, it always comes back to bloody Cora and the magic and the Morgans . . ."

"Tom—"

He raises his hands. "I'm sorry. I'm a shit and I'm sorry. I shouldn't have yelled. You don't—you don't deserve that." His face crumples, and she sees just how tired he is. How this winter has dragged him down, drowning him, pulling him back, when all they ever wanted was to move forward. He's right. She never should have gone to Cora all those years ago. Too many times in Woodsmoke people have gone to Cora and the outcome has sent ripples through them all. "Please sit down," he says. "Please."

She stands there for a beat before slinking toward the chair and sliding into it, her hands staying clamped on her belly. She rubs it in soothing circles, calming them both, as Tom takes the seat opposite. This feels like judgment day. She feels like she's thrown herself over a cliff, with only the slightest hope that the sea will allow her to plunge into the water and then resurface.

"Are you going to control your temper?"

"I will, I'm sorry. Just—just explain what happened. From the beginning. Please." His voice fades into desperation, his gaze fixed on her, as she stares down at the wood grain of the table. She follows the pattern of it, the eddying whirls, the black knot that looks like an eye. Jess swallows, clearing her throat and her thoughts.

"I went to Cora a month or so before you were meant to marry Carrie." She fidgets with the tassel on the end of her scarf. The storm of her migraine has dulled to a continuous growl. "When Carrie told me you were both planning on leaving Woodsmoke after the wedding and that you didn't intend to come back, I just . . . snapped. I was terrified of losing you both. I—I told Cora that it was all wrong and that you both couldn't leave. I wanted her to do something. Anything."

Tom frowns, creasing his face, but he doesn't say anything.

"Cora said . . . she said she would handle it. When I left, she was holding the book, and she had this look about her, this determined look. Can you remember when we snuck in and Carrie showed it to us? We must have been fifteen."

"I remember. You kept asking Carrie if we could leave. You didn't want to get too close to it, like you were afraid, or spooked by it."

"I was afraid for good reason," Jess says numbly. "We should *all* be afraid of that book. Of the old tales."

"Go on."

Jess breathes in through her nose and shrugs. "After Carrie left, I cried myself to sleep every night. I was heartbroken. I've never known pain like it, knowing that Carrie was gone and it was my fault. I thought you'd both stay, I never thought . . ."

"You cursed us. You—you meddled with my feelings, my emotions—"

"No, absolutely not," Jess says, her voice intense. "I would never, ever do that."

Tom is quiet for a moment, and Jess wonders if his memories are clicking into place in a new way, rearranging themselves to fit with this revelation. Is he remembering that morning when it seemed as though a hole had been rent in a gauzy panel, letting in the stark colors of the world, rushing in sharp as knives?

As Jess watches him, Tom remembers cringing away from the path laid before him. The plan with Carrie to move away and leave behind everything they had always known. He didn't want to leave, but he wanted Carrie, he was sure of it. He wanted to hold her hand in his, to make her happy. But he hadn't told her about the apprenticeship, about the deposit on the house . . . and it plagued him. He woke up one morning a month before the wedding and it was like he was seeing clearly, *feeling* clearly. When he saw Carrie later that day, sunlight no longer danced around her.

It danced around Jess.

He draws in a shaky breath, pushing his fists into his eyes. "After Carrie left, you and I kissed. That night at the bar, when I was playing in the band still. And it felt so right, being with you . . ."

"I'm sorry, Tom. Truly," Jess says, tears prickling her eyes. "But at the same time, I'm not at all. I love what we have here. I love what we've built together."

Tom slowly lowers his fists, placing them on the kitchen table and stands, pushing the chair back suddenly. "I have to end this, Jess. Once and for all. This all has to end."

Jess gulps, swiping at her tears, standing up to follow after him as he lunges for the door. "Tom, wait, please—"

"Not this time," Tom says sadly. "Not this time. It's my choice. My decision and my life. We're all too tangled up, and it's holding us back, isn't it? I have to fix this."

"How?"

"However I want to, Jess," he says. He turns to her, features regretful, drawn in lines of sorrow. "However I think is best."

Then he's gone.

Jess stands in the doorway, blood-hot panic coursing through her. She shivers as she clutches her belly and watches the car as it pulls down the road. Watching her first love, her only love, leave her.

"No, no, no . . ." she whimpers, pushing the door closed on the night. She hunkers down on the other side of it, tipping her head back as her migraine takes over, exploding like a bomb. All she can do is sit there, trapped in the tempest he has left her in.

Chapter 41
Carrie

When I hear the knock, my mind leaps to Matthieu. I trip over my own feet on the way to the door and throw out a hand to catch myself. My breath is uneven as I grip the handle, pulling it open, heart pounding in my ears—

"Oh," I say, deflating against the doorframe. "It's you."

"Can I come in?" Tom asks, face set in stone, just like the last time. I haven't seen him since that night he sat in my car, which feels like a lifetime ago now. Only a handful of months have passed, but everything is different. And somehow we have managed to avoid each other in this small, sleepy town.

I shrug, not bothering to show him false politeness—we're too far past that now—and move off into the cottage, beckoning with a hand. He shrugs off his coat, unlaces his boots, and then follows me to the kitchen. I sit on a barstool at the island, and he takes the other and drags it a few paces away. We eye each other, and I wonder what he'll hurl at me this time. What I've done to overstep some invisible line he's drawn around himself and Jess.

"There's no easy way of saying this," he begins, clearing his throat. He breaks eye contact, gazing toward the window, a dark maw opening onto the night. "But it has to be said."

I reach for the bottle of wine in front of me, tipping a couple more inches into a long-stemmed glass. I swirl it around, watching the ruby liquid stick to the sides like a rising tide. "Do you want some?"

"I'm driving."

"Sure." I pause, taking a tiny sip, and look over to find him staring at me. "Well, go on, then. Tell me."

"It's about Jess."

"Isn't it always?"

He curses under his breath, shifting in his seat. "Yes, Carrie. Yes, it's always about Jess . . . because it's always been about Jess. I love her. I love her so damn much, and all I do is hurt her, all the time—"

"And what do you think you're doing right now? Coming here?"

"Straightening things out." He wets his lips, a slight frown dimpling his forehead. "I'm sorry I asked you to leave a few months ago. I—I can't take that back, just like I can't expect you to vanish like smoke. I thought it would be the best thing for Jess. For . . . us. But it isn't. She misses you, and when you left, it was what she was most afraid of. She won't make the first move, Carrie. You have to."

I place the wineglass down carefully and push it away with the tips of my fingers. It slides across the surface of the kitchen island, and I allow his words to echo around us. When I speak, my voice comes out thicker than I intended. Rife with a decade, a lifetime, of emotions. "I've been back for months. Why tonight?"

"Jess is pregnant."

I still a hiss on my tongue, eyes snapping to his. "And she's all right?"

"She's fine." He sighs. "Baby's fine. It's me. I—I didn't handle things right at all."

I take a deep breath. "What do you want, Tom?"

"Can you . . . speak to her?" he asks, opening his arms wide. "See a way of patching things up? Find some common ground, be civil with each other. Something. You're both too big a presence in Woodsmoke to exist apart. There's too much history. This will keep simmering away, and it's already a weight on her, it's already affecting her. If you're staying, then at some point you'll bump into each other. You have to fix—"

"Does she want that? Did she send you?"

"No, no, she didn't—"

I laugh, reaching again for my wineglass. I bury my hurt in a quick sip, letting the taste linger on my tongue before swallowing. If Jess had wanted to see me, if she had wanted this . . . but no. This is about Tom wanting his life to go smoothly. His stumbling way of making his wife happy. "Time to go, Tom."

He swears again, dropping his gaze to the floor. He keeps it pinned there for a moment, and I can feel the desperation seeping from him. "I don't want to lose her. I don't want to lose what we have, Carrie. And I realize now that I shouldn't have told you that you shouldn't have come back. This is your home too, Woodsmoke is yours as much as ours. I see that now."

A part of me thaws, just a little. "Go on."

"I think Jess has been looking over her shoulder this whole time, hoping to see you, missing you. I don't know. I can see how that would cut a person up, make them miserable. And what if you did come back looking to stir things up? Maybe that's what she's afraid of."

In a way, he's right. Maybe Jess was right to be afraid, maybe there was a part of me that wanted this town to implode with my homecoming. I always felt like I was out of step, like Woodsmoke didn't accept me. But as soon as I got engaged, when I agreed to wear that pretty white dress, suddenly I was the golden girl. Suddenly I was valued. But I couldn't fit into a version of myself that wasn't real. And the bitterness of feeling that I couldn't just belong as *me*, that I had to be what folk *wanted* me to be, lasted for years and years.

But I don't feel like that anymore. Not after this winter. It's as though the frost has cooled the bile inside me, allowing this homecoming to be more healing than I ever imagined it could be. I think of Matthieu, of the shop in town that could become something else. I think about the spring and how the mountains are changing. And about how I've changed since I returned, how I've begun to feel like this is home. Like I've found it. Like I belong somewhere and with someone. "I'll talk to her," I say quietly. "Not tonight, but I will. You have my word."

He blows out a breath, and I swear his edges sharpen. He sits up straighter, regaining some of the old Tom. The apple thief. The boy who hopped the wall of the Morgan garden on a dare, even though the town whispered of curses and witches. Who played bass in a band, swaggering around town like he would conquer the world one day. "Thank you."

"You should probably go home. She'll—Jess will be worried."

He hesitates, his eyes flicking up to meet mine. There are still shadows there, ghosts that have not been dispelled. I brace myself. "There's one more thing. You have to know . . . it's about Cora." Our eyes meet, and I nod slowly. "Jess went to her before the wedding, and Cora said she'd take care of it. Of us. And that was when I saw Jess properly; it was like a gauze had been ripped away. I didn't want to leave Woodsmoke, like we planned anyway, and after that day, I was even more sure about that. And then you ran on our wedding day . . . and I don't know. I guess Jess has been in torment ever since. She told me tonight. And I don't know how much of it I believe, but deep down I've always loved Jess. I know this is important for her that you know what she did, so that she can let go of the guilt . . ."

My breath catches and I swallow. Jess went to Cora. She went to Cora knowing full well what that would mean, after seeing glimpses of the magic herself throughout our childhood . . . she went to my great-aunt and asked for her help. I take a sip of wine and feel it burn all the way down my throat. Cora, with her bony, pinching fingers. Cora, with her intense, strangling love . . .

"Of course," I say quietly. "It always comes back to her. Always."

"I'm sorry, I just thought you should know the whole truth, Jess is in bits—"

"It's okay." I run my hand over my forehead. "Please tell her it's okay, and I'll come over there and see her soon."

Tom nods, saying nothing, and begins to slide off the barstool. "I know we can't . . . it's impossible to make it right between us. But Carrie, you were my friend too. I shouldn't have implied you shouldn't stay when you got back. I'm sorry."

I breathe through my nose and fix on a smile for him. "Honestly, put it out of your mind. It all makes sense now. More than you know." I frown down at my wineglass. Piecing together the weeks leading up to the wedding, piecing everything together. "Cora warned me about Matthieu, how he could disappear, and now he's missing. I can't help thinking . . . I . . ."

"Who's Matthieu?"

"A friend." I smile, feeling the ghost of a kiss, the touch of his hand. "More than a friend. Cora told me he wasn't real, and that he would disappear as the frost thaws, and I haven't seen him since yesterday. Haven't heard from him. Maybe it sounds unbelievable—"

"Since the frost thawed . . ." Tom says softly.

I nod and sniff. "Exactly."

Tom rubs a hand over the back of his neck. "Look, we both know Woodsmoke and the mountains are . . . an unusual place."

"To put it mildly."

"And I know Cora meddles in people's lives when she shouldn't. But real people don't just . . . disappear like they're a spirit in the old tales. They don't." He bites his lip. "Where does he live?"

"He's got a cabin up in the mountains. You remember that one we found when we were kids? Past the lookout, up in that clearing?"

"I remember. The Vickers place," Tom says, a faint smile whispering over his features. "Have you gone up there?"

"Not yet. I didn't want to hassle him. He might just need time or space—"

"Has he done this before?"

"No—" But I stop, suddenly remembering the last time the frost thawed, that day I went to the cabin to find him. How the place was deserted, how I felt eyes pressing into me . . . "Actually, yes. He's done this before."

Tom nods. "All right. Well, there's not a lot you can do tonight. If this is a pattern, Carrie, I've got to say—"

"It was the last time the frost thawed." I frown, blinking back sudden tears. "Tom, what if Cora's right? What if he is . . . a curse? What if the mountains have cursed me for leaving and Matthieu isn't . . . real?"

Tom stands staring up at the ceiling for a minute, as though gathering his words. Both of us have seen what Cora is capable of. And neither of us fully grasps why there are things we can't explain—in our own lives, in the stories, in the snatches of fable woven into the fabric of Woodsmoke. The warnings we were given as children to not stray from the mountain paths, to always greet the mountains when we return, to never trust our eyes and ears . . . and to never fall in love if we know it's a love that could be cursed.

"There's a chance of that," he finally says. "But . . . there's also a chance she's wrong."

I stand as well, crossing my arms over my chest. The cold has crept in, stealing into my heart, and all I can think about is Matthieu. "I'll go up there. Tomorrow. I'll go to the cabin."

"Carrie, I know you know the mountains, but . . ." Tom stares at the dark window. The one facing the mountains. All those old warnings, those old tales, are in his mind too, swirling behind his eyes. It's a shared understanding we all have here. Finally, he looks at me. "The snow will have thawed, ground will be slippery. Don't . . . don't leave the path. If you hear a voice, or a cry, don't follow it. Be careful."

I LEAVE AT dawn.

This time I pack a rucksack with more than just a day's worth of food. I pack medicine, bandages, and a torch. And as I pack, I tell myself it's unnecessary. He'll be there, in the cabin, probably absorbed in another project. Or he's taken on work at another site, or he's just ill, as I thought last time. I can't believe Cora's tales. I can't believe in my legacy, the old stories threaded through the mountains. I can't believe in any of that and still know that he is real. He's a new beginning. A fresh start. He's the first man I've truly cared for since Tom, and I'm not ready to give that up.

As I climb, my breath hangs in uneasy clouds, materializing like little ghosts before disappearing in my wake. I climb steadily, walking with the rhythm of the thoughts driving me forward. I picture him, his hand holding mine, the night under the stars, the scrape of ice under our skates on the frozen lake. I picture all of this and never falter, never flag. And as the sun climbs the ladder of the sky, casting the mountain in an eerie glow, I reach the clearing and the cabin.

The quiet is deafening. As it did the last time I was here, unease steals over me. I step forward, and the mountains ruffle and sigh. I can almost imagine them breathing my name, whether in warning or as a greeting, I'm not sure. All I know is that the mountains are on edge. That I'm standing on the threshold of something I do not fully understand.

"Matthieu?" I say softly, my gaze tracking right and left as I cross the clearing. Unseen eyes, pressing, burning into my spine, send shivers skittering over the back of my neck, and I have to force myself to walk evenly. To breathe evenly. It's instinct. It's that gut feeling you can't easily explain. It's that needling, that insistent finger tap of fear or excitement or panic that tells you what you should do.

Mine is telling me that something is very wrong.

I knock first, listening for any sound, any sign at all that he is here. When there's no response, I close my fingers over the door handle and shake it, leaning my forearm against the old wood to shove the door in. "Come on, bloody thing."

Heat prickles along my hairline, but when I snap my gaze back to the clearing, there's no one there. All is silent. Watchful. The mountains are waiting for something . . . but I don't know what.

With a groan, the door gives, and I fall inside, my boots clattering on the floorboards. I quickly right myself and push the door closed. My whole body is heaving, my lungs tight with the need for air, and I breath wide and deep, flooding them with oxygen. The feeling of unseen eyes fades, leaving only the imprint behind. The mountains are far too watchful today. As though waiting to see what I discover.

I turn to the room, looking first to the kitchen, then the lounge, then the door left ajar that I know leads to the bedroom. I swallow, wetting my dry throat. "Matthieu? Are you here?"

Silence.

It's dense as fog, and I'm wary of walking to the bedroom, of what I will find there. I cross to the door in only a few steps, though it feels like a mile, an endless stretch of floorboards to the other side of the room. I steel myself, then push the door open wider. All I find is a well-made bed and a stack of well-thumbed paperbacks with cracked, weary spines. The window is slightly open, and damp air is whirling in with the scents of pine and loam. I breathe out a sigh, releasing the tension in my shoulders, and walk to the window. I pull it closed, fastening the handle, and stare out at the tightly packed trees. Shadows form between them, taking the shapes of men, of monsters, of the things in the old tales that are always hungry, forever restless.

"Where are you?" I ask the silent room. "Where have you gone?"

The cabin is more homely than it was the last time I was here. As though warmth and life have suffused the space, flooding the corners, softening its jagged edges. I brush my fingertips along the stack of paperbacks at his bedside. All nature and history books, they're creased and have frayed covers, as though handled many times. There are no photographs displayed on the chest of drawers, only a comb. A half-used bottle of shampoo. No indication of what he was before I met him. *Who* he was.

I know who he is now after working alongside him this winter, sharing everyday moments and stories from my past. Someone whose mouth and hands and skin I am discovering, whose soul is slowly cleaving to mine. With his absence now, with this fear that he is not quite real, I'm afraid he may be the person I've been unconsciously searching for—a soul that matches my own.

In this room, I see pieces of Matthieu now. In the woven blanket tucked over his bed, in the clothes in the dresser. I smell the scent of his skin lingering on the pillows. I pick up little clues of who he is to me, and yet nothing here tells me of his history. No breadcrumb trail planted in my memories runs through here, telling me where he could have gone.

I move back into the lounge and eye the map taking up the far wall. It takes me a moment to register that it's different now. The crisscrossed lines have grown frantic, and the map is now covered, practically coated, in handwritten notes. I step forward and time slows around me, dripping like honey. He's searching for something. Searching across the length and breadth of the mountains, each careful handwritten note a question, an answer, a date—

My head swims and the ground tilts under me. There's a note stuck to the left edge of the map, where there's no place mark on the map itself. It has yesterday's date on it—and an answer.

The last trail we were going to explore together.

This must be it.

He's still searching for clues about Henri's disappearance.

I breathe out, tremors shivering to my fingertips as I pull the note off and examine the place it was tacked to. My eyes trace the lines, back and forth, feathering out from the cabin like veins.

Matthieu isn't fine. He isn't safe, and he isn't well. If this note was made yesterday, if he set out early and never returned—

He's missing.

If what I believe is true, he's somewhere in the mountains. And no one has seen him in two days. And . . . he's real. Very real. Not some tale conjured from the frost and the mountains, not some phantom or spirit that disappears with the spring.

This is real.

Stars explode, clouding my vision, and I sink to the floor. I clutch the note in my fist, trying to steady my breathing, even as the panic, the absolute terror, sets in . . .

"Breathe. Just breathe," I say to myself, as though it can somehow slow my racing pulse, the quickening of my fear. I fumble for my phone and curse the lack of signal as I register the time. It's just past ten in the morning. The last time I saw Matthieu was yesterday morning, my mouth still swollen with his kisses as I left to meet Cora at the shop in town.

I assumed . . . I thought . . . I swallow, closing my eyes. I was the last person to see him or hear from him, and now he's been missing for nearly thirty hours. Knowing these mountains, knowing the number of people who have gone missing, never to be found again . . .

"Oh God," I say into the strangled silence. "Matthieu, where have you gone?"

Chapter 42
Cora

Howard has taken Kep for a walk. Cora offered to go with him, to tread the fields at his side, but he huffed in that impatient way that means he needs space. Time. A lungful of new spring air not perfumed by her words. So she washes up the breakfast things, muttering to herself, taking her time over the caked-on egg yolk on their plates. She's fastidious, always has been, scrubbing at her life until it's pink and shiny and just so.

She never really felt the absence of a baby in her life until Carrie. Never wondered too much what that weight would feel like in her arms. Most of her friends were enthusiastically filling their arms and their lives with children, their worlds revolving around playdates and new bikes and family camping trips. Cora never quite understood it, never felt that internal tug from some cord draped around her heart. She knew Howard wanted a big family—a loud, shouty, messy family—to help on the farm and to surround himself with. But as every month passed and it still didn't happen, she would try not to dwell on it for too long. After Carrie, though, all that changed.

But by then it was too late.

"You're a silly old woman. A silly, *silly* old woman," she berates herself now, the teaspoons, covered in soap suds, clattering on the drainboard. She can usually pull herself out of this spiral, raise her chin, and get on with things. But this morning . . . not this morning.

She stares out at the chickens, now gone back to their lazy clucking, and feels a pang of something. Is it remorse, or shame, about those chickens? But she can't put her finger on it. She's lost again, lost in a labyrinth of yesterdays, feeling her way through dimly lit tunnels, clutching a spool of unwinding thread.

She's searching for the moments with Carrie, the times that light up her memories like flares. The first time Carrie chose her instead of Ivy to bandage a skinned knee. The times Carrie cycled over on the weekends and Cora would feed her apple pie and custard, lend her books, show her the latest sepia photograph find, or a trinket from a car boot sale. Anything to lure her back, her magpie findings for a girl who loved glitter. She would tell Carrie the old tales, giving her a glimpse of the book, turning a blind eye whenever she and Jess leafed through the pages. She wondered if this was what it would have been like, to have her own daughter. If this was what she gave up to have the book all to herself. She would do anything on those days to keep her grandniece lingering, to keep Carrie near her, if only for a few minutes more.

Cora is so lost in days gone by, in all those memories of Carrie, that she doesn't hear it at first. There's a scratching, yipping sound coming from the front door. She blinks, vaguely aware of a bark, of more scratching, and she dries her hands, muttering as she walks to the door. She pictures Jess, her nails and her wide, pleading eyes. She mutters again as she fumbles with the door handle, readying herself for an onslaught of desperation from Jess or someone else from Woodsmoke. But when she pulls the door open, letting in a gust of sharp air, it's not Jess at all, or anyone else.

"Kep?" she says, confusion pooling in her gut. She leans down to scratch the dog's head, feeling the silky warmth of her fur. "But you're with Howard, you're not meant to be here . . . you're not . . ."

Cora feels the first stirrings of alarm as Kep stares at her, eyes doleful and brimming. Cold creeps over her, as though the frost has returned.

"You're not supposed to be here."

Cora turns, finds her jacket, and stuffs her mobile phone in her pocket.

"Come along, then," she says to Kep in false, bright tones as Howard's dog yips, checking that she's following. Cora makes her way on stiffened joints into the fields, the mud sucking at her boots as she stumbles after Kep. Twice she has to stop to gulp down air as fire burns in her chest, unease builds in her belly, and sharp twangs knot in her joints. Kep circles back each time, waits for her, waits as she stifles a gasp of pain, then continues to hobble after the dog.

It's his back she sees first. He's lying on his side in the grass, like a lump of abandoned sacking. She's never liked that coat of his, how it blends into the landscape, how shabby and unkempt it appears. She's had to stitch up tiny tears in the lining, patch up a hole that appeared on the left elbow. But Howard still wears it, still reaches for it, just as he did this morning. Kep races ahead, tail brushing to and fro, barking at the lump of him, nuzzling his still form.

"Howard?" she croaks, dread whipping up inside her, closing the space between them, ten paces, five, two—

She topples over to her knees, joints barking as she slams her palms on the ground. The soft mud and grass give beneath her, and she breathes heavily, trying to turn him from his side.

"Howard, you old fool, give over, *turn*, damn it," she mutters at him, dragging his body over so his face is raised to the clouds. She drops her cheek to his chest, finds a fast rise and fall, like a rabbit caught in a snare. "Oh, Howard."

He blinks, looking at her, as though trying to fix his gaze on her face. He's sweating, and his breath is a stale muddle of toast and copper. Blood, she realizes. "Cora. Why are you here? I don't know . . . I don't know what happened . . ."

She drags the mobile phone from her pocket, squinting at the screen. It takes a few stabs of her index finger, but finally the phone slowly churns to life and the screen lights up. "I told you not to go too far. What did I tell you? You're a fool, a damn fool," she says, her voice filled with breathy tremors. She finds Carrie's number in the address book, presses it firmly, waits for the tinny dial tone . . .

It rings out once, twice, while Cora holds her breath, holds everything inside herself, focused only on Carrie, on her hope—

"Damn thing. Damn bloody thing!" she says, wet tears threatening to rise up from her throat, from her chest. She sniffs, looking down at him, this man she's traveled through the years with, this man who was always her sensible choice. She does love him. She knows that now. Maybe not in that fiery way shown in films and novels, but she truly does. "Howard, I don't know what to do. Tell me what to do."

Her fingers are moving to another name, another number, before the thought is fully formed in her mind.

"Woodsmoke library. How can I help?"

"Jess. Jess, it's Cora."

"C—Cora?" There's a static buzz, a brief whistle down the line. "Is everything okay?"

Cora looks down at Howard, fumbles for what to say. "The mountains . . . they always want something. I'm afraid, I'm afraid that maybe I asked too much over the years—"

"Cora, where are you?"

"With Howard," she says, patting his cheek. "He needs help this time. We need help."

"Stay where you are. Are you at home?"

"No, I followed Kep into the fields. He was just out for a walk, silly sod . . . just out walking."

"Stay where you are, don't try to move him. I'm going to hang

bothered. She wants to turn up just as she is. Seething and imperious, her tongue sharpened and ready.

Cora hops the stile, mud spattering her legs when she lands on the other side, and heads for the yard at the back of the farmhouse. Howard, his back to her as she approaches, is feeding the chickens, talking to them, encouraging them. She stops for a moment to watch him as he bends to scatter more feed, emptying the bucket out as the chickens scratch and squark. He's wearing what looks like a brown jacket. She hasn't seen it before. Then he turns toward her, eyes squinting against the sunlight, and his constant smile turns into a full grin.

Her mouth puckers in response, and his shoulders lift in a lazy shrug as he ambles over to her. "What can I do for you today, Miss Morgan?"

"It's Cora," she says, drawing herself up to her full height. "And you know full well, Howard Price. You know full well what you've got of ours. Where have you hidden her? Hmm?"

"Is this about that pig of yours?"

Cora stifles a snort. "Would I be over here every blessed week if it was about anything else?"

"Would you like some lemonade? Mother made it this morning. It's got a lovely tang—"

"The pig, if you would!"

Howard chuckles quietly as he moves to the gate, then closes it carefully behind him. "Right you are, Coraline."

She trails after him as he walks past the farmhouse, over to another path set between the fields. He takes her through another gate, then points at a field that's been dug and scattered with straw, which looks like it's been wallowed in. In the middle is the pig house, several of their snouts nudging out before they race toward the gate. Howard leans against it, forearms resting on the top. "You have to go in there and get it. Don't fancy the state of that dress afterward, though."

Cora splutters, eyeing the pigs, then him. "You what?"

"Unless you want me to go in there and fetch it. Save your pretty dress?" He eyes her, a glint in his eye she hasn't noticed before. A glint that says he's playing with her. Her composure slips into fury.

"Howard Price, you fetch that damn pig, and you stop putting it in there with your others when it strays. You're doing this on purpose, you—"

"A date."

"What?"

"That's the price." He shrugs. "If you want me to go in there and get your pig, and no doubt drop it back at your place, I want you to come on a date with me, Coraline Morgan."

She splutters again, saying nothing, eyeing the pig, then him. She understands the glint in his eye now. She's turned down half a dozen boys with that same look. But Howard Price . . . She swallows. Maybe he's different. She could see that, even in school. She crosses her arms, fixing him with a glare.

"A date of my choosing."

"All right."

"And only one, mind."

"Yes."

"Absolutely no taking any liberties. I'm not going to the pictures with you if *that's* what you're planning."

He holds up his hands, that grin lighting up his face again. "I swear it."

She looks at the pigs, all nosing up to the gate. Then she looks back at him. "I haven't been to that fancy restaurant in town. And I do have other nice dresses."

"I'll make a reservation."

"No catch? No . . . nothing?"

"Just a date, Cora," he says, already climbing the gate to get Cora's pig. "Just one date, that's all I'll need."

Chapter 44
Carrie

No one else had met him. No one had heard of this trapper. And Sylba, to the end of her days, searched for the man who arrived with the frost and stole her heart.

—Tabitha Morgan, July 19, 1929

I take a photo of the map, make a few feverish notes. I try again, fruitlessly, to call someone, anyone. In a frenzy, I search for a landline, for a handset that will connect. But there's no phone to be found. I cast a look at the trees waiting outside, at the mountains holding their breath.

I know what I have to do.

I've known it would come to this ever since I pulled up to Ivy's cottage in the autumn. The mountains, the looming, ever-present mountains, have wanted me to return to them, to walk the old ways under silent trees. I've resisted, not wanting to stray too far, especially not alone. But now they have the perfect lure—Matthieu stuck on the end of their hook. I wonder if this is the price of leaving this place all those years ago. If this is somehow my penance for not turning back and coming home. By rejecting Woodsmoke, I was also rejecting my legacy as the next Morgan woman to inherit the book and all its strange, wild magic. I wonder if I *am* cursed, as Cora believes. If so, I have no idea how to break it.

Shouldering my rucksack, I cast one last glance around the

cabin. I move to the kitchen, scribble a few words on the back of an envelope, and place it by the sink. Then I leave the way I came in, closing the door softly behind me. When I face the trees, the paths snaking away beneath their branches, I choose the one that calls to me. The one I believe Matthieu has taken if his final note on the map can be believed.

I keep my phone in my hand, monitoring the screen, hoping for just one solitary bar of signal. I could go back to Woodsmoke, but what would I say? I don't know if he's definitely lost out here. Would I be convincing enough to rally the town into a search? Perhaps they wouldn't even consider him a missing person. With a jolt, I realize that they might not believe he exists at all. We've all heard the stories, so doesn't this fit the pattern? I push the first branch from my face, the scent of evergreen and spring hitting the back of my throat. I doubt that anyone will listen to me or be inclined to help search for a man who may or may not be entirely real.

The sun climbs quickly, as though racing me to nightfall. I begin at a measured pace, stopping only so often to eat and drink some water. I know a lot of these trails, having explored great swaths of them, and as I walk the map opens up in my head. I call out his name every so often, checking for any sign that he's brushed through, or that he might have slipped and fallen from the path. Later, as the sun wanes, drifting lower, I try to pick up my pace. But pausing to look for signs slows me down, and I'm horribly aware that time is against me. Still, finding the occasional mark—a pushed-back branch, a fresh boot print that hasn't been washed away by the rain or the winter—spurs me on, making me hopeful that I've chosen the right way.

By late afternoon, my thighs are aching and I keep having to pull down the straps of my rucksack to give my shoulders some relief. I've drunk nearly all the water and have only a few snacks left. And yet the occasional boot print or other sign—such as a discarded chocolate wrapper, recently crumpled and accidentally dropped—tells me that I'm still going the right way.

"You have to be close," I say, eyeing the dense trees, the slice of path cutting a jagged line through them. "You *have* to be."

As the shadows lengthen, creating monsters at the edge of my vision, I pause to pull my head torch from the rucksack. I could sit down right here on the bed of pine needles beneath a tree, tip my head back against its trunk, close my eyes, and allow my bones to rest. After walking all day, I want that—need that. Every part of me is laced with tremors, cold and then hot with a pulsing ache. I'm reaching the furthest stretches of the map in my head. Beyond this point, I don't know the terrain, and that terrifies me.

But I can't stop. I've come too far. It's just me here now. Me and the endless mountains. With every shaking step, this feels more and more like a test.

Memories surface as though from an inky lake as I stumble on, more slowly now, much more slowly. Memories of Tom and Jess when we were younger and would explore these mountains with wonder. Of myself in that wedding dress—too pale, too skinny, with my collarbone jutting out—as my mother told me I didn't have to go through with it. Of how I ripped all those bobby pins out of my hair, discarding them at Cora's, and how she helped me remove the veil. How my heart was broken, and had been since I knew I wanted to leave and Tom didn't really want to go with me. How it was like tearing a veil away from my own eyes, my own sight, that day. And how I've felt the press and pull of Woodsmoke ever since, however far I've run, telling me to come home.

And then I remember that night in the car sitting next to Tom, his features all distorted and wrong, telling me to leave. And Jess coming to the cottage, angry, upset, both of us knowing it was never meant to be that way between us.

Then comes a memory of Howard, like a pillar, like an ancient, weathered tree, telling me I should stay and should never have left for so long. All of them, Tom, Jess, Howard, believing I didn't handle any of it right—not my departure, and not my return.

I struggle on as night grows thick and deep, too dark for my eyes to see beyond the feeble pool of light the head torch kicks out. I wonder if I'm losing my mind a bit. If the mountains have somehow beguiled me, worked their way into my thoughts until I've lost all sense of reason. For a moment, I'm sure I hear a human cry of pain and I freeze, blood pounding in my ears, before I continue on, shaking.

This search is no longer just about finding Matthieu. It's about me, and about Woodsmoke. With every step I'm pitted against all of them, all the voices telling me I should leave. Or that I should have stayed. Some telling me that I don't belong here in the place where I was born, in the mountains and loam and trees I grew from. Others tell me that, with the Morgan blood running in my veins, I'm so entwined with this place that I have a duty to stay. To carry the book after Cora, to stay and keep the old ways alive. With every step I hear each voice, each opinion, and search for clarity.

The loudest and most treacherous of all these voices, the one dragging me back, pushing me into that cage of a person I escaped—the person wearing the wedding dress with the froth of tulle and lace—is my own. With every footstep I am battling against myself. Against the fears that have plagued me, hounded me, and followed me. I am fighting to find my roots, to plunge them back into the earth in this place and tell the mountains: *I'm not done.*

I'm not going anywhere. This is my home too, and these past few months have been my homecoming. It's taken me a winter to realize that this is where I belong. I'm not afraid of Woodsmoke anymore. I can face the town and stake my claim. I can face the mountains, even as they try to loosen the grip I have on my own sanity. I can face what becomes of the people in the old tales and come out on the other side, stronger.

The fire grows inside me, scorching my veins, reminding me that my heart still beats, that even as this place took everything, *everything*, ten years ago and left me with this cold, quiet nothing that I've been dragging around for years, this lack of home, this lack of belonging, I won't give in.

"You want my bones as well? Is that it? You want another missing hiker in this place?" I rasp, laughing. Then I pause again. Another human wail is piercing the dark night around me. Fear sparks in my veins, but I bunch my hands into fists. I lift my chin and force my feet to continue, one in front of the other. "Not enough for you to have Cora, not enough to have her fanatical soul, and all the souls of the Morgan women before her. You have to have *me* as well." I sniff, stopping to brace my hands on my thighs. My lungs are aflame, my entire body shaking, and yet still it's not enough. Not enough for my hometown, for these ancient, blood-soaked mountains. I realize now that there was no welcome here back in the autumn.

Only a final test.

Only a curse.

"Where is he?" I breathe. "You can't keep him. He's not yours to keep, just as I never was. It was my choice to leave, and my choice to return." Then louder, firmer, I scrape together my strength and bellow, "*Matthieu! Where are you?*"

My voice is a roar, a battle cry, defying the might of the mountains as it echoes through the night. I stretch up, standing tall, and peer into the darkness. "Where are you?" I yell again, voice cracking. "*Where are you?*"

I have been stripped bare, every piece of me, the armor, the years, all of it shed like a second skin. All I am is a pile of ragged thoughts wandering the vastness of the mountains. To find the man I love, to find myself. To gather up what is left of us and show the mountains they can't have the remaining pieces. I've paid the price, over and over. I've wandered the world with that hollow in the center of my chest. I've searched everywhere for a place to feel rooted, to belong. Woodsmoke is that place. And these mountains will not break me.

They *will* yield.

An owl hoots, low and long, and I hear prey scurrying in the thicket. I lay aside my tumble of muddied thoughts and attune myself to the outer world. Pinpricks of stars pierce the roof of the world, gleaming and shimmering. Slowly, as though a cloud has shifted, more stars appear, strewn like silver paint flecks over the dark sky. Even in my exhaustion, I smile up at them, picturing that night with Matthieu.

"Are you watching them too?" I ask Matthieu. "Are you somewhere seeing what I see?"

My phone chugs toward the last of its battery power, and I realize I am truly cast off from the world. I've cut myself loose, cut away every net and anchor. I've wandered far beyond the paths I've trodden before, into a wilderness of overgrown trapper trails. With the last trickle of power on my phone, I scrutinize the picture of the map I took in Matthieu's cabin and have a chilling realization.

The only way out of these mountains is through.

The hour circles toward midnight, the witching hour. I try not to dwell on all the tales in the book, the ones of people vanishing on these mountains. Of women coming back after searching for someone lost and never being quite right afterward. I pause to rest for a moment, turning off my head torch so it's only me and the stars.

Then I hear it.

A low panting, a groan. More animal than human. Stripped down, as bare as I am, all the human veneer scraped away and taken by the mountains.

"Matthieu?" I say, hope beating in my chest. "Matthieu?"

I hold myself still, listening beyond the drum of my own heart.

Then—

"Carrie?"

I gasp, hands flying to my mouth as I stumble around, my gaze raking over everything.

"Carrie, is that you?"

"I—I'm here! Matthieu, I'm here!" I say, tears blurring my words as they thicken in my chest. I fumble for the head torch, switching it on with twitching fingers. "Keep talking, describe what you see, I'm coming."

Matthieu groans again but begins talking, finding the words for the dark surrounding him, trapping him. I scramble down and, finding a ledge too high to jump, lower myself slowly, easing around the edges—

"Matthieu!" I cry out as I find the shape of him. He's below the high ledge, like he's fallen off it, and is sitting in the crook of an exposed tree root. He laughs, panting, as his face tilts toward mine. I'm weeping, shaking with the sheer relief of it being over, this all being over, I've found him, *I've found him*—

Then I see it. His leg, all bent and full of angles. The dark sweep of something too similar to blood—

"Carrie, my love, I can't move."

Chapter 45
Jess

"Tom, I need you to meet me at the hospital. I need—I need you."

"What's wrong? Is it—is it the baby?"

"I'm fine. It's not me . . . it's Cora Morgan's husband . . . Howard. He's had a heart attack. Mum's picking up Elodie from school."

"Okay. I'll meet you there."

"Cora's babbling, and I don't know if I can handle her solo. She keeps saying . . . Christ, this is hard. I don't know what to make of it. She thinks Carrie's missing. She keeps saying she'll follow him to the mountains and never return. Tom, tell me, did she say anything to you last night about someone she's met?"

"Yes, she did, but . . ."

"What? Tom, what did she say?"

"She said something about someone called Matthieu. She was worried about him, wanted to find him. He lives in the mountains, in a cabin—"

"Oh shit."

"Has anyone heard from her today?"

"I don't know. I honestly don't know."

Chapter 46
Carrie

"I don't think I can make it back down."

I fall to my knees at his side, sweeping my eyes critically over his body, his chalk-white features. He's alive. I've found him and he's alive. Relief rushes through me, heady and brimming. If he's alive, I can keep him alive, I can get help, I can—

"My leg, Carrie. I can't walk. I—I think I passed out, I don't know. It's not cold anymore."

A chill runs through me. I blink slowly, ransacking my mind, trying to remember anything I might have picked up in all my years. Anything about fractures, about blood loss. Anything about exposure and survival.

"Drink this," I say quietly, passing him my water bottle with the trickle of water left in it. His features pinch as he moves his arms, the slightest shift of his weight sending pain reverberating through his whole body. I assess him quickly, taking in the shard of bone, the blood, the ledge above us he must have slipped from. "How long have you been out here?"

He closes his eyes briefly after draining the last of the water. "I think this is the second night. It's been dark before, I'm sure."

I nod, not trusting myself to speak. He's been out here too long, utterly alone. "Did you bring any water with you, any food?"

He shakes his head. No water, no food all this time, and the blood loss as well as the shock . . . I swallow, trying to hide my fear, trying to remain calm.

"I have to get you help. We have to get you to a hospital—"

His laugh is a husky shadow. "It's too late for that, I think. It's—it's a miracle you're here." He lifts his hand to my face, runs his palm over my cheek. His fingertips scrape against my skin, leaving a trail behind that's limned with a bright flame. "I can't believe you're real."

"I'm right here, and I'm real. And so are you." I release a shuddering breath, then hunker down next to him, aligning my body with his. I can't take my eyes from his face, his bent frame as I constantly assess the shifts in him, the changes and all they could mean. I wish I had come better prepared. I wish I had told someone where I was going. If I leave him here now, will I be able to find my way back? Will I be able to get help in time? "Please don't give up, not yet. Not now."

"It's warm now at least. You'll be warm enough," he says slowly, his voice thick as treacle. Fresh fear courses through me. It's not warm. It's not warm at all. At night on the mountains the temperature drops to near freezing, and my exposed skin is coated in a nettling cold.

I try to keep him awake, try to keep him talking. I can't share any more body heat with him without the risk of jostling his broken bones, and I don't know if there's further damage from his fall. What if he's bleeding internally?

"Tell me more about the trails, Matthieu. Have you come this way before?"

"Once, just once. With Henri."

"Your brother."

"He was here . . . I'm sure of it."

"You left a note on the map. You've been searching for him? All this winter?"

He swallows painfully. "I hoped with the stories of magic, I hoped I would somehow find him. How foolish. What a desperate fool I've been. These mountains . . . they do not give back those who are lost."

Before I can answer, the wind whips up, and the trees moan as they shift overhead. Sharp cold hits my face, and I catch Matthieu's flinch in the dark. His words are so eerily similar to Cora's warnings that I wonder if now we are lost too. We are the lost ones this time, and I know how that tale ends.

He drifts in and out, talking about the creatures of the mountains, the cabin. Me. When he begins to talk about me as though I am not here, I pass a hand over his forehead and feel the scorch of fever. After a while, I'm not sure if he knows I'm here beside him at all. He screams at one point, flinching away from something that's not there. I try to tell him it's okay. I try to calm him; I even sing, digging a French lullaby from the edges of my mind that perhaps was sung to him as a child. Anything to keep him still, to stop that blood from flowing afresh from his leg.

Anything to anchor him to this world.

When he finally falls into a fitful slumber, his head against my shoulder, I cry quietly. My tears are tiny flashes of heat stinging my skin before I wipe at them with shaking fingers. I begin to talk then. To the mountains. I know what I have to ask for.

Somehow I've always known it would end this way. The mountains demand bargains. They require beating hearts and blood. They've been the subject of too many stories to ignore. There are too many unexplained things that could be magic, that could be *something*, and maybe I should have paid better attention. Maybe I should have had a bit more fear.

I know what I might need to offer in return.

Cora let me see enough of the book over the years that I came to know how bargains work. The magic of this place requires—is thirsty for—balance. It seeks life. And only a Morgan woman can give the place what it requires.

"How much blood is soaked into this place? How much have you taken over the centuries?" I croak, searching my rucksack for the pocketknife I carry. Opening the blade, I see that the edge is only a shade sharper than dull and useless. I hesitate, readying myself for the next part. Jess and I whispered it to each other as children, glancing up from huddled groups on the playground to eye their looming presence. We'd cast what we believed to be spells, and sometimes I'd wondered if they worked. Cora made potions with us, scattered salt and lavender to create wardings, but these were lesser things, fripperies and fancies, in comparison to the real bargains. I know what they truly require in moments like these. What the Morgan women have sacrificed before me. Every bargain steals something from you and is always sealed with a drop of blood.

"You know what I ask for. For his life, for his heart. And for my own heart not to break." I stifle a gasp as I slice down the edge of my palm, just below where my thumb connects with my hand, parallel to the scar from the cut that Jess and I made many years ago, in a pale imitation of this act. The blood pools, warm and rich, and I let it drip on the ground, into the shaft of silver moonlight, just as I know it says to do in the book. "Take this, and take whatever else you want. But do not take him. Please, *please*, don't take him from me. Not like this. I—I've only just found him."

I bandage up my hand, aware of how watchful, how still, the small hours of the night have grown. As though the mountains have leaned in and are listening to every syllable and silently counting the drops of blood falling from my veins into the silver moonlight. I lean back, closing my eyes for a moment as the tiredness seeps into my very bones. "Please," I say softly. "Whatever the cost, whatever the price, I'll pay it."

This is the way of the mountains, the way it has always been. This is the truth we learned as children, the truth that followed us into adulthood, through whispers that bound us. A Morgan woman can cast a wish. She can scratch at the door of the mountains and ask for the world, but if they agree to help, she must give something of equal importance in return. An eye for an eye. A secret for a secret.

A life for a life.

I hope the mountains extract payment from me when I've lived a full, rich life. I search for Matthieu's cold hand, cradle it in my own, and lean my forehead into his, which is still blisteringly hot. For maybe the only time I'll ever get to say it, I whisper to him, realizing that it's true. *I love you.*

As dawn finds us, searching through the trees with golden, watery fingers, I regret nothing. I have fought my way back, across oceans, over vast distances, and I deserve to be here on this mountainside. Next to Matthieu, next to this man who has made me want to stay, who has walked every step with me through this winter.

I have finally found my way home.

I close my eyes, allowing my own soul to drift and wander, Matthieu's hand tucked in mine.

Chapter 47
Cora

Too many tubes. Too much beeping, too much movement and light so bright it makes her eyes ache. She clings to his bedside, her eyes snapping back and forth, trying to understand all that's happening, feeling like she's drowning.

"Speak up!' she says crossly when a young woman comes to dance around Howard's bed as she idly chats, asking him questions, plumping his pillow, and staring intently at the machines around him. Cora pushes a pair of spectacles up the bridge of her nose, blinking owlishly and grimacing. "Speak up! What doctor? What did they say?"

She wants her home, her kitchen, the familiar comfort of her well-worn routine. Mostly she wants Carrie. She wants Carrie to be here with her, to translate the world around her until it all makes sense. She seeks Howard's hand as she sits ramrod straight in the standard-issue hospital chair and winces when her fingertips brush the cannula at the back of his wrist, the rigid plastic taped down to fasten around his hand.

Howard is alive. That's what she keeps telling herself. He's alive, he's still breathing, and this is all a nightmare that they can wake up from very soon. Until she found him in that field, his eyes turned to the wide bowl of sky, she hadn't realized how much she loved him. How much she needed him. How her life had grown around his and, fused together, they had collected memories and age like lichen. How her life without him wouldn't make any sense.

Really, she's wasted a lifetime. Ever since that first date, the one Howard wrangled from her in exchange for that damn pig that kept escaping, she's been smitten and hasn't wanted anyone but him. She's a fool, for not seeing that he's the love of her life. He has been everything—her best friend, her partner, the person she snarks at, the person she sleeps next to every night. Everything about him—the slippers he wears, the newspaper he reads, the way he likes his eggs cooked for breakfast—is more important than she ever realized. And now . . . now . . .

"Is Carrie here yet? Did you call her?" she asks the woman with the kind eyes and light brown skin. She grips Howard's hand a little tighter, gazing at him intently. She's not ready to let him go.

Cora is left alone again, Howard asleep at her side. She lets his hand slip from hers and places it on the bed beside him. The green curtains are pulled around their cubicle, creating a kind of life raft, a space of muffled quiet in this vast sea of people. She feels as though this hospital is endless, and that they're drifting through it with no shore in sight. Vaguely, she's aware of her heart thumping too fast, of a buzzing sound like a bee trapped in her ears. She gets up, her head swaying, vision tunneling and turning dark before coming back to her. She needs to rest. To lie down.

Cora crawls onto the hospital bed next to Howard, carving a slight space next to him to drop her slender frame. He mutters in his sleep, and she's sure he says, *I love you*. So she says it back, murmuring in his ear, drawing the blankets and sheets around her body too as she pats his arm. She sinks into his side, avoiding the tubes, and balances a featherlight hand on his chest. She watches the way it rises and falls, their world shrinking to this hospital bed, their shared warmth, this movement.

As Cora closes her eyes, she hears her. Her Carrie. She's asking for something, pleading. Begging in a way that wrenches at her heart. Cora tries to reply, tries to fight through the cobweb of tiredness to find her. She realizes, with sudden, horrible clarity, why Carrie never answered her phone call, why Carrie hasn't come to find them in the hospital.

"She's in the mountains, she—she . . . Howard, Carrie's gone there—"

She tries to get up, force her limbs to fight the fatigue. But her heart thumps once, twice, too loud, like a clenched fist against a door, and she gasps. She clutches at Howard, clinging to him in confusion as the hospital floats away.

She closes her eyes and suddenly she's in the mountains. She's there, standing next to Carrie, or at least she thinks she is, and Carrie's body is wrapped around the man Cora was so sure wasn't real. Cora kneels down beside her, shakes her arm, screaming her name. But Carrie only mutters, shrugging her off. Cora looks around at the darkness, listening to the silence, and notices the dribble of blood from Carrie's hand. She suddenly realizes why she's here. Why she's on the mountain somehow, not on the hospital bed lying next to Howard.

"Carrie, you made a bargain," she whispers, looking at her face. So young, so tired, so pale in the silver moonlight. "All right," she says, her gaze sliding to the man at her grandniece's side. This man she was so sure would break Carrie's heart, who would disappear as the frost thawed. "All right."

She agrees to what's being asked of her. She listens to the mountains, the tolling bell growing steadily louder. It's not Carrie's time, nor is it Matthieu's. Not yet. But she felt that pinch in her chest, felt it dragging down her arm, that muscle in her chest giving out.

It's not their time.

But it is hers.

She hears them, the people searching for her Carrie, and runs with a fleetness she hasn't had since her youth, guiding them, pressing back the branches to lure them farther down the path. When they find her, Carrie's breath is a huff, a small sigh. Cora's fingers press against her mouth as they lift her, as they move her. They carry them both, Carrie and this man, this Matthieu, calling out to one another as the sun dusts a lazy haze across the mountain.

Cora is left behind, left in the frost and the cold. She lowers her fingers from her mouth, breathes in the scent of spring. She closes her eyes, once more feeling the warmth at her side, of Howard on the hospital bed beside her. And she knows it was the mountains, the final slip of Morgan magic, that guided her to Carrie's side. She smiles, nuzzling in closer to the man she loves, breathing in his scent.

Then she gives herself, all of herself, knowing her time is coming.

Chapter 48
Cora

Fifty-Nine Years Ago

As the band strikes up, Howard holds out a hand. She arches an eyebrow, letting him lift her from the chair, drawing her over to the space in front of the band, to the dance floor, with all of Woodsmoke looking on. He spins her once, placing his hand on her waist to catch her, and the band sinks into an old, familiar song by Frank Sinatra.

"Howard Price, you young fool," Cora says quietly, recognizing the song. "It's the one you chose on the jukebox after our first date."

"When I wouldn't take you home straightaway. We went for Coke floats at Benny's."

She laughs breathlessly, leaning her cheek on his shoulder. "You young fool."

She likes how he smells. All forest and earth and clean laundry. She likes how his hands are always warm, how solid he feels to her. She's grown to love the steady glow of his quiet strength and goodness these past few months. They've had a short courtship by the usual standards, but after all, she's known Howard since they were at school together. In her mind, the final steps that led them to this day, to this dance floor, were just formalities. She knew what she wanted the moment she heard this song playing on the jukebox at Benny's.

He twirls her around, and a few more couples join them. Ivy winks at her, and her mother gives her a small, proud smile. But somehow, it's still just him and her. She likes how he makes her feel, like she's someone important. Like she's the only person in the room.

"I want five kids at least," he murmurs in her ear. "I want to raise them right here in Woodsmoke, and they can help on the farm, and we'll all be together. Always. You think you can handle that?"

She snorts, leaning in closer to nuzzle against his neck. "You even need to ask?"

He chuckles, dipping her like they do in the black-and-white films, like they saw at the pictures last week. He dips her and kisses her, and she's distantly aware of whoops and cheers, of clapping. But she doesn't push him away. She throws her arms around him and lets that kiss linger on her lips.

She pictures it, all of it. Their shared future together, this path opening up before her, and for the first time in her life she feels like it could be enough. As he brings her back up, the band is moving to the next song, and they slow-dance across a crowded dance floor. She hides a smile, ducking her head against his shoulder, and says, "You know what, Howard Price? I actually think I love you."

Chapter 49

Jess

Jess makes the call the moment her gaze hits the map. Standing in the center of the cabin, she is transfixed by the vastness of it. The trails and routes Matthieu has carefully staked out, the intersections, the research. She feels for Tom's hand, whimpers when his fingers close around hers.

"No . . ." she breathes. They both stare at the map silently, barely moving. The sheer scale of the mountains, of the danger, eclipses everything and brings her right back to her teenage self. When she and Carrie were as close as sisters, when she couldn't imagine a space or time in her life that wasn't inhabited by Carrie. The past decade of silence between them vanishes in her mind as her heart focuses like an arrow. None of that matters now.

"She—she's out there, she could be anywhere—"

"We'll find her," Tom says, even as his voice shakes.

Jess can't even nod, can't articulate the landslide of fear that holds her in its grip. She doesn't know this time. She doesn't know. She shifts her eyes away from the map, to the sofa, the kitchen, the door leading to the back room . . . it's all so ordinary. There's no imprint of a life here, no clutter to indicate the history of a person. She drifts over to the kitchen, opens a cupboard at random, and finds four plates, four bowls, four mugs neatly stacked. She bites her lip, a prickle rising along her hairline, trickling down the back of her neck. This man Carrie is searching for . . . was he ever really here? She hasn't heard his name mentioned around Woodsmoke. Hasn't seen a stranger in the supermarket or wandering the market square. Usually there would be gossip, threads of whispers surrounding a newcomer. But she hasn't heard a thing.

She doesn't want to voice that kind of fear aloud, not here. Not when the mountains are listening. She glances around, hoping for some sign of life, a used coffee cup, a crumpled crisp packet, *anything*—

Then she sees it.

A carelessly discarded old envelope, one corner folded down, as though rubbed with a frantic thumb. An image floats before her eyes, summoning a memory. Carrie used to do that. As the chemistry teacher droned on about something obtuse, she looked over at Carrie and saw that she was folding the corner of the page on her notebook and then smoothing it out, folding it over, creating a tiny triangle, and then smoothing it out, over and over. Jess snaps back, blinking quickly. The note had been left on the kitchen counter. Abandoned. Or . . .

She rushes for the envelope and snatches it up, and her heart bursts when she sees the writing scrawled across it. "It—it's Carrie's handwriting! Oh God, she was here, you were right." She gulps, forcing back the tears, focusing her mind like a needle. "She's gone looking for him—for this Matthieu. Says she'll take the trail across to the three peaks—"

"Shit . . ."

Jess swallows, passes the note to Tom. She looks at him, the agony on his features reflecting her own. Neither of them says it yet. That they are partly to blame, that they should have been the people she could turn to when she returned. Her people. Instead of pushing her, *shoving* her away—

Jess blows out a breath and holds up her phone. "I'm going to find signal. I bet she couldn't; I bet she's not on the right network anymore." Jess gathers herself, creating a mental bullet list, the salient points she'll relay on the call. "Search for anything else, any clue—I don't want to go the wrong way. I don't want to give search-and-rescue the wrong information to find her."

Tom only nods as Jess steps outside, already punching a number into her phone. She cradles it to her ear, praying for the tinny dial tone, almost passing out with relief when someone answers at the other end. She rattles it all off, where the cabin is, who has gone missing. And finally, she confesses, in her clipped, librarian tone, her worst fear. That no one has seen her since the night before.

The wait for search-and-rescue is the darkest hour of Jess's life. She scans the skies, as though search-and-rescue will suddenly appear, as she paces back and forth, bile curling and writhing in her stomach.

"You should sit down, Jess. You should drink some water—"

"Don't. Just please . . . don't."

Tom blinks steadily. "Okay, fair enough. But all the same."

"You literally walked out last night, and I didn't have a clue where you'd gone. So no. You do not get to tell me to sit down."

Tom blanches. "All right, point taken."

She stifles a scream, stalks back inside, and sits on the sofa. For a moment, the nausea wanes, leaving her temporarily suspended in the hope that it won't return. But then it comes shuddering back, slamming into her middle, the back of her throat, like a fist. She groans, placing her hands on her stomach. "It's like I'm in a car—or on a boat, and it's moving too fast, and my body can never keep up."

Tom sinks down next to her, rubbing a hand up and down her arm. "It's shit, I know."

"You don't know."

"You're right, I really don't." He cracks a smile, and Jess catches it. Then her mouth lifts too, and suddenly she can't help herself. They're both laughing, hysteria clutching their sides.

"We shouldn't be laughing," Jess says, sniffing. "Why the hell are we laughing? Think of something serious!"

"I can't," Tom says, pressing his hands into his face. "I can't believe any of this is happening. I mean . . . what *happened* this winter?"

"I know," Jess says, then looks over at him. A squeak escapes her, and she's laughing again, so much so that bile rises up her throat.

After a few minutes, their laughter subsides into silence. The nerves, the adrenaline, have left them cold. Tom wraps his hand around hers and looks over at her. "I'm so sorry, Jess. You cannot believe how sorry I am for leaving last night, for being so cross I couldn't see how it would look, what you would think . . ."

"It's all right," Jess says, closing her eyes. "It's all right."

They sit for a moment in the silence, thicker than fog in the cabin.

"I think it's a girl again," she says. "I feel as sick as a dog, just like last time."

"When will we . . ."

"Twenty-week scan." She sighs. "Not long. If we want to know, that is. We could keep it a surprise."

"Been a lot of surprises recently, don't you think?" Tom says bleakly. "For once, I'd like a heads-up on something."

"When—when you went to her the other night—"

"You thought I was leaving you. For Carrie."

"Well, possibly."

"Jess," Tom says, turning to her. "I'm a fool. You're the love of my life. Always have been, always will be. That I ever made you doubt that, that Carrie coming back ever made you question . . .

I've been distant since she got back, I know. I've just been in my own head, and I should have looked up, *noticed* more.

"What you did when we were kids, before the wedding? Going to Cora and all of that? I forgive you. I was angry, but my anger was misdirected. It was really about Cora. She's always meddling, always involved, and I guess I just snapped last night and took it out on you." He stops himself, shaking his head. "I would have loved you anyway, I'm sure of it. I would have found my way to you, like it was always supposed to be. Carrie and I wouldn't have lasted, and it would have done more damage if we'd gotten married. I have a lot to make up for. Starting now. Right this minute."

"Yeah?"

"Yeah." Tom leans over, kisses her cheek. He lowers his face to her shoulder, breathing in her scent, all vanilla and mint and fresh linen. She's always smelled like this to him, even when they were young. "Tell me what I should do to make it up to you."

"Find Carrie. Find her and help me mend it between us. That's what I want. That's all I've wanted since she left. It's like there's been this hole. I love you, and Elodie, and the life we have, but I can't fill that space with anyone else. Only she can fill it."

"All right."

"I'm afraid," she says suddenly. "More than anything, I'm afraid it's too late. That I left it too late and got too caught up in thinking I hated her, when really it was only my guilt and fear I hated."

"They'll find her."

Jess sniffs as her entire being fills with tears, and she curves herself into Tom's side. "You forgive me, then? For everything? Truly?"

"Of course."

"But . . . you believe it all, don't you? The Morgans, the book, the old stories . . ."

Tom is quiet for a minute as he still holds her. He's been trying to work this out for years, to unravel the threads that bind them all, trying to unpick the real from the imagined. It's true that the stories can't be ignored in Woodsmoke, that trying to explain them to anyone from outside of town would be futile. But Jess and Tom and Carrie have all grown up with it. They've seen the seemingly magical effects, the unexplained things that happen. As much as he'd like to brush it all aside as superstition, he simply can't.

"I believe that Carrie and I weren't meant to be, and we never should have gone along with that wedding. We never should have let it get so far along. And I know, without any doubt, not even a shadow of it, that I love you. That I loved you as soon as I really saw you. And I should have welcomed Carrie home this autumn. I should have talked to her years ago. I should have called the wedding off myself and—and tried to make amends. For your sake."

Jess breathes out, the air in the deepest part of her lungs expelling as she exhales. "It feels like we've all been suspended in that wedding day for a decade. Like we're all trapped in the wedding that should have been. Not just us, but the whole town."

"Yeah."

Jess's phone rings and she grabs for it, and Tom helps her stand as they both huddle over the bars of signal. When the voice connects on the other end, she cries.

They've found her.

She's still alive.

Chapter 50
Carrie

At first, it feels like a dream. Like I am being lifted out of the real world, out of my own body. I can't pin myself to my own existence anymore, it is just a rush of words and colors and faint prickles of sensation. All I remember is my arms curled around him, and how quickly the warmth of our shared bodies drained away. I'm in an in-between space—not dreaming, yet not awake either, and the imprint of his body, the ghost of it, is all I'm clinging to as I'm wrenched across that threshold.

"Water?" I croak. My tongue lolls behind my gums, ten times thicker than normal. My throat is as slender as a needle, swollen, and filled with sandpaper as I blink into the quiet. I last had a drink as the sun set, before I found Matthieu. The rest I gave to him. I slowly begin to stir, begin to see that the world around me is no longer filled with frost and darkness. Everything is coated in a fine haze, but the smell is antiseptic, like lemons and cleaning products.

"Shit, she's awake. What do I press? Do I call someone? Tom, get a nurse, get that doctor."

I frown as a face hovers over me. "Jess, your hair's in my face."

"Sorry, sorry! Tom! She's lucid! Get that nurse!" Jess's face comes into view again, and her shaking palm strokes my cheek. "Carrie? Carrie, I'm here. We're both here. Say something else, anything—"

"My throat hurts."

Jess releases a sob and drops her head to my chest. I smile, at least I think I do, and move my arms, trying to embrace her. They're heavy, limp, and tired, but I manage to balance them on her shoulder blades. She sighs heavily, releasing a long breath. "Don't do that again. Never, ever do that again. You scared the shit out of me."

"Jess . . ." My whole being wells up, and I don't know if I'm dreaming, if I'm awake, if this is something I'm willing into being, having her here with me, but I want to cling to it. I want to stay in this moment, with this woman I've missed like a hollow in my heart. If I am dreaming this moment, if my body is still slumped beside Matthieu's on the mountain, then at least I have this. At least my memories, my mind, have pieced this together for me.

At least I now have peace.

"Jess, I missed you. I missed you so much."

She clings to me, crying quietly, and the heaviness is too hard to lift any longer. My eyes shutter closed, and an ache spreads out, coating me, pressing me lower. I'm so tired. I'm so, so tired. From the hike across the mountains, from the worry gripping my chest . . . I slip beneath the fatigue, as though into an inky lake, and my world goes dark with sleep once more.

IN THAT INKY lake, there is only me and the quiet. A vastness surrounds me, warm, soft as velvet. Memories surface, of Jess, of the two of us, of Tom and the mountains and Ivy. I'm standing in my grandmother's kitchen. The radio is tuned to some tinny classical concerto, and Ivy is nursing a batch of griddle cakes on the stovetop. I can smell them, that bready, sweet scent hanging like a cloud.

"Ivy?" I say, my voice fainter than I've ever heard it.

She smiles and turns toward me, rubbing her hands down her

red-and-white-striped apron. "You're not meant to be here yet. You have to go back."

I blink, and I'm with Jess. We're walking to school, our arms linked, my rucksack bumping against the small of my back. She's talking really fast about a book she read, about how maybe she wants to be an author one day, about how Woodsmoke is so small, how the world is so big—

Then we're standing at the lookout, and the whole of Woodsmoke is bathed in moonlight beneath us. Blood wells from a tiny cut in her outstretched hand, and when she clasps my hand, the cut on my own a twin to hers, we grin in the dark as we whisper, *Sisters.*

And we're just eighteen, in the bar on the edge of town, screaming along to Tom's band with our sticky drinks and sweaty faces, all red and different, as if the night has turned us into ghouls—

Then I'm alone, on the mountain. Standing at the lookout once more, staring down at Woodsmoke, and it's spring. The frost has thawed, and there's green in the fields. I cup my hands around my mouth, draw in a fresh gulp of air and bellow—

There is beeping, and a sterile sweetness to the air. I glance around and see I'm not in Ivy's cottage, or walking the track to school, or at the lookout. I look down at myself and see a white hospital gown stretching over my chest. I move my hand, run my fingers along the scratchy fabric of the bedcovers. Then I notice people. Voices. A hand reaches for mine and carefully pulls it into a clasp. When I look up, I see it's Jess, holding my hand, and I don't fully understand.

"Two days," the doctor is telling me, and telling Jess, who sits at my side, her hand now tight around mine. I snap my eyes to the doctor, the one with a buzz cut and heavy features. I've met him before, I'm sure of it. Maybe yesterday, maybe this morning . . . I nibble on my bottom lip, tugging at the dry skin, trying to anchor myself, to convince myself that this hospital, this gown I'm wearing, it's all real. "She's going to slip in and out, but everything is looking good. Heart rate steady, no signs of infection. We're going to push fluids, and you can start to get her talking."

"Will there be permanent damage?" Jess asks, then swallows, looking down at me. "Sorry, that was insensitive."

"It's okay," I manage, my words slurring together.

"We won't know yet. But nothing indicates there is right now. She just needs rest; her body had a shock. She might be confused, ask repetitive questions, that sort of thing. Be patient. With the hike, then the exposure overnight and the dehydration, she really put her body through it."

"Matthieu . . ." I say, his name trailing across my tongue. I was with him, on the mountain, in the loam and the cold and the dark. "Is he here?"

Jess glances down at me, the conversation stuttering out. After a pause, they keep talking, about temperatures, about blood flow, about fluids and getting me to begin moving . . . but I'm slipping again. Slipping below the surface, the eddying lake rises up to submerge me. I try to move my lips, try to frame the question again, try to keep my hand gripped in Jess's as the room slides away, my thoughts fracturing, sinking—

Matthieu.

Are you here?

Are you real?

Matthieu . . .

Chapter 51
Carrie

"He's real."

I crane my neck, focusing on wrapping my fingers around the mug offered to me. "What?"

"You kept saying, 'I don't know if he's real, what if Matthieu's not real?' And I've been telling you every time you wake up," Jess says, taking a breath. "He's real, he's recovering. You can see him . . . if you want to."

I'm still in the hospital, but in a different ward. I'm in a room all my own, and I'm waiting for the all-clear to get discharged. Jess is fussing around me as Tom hovers by the door. She keeps turning to him, giving swift orders as she turns back the blanket on the bed, smoothing out the folds around me. My breath hitches, and I stare down into the mug, turning her words over and over. I was moved an hour ago, Jess pushing me in a wheelchair, Tom walking behind us with a bag of my things against his chest. I didn't like being in a wheelchair, but apparently it's hospital policy for transporting patients between wards.

They discussed over my head when their daughter, Elodie, needed picking up from school. Which clubs she was doing today, what extra items she needed in her backpack. I zoned in and out, the world of the hospital around me still a fuzzy blur of light. I was still bewildered by their presence, by both of them being here. Just thinking about it clogged up my throat, making my chest ache.

"Now? Can I see him now?" I ask, looking at Jess hopefully. "He—he doesn't know anyone else in Woodsmoke. I should have stayed with him. We should be here together. I don't even know if he has any family left to call."

"We know," Tom says from the doorway. "I tried, went through his phone, talked to him when he was awake briefly. But he just kept asking for you. Saying we'd left you on the mountain."

I close my eyes, a sigh brushing my lips. I keep feeling like the world will tilt and fall into a dream at any minute, and I still can't handle much more than the basics of eating and sleeping. I want to get out of this hospital, back to the cottage, back in my own space, to process it all. "How long have I been here?"

"Two days," Jess says. "The doctor said that time will feel weird, like it could be months, or minutes, that you've been here. Or you might think you're still . . . up there."

I sip the tea, remembering that the cup is in my hand, a slight tang of chemicals lingering at the edges. "I won't believe we both actually left the mountain until I see him. I need to see him. All of this . . . I don't know." I drop my gaze to the tepid tea in my hands. "Nothing feels real."

I catch Jess's glance at Tom out of the corner of my eye. She raises her eyebrows at him, then looks to me and nods. "Okay. We'll go now."

TOM LEAVES TO pick up Elodie, and Jess wheels me to another ward, inquiring for directions along the way at a nurses' station. I can feel slumber dragging at me, tugging at my hand, but I shake it off. I can't slip away yet, not until I've seen him, not until I've touched him. I need to know it's true—that we both survived the night.

He's on an open ward. Some curtains divide up the space, but the curtains around his cubicle are thrust open. A small shudder rushes through me as Jess and I approach, relief and a strange dread mingling beneath my ribs. I lean forward when I catch sight of his features, his eyes staring into the middle distance. My fingers flutter at my throat, choking down a sob.

He's real.

I didn't dream him up from the frost and my own longing. Cora's worries, the frost tale, none of it was true. He didn't disappear as the frost thawed. My heart beats harder, straining against my chest. I reach for him, my hands clutching at thin air, then his blanket, then his face. Tears leave salty tracks down my skin, and he blinks, then locks his eyes with mine.

All there is in that moment is him.

"Carrie," he says, his voice flecked with cold. As though the frost crept inside him on that mountain and hasn't melted since. "You're here."

"I—" My throat closes up before I can get my words out. I bury my face in his shoulder, sobbing and sobbing, tears soaking into his skin. I really thought he might die up there. I thought that, if I left him at daybreak to find help, he wouldn't be alive when I returned . . . or that I wouldn't have been able to find him at all.

"I'm going to leave you two to, er . . ." Jess says over my head. "I'll be back in a bit."

I stay there for a few moments, aware of the rattle of his breath in his lungs, of my own tiny sips of air as my sobbing subsides. "I thought you were going to die, your leg was so bad, and there was blood, and you had a fever . . . I, I can't believe—"

"I'm here. We're both here," he says, stroking my hair. "Could have lost my leg if it wasn't for you. Could have lost more than that if you hadn't found me, if Jess and Tom hadn't called search-and-rescue to get out there . . ."

My eyes trail down to his leg, now bound in plaster. I shudder again, picturing how it was when I found him. "You're safe, that's all that matters." I burrow my face back into his shoulder, breathing in his scent, the evergreens and fir and midnights enveloping my senses. Then I move away, wiping my face, and smile at him. "Have they told you how long you'll be in for?"

"They've not been specific . . . it depends on the leg. I picked up an infection—that's why I'm attached to this bag and all these tubes." He shrugs, and my heart lifts at the corners. "It is what it is."

"I can visit you every day. Bring you whatever you want, or—or need." I sniff, grabbing for his hand. "It doesn't matter if it takes time. I'm here."

Matthieu's eyes crinkle, then he carefully pulls his hand away. "Listen, Carrie . . . we need to talk about what happened. How it happened. You coming after me like that . . . I've never been so scared in my life. You could have died, Carrie."

"*You* could have died—"

"That was my risk. My stupidity." He takes a breath, glancing around us. "Pass me my wallet? It's right there, yes, that's it."

I scoop up the old leather wallet that I've seen before, sitting on the bedside table next to a water jug. He opens it, pulling out an old, battered Polaroid, and hands it to me.

I gasp.

"This . . . this is Henri?"

"Yes."

I trace the shape of his features, the haunting eyes. They're so much like Matthieu's, but different. More pronounced. "Did he sit for a photographer when you visited Woodsmoke?"

Matthieu's forehead creases into a frown. "He did, on a family visit in the autumn before he disappeared in the mountains. A local reporter was writing a story about the hiking trails and thought a photo of Henri would be a good lead image for a short interview. Why?"

"Cora . . . my great-aunt? She collects things. Photos, memorabilia, anything she's worried will get lost and forgotten in Woodsmoke." I pass the Polaroid back to Matthieu. "Henri is in a photograph in her hallway."

"We gave the reporter a photo of Henri taken at a fair," Matthieu says, replacing the picture in his wallet. "You know, one of those touring ones with the old-fashioned sweets stalls and merry-go-rounds? I was forever taking Polaroids with a camera I got for my birthday from my parents the year before. So I took this one of him while he sat there, posing, and I kept it. They used the photo in the newspaper article," Matthieu says with a sigh. "And I've seen it in Cora's collection. I know she's got it. I told her to keep it when I went to ask her if she could bring him back last winter."

All the air leaves my lungs at once. "What?"

He looks at me then, sadness straining his features. "This was when my brother disappeared, when no one could find him and all I had was that Polaroid photo to show around. All the folks here told me to go and see Cora Morgan. They avoided my gaze themselves. They were sympathetic, but wary. The police searched, but it's a vast range and they never found a body. My family . . . we didn't believe what we were hearing from folks here, the whispers about missing people and bargains. It sounded like superstition. Folktales. But after Mum died, I couldn't shake it off. I had to know. I had to return and put that ghost to rest in my mind. So I found Cora last winter and went to see her. Went to ask her if Henri could still somehow just be lost . . . and still alive . . . all these years later. If she could find him."

I press my lips together, reaching again for his hand. "So you came back . . . for answers?"

"Yes. And this is the part you're not going to like," he says, moving his hand away, just an inch.

I draw back my hand, closing it into a fist. Waiting. "Go on."

"Cora refused. She told me not to go looking for those who are lost to the mountains. She told me to leave and not return. So I asked around and learned that there was another Morgan woman living here, her sister. I offered to help Ivy with the cottage, and I was hoping she'd know, that she'd have some answers that Cora wouldn't give me. And she did, in a way. She told me some more about the old tales, the old ways. At first, I couldn't believe her. But after a while, I began to see that Henri's disappearance couldn't be explained in the usual way. That there might be some explanation that wouldn't seem reasonable or logical anywhere but in Woodsmoke."

"So you started searching the mountain," I say. "For evidence. For signs. Checking the trails, marking your routes . . ."

"I came back for a second winter, hoping Ivy would be able to give me more clues. That finally I could at least find his body. I figured, if I scoured every trail, every path, I'd find *something*. I even searched along the ones we hadn't walked together, just to see if somehow he had disappeared somewhere I'd never seen.

"Henri left in the night. We were staying at a guesthouse, had a whole route planned for the next day, and he wasn't there when I woke up." Matthieu shakes his head. "It was the worst moment of my life. I was so scared. I felt so powerless and young and utterly alone. That was . . . thirteen years ago."

"Oh, Matthieu."

"So I came back. But then, when you told me that Ivy had passed, I didn't bother going to Cora again to ask for her help. I knew she would be as tight-lipped with an outsider as she'd been the last time, not telling me anything about the old tales or suggesting why he could have gone missing. I figured, since you were Ivy's granddaughter, a Morgan, I might learn something from you . . ."

He shakes his head again. "It felt deceitful at first, offering to help with the renovation. Staying close to you, earning your trust. But I felt like it was all right, because I was doing it for Henri. I was doing it to find closure. And I didn't hide the fact from you that he had gone missing. I was just selective about how much I shared with you. But then, of course, I didn't expect you to be, well, *you*. Carrie Morgan. The woman you are."

I frown, looking down at the cast on his leg. At the hospital blanket, then at my own hands. "I don't know what to make of all this."

"There's nothing to make of it. I should never have returned to Woodsmoke. There aren't any answers here. And if I hadn't met you, maybe I would have given up and moved on by now."

I sniff, finally looking up and search his eyes for the man I've been falling for this winter. "Was it real between us?"

"Yes," he breathes, at last reaching for my hands. "Yes, Carrie. And that made it so much more complicated. How could I leave when you were here? And yet . . . how can I stay when all I feel around me is Henri's ghost?" He shakes his head. "I can't stay in Woodsmoke. I want to, for you. But I feel like I failed him."

I nod, biting my lip. His hands are so warm, cradling my own as I process everything he's told me. Everything about Matthieu now slots into place, the puzzle pieces clicking quietly. I can see the full picture now, the sadness he's dragged around with him. The hope. And in a way, the frost tale is true. This man I met as the frost formed will leave as it thaws. He'll break my heart and take it with him when he goes.

"Did you ever intend to stay?" I ask softly.

"I hoped, in time, I might be able to leave Henri behind, especially as you became sure about staying, but . . ." He sighs. "Look at what I've done. And putting you in danger . . . that cannot happen again. Ever. Carrie, I have to leave. I have to figure this out in my own way, in my own time. I don't think I'll ever find Henri's body or any answers about why he left that morning, and I have to make my peace with that."

I nod quickly, sniffing back tears. "You'll be haunted until you come to terms with his death."

"Yes," he says softly.

I brush a tear away, then another, not able to look at him. How can I hold this against him? But equally, how can I convince him to stay if every corner of Woodsmoke reminds him of what he's lost?

"Do you want me to visit you again here? Or is it better if—if—"

"We say goodbye now?"

I don't trust myself to speak.

"I don't want to say goodbye. I love you. This winter together, what we have . . ." He swallows. "I want to say I'll be back, but I need time."

I stifle a small sob, but nod and move closer, leaning in so I'm resting beside him, my head beside his. His fingers stay entwined in mine, and we lie there together as the hospital moves around us, as lives begin and lives end, talking about the cottage and ice-skating and our midnights. We talk until I see he is growing tired. I watch his eyes close and the world drift away from him. Then I press a kiss to his cheek, wishing our lives could have been different. Wishing Woodsmoke, my home, my anchor, wasn't the one thing standing between us.

Wishing more than anything that he didn't have the burden of this ghost.

"Goodbye," I whisper, turning away and feeling my fragile heart begin to crack.

Chapter 52
Jess

"I want to go home now" are the first words Carrie says when she leaves Matthieu's side. Her face, already wrecked from the cold night she spent on the mountain, swells with more tears as Jess wheels her back to her room. "Can you speak to the doctor? Get them to speed up with their final checks and get me discharged? I need to go and see Cora and Howard, go and check on them in the ward Howard's in. I shouldn't stay here. I need to pull myself together, be strong for them . . ."

"Sure," Jess says, glancing quickly back at Matthieu, asleep on the hospital bed. His features are just as wrecked, just as hollowed out. As though the mountain took and took from him, leaving nothing else for him to give. She doesn't know what Carrie has found in this man over the winter. Jess doesn't know him at all. She's never seen Carrie devastated, not in all the years they grew up together.

But . . . she's missed the last decade. That's ten years of cracked hearts, of misery and grief and loneliness. Guilt holds a blade to her chest, slowly sinking between her ribs. Suppressing her own feelings, the nausea grows in her belly. But she chooses to be the friend she should have been all along. "Whatever you need."

"Should I have come back? I don't know anymore. I thought, I guess I thought, he was the one. That it all suddenly made sense. The cottage, the wildflowers . . . it was like Ivy left it all there for me to find."

"And he's not . . . the one?"

"He's leaving."

"Shit."

Carrie's breath stutters in her chest, and she quietly cries, pressing her fingers into her eyes. No one looks at either of them, no one bothers with them as Jess wheels Carrie slowly along the fluorescent-lit corridors, trying to figure out what to say.

"I can't go with him. Not after this winter, not after finding what I've been missing all these years. Roots. A home. But he—he wouldn't want me to anyway."

"You're meant to stay, Carrie," Jess says, stopping suddenly. She walks around to the front of the wheelchair and kneels down before her. After a brief hesitation, she reaches across, gripping Carrie's hands in hers. They're cold, so much colder than her own, but a faint thrill goes through her, a connection she hasn't felt in too long. She steadies herself, looking down at their hands, then up into Carrie's eyes. She suppresses a wave of mourning for the woman she never saw Carrie grow into. "You're meant to stay. In fact, you should never have left. It's the biggest regret of my life, letting you go like that. Not speaking to you, not trying harder to search for you."

"You . . . searched for me?"

Jess's nose wrinkles. "Online mostly. Just every now and then. Ivy told me once you were in St. Ives, renting a cottage, and I went to go and find you. I guess I was beginning to think that you didn't care anymore, that you had moved on. But I didn't move on. Not ever. I know it seemed that way, but I was scared, Carrie. And guilty." Jess shakes her head. "It's amazing what guilt will do.

"So I told Tom I wanted a few days to myself, to be by the sea. I caught the train, checked into a B&B, and the whole time I kept telling myself I should turn back. But I couldn't stop myself. I . . . I had to see you." She clears her throat, looking down at their hands again. "On the second morning I saw you across the beach, batting away a seagull, laughing with some guy over cones of ice cream. It was . . . I couldn't breathe. I remember just standing there, watching you like some kind of ghost. I imagined myself going over, talking to you, but that little strip of sand seemed impossible to cross. Anyway, you just wandered off with him after a while, and I didn't follow."

Carrie frowns, quiet for a moment. "That might have been Ian."

"Might have been?"

"None of them really mattered after I left." Carrie smiles, the corners of her mouth twitching upward sadly. "None of them mattered, until Matthieu."

"Come and meet Elodie. Please. Let's get you discharged, and I can bring Elodie over to meet you. You'll love her, she's a little monster in human form. Please, Carrie . . . just, please."

Carrie's smile grows more real, then she sighs, leaning forward to touch her forehead to Jess's. Jess's heart stutters. She remembers . . . oh, how she remembers . . . the way they used to stand like this, how it used to be with the two of them, how she used to feel complete with Carrie next to her.

"God, I've missed you," Carrie says with a sigh. "You have no fucking idea how much I've missed you."

Jess stifles a sob and wraps her arms around Carrie, her hot tears leaking into Carrie's hair. "I'm sorry. That night when I came to see you—"

"It doesn't matter."

"But—"

"It really, really doesn't matter," Carrie says, her voice muffled by Jess's jumper. "All that matters is this. Now. We've lost ten years. I don't want to lose another ten years."

Jess's phone vibrates in her pocket and she reaches down, pulling away from Carrie. She frowns down at the screen, at the flashing words NO CALLER ID peering up at her, and swipes to answer. "Hello?"

Her features sink as she listens to the voice on the other end. She blinks quickly, taking it in, fighting back the nausea writhing inside her. Blowing out a quick breath, she answers as calmly as she can, her gaze slicing to Carrie, the nausea clawing up her throat. When she hangs up, she takes a moment to gather herself, placing her hands on her belly, fighting for strength.

"Jess . . ." Carrie says, knowing it's bad, both wanting and not wanting to know.

"It's Cora. And—and Howard." Jess's eyes fly open, fixing on Carrie's. She reaches once more for Carrie's hands, as though to brace her. As though bracing herself. "I'm so sorry. So very, very sorry."

Chapter 53
Carrie

Two Weeks Later

I drive over to their house after the wake, going alone with Kep. I need to feel close to them. When I kick off my black heels in the hallway, my presence ripples through the silence. Kep whines and wanders away to search for them, nosing his way into the kitchen, and I let her. This is her goodbye as well, after all.

I can feel the house stirring beneath my stockinged feet, and maybe it's them here with me. Maybe Cora is trailing her fingertips along the wall, walking behind me as I step like a ghost through the rooms. I stand on the threshold of the lounge, holding the keys to the front door in my palm. It's all so perfect, so neat and orderly. Just like Cora. I sniff, pressing my rouged lips together. I didn't wear mascara today. My eyes are red and raw from the past two weeks, and the red slash of lipstick was the only color I could stand.

"You know why I'm here," I say into the listening quiet. "I know you will have left it for me, and I've come to collect."

I move into the kitchen, eyeing the now-empty yard out back. The chickens were collected, taken to a local farm, and Kep came to live with me, so we could walk the old ways between the fields together. It's what Howard would have wanted.

I run a hand over Cora's favorite mug, pressing my fingertip into the chip near the handle. There are certain things in this house that I won't be able to let go of. Not costly items, but things that I know she loved. Things like this mug, and Howard's. Items that still carry the imprint of their souls.

I turn to the bedroom, the room that is beckoning, calling to me. It takes only a handful of heartbeats to find the book, on top of the wardrobe. It's like Cora is guiding me, showing me the path I need to follow to find it, where to reach for it.

How to claim it.

It's heavy, weighed down by the many stories of the mountains. The many moments pressed into it in fading, handwritten ink. I cradle it to my chest and sniff again, knowing I can't turn it to ash, as Howard wanted. I can't set fire to Cora's legacy, the legacy of so many Morgan women before me, to the thread binding me to her. It feels like I'm holding her life right here in my arms. As though the body we buried today was just a vessel, just a fleeting cage, and this is the real her. The truth of her is right here, nestled in these pages.

I imagine her watching me, willing me to take a look. To seek out the secrets inside, to finally understand what the Morgan women have carried with them, generation after generation—the ancient ways of the mountains. I sink to the floor, lean against the bed, and open to the beginning. Some of the pages are so old and frail that I'm worried they will tear like tissue beneath my fingertips. I've read a few of these stories before, but that was years ago. Today, reading this book as an adult, and knowing I am its keeper, feels different. Monumental. I read a few words, carefully turning the pages, then move quickly to the back.

To the final story.

"Of course," I breathe. Cora has written the last story in the book. Her careful script, slightly slanted, crawls across the pages, detailing a story about two sisters, one tall and fair, one brittle and bitter. The book is given to the fair sister, who does not care for it. The other sister covets it, and a chasm opens between them, growing wider with each passing year.

Then the fair sister offers up the book to the bitter sister. She gives her the book, wanting her to be happy. They seal the gift of the book with blood from a slash across their palms. The bitter sister believes that there was no cost to this transaction, that somehow she had paid no price for accepting the book from her sister.

Until . . .

I gasp.

The fair sister has a grandchild. A girl with stars for eyes, who loves adventure, who falls in love with an apple thief, who paints and draws and creates and wonders . . .

That grandchild is *me*.

"Oh, Cora," I say, a sob catching in my throat. I read on. The bitter sister knows the mountains did not claim a price from her sister—they claimed it from *her.* They robbed her of the chance to hold her own child, to ever have children. The bitter sister believed that the child who had stars for eyes and loved the mountains should have been hers, but was gifted to another. To the fair sister's daughter, who had no lasting love for Woodsmoke.

My fingers stray to my throat, eyes growing wide as I read on.

When the bitter sister learns that the child plans to leave, she cannot stand it. She makes a new deal with the mountains, offers fresh blood in the moonlight. To cut the tie she had made with that love potion to the apple thief, to stop her from leaving Woodsmoke and her. But the bargain sours, turning into a curse, a curse that robs the child of all she loves, and all who love her. She leaves the apple thief, her home, the bitter sister, and the fair sister. She leaves every love of her life; she leaves the mountains…

I turn the page with shaking fingers.

Then the fair sister dies, and the child is beckoned back. But the mountains do not welcome her. Instead, they punish her for leaving. They curse her to fall in love with the man who appears with the frost... who disappears as the frost thaws.

I run a finger over these words, seeing the faint markings of a footnote, the reference at the end to the page where the frost tale begins. Cora believed it. She truly believed it.

"Matthieu," I say, running my finger back over the words. "You mean Matthieu."

I turn another page, expecting the tale to continue. But it's blank. I turn the next page, the next, my fingers frenzied and trembling, searching for the ending. But there's no ending to the story. Only empty space, dozens of blank pages. I laugh, tipping my head back, and wonder if she didn't know.

But maybe she wanted me to find my story unfinished. To carry our collected stories and write my own. The story of the girl who finally found where she belonged. Who came home.

Epilogue

Carrie

The Following Autumn, as the Frost Forms . . .

She was easy to love, easy to laugh with. Her soul shone like that full moon under which she was born.

—Cora Morgan, February 1, 2013

I get up with the dawn. The frost has formed overnight, weaving lace and ice over the fields. I throw on an extra jumper, pull my hair up into a bun, and stretch, feeling the spaces between my ribs fill with light. I walk downstairs, flick on the kettle in the kitchen, and eye the looming giants through the back window as Kep stirs at my feet. It feels as though they're waiting.

I drink my tea quickly, after letting it cool just to a temperature that burns but doesn't scald. I feel the hot liquid trickling down my throat, into my chest. Taking a breath, I welcome the winter. Remembering the winters that have gone before, I know that this winter will be all mine.

My breath fogs out before me as I walk, boots crunching, like treading on glass. I thrust my hands into my pockets, tip my head back, and breathe in the air. It's cold and sweet like the first taste of winter. I drink and drink it in, smiling as the sun dances through the sky, as Kep barks, haring off into the grass to stretch her legs in all the frost.

There's only one place I want to go this morning. Only one

Pewter slings a cloth from his shoulder, wiping away a puddle of spilled rhyn. 'None yet. I heard though—'

'Yes?'

He frowns. 'That Killmarth entrance exam is soon. Wouldn't be surprised if there's a few hopefuls in here today. A round for courage, you know? It always happens towards the end of September.'

I pass him another floren note, and he adds a generous pour into my glass. His attention is snagged by a woman asking for toquay and I move away from the bar, threading my way through the scholars. Pewter told me exactly what I needed to hear. I've been tracking down information since I heard of the college, Killmarth, nine months ago. Perhaps today, at last, I'm in the right place to learn more. And if the entrance exam happens each year towards the end of September, they're cutting it fine. It's already the 28th.

Pewter puts an alchemist-made record on the music amplifier and the whole space fills with the soft crooning notes of a female singer from unseen speakers. It's busier than even a few moments ago, but still none of the scholars are the kind I'm looking for. Too puffed up on poetry and self-importance and none of them, as far as I can tell, wield magic. I swirl the dark green drink in my glass, stepping carefully around their elbows, the frothing rhyn dripping from their tankards. There's a young woman practically boxed in by two of them, men yapping about their interpretation of the Attestations of the gods, trying to impress her, like their opinions are the only ones that matter. Our eyes meet as I brush past them and she's got that look, glazed with boredom. Like she wants to escape.

That's when I twist my hand, like I'm twisting a doorknob, and the bar cuts to darkness. For those two scholars anyway.

I hold the illusion, clenching my jaw, even as the telltale headache begins to nag at my temples. The young woman grabs the opportunity, with them swearing and fumbling, and slips away.

I release their minds from the illusion, and they blink at each other, seeing their quarry has bolted. Allowing myself a small smile, I sink into the cushioned seat at a table in one of the alcoves at the back.

And I wait.

I've trained for moments like this my whole life, blending with a crowd, waiting for a mark the Collector wants, or someone I have a keen interest in. For the past few months since I learned of Killmarth, I've gleaned that it is a place for magic wielders to train. And best of all, fully funded by the Crown, the rulers of Kellend, which to a person like me, means it is *possible*. But it wasn't until recently that I overheard a snippet that changed everything.

When you walk through the gates of Killmarth College, all outside magical interference falls away. No one can follow you through their wards, no matter how strong a wielder. I've been hunting for more information ever since and, with whisperings that the next intake of hopefuls is about to be chosen, I'm ready to take my place amongst them.

Sipping my velvane, I toy with the silver bracelet on my left wrist, the one that shackles me to the Collector. My uncle, my boss, my keeper. The man who'll be impatiently waiting even now for me to deliver the vial of blood from today's assignment. And just as I'm about to give up on this bar and move on to the next one, I hear two voices at the next table.

place I can go to greet the frost and the change in the season. I whistle to Kep and she stalks over, staying at my heels. The trail leading up the mountain is still overgrown with the remnants of summer. Autumn beat back a little of it, but only enough to change the color of the foliage. Bronze and gold and scarlet leaves litter the ground, leaving the limbs of the trees bare and expectant. Waiting for winter. Waiting for the snow and ice to cover their naked forms.

I walk slowly, swaying with each step as my feet get used to the new boots I'm breaking in. Once I decided to stay, I knew I had to match my wardrobe to the seasons. Dresses in the summer, and wide-brimmed straw hats. In autumn, layers of long-sleeved shirts and woolen jumpers, with boots sturdy enough for the mud coating the trails. I kept my old shirts to paint in. I'd set up an easel in the back room, just as I'd pictured. And now, at the beginning of winter, I'm wearing a coat that's thick enough to turn away the cold. One I chose with Jess a couple of weeks ago as she cuddled the new baby into her chest.

Elodie has been the biggest surprise. When I look at her, all I see is springtime. She's an unexpected anchor here, a tie I can't just cut loose and sail away from. I pick her up from school so Jess can stay at home instead of bundling up the baby to make the school run twice a day. Elodie and I thread daisy chains and play hopscotch, and I carry a bag of penny sweets just for her. When I told Jess that I was definitely staying, that I had no plans to leave with the summer sun, she turned to Elodie and said, "Isn't that wonderful? Auntie Carrie isn't going anywhere." And I had to turn away, sniffling as my eyes quickly misted with tears.

Auntie Carrie.

Just those two words, twined together. That is the greatest gift of all.

Pausing at the fork in the trail, I turn to the lookout. The view steals my breath, even now. The view over Woodsmoke, and beyond it, growing indistinct, the endless horizon. All the lives in those little houses, their chimneys freshly lit with the arrival of winter.

My gaze roves over the tapestry of houses, the market square, the cobblestone heart of the town, and lands on the crooked shop off the town center. Ivy's shop. *My* shop. Or rather, my art gallery. Cora left the property to me in her will, so all I have to do is pay the scant bills. It's the perfect space to fill with my sketches and prints, with a couple of bolder pieces I've tentatively placed on the walls to sell. The tourists seemed to like them this summer. They flocked through Woodsmoke in their hikers' boots, binoculars slung around their necks, and some came in to ask after Ivy. Finding no candles to purchase, they bought a print or a postcard instead. I couldn't help thinking of Matthieu and his brother, though, when I saw those hikers and heard their plans.

Cora would have loved what the shop has become. Ivy would have snuck in after I turned the sign to CLOSED and stuffed her candles into every little bit of spare space. But they both would have handed me the old iron key, patted my hand, and wanted me to keep going. The fair sister and the bitter sister.

The Morgan women who came before me.

A whisper stirs at my back, and I close my eyes, imagining it's him. Just for a moment, I picture his face, the way his eyes crinkle at the corners. The way last winter he tucked a smile away, just for me, as we grew to know each other. The way the trail of his kisses lit me on fire. *I still love you*, I whisper back, wondering if he'll hear it, wherever he is now. Whether my words will carry across continents, a whisper on the wind in his ear.

I could make a bargain with the mountains. I could pull him to me, hand over pieces of myself as a trade. But I've seen the other side of that coin, experienced it for myself. The mountains may give, but they ask so much in return. An eye for an eye. A life for a life.

A love . . . for a love.

I sigh and turn back toward home, not looking at the trail that peels upward to the Vickers cabin. I heard that it was sold not long ago. That it's been empty all this time.

I walk down the mountain as I walked up, slowly and ponderously, with Kep at my side, greeting winter with my head held high. I no longer fear this place and the tricks it can play. I've read all the stories in the book, and for me there's no longer any mystery about them. Only sadness at all the curses, all the downfalls. All the fools who lusted after more than their share. The mountains are so ancient, so soaked in blood and stories, that they're almost alive. Almost sentient. And I know never to cross them again.

As I reach the field, I feel the press of their eyes against my spine. The unseeing kind, the hungry kind. But I know better than to offer blood in the silver moonlight. I know better than to pass on the book to anyone who thirsts for more.

There's something on my doorstep. A tiny bundle, tied with a green ribbon. My breath hitches as I bend down to pick it up. The posy of wildflowers casts warmth up my wrist. There's yarrow, aster, dahlias . . .

"Matthieu . . ." I say, swallowing down the ache in my chest. It can't be him. He's somewhere far away, surely—

"Carrie."

I whip around and see him standing there.

My heart explodes.

The posy drops from my fingers as I go to him, closing the distance between us. One step, two, and his arms come around me. "You're here, you're really *here*—"

"Yes. I've had . . . time. Time I needed."

I lift my face to his, feel a blaze of heat as his mouth finds mine. The world drops away, leaving only us, only this. I kiss him harder, deeper, pulling him into me. When I come up for air, he's watching, waiting.

"What are you doing back?"

He knows what I'm asking of him. Whether he's found some peace over the past few months. Whether he's confronted Henri's ghost and found a way to let his brother go. "I bought the cabin. It—it felt right somehow. I won't go searching for Henri, but he'll know I'm here. This feels right, being here."

Tears catch in my throat, clawing up from my chest. "If you're sure, if you're sure you don't need more time—"

"I'm sure. I want to be here with you, Carrie."

I laugh, my lips finding his, pressing the joy between us.

"I realized this past summer what I was giving up by staying in the past. I've never met anyone like you, Carrie. There's never been a single soul like you. I love you. I shouldn't have left, I should have tried—"

"It's all right," I say. "It's all right. You needed to leave. But you came back."

Then I feel it.

The curse recorded in the book, the curse that has lingered far too long in this place, curling around the frost, squatting like a toad in the mountains. I feel how fragile it is, how frail it has become. As I lean back, I feel the roots and shoots weaving around us, binding us, and I lock my gaze with his. Then I say the words that I know will finally break the curse.

"I love you too, Matthieu. I'm not going anywhere either."

And the lingering, lonely curse shatters, splintering all around us.

With the frost.

Acknowledgments

This story was one that needed coaxing out, piece by piece. Perhaps it's because it's the cursed sophomore novel, and this story is all about the curses; or perhaps it's because these characters didn't want to give up their secrets. But I owe so many thanks to the following people for helping me get it into your hands.

To Maddalena Cavaciuti, always. It's a joy working with you; thank you for being my publishing wing woman. And to the team at DHA, particularly Rachael Sharples, Ilaria Albani, Rhian Kane, and Clare Israel; and to Allison Hunter and Natalie Edwards at Trellis Literary, thank you for championing this book, everything you do behind the scenes, and for believing in it.

To Ariana Sinclair, we've made it to two books together and I adore you. Thank you for seeing the true heart of this story and helping me peel back the layers. To Seema Mitra, I am so thrilled you joined Ariana and me and elevated this book even further. This story wouldn't be what it is without both of you.

To my incredible publishing teams at HQ and Avon, particularly Sarah Lundy, Emma Packard, Samantha Larrabee, and DJ DeSmyter, thank you for loving this book and for the many ways, both seen and unseen, that you get my work into readers' hands. You are all truly a force.

To my family and friends, the people in my life and that of my little family's lives, for scooping up my wildlings, cooking us dinners, getting just as hyped as me about this wild journey through publishing, and for really caring, thank you. Suz, Helena, Issy,

Lucy, Sian, Beth, Phil, Liam, Rob, Angie, Mark, Meriel, Carri, Vik, and many more.

To Cyla Panin and Marina Green for being the people I trust most with messy first chapters, new ideas, and anxious messaging about anything and everything—you're both utter gems and I wouldn't be without you.

To the booksellers and book champions who handsell my books, who are genuine and kind and just love reading, thank you. And to Michelle Donavon and the whole WWTS fam, every win of yours is magic. Thank you for celebrating with me. I appreciate you all so much.

To Rosie and Izzy, I'm your number one fan. Watching you grow into yourselves is a constant joy, and I love you to the moon and back and all the stars in between.

To Joe, thank you always. Utterly selfless, terrible dad jokes, always and forever, my favorite person. Thanks for taking the kids out so I could get this book written.

And finally, thank you to you, the reader of this story. Thank you for picking it up and spending your time in Woodsmoke, for meeting Carrie, Matthieu, Jess, and Cora. The further away I get from childhood, the more I realize magic does exist, just maybe not in the form we believed as children. I hope this story lifts you away, even briefly, and you turn the last page feeling like you've just found a glint of real magic in your own life.

Another magical, compelling read from Rachel Greenlaw

Sophia DeWinter has been bound to her cruel uncle, the Collector since he exacted a blood bond from her as a child. When she learns of Killmarth, an elite academy for magic wielders outside of the Collector's control, she grabs it as her only chance to break free.

Each hopeful must prove their worth by competing in brutal and deadly challenges - the Ordeals. And that's just the beginning, because hopefuls are also being viciously picked off one-by-one. To survive, Sophia could team up with another challenger. Perhaps the powerful wielder Alden Locke. But how to identify an ally from a rival? Or even a murderer?

In her haste to escape the Collector's power over her, has Sophia risked everything only to run from the flames and into the fire?

Available to order now!

Turn over to read an extract . . .

Chapter 1

The Pickled Gargoyle

On a Thursday afternoon, around three o'clock, the Pickled Gargoyle is alive with scholars. I wander in as if on a whim, stepping towards the bar as I discreetly eye the room and the gathering of flushed faces. They're clutching tankards of frothing, ruby rhyn, delivering opinions in drawling nasal tones and I realise, the brand of scholar I seek isn't here yet. I signal to Pewter, the barman and he half turns, revealing an array of drinks at his back. Honey-gold toquay in glinting, chilled bottles, a blackcurrant variety steeped to taste like autumn, and my drink of choice, forest-green velvane, smoky and silky smooth, with a lingering taste of toffees.

Pewter raises an eyebrow, grabbing an octagonal glass, and pours two fingers of velvane before sliding it my way. 'Not your usual haunt at this hour, Sophia.'

I pick up the glass and take my first sip, the feel of warmth and silk slipping deliciously down my throat. 'Just came to see my favourite barman.'

'Liar.'

I grin, sliding over a floren note and he tops up my glass. 'Yours is the best velvane in the city?'

He chuckles. 'Still a lie, but I'll take it.'

'Any wielders here today?' I ask casually, taking another sip as I survey the bar.